THE
WINDS
OF SONOMA

REGALO GRANDE

THE
WINDS
OF SONOMA

NIKKI ARANA

Revell

Grand Rapids, Michigan

© 2005 by Nikki Arana

Published by Fleming H. Revell
a division of Baker Publishing Group
P.O. Box 6287, Grand Rapids, MI 49516-6287

Printed in the United States of America

Library of Congress Cataloging-in-Publication Data
Arana, Nikki, 1949-
    The winds of Sonoma / Nikki Arana.
        p.   cm.—(Regalo Grande ; bk. 1)
    ISBN 0-8007-3048-8 (pbk.)
    1. Women lawyers—Fiction. 2. Horse breeders—Fiction. 3. Sonoma (Calif.)—Fiction. 4. Rich people—Fiction. I. Title.
PS3601.R35W56 2005
813'.6—dc22   2005015728

For my father and mother.
I love and esteem you for who you are,
a wise mentor, a sweet spirit.

The wind blows where it wishes, and you hear the sound of it, but cannot tell where it comes from and where it goes.

—*The Book of John*

PROLOGUE

August
Guadalajara, Mexico

She laid wood on the fire. The morning sun was just beginning to light the countryside that surrounded Guadalajara. It wouldn't be long before daylight awakened her children sleeping under the tarp that stretched across the lowest branches of the jacaranda tree. She placed the rusted barrel lid across the stones, just above the flames, and patted tortilla dough between her palms. Her lips moved in silent prayer as she cooked. She prayed and listened, waiting for the whisper of the wind. One by one she laid the tortillas on the lid. When both sides were lightly browned, she took them from the fire, putting the best ones on a worn cloth to her right, the others on a tin platter to her left.

This was the day and the hour. She'd known it would come, as it had before, as it would again. First it had been her husband, now it was her oldest son. Soon it would be his brother. The birth of each of her ten children was a blessing and a curse, the joy they brought her allowed only for a measured time. Each would learn what she had learned as a child, there would never be enough food or enough work or enough money to care for the family. There was only the border and the coyotes who knew about the tunnels and passes where a Mexican could run and crawl and hide, straining toward that desperate hope to the north.

The woman reached to her right, carefully folding the faded cloth around the pile of tortillas to form a sack. She knotted the top. Hearing footsteps, she turned. It was her oldest son.

"*Vaya con Dios, mi hijo*," she said. If God heard her prayers, the boy would find favor on his journey. She listened again for the whispering wind.

He was tall, like his great-grandfather. The boy's black hair, broad shoulders, and square jaw were the only remnant of the Aztec royalty that was his heritage. He bent and kissed her cheek, took the sack, and put it under his arm. There was nothing to say. They both knew he must go. It would be days of walking and, with luck, some days of riding. Whatever it took, he must get to the border and find the coyotes who could take him to America.

She watched him turn and walk down the dusty road, leaving his country, his family, and his life behind. He was proud to be the first son to go, not for himself but for them. He would send them whatever money he made, and maybe someday he would find a way to come back. But she was not sure of his fate. Others had left the fields and never returned.

She fingered the primitive, metal cross she wore around her neck. "*Vaya con Dios, Antonio*," she called after him. If only he would turn and she could see his face one last time, but he couldn't hear her. A wind had begun to blow. No longer able to control her tears, she put her face in her hands and knelt on the ground, sobbing.

As clear as the sound of the wind, she heard a whisper, "Fear not."

THERE WASN'T ANY more time to think about it.

Angelica Amante sat at the ornate desk of the late William O'Connell and stared at the bold print stamped across the paper on top of the open file. "U.S. Immigration and Customs Enforcement." If she signed the paper, it would move on through the system and result in legalizing the exploitation of hundreds of illegal Mexicans. If she didn't, her job and career would be in jeopardy. She sat back in the deep, leather chair and turned toward the floor-to-ceiling windows that framed the view of Manhattan from the seventy-seventh floor of the International Commerce Building.

Her gaze drifted to the spire of St. Pius Cathedral, visible in the distance behind the wavy heat of the summer sun. The funeral had been held there two weeks ago. She'd hardly known Bill O'Connell—they worked in different divisions—but every employee of Czervenka and Zergonos, one of New York's most prestigious law firms, had attended. They'd all received the brief note, typed on the gilded letterhead of C. Czervenka, Esquire, that read in part, "It is important we show our support for the O'Connell family during their time of loss. They have requested all donations be made to the American Heart Association."

Angelica rose and walked to the windows, leaned her forehead against the glass wall, and closed her eyes. Constantine Czervenka had insisted she ride with him to the funeral. He had told her that her work ethic and ability to choose the right strategy for the cases she'd researched made her his only choice to take over the precedent-setting work that Bill O'Connell had been handling. He'd said she was one of the "brightest young attorneys" working for the firm. Her heart had skipped a beat. She'd hardly believed her good fortune.

A promotion like this brought her one big step closer to her dream of partnership. The sacrifices she'd made to get to this point in her career had been huge, some intended, some unintended. Years of study, weeks spent sequestered in her office as she researched cutting-edge legal questions, and the loss of the man she'd hoped to marry, a man she still thought about. This promotion had promised to be worth all that.

When they had returned from the service and burial, Constantine Czervenka had shown her the office. Her nameplate, newly etched in shiny brass, shone in the center of the mahogany door as it swung open. "We have great expectations for your career. This is just the beginning."

She stepped away from the windows and moved toward the open file. A sense of dread filled her. She'd agonized night and day over her decision. She turned the paper face down and closed the file. She would ask to be taken off the case. She looked at her watch, 9:21. The appointment with her boss was in nine minutes.

Rehearsed words and phrases ran through her mind. *I*

appreciate this opportunity you've given me. . . . This is an important case, however . . . Everything is in order for reassignment. . . . Again, thank you. . . . This had to go well. It would take all her negotiating skill to remain honest while laying out an acceptable position as to why she could not continue on the case. A moment of moral clarity injected into the high stakes game of a federal court case would be admired about as much as honor among thieves. Yet, it had been her desire to make a positive difference in people's lives that had drawn her to the legal profession in the first place. The irony didn't escape her.

She knew this meeting wouldn't surprise her boss. She'd tried to speak to him several times since she had first realized what Bill O'Connell's cases entailed. But Constantine always cut their conversations short with the same clipped tone she'd heard him use with his wife when she called during business hours.

The cases of the late Bill O'Connell, if won, would make it possible for the largest produce company in the United States to hire illegal Mexicans to work the crops and then to delay their pay for months, having them deported in the interim. This amounted to, no, in fact was, using the most brilliant legal minds in the country to steal the only thing the desperate immigrants possessed, hope for a better life. Angelica could no longer bring herself to read, much less support, the cases as they outlined in cold detail timetables to destroy lives, legal freight trains running on precise schedules and heading south of the border every payday.

Angelica picked up the files she'd stacked on the corner of her desk and started toward the door. She stopped. Turning slowly, she walked to the glass wall for one last look at the Manhattan skyline and the vast business empire that lay at her feet. Lifting her eyes, she looked south. Minutes passed. The names on the files she held in her hands filled her thoughts: Ortega, Ramirez, Martinez, Herrera. *God, be with me. I'm trusting You to go before me.* She took a deep breath, turned, and walked out the door.

She pushed the call button for the elevator. As she waited in the plush lobby, she caught her image in the gilded mirror that hung above a cherry, bombé chest—dark hazel eyes, flecked green, high cheekbones, thick, shoulder-length hair. She knew others thought her a striking beauty, but that fact was as much a hindrance as a help, working in a man's world. She had worked harder, longer, and smarter than her male counterparts to climb the corporate ladder.

"Good morning, Ms. Amante. How may I help you?" Deirdre, full lips parting for a perfect smile as always, greeted Angelica as she approached the reception desk.

"I have an appointment with Mr. Czervenka."

"Yes, he called. He's running late. He'll be here any minute."

Angelica thanked her and took a seat. She looked toward the conference room adjoining the reception area. The senior partners were in a meeting. She'd attended meetings there, going over daily research assignments and participating in strategy meetings where ruthless litigation and devastating defenses were plotted. The ends justified the means. Guilt or innocence was a nonissue. Winning was everything. Who was being set up for a fall today?

"Good morning, Angelica."

She turned at the booming voice behind her. Constantine Czervenka looked like a statesman. His silver hair, deep tan, and thousand-dollar suit told everyone who met him exactly who he was. The taut skin that stretched to the faint scars just behind his hairline revealed the secret of who he pretended to be.

14

"Good morning." Angelica stood and extended her hand.

He took it with casual authority and an engaging smile. "Before we meet, Angelica, I'd like you to step into the conference room. There's something we want to talk to you about."

Nicolaus Zergonos opened the conference room door. He winked at her and swept his hand toward the table. "After you."

She felt trapped in a freeze-frame of time. What could this be about? Did they know? They were all smiling at her, that was a good sign. He continued standing, looking at her. She willed her feet to move.

"Have a seat." Jack Lauer, head of the International Division, motioned to the open chair next to the head of the table.

All eyes were on her as she sat. Everyone else took their seats. She laid her files on the table.

"Angelica. When you joined us, we had high expectations, and you haven't disappointed us." Constantine leaned forward in his chair. "You came to us with outstanding personal and professional references. I've had the opportunity to thank some of those people personally, I might add."

She sensed a power play.

"During your time here, you've taken everything we've thrown at you and handed it back tied up in a neat package."

There were chuckles from around the table.

"We're putting you on the fast track to a junior partnership."

Angelica's heart started to pound. "I don't know what to say."

Constantine's eyes narrowed slightly. "You know the minimum track here for partnership is seven years."

"Yes, I know. I mean . . . I'm flattered, of course."

Someone cleared his throat. A chair squeaked.

Angelica's mind raced. What were her options? This was not the time or place to ask to be taken off a precedent-setting case.

"Well?" Constantine sat back in his chair.

Seconds seemed like hours. Every argument she'd made to herself over the last two weeks crowded into her mind. *You could be jeopardizing your career. . . . Your reasons are legitimate. . . . You've got too much at stake. . . . God opened this door, and He'll make a way. . . . You're in the big leagues now.*

"Could I have a word with you privately?" Angelica picked up the files and stood.

Constantine studied her. His jaw tightened.

"Excuse us." Constantine pushed his chair back.

She followed him to his office.

"What's this about?" He sat on the edge of his desk and folded his arms.

"There's something I need to clear up before I can continue that meeting in good conscience. I don't think this is unexpected. I—"

"What do you mean by that?"

"Well . . . I've spoken to you before about these deportation cases. I—"

His mouth tightened into a stubborn line. "Whatever you've said in the past, I took as a young attorney's naïveté about how things work in the big city. This offer today *should* make things crystal clear."

"I understand what you're saying. I certainly haven't

16

made this decision lightly. I've thought about nothing else since—"

"What is there to think about?" Red tinged his cheeks.

"It's a matter of principle. I—"

"Principle? Those people you're so worried about are here illegally." He spoke with menacing calm. "Deportation is the natural consequence of their choice to live outside the laws of the United States."

Twisting the truth was an ethical sophistication she knew she would never be able to defer to. "Yes, they have broken the law, and they should be held accountable, not exploited. I'd like to be reassigned."

"Are you saying you want to be taken off this case?" Anger flashed across his face.

"All the files are in order. It will be an easy handoff."

"The prestige and financial rewards of being put on the fast track are something that only come along once in a lifetime. And rarely at the age of twenty-five."

She recognized his offer to reconsider and the clipped tone that had crept into his voice. Seconds passed. The only sound in the room was his short, rapid breathing. She noticed a bead of sweat near his temple.

"Really, I appreciate the opportunity. It's just that—"

"So, you're walking out."

"No, not at all."

"Yes. You are. You'll be gone by noon. Your career is finished. Here and everywhere we do business. Now, if you'll excuse me. I have the rather irksome task of telling my partners I apparently made a huge error in judgment."

She caught her breath. How could this be happening? She was doing the right thing. She had asked God to be with her.

Angelica stepped through the doors of her firm's lobby into the miserable, sucking heat of a New York summer with everything she'd been allowed to take from her office in the crook of her arm, crammed into an empty envelope box she'd found in the supply room. Cab after cab flew past her outstretched arm.

Finally, she moved back onto the crowded sidewalk and started the long walk home to her apartment. As the blocks stretched behind her, the enormity of her decision pressed upon her. By the time she reached her apartment building, she'd begun to press back. The heavy hand of Constantine Czervenka wasn't going to shape her future. She would find another job.

She stepped into the cooled air of her one-bedroom apartment, dropped her keys, purse, and box on the floor, then plopped down in the big, overstuffed high-back chair that furnished most of the small front room. She drummed her fingers on the arm of the chair. She'd have to tell her parents, but first she needed to find another job, to get back on track with a different firm, one that needed her experience and would value her ethics.

She picked up the picture that stood on the table next to her chair. "Congratulations" was engraved in script across the bottom. It had been taken the day she graduated from Hastings law school. Her father stood with his arm around her, his hand resting on the gold sash she wore as the class valedictorian. Her mother stood at an angle to his left, face slightly tilted, smile perfect, pose practiced. After the camera shutter clicked, he'd bent down and whispered to Angelica, "This is the proudest day of my life, Angel."

What would he think now? How many times had he told her, "You're an Amante. We never quit"? Would he understand why she'd had to take a stand, even though she was living the dream he'd always had for her, the dream she'd made her own? Would anyone understand—the professors who wrote her letters of recommendation, the organizations that lauded her leadership and loyalty? Would they think she'd naively embraced some altruistic ideal, some moral absolute? The legal profession was all about hardball, and she'd accepted the challenge, with its uncompromising directive—advocate for the client—regardless.

As she set the picture down, the bold print of a clipped news column taped to the back caught her eye: A RISING STAR. Immediately, the moment was with her again . . . walking to the podium, addressing the overflowing audience, her parents' faces in the front row, the thunderous applause when she finished her speech. She continued to read:

Valedictorian Angelica Amante wowed the crowd with her inspiring speech at the University of California Hastings College of the Law graduation ceremony Saturday. The event marked the culmination of a stellar academic career that began when she enrolled as a freshman at the age of sixteen.

She told her fellow graduates, "We must not only defend the letter of the law, we must never forget the intent of the law, because we know the great principles on which it was founded." The final words of her speech summed up the passion that has made this idealistic young woman someone to watch. "The heart of America beats in the words of the lady in the harbor: 'Give me your tired, your poor, your huddled masses yearning to breathe free.' We must never forget it is our duty, our charge, to protect the principles that have made our country great."

Angelica shook her head. Things had been so clear then, so simple, with the dream of her heart within her reach. The dream to redress the terrible wrong that had so profoundly touched her.

But somewhere along the way she'd gotten caught up in the glamour and excitement of a high-profile job. Now her job description included preparing deportation briefs, stripping jobs and income, destroying families. Why had she allowed it? She peeled the paper off the back of the picture and crumpled it. She couldn't call home. Not until she'd pulled her life together.

As the weeks passed, the prediction of her former boss proved to be true. The long reach of Czervenka and Zergonos caused her final interview with Sterling, Marchand, and Hunt to be canceled, prevented the first callback at Wyndham and Fischer, and finally filled all available positions just when she applied for them. She moved her circle of inquiry farther and farther from the city.

Angelica stepped out of the elevator, having just dropped her last month's rent and the neatly typed thirty-day notice at the manager's desk. A faint ringing of a phone somewhere down the hallway interrupted her thoughts. She raised her head, listening. Her steps quickened. It was coming from her apartment.

She fumbled with her keys, got the door unlocked, and raced to the phone. Maybe this was a callback on one of her applications. The call that would restart her career. "Hello."

"This is Ms. Beutler, human resource director for Solomon and Walker."

She gripped the phone. Solomon and Walker, the midsize

firm that was just beginning to expand. Exactly the kind of position she was looking for. She'd had a very good feeling when she'd left the interview. "This is Angelica."

"We have finished reviewing your application and don't think this is a good fit right now. We'll keep you on file, and thank you for your interest."

Anger flooded through her as she took control of her voice. "Thank you for getting back to me." She dropped the phone in its cradle and stood staring at it.

As the moments passed, her anger gave way to grim reality. The seriousness of her situation settled on her. She sank onto the edge of the big chair next to the phone. So this was the way the game was played. And apparently every law firm of any consequence willingly participated.

Her mind replayed this latest interview. The interested, smiling faces she sat before. The sincere admiration expressed for her accomplishments in law school and her advancements in her career. Had they already been clued in? Or was it done later, when references were checked? Some interviews had been canceled before she could keep them, so either option was possible.

She settled back into the chair and threw her feet up on the footstool. She needed to make some decisions. She had left a firm because she couldn't reconcile her job with her principles. Yet, she had spent the last few weeks doing everything in her power to find another job with companies that found it in their best interest to align themselves with Czervenka and Zergonos. The truth began to crystallize in her mind. It was a vicious circle. If she continued to pursue her career with companies of power and influence, she was going to be required to play the game. That probably meant calling her former boss and explaining how she now realized she'd made a mistake. Her stomach turned.

Thoughts of facing her parents pulled at her. Telling them she didn't have a job, worse, couldn't get one, would crush them. They'd been so proud of her. Making her father proud was why she had pursued the opportunity offered by Czervenka and Zergonos in the first place, instead of keeping the promise she'd made to herself.

Oh God, what a mess I've made. Poppy and I prayed that You would show me Your plan for my life. It seemed so much easier to trust God with Poppy holding her hand, kneeling beside her.

She reached for the phone beside her chair and dialed. After the third ring, she heard the familiar voice. A wave of emotions flooded through her.

"Hi, Poppy, it's Angelica."

"Oh, Miss Angel, it so good to hear your voice. Just this morning I telling Jesus I miss you and be sure He watch out for you."

She struggled to control her voice. "Oh, Poppy, everything is going wrong. I got fired. Worse than that, I can't find another job." She burst into tears.

As she tried to get ahold of herself, she heard Poppy's comforting voice. "Now, you just tell me all about it."

The words tumbled out through tears and sniffles as she filled him in on the events of the previous few weeks. "I've spent the past two years building a career, and now it seems like everything is being taken away from me. But, you know, it's given me time to take stock of where I am . . . and where I want to be."

"You've worked hard for your career. No let doubt come in now. Satan love to shoot those fiery darts of fear where God working."

"Don't you see, Poppy. That's what I'm saying. God is working. He's giving me a second chance, and I'm going to take it." The afternoon at the gravesite, the depth of Poppy's pain—suddenly, it was as real to her as the day she had witnessed it.

"Take some time alone with the Lord. He speak to you about this."

Poppy's words began to give her perspective. "I know you're right. Things seem so confusing right now." She sighed. She could have talked to him another hour. The sound of his voice lifted her spirits, but there was really nothing more to say. "I'll call you soon and let you know what's happening."

"You no worry, Miss Angel. God have a plan for you. I put this at top of my prayer list."

"Please do. And Poppy, of course you'll keep this between us."

"Just between you, me, and my Jesus."

She hung up the phone and took a deep breath. She would stick with her decision. She would trust God to open a new path for her. Surely He was with her. She felt a weight lift from her shoulders.

As she sat quietly, she began to form a plan. She would go to the West Coast, where people knew her and her family. Where *she* had connections. Where she could pursue the dream of her heart. Where Czervenka and Zergonos didn't have any influence . . . she hoped.

Three days later, Angelica was aboard United Flight 5236, headed home. She settled into the blue cushions, put her head back, and closed her eyes. The rolling hills and quieter life of the wine country nestled in the Sonoma Mountains of northern California were only hours away. She let her mind wander to the lush hills that surrounded the ranch, recalling the many afternoons she rode her Arabian stallion, Pasha, her hand wrapped in his mane, urging him on, exploring every hill and meadow on the 175-acre spread her father had named Regalo Grande. Her father, Benito Amante, a successful surgeon specializing in heart transplants, had indulged Angelica in her passion for horses, and to please her, he dabbled in a breeding program.

The beauty and innocence of those growing-up years called to Angelica now. Going home would give her the space and time she needed to get her career back on track and moving in the direction *she* wanted. She hoped her decision not to tell her family the details of her situation had been the right one. She wanted to tell them the whole thing face-to-face. It would feel good to get everything out in the open.

Angelica pressed the bell for the flight attendant. "Would you bring me a paper?"

"Certainly, Ms. Amante. Would you like *USA Today, The New York Times*, or the *San Francisco Chronicle*?"

"The *Chronicle*."

"Ladies and gentlemen, this is your captain speaking. We're heading into clear skies, and the weather forecast indicates a smooth flight all the way. The temperature in San Francisco is seventy degrees. Enjoy your flight, and thank you for flying United."

With the paper in hand, she settled in for the inevitable wait for takeoff. THE PRESIDENT ADDRESSES A JOINT SESSION OF CONGRESS was the headline. Macy's was having a sale. Weather forecast: sunny, seventy-two. Then her eye fell on bold type near the bottom of page 4. ILLEGAL IMMIGRANTS DIE IN DESERT. She read on:

Associated Press, Borrego Springs, California—Sixteen illegal immigrants were found dead after being abandoned by smugglers in the blistering heat of the California desert. The

24

Border Patrol found the abandoned U-Haul trailer south of Borrego Springs, in the rugged terrain of the Anza-Borrego Desert State Park, after receiving a report from park rangers, Agent Hector Gonzalez stated. The occupants died of heat exhaustion and severe dehydration, having been left there in temperatures as high as 115 degrees. Their ages were estimated to be between 15 and 35.

One of the immigrants, still conscious when found, died on the way to the hospital. Information he gave revealed they had been brought across the border near Tecate, Mexico, after giving their money to coyotes, smugglers of human cargo. He also said that just hours before the rescuers arrived, three of the men with him had tried to walk out. Rescuers reported they searched the nearby area and found two bodies several miles north. Border Patrol agents trained as trackers were being brought in. They would use government-issued ATC Honda motorcycles to expedite the search. "If there is still someone out there, we'll find him," said Agent Gonzalez.

The roar of the engines brought her back to the present. *Sure, if he were out there, they'd find him. They'd find him and send him back to Mexico, dead or alive.*

She shifted in her seat, the familiar sense of dread returning. Ortega, Ramirez, Martinez, Herrera. The names marched through her mind. Her heart went out to them. Had some of them tried to return? Were they living or dead?

Her thoughts drifted back to Poppy and his wife and child. She had begged him to take her to visit their grave. When he had kneeled and kissed the marker, she'd witnessed a sorrow so deep and raw, it left a mark on her own heart. What had happened to them should not happen to anyone. But there was nothing a ten-year-old girl could do about it. Nothing, but make a promise.

The plane was gathering speed for takeoff. She put the paper down and turned to look out her window. Within seconds the blanket of asphalt, steel, and concrete that was New York City stretched as far as she could see, but clouds were closing in under the plane. The turbulence caused the plastic window shade to drop down, blocking her view. Why the wind? The pilot had just said they were heading into clear skies.

She pushed the shade back up, straining for one last look. But the wind had thickened the clouds beneath her, leaving nothing but a distant opening, seemingly pierced by a blade of light. There, in stark relief, stood the Statue of Liberty.

The words of her speech returned to her, "Give me your tired, your poor, your huddled masses yearning to breathe free." What for years had been a hunger in her spirit became a certainty. She would follow her heart. She would keep the vow she'd made to herself that summer afternoon when she had first discovered the terrible details surrounding the young immigrant who had come to America in the 1940s and lost everything. The man who, in the face of his own adversity, had taught her to love this land, its laws, and the God who was the foundation of both.

Not her father, but the man who had raised her. Poppy.

2

Antonio spent the night in a small outcropping of rock under a lone elephant tree, its short, stout trunk and branches providing nothing more than a marker of where he slept. Light crept over the horizon. He struggled to his feet. He lifted one foot and set it down, then the other. Step by step, he continued on, hoping to find water, shelter, a road . . . anything. Step by step, hours passed.

As the sun rose high overhead, he heard no sounds of life anywhere in the desert wasteland. Its blistering heat withered the earth beneath his feet and made the air thick. He felt as though he were breathing through mud. He willed each short, convulsive breath that transformed death into life.

Leg cramps tormented him with each footfall. The smallest effort was an incredible hardship, draining what was left of his courage and spirit. He pulled off the bandanna, tied around his head since leaving Mexico, and dropped it. With slow, jerking movements, he replaced it with his shirt, letting the shirttail fall across his shoulders. He'd been sweating profusely for hours, but now his skin was dry.

One more step.

And with that thought came just enough strength to take it.

He must go on, not just for himself but for the other men stranded where the coyotes had left them.

His mind drifted to his mother and the last time he saw her, cooking by the fire, praying for him. The memory strengthened his resolve. He knew the God she prayed to, the God of all creation. When his mother had held him as a child, watching the morning sun rise, she told him that God held the light in His hands at night so they could rest and He released it every morning so they could work. She often pointed out beautiful birds God had created just for them. She showed him how God shut the rivers in their banks so she could collect the water they needed each day; how He wearied the ominous, dark clouds that argued in voices of thunder and lightning, making them rain on the crops. He had spent many nights under the endless, Cimmerian sky watching diamonds spill from the treasures stored in heaven, flashing through the night, sparkling, melting, vanishing, stirring something in his heart.

He stumbled and fell to his knees. He reached out, dug his fingers into the dirt. If he could not walk, he would drag himself forward. The gritty earth clung to his face, working its way into the creases of his eyes and mouth. The certainty of his circumstances pressed upon him, but he would not surrender. The air was still as death, yet he felt a presence. As gentle as an angel's wing, the Spirit covered him, dispersing the blistering rays, sustaining life, manifesting the will of God. His last, lucid thought brought recognition. He was not alone.

Agent Hector Gonzalez sat on the bumper of the abandoned U-Haul. The empty truck and a few articles of clothing were the only evidence of the carnage found the day before. The last of four Border Patrol tracking teams had left to continue the search to the north, toward Anza.

"Think you can fix it, Mick?"

"I told you last time this happened, I'm not the on-call mechanic for the agency," Mick said, pulling a spark plug from the Honda motorcycle.

Hector smiled at his friend. "Yeah, that's true. Just like you told me you'd never cheat on your wife again."

"Very funny. If she hadn't let herself go after the baby was born, stuff like that wouldn't happen." He wiped the plug on his pants. "This thing's fouled." He threw it down and pulled the tool kit out from under the seat of the bike.

Hector's gaze wandered across the horizon. "S-2 is the nearest county road that gets any traffic, and it's over five miles from here. I bet we find him."

Mick pulled another plug. "I'd like to find the coyotes that brought 'em here. They've got the money. At four hundred bucks a head, that's at least $6,800. I could use $6,800. It'd take me six months to make that. If we found 'em, they'd pay, know what I mean? Just between you and me. They've got to be around here someplace, and they're gonna come back here looking for that truck."

Hector shrugged. "Even if they are, they're not going to come around as long as we're here."

"Yeah, but I bet we could find 'em. If we catch 'em, we can take that money from 'em. They'll just go back and pick up another load down in Tecate. These Mexicans are a dime a dozen. Hey, they mess up, they pay for their mistake, they move on. No one's the wiser, and me and you have a little extra cash."

Hector climbed into his Jeep. "Forget it. I'm going back to the yard to pick up a flatbed. I'll be back within the hour. If you get that thing running, radio me so I don't have to come back and get you. You can drive over and join Team Four. They're covering Search Grid D, where you were yesterday."

"You think about what I said, buddy. It's a good idea."

Hector shook his head.

Mick watched as Hector drove away, then turned back to the work at hand.

"If it wasn't for these worthless Mexicans," he mumbled, "I wouldn't be out in this godforsaken desert working on an engine that will be too hot to touch in a matter of minutes. It's got to be over 110 out here." His tongue darted across his top lip, catching a bead of sweat.

He found the spare plugs in the tool kit and put them in. The engine roared to life. He repacked the kit and put it back under the seat of the bike.

If I find this guy, he could tell me what the routine is: where the Mexicans get picked up, who they pay, when they travel. He grabbed binoculars from his backpack and got into the seat. *Everyone seems to think he headed north toward Anza. But what if he didn't? What if he headed west?*

Mick hesitated. He was an experienced tracker. He'd spent time in Australia in the late '60s as a member of an elite Special Forces team formed at the request of the CIA in anticipation of an Arab oil embargo. The team trained with Aboriginal guides who took them into the Great Sandy Desert and taught them arid-land survival techniques and tracking skills. He learned how to ensure that any unfortunate encounters with the enemy would never be discovered. The thought of killing the enemy had kept him going through the hellish training.

He knew how to read the subtlest impression in the sand. If he picked up the Mexican's tracks, he could tell how long he'd rested, how strong he was, if he was wandering, or if he was moving deliberately. Mick knew if he got any break at all, any clue as to the direction the man had taken, he'd have a good chance of finding him—and a good chance of making a little extra money. He turned the handles of the bike, gunned it, and started west.

Leaning first to the left, then to the right, Mick examined the surface of the desert floor for any telltale signs of a human passing through: a flat spot in the soil, a pebble pressed into the dirt. He walked, pushing the bike, then rode at measured intervals.

Suddenly, he saw something up ahead. It looked like a piece of cloth. He rode over to it. A bandanna. He bent down, examining the ground. Faintly outlined in the dirt was a single set of shoe prints without much distance between steps. The person was clearly struggling to walk. It had to be the Mexican.

Mick grinned. "Hey, am I the best or what?"

The county road wasn't too far from here. He could radio Hector and have him notify the search teams to come and help. Or . . . He smiled. He could just keep going, find the guy, get the information from him, then go for help. No one would be the wiser. He'd have the information he needed to work out something with the coyotes, and if he took his time, the state of California would have one less Mexican to worry about. A real win-win situation.

He raised his binoculars and surveyed the area in the direction of the last toe dig. Inch by inch, he scanned the desert. His eyes settled on an outcropping of rocks, cholla, and an elephant tree about a mile ahead.

I bet the Mexican saw the tree and headed that way for shade. He glanced up at the sky. Clouds were gathering. He wouldn't take the time to follow the tracks. Seconds could be the difference between getting the information or losing the trail completely. Thunder rumbled in the distance. Mick revved the engine and headed toward the oasis at full speed, a broad grin across his face. The Honda lurched and slid over the rutted desert floor. He was almost there. Nothing was going to stop him now.

The speedometer needle was just passing fifty when the front tire hit a berm head-on. Suddenly, Mick was airborne. Everything seemed to move in slow motion. The cycle rotated to the right, metal and rubber spinning out of control. His hands were still on the grips. He tried to let go, to push himself away from the machine. His feet swung free, but the handlebars seemed sealed to his palms, holding him in a maniacal, midair dance. His heart hammered in his chest as he struggled to break free, but it was as if he were in the grip of the devil himself. He hit the bottom of the wash and pulled his partner to him.

Lightning flashed directly above him. A drop of rain fell on his face. He clawed at the ground, trying to pull himself out from under the twisted machine. He couldn't feel his legs. Fighting to stay conscious, he drew a ragged breath. *The walkie-talkie. Where is it?* His hand found his gun belt, then the walkie-talkie, still fastened there. He pulled it out and signaled for Hector. Nothing. Mick cursed the storm. He knew he was in range of the repeater tower; it had to be the storm messing up reception. He tried again.

The answer crackled over the speaker. "I read you."

"Hector, it's Mick." The thunder crashed, and the transmission broke up. Mick couldn't concentrate.

"Hector. It's Mick. I . . . I got the cycle running. I was heading for S-2. . . ." More thunder and lightning split the sky, garbling his transmission.

"I read you. I was about to start up there with the flatbed. You caught me just in time. I'm glad you got it running. I'll talk to you when you get back." Lightning zigzagged through the sky, filling Mick with fear.

Hector's final words crackled over the receiver. "Over and out."

It was raining in earnest now. Mick tried to raise the top half of his body to get a better look at where he was. He saw only the sides of the wash, cradling him like arms of death as they embraced the torrential downpour. The ground under him vibrated. Then in one sickening moment, he realized it wasn't thunder reverberating down the walls of the arroyo; it was the sound of boulders being torn from the mountain above, making way for the water flashing down the wash, cleansing the earth of everything in its path.

Ron Kaye searched the desert highway for a place to pull over. The sky was clouding up, and it looked like a summer thunderstorm was brewing. The feed door on the horse trailer had come open; he could see it in his rearview mirror. The mare he was trailering was the last of four cross-country deliveries from a breeding farm in Texas. She was in foal to the Arabian National Champion, which made her even more high-strung and skittish than usual. The last thing he needed was hay blowing in her eyes and causing an injury or, worse, throwing her into a panic.

If it wasn't one thing, it was another. He rarely hauled

long distances alone, but Neva, his partner and wife, had stayed at home to meet with college recruiters interested in offering their son a football scholarship. Thinking about her, he smiled. They'd built their business from nothing. In the early days, the three of them had traveled together when they hauled.

Life was funny. Here they were, hoping for a scholarship, when the price of the mare he was hauling would pay for all four years at the finest college in the country. He wasn't complaining, though. They'd been professional haulers for twenty-five years, and God had blessed their business.

He looked up the side of the road as far as he could see and spotted a turnout about a quarter mile ahead on the right.

He pulled into the turnout, set the brake, and jumped out, his stocky legs fully extended as they touched the ground. When he tried to shut the feed door, he found it was bent. *Must've happened when it blew open.* Ron bent it back in shape the best he could and managed to get it latched. He walked around to the back of the trailer and unfastened the right door from the center post. The mare was in the front, left stall.

"Hey, girl. You getting tired of standing? It won't be much longer. We should be in Sonoma by midmorning tomorrow." He patted her neck, retied her halter, and checked her feed. Stepping in front of her, he made sure the feed door was secure. Satisfied it would stay shut, he walked to the back of the rig, shut the tailgate, and dropped the bolt.

"Boy, look at those thunderheads. We could be in for a real storm."

He scanned the horizon. A flickering movement. Ron squinted and walked forward a few steps. The heat rising from the desert floor could be playing tricks on him. He chuckled. It'd happened to him before. Last summer, on a long haul through this same desert, he'd been sure he saw a family about a hundred yards off the road, bent over tending to someone on the ground. And what did he find after pulling over and running the distance in the heat of the day? A group of flowering cacti enjoying the sun. Life. Sometimes things weren't what they seemed.

He turned to get back into the truck, but the flickering motion began again. It looked like something waving in the breeze, but the air was still.

"Boy, I've been standing here too long." He walked around the truck, opened the door, and stepped up on the running board. Now, standing just a little bit higher, he took one last look. There it was again. Something *was* moving out there. Better safe than sorry. He grabbed his hat and water bottle from the truck.

As he closed the distance, he made out a form. A man lay sprawled in the dust. Ron stopped and crossed himself, observing the outstretched arms, one leg bent, ready to push forward—poignant evidence of the solitary struggle waged by the will to live. He didn't hear a sound. Nothing moved. There was something wrapped around the man's head, some kind of hat. No, it was a shirt, the tail of it across his back. He bent down and pushed the shirt away from the face.

Just a kid. Twentysomething. Ron brushed the dirt off the young man's face, looking for some sign of life. The man was breathing. Ron opened the water bottle and poured some on the man's forehead.

"Hey, buddy. *Amigo*." No response. He sprinkled a little more water on the man's face. "Hey, buddy." He shook him gently. He looked back toward his truck, there wasn't another car in sight. The man moaned as thunder rumbled and rain began to fall.

"Hey, *amigo*." Ron shook him again.

The young man's eyes opened. He looked at Ron for a moment, then seemed to realize where he was. He tried to get up.

"*Hombre. Los hombres están muertos!*" He pointed up into the mountains and tried to stand.

"Are there men after you? *Hombres por usted?*" Ron wished he knew more Spanish.

"*Hombres muertos.*" The man pointed to the mountains again.

"Don't worry. No one is after you. *De dónde?*"

"*De Guadalajara.*"

The kid had to be an illegal. There was no other explanation for him being out in the desert alone. Maybe the Border Patrol had been chasing him. Ron helped the young man up and felt the tattered pants pockets. Nothing. No papers, no money, nothing. Ron noticed the pants were far too big and fell in folds across the young man's bony hips. An old rope was woven through the few belt loops that weren't torn off and tied in a knot at the side. Ron had seen many of these young Mexicans working on the horse ranches, sending home whatever money they got. Some were treated well, but most were kept in substandard housing and treated as slave labor. His heart went out to the guy. What if it were his boy who needed help? Ron would want someone to help him.

He gave the exhausted man a few sips of water. The rain was becoming heavy. He pointed to his truck. "Come. Come." He put his shoulder under the man's arm and half-dragged, half-carried him to the truck. He opened the passenger door and lifted him onto the seat, where the young Mexican slumped forward. "Whoa there, *amigo*. Man, this isn't going to work."

Ron ran to the back of the trailer, opened it up, grabbed some fresh hay, and spread it on the empty side of the trailer. By the time he got back to the truck, the man had lost consciousness. Ron pulled him off the seat and managed to get him in a fireman's carry. The rain came down in sheets now, and they were drenched. Ron walked into the back of the trailer and, as gently as he could, laid the boy down in the hay. He knelt beside the man, raised his head, and managed to get him to take a little more water. He tucked the water bottle under the man's arm. "Rest, *amigo*."

Ron went back to the truck and opened the glove compartment. He took out the jar of roasted peanuts he always kept there, returned to the Mexican, and laid them next to the water bottle. "I'll stop soon and get you something better to eat." Ron shut the trailer door.

He got in the truck. Should he look for a hospital? What kind of questions would be asked? Still, wouldn't it be better to risk the man's freedom than to risk his life?

Ron tapped the steering wheel, then got back out of the truck and opened the trailer door. The young man opened his eyes. The look of trust and hope that filled the drawn face gave Ron his answer. He patted the young man's leg and bolted the door.

Ron started the truck and pulled back onto S-2. His eye caught a flash in his side mirror. A state police car was behind him, lights flashing.

Antonio struggled to sit up. As the truck slowed and stopped, he opened the jar of peanuts and shoveled a handful into his mouth. Outside, he heard voices. One belonged to the man who had helped him. He used the divider post to pull himself to his feet. He couldn't see anything through the small, opaque windows on the sides of the trailer.

Hanging on the divider, he looked toward the stall where a horse stood. A sliver of light shone near its head. He listened to the voices, but the words were meaningless. Slowly, he eased himself in front of the horse, lining up his eye with the crack in the feed door. He saw part of a man's back and side. He moved his gaze down the back. His eye widened. A club hung from a black belt, next to it, the handle of a revolver. The man's hand rested on it.

Was the man asking about him? Would he kill him? He used what little strength he had to move away from the feed door. Leaning heavily on the divider, he inched toward the back of the trailer. He would accept his fate, whatever it was. But he would be on his feet, not on his knees. He stood waiting, his eyes fastened on the door's bolt.

The trooper handed the driver's license back to Ron. "We're assisting the Border Patrol with a search for a missing man. Someone abandoned a truck full of illegals up in the mountains yesterday. We believe one of them walked out. This is the nearest road he could've reached. Seen anybody walking?"

"Can't say I have. No, nobody walking. I'm just passing through. Kind of in a hurry though. Got to get this horse up to Sonoma by tomorrow morning." Ron dropped his license as he tried to put it back in his wallet.

The trooper's eyes narrowed slightly. "Drive carefully. Looks like the rain's quit, but the way this wind is blowing, I don't think this storm's over."

Ron smiled. "Oh, you never can be too careful, sir."

He watched in his rearview mirror as the trooper got in

his cruiser, slammed the door, and switched off the flashing lights. Instead of starting the car, however, the trooper leaned over the steering wheel, looking at the trailer.

Ron turned on his signal and eased onto the road. He checked his rearview mirror. The trooper was still parked. It had been just plain lucky that the trooper hadn't asked to look in the trailer. Ron checked his mirror again. The cruiser's overhead lights were flashing.

Maybe the trooper had another call. Ron stepped on the gas until he hit the speed limit, putting distance between himself and the cruiser. He looked in his side mirror. Far behind him he could see the police car pulling out.

He turned his eyes back to the road, leaned forward over the steering wheel, and squinted at the reddish haze coming toward him. His grip tightened. What was that? He glanced in his rearview mirror again. The flashing lights were still there.

He turned on his headlights, gritted his teeth, and drove into the billowing cloud of sand that rolled toward him.

3

PLUTARCHO "POPPY" MENDOPOULOS hurried down the concourse of the United Airlines terminal. The "Departures/Arrivals" screen told him the plane was on time and would be landing in fifteen minutes at Gate 80. He knew right where to go. How many times had he bid one of the Amantes farewell or patiently waited to greet them? It seemed that someone in the family was always on the way somewhere. This time, his Angel was on her way home.

He stood near the security checkpoint, the small, square, white sign he'd meticulously lettered A M A N T E clutched in his hands. Craning his neck, he tried to see down the concourse. *Jesus, You bring my Angel home safe.*

He looked around at the other people who were waiting. *Lord, use me today.* He pressed one hand to his shirt pocket, *The Four Spiritual Laws* booklet and peppermint candy were there, ready to help whomever needed them. The unsaved or a fussy toddler, they were all God's children.

His eyes rested a moment on each face: a young man crouched down, holding a toddler awkwardly on his knee;

an old man stood alone, rubbing his whiskered chin with calloused hands; a boy in fatigues fingered a small, blue velvet box as he shifted from one foot to the other; a middle-aged woman dressed in black held a child in her arms, tears glistening in her eyes. He could just make out the heading of the tract clenched in her fingers, "In Memory of . . ." *Lord, send Your ministering angels to comfort her.* He made a mental note to pray for her during his evening prayer time. The Lord often put him in the path of people suffering a loss. He had known their pain firsthand, but he'd also known the healing love of Jesus Christ.

The young man with the toddler stood and pointed down the concourse. "There's Mommy."

People began moving toward the security station. Poppy picked up his sign, eager to find his Angel and comfort her.

A woman tapped him on the shoulder. "Excuse me, sir."

Poppy moved aside.

A man bumped him. "Pardon, I need to get through."

Poppy stepped out of the way.

A boy pushed past him. "Move it, old man."

Poppy edged back.

The arriving passengers began pouring through the security checkpoint. From the farthest edge of the excited onlookers, Poppy squared his shoulders, stretched up on his toes, and raised his sign with both hands above his head. *Oh Lord, please don't let her ask me where her mama is.*

As Angelica stepped into the open terminal, she scanned the area for her parents. Caught in the stream of deplaning passengers, she stood on her tiptoes, trying to spot their familiar faces. As the travelers began to disperse, she saw the white board with big black letters. Her heart soared. *Poppy*. She took note of the people standing next to him. No one she recognized. Where were her parents?

She shouted, waving her hand. "Poppy!"

He lowered the sign, scanning the crowd, unable to see exactly where she was.

Angelica threaded her way toward him, finally catching his eye as she neared him. She noticed his silver hair had been recently cut, his thin mustache neatly trimmed, a bowtie carefully tied at his neck. It touched her heart. Though he always took pride in his appearance, he'd dressed up for this special occasion.

He dropped the sign and wrapped his arms around her. The wisp of a man pressed his cheek against hers. "Oh, Miss Angel. You look beautiful. Praise Jesus, He bring my girl home safe." His dark eyes sparkled.

"You look great." It was hard to believe he'd turned seventy-five on his last birthday.

Memories of her childhood flooded through Angelica. Poppy had worked for the family since before she was born. He was in charge of the gardens, the meals, and the household help, and he often served as a chauffeur. But when her mother brought Angelica home from the hospital, it became clear to everyone that Poppy's other duties would take second place to her happiness. He spent so much time with her that her childish interpretation of his Greek name, Peter, was her first word. He'd been "Poppy" ever since.

As the years had passed, he'd dried her tears as a toddler, helped her with homework through elementary school, and listened patiently to her teenage tales of first crushes. Poppy was a constant presence in her life, always available when her parents were not.

He was the one who had stood just offstage at the school play, prompting her lines when she'd frozen with fright at her third grade Christmas pageant. He was the one who had run along the sidelines of the soccer field cheering her on. He was the one who had helped her gently lay Goldie to rest in the little box they had decorated together. She smiled at the memory, knowing now that the tears in his eyes as he comforted her had not been for the shiny fish, but for the loss of innocence.

He'd taken her to church and taught her about God's unceasing love. By his example, he'd shown her the fruit of the indwelling Spirit and taught her about the purpose and power of prayer. Was life really as simple as faith and prayer?

Knowing how he'd rebuilt his life from ashes never failed to inspire her. Alone, without his country or culture, he'd refused to be destroyed by the thoughtless acts of one man. He'd rebuilt a life that transcended the physical world.

She stepped away from him. "Where's Mom and Dad?"

"They fly to Los Angeles this morning. Your father, he have emergency board meeting for his drug company. He say he have big investment in New Life, and he worry about drug approval. Your mother go too. She must go."

"What do you mean, Mother must go? She's never been involved with Dad's company."

"They come home Friday. They say they call you tonight."

She laughed. "Poppy, you didn't answer me." She often teased him about his unusual use of the English language, to which he usually replied, "You cross-examine me, Miss Angel?"

But instead, his voice was serious. "She no want me say anything. She say it's better she talk to you face-to-face."

Poppy was clearly uncomfortable with the conversation. There was no point in pressing him. If he'd given her mother his word to be silent, he would go to his grave with the secret. An uneasy feeling gripped her. "Oh, Poppy, everything's a mess." Her voice caught in her throat.

No taller than she, Poppy stepped back and put his hands on her shoulders. His wise eyes studied her face. The familiar smell of peppermint, his leathery skin, the look of concern and care . . . Her lips began to tremble. She closed her eyes and stepped back into his arms. No words were necessary. She was home.

Pulling herself together with a deep breath, she finally stepped away from him. "Sorry. I don't know what came over me."

"We talk in car. You tell Poppy all about it." He fished in his pocket for a peppermint and unwrapped it for her.

Angelica burst out laughing. "No, really. It's okay." But she accepted the candy, then took his hand as they moved through the crowds toward baggage claim.

While Poppy went to get the car, she waited for her luggage. By the time she found a porter and got to the curb, Poppy was waiting. He stood by the opened back door of the Lincoln Town Car, waiting for her to get in.

"No way, Poppy. I'm sitting right up front with you." She opened the passenger door and jumped into the front seat.

As he shut the door for her, she heard him say, "Praise You, Jesus. You give me such a good girl."

He got in and started the car. Smiling ear to ear, he eased into the airport traffic.

Angelica turned toward him. "Now tell me, what's happened with Thrombexx?"

"Your father say no drug approval yet. He think it taking too long."

She'd been in high school when her father began the project. He believed the drug had the potential to eliminate organ rejection in transplant patients. He'd finally formed a company, New Life, and begun the process that would get FDA approval.

"Well, now that I'm home, maybe I can help in some way."

Poppy nodded in agreement. "That what Dr. Amante say. You plan your *visit* just right." He glanced at her, as if to confirm his words.

Visit. The word hit her like the blow of a sledgehammer. He glanced at her again.

She dug in her purse for her sunglasses. "Why are you looking at me like that?"

"You still no tell your mom and dad what happened." He reached across the seat and patted her hand. "You need tell them."

His gentle touch brushed away the two years she'd been gone, and she was immediately aware of his unconditional love for her. "Oh, Poppy, after I talked to you I realized that if I didn't leave, I'd never be able to overcome my situation. Every law firm of any stature is in bed with Czervenka and Zergonos."

"Oh, my. That trouble for you."

"And it's more than that. I've thought a lot about it since it happened, and it may be a blessing in disguise. It's really made me think about my career. About where I'm going and how I'm getting there. It made me realize I've just jumped through hoop after hoop, being the best of everything. The best daughter, the best student, the best employee. And in the process I lost myself."

"I pray for you every day, Miss Angel. I ask God to show you what He want. Maybe this is His timing. Maybe He have something for you here."

"Well, we'll soon see. I came to a decision."

Poppy kept his eyes on the road.

"I'm going to apply for a position as a public defender. I want to advocate for the poor, and after I have some experience I'm going to open my own office and serve the people who can't afford high-priced attorneys. I'll use my trust account to help subsidize the pro bono cases."

Poppy glanced at her again. "That a big decision. You still young. You have time for that maybe later in your life."

"No, I put it off once, and I ended up hurting the very people I have always wanted to help. I compromised, and I regret it."

Poppy's face filled with understanding. "I pray for you, whatever you decide, I pray the Lord go before you. You talk to Him too, Miss Angel. Spend time with the Lord. Then you must tell your parents everything. It no good having a secret like this."

"I know, Poppy, I'll tell them as soon as they get home. And, believe me, I'm trusting God in this whole thing." She turned and settled into her seat. "Now, what's new at the ranch? Who's taking care of the horses? Did Dad breed Sari to the Sheik?"

"Your father hire a new man to run breeding program. His name Dr. Jim Williams. He come up here from big school in Davis. He send Sari down to Texas. She coming home tomorrow."

"How's Pasha? I've missed him. As soon as I get home, I want to take a ride." She could already feel his mane in her hand, the wind in her hair, the world fading away as he flew over the ground. "It won't be too late. No one's home anyway."

Poppy nodded his head. "Yes, Miss Angel. You go for a ride."

As they passed the downtown exit, Angelica quickly glanced at Poppy's face. She knew that was the exit that led to the alley, a home for the homeless, where his wife and child had died. But his face was serene, and his eyes never left the road.

It was four o'clock by the time they turned through the big, white gates that marked the entrance to Regalo Grande. The long, paved drive followed the quiet stream that flowed on the ranch year round. Ancient oaks shaded the banks, and lupine and roses grew wild in the natural surroundings. She'd forgotten how beautiful it was.

She rolled down her window, pushed her sunglasses back in her hair, and took a deep breath of the fresh air. "Absolutely heaven. It smells just like I remember."

The red-tile roof that spread across the massive, stucco home that sat atop the ridge was visible even from the valley. As they approached, Poppy pressed the remote control to open the black wrought-iron gates. They were anchored in a gray, fieldstone wall that had been built to define the southern boundary of the estate's formal grounds. Angelica watched the R and G medallions swing back with the gate. When they first moved there, her father had told her he'd named the ranch Regalo Grande for a very special reason. It meant "The Big Gift" in Spanish. The ranch was his gift to her and her mother. It would always be there for her. She knew it was his way of showing his love for them.

Poppy parked the car in front of the arched, stucco entryway. Bougainvilleas planted on each side were in full bloom, a wall of living lace. Tropical flowers flourished in the sheltered setting. Their bright colors and delightful fragrance added to the sense of beauty and peace she'd so desperately missed.

Angelica didn't wait for Poppy. She jumped out of the car, leaving the door agape. Her feet flew down the wide path beneath the arches and across the Mexican pavers. Approaching the circular fountain that sprang out of a split boulder in the middle of the entryway, she slowed her steps. The sound of the trickling water transported her to warm summer afternoons spent playing in the fountain pond. The fragrance of jasmine that grew in profusion along the drive filled the air. This was the enchanted place of her childhood. She stopped and watched as a red-winged blackbird landed on the base of the fountain to drink the cool water.

She quickly walked the rest of the way to the massive, double-front doors and pushed them open, then sprinted up the stairs to her room. No matter when she visited, she always found it just as she remembered. The queen-size bed, topped by a big canopy, was made up with a thick, white comforter and overstuffed pillows, all covered in Battenberg lace. Sheer drapes fell from the twelve-foot ceiling to a casual gathering on the tiled floors, framing a huge, glass sliding door that opened to a private, redwood deck overlooking the Sonoma Valley. But her favorite place was what she called her nook. The bay window at the far end of the room with a deep seat, lined with pillows. It faced the rolling hills and pastures of Regalo Grande.

She walked over, knelt on the window seat, and cranked open the big windows that formed the sides of the oriel. The stables and arena were just below, and behind them were the white fences that outlined the five-acre pasture her father had enclosed for Pasha when he bought him for her twelfth birthday.

"Where is he?" She put her fingers between her lips and let out a piercing whistle. From behind the stables that blocked her view of part of the pasture came a white blur headed at a dead run for the fence gate. When it seemed too late for him to stop, Pasha peeled to the right, breaking into a high-stepping prance, tail up and nostrils flaring. He tossed his head and snorted.

"I'm coming, Pash!" Angelica jumped from the window seat. She hunted through the big chest of drawers next to her bed, pulling out a pair of her old Levis and a pink cotton top. She changed her clothes and grabbed her boots from the closet. Within minutes she was at the pasture gate.

Pasha nickered and pranced when he saw her.

"Hey, good buddy." She patted his neck, and he quieted down, his brown eyes intent on her. She knotted his mane just above his withers and gave a quick pull. On cue, he kneeled down on his left knee, and she slid onto his back. They were off, out the gate and across the ridge. With her cheek against his neck, her legs gripping his sides, they were a synergistic force moving through suspended time, independent of mere mortals.

Perhaps ten minutes had passed when she finally sat up and leaned back, signaling Pasha to slow down. "Easy, boy." He nodded his head up and down, as if to agree, and broke into a choppy trot.

"Easy now." He slowed to a walk but pranced in protest. With a grin, she walked him south until they reached the big, shady oaks that marked the path of the mountain stream. They stopped for a drink, then continued on to the stables.

"Hey, Ms. Amante." She closed the pasture gate and turned around. It was Chick, the ranch manager who'd been hired shortly before she moved to New York. He took care of the horses and hired and fired the laborers needed to run the ranch. He gave her a polite smile that did little to soften the hard angles of his face. "When'd you get back?"

"Just an hour ago. I couldn't wait to take Pasha out for a ride." She'd forgotten about Chick's mismatched eyes. They reminded her of an Australian shepherd.

"Your dad had the guy takin' care of Sari take special care of Pasha too. But when Sari went to Texas for breeding, the guy just up and left. So, I've been takin' care of Pasha to fill in. Eh, boy?" He stepped up on the bottom fence rail and reached over to stroke Pasha's neck, but the horse put his ears back and stepped away, causing Chick to lose his balance and flop over the top board.

"Whoa, Pash. What's that about?" Angelica stepped toward Chick. "You okay?"

Chick got his feet back on the ground. "Yeah, fine."

Angelica frowned and glanced at her horse. In all the years she had owned him, Pasha had *never* acted this way. "Guess he just wants me to know he expects me to take care of him now that I'm home."

"Guess so." Chick chuckled as he checked himself over.

"Are you going to get someone else to take care of Sari? Poppy said she'd be here tomorrow."

Chick shrugged. "Don't know. I've been trying to hire another Mexican." He stuck his thumbs in the top of his pants and cocked one of his bowed legs at the knee. "They just never stay around. Always sneakin' off. Just about the time I've got 'em trained on handling the horses, they take off. I've got some calls out to see if we can find somebody. That mare's hard to handle. Be best if we could get someone with experience."

"I know, and now she's in foal she'll probably be even more skittish. It's important you find someone good. Keep trying."

Chick's lip twitched. "As a matter of fact, I was just goin' in to make a call to Mario at the Lo Bianco Vineyard when I saw you. He's supposed to be looking for me."

"Who's working here now?"

"I've got a college kid from Sonoma State helpin' out with exercising and feeding while we're lookin' for somebody permanent, and the yard man helps out if I need him."

"Please, have someone clean my saddle and bridle. I'll be using it now that I'm home. And I noticed there's quite a bit that needs to be done on the place. Fences painted, hay stacked, and Pasha's water trough is filthy. It really needs to be cleaned . . . soon."

"Sure, Ms. Amanté. I'll get to work on that stuff right away." His grin tightened.

Angelica scanned the property. It wasn't in the kind of condition her father had always insisted it be. "Thrombexx must be taking more of Dad's time than I realized."

"Your father's a busy man all right. Well, I need to get back to work. It's good seeing you again." Chick turned and walked toward the barn.

Pasha stepped up to the fence and stretched his neck toward Angelica. She gently rubbed his velvety nose. "What was that about, Pash?" She studied the animal's face. "What are you trying to tell me about him?"

Pasha snorted and pranced, nodding his head up and down, then trotted off to the water trough. Angelica folded her arms on the top rail of the fence, rested her chin on the back of her hands, and watched him drink. Thoughts of her father's investment in Thrombexx, her mother's absence at the airport, and the unkempt look of the ranch jockeyed for her attention. As she stood beneath the blue California skies, surrounded by the pastoral mountains of Sonoma, a strong feeling of apprehension rose within her.

51

Chick watched from just inside the barn door as Angelica Amante walked up the hill to the main house. When she disappeared through the kitchen door, he walked to the barn and went into the tack room. He picked up the phone.

"Hey, Mario. It's Chick. You got a line on any Mexicans?"

"Why'd you ask? I thought you just sent your Mexican down to Hell's Canyon."

Chick sat down on a bale of hay. "I don't mean for our little business in Texas. I mean somebody I can use here for a while. The doctor's daughter is home for a visit, and she's already stickin' her nose where it don't belong about work to be done around here."

"I got no one right now, but I'll keep you in mind."

"I don't want nobody too smart. Give me a beaner that'll work cheap, sleep in the barn, and thank his God if he don't get slapped around." He ran his free hand over his stomach where it had hit the fence rail. *Too bad Miss Prissy was there, or that horse woulda regretted his little tantrum.*

"Why don't you call me again in a week or so," Mario said.

"I'll do that."

Chick hung up the phone and looked with disdain at the tack lining the walls. Bridles needed cleaning, saddles needed oiling. Yep. What he needed was someone not too smart and not too good at countin' his money.

Angelica's saddle was mounted on a wooden V. He fingered the silver conchos that needed polishing. "I'll get 'im trained, and by the time that woman goes back to New York, he'll be ready to go to Hell."

4

THE TRUCK'S HEADLIGHTS revealed a swirling curtain of sand. The blacktop faded from sight. Ron slowly applied the brakes, brought the rig to a stop, and turned off the headlights. He checked to be sure the windows were closed tight and the vents shut. Still, the gritty particles sifted into the cab as though through a sieve. The truck rocked side to side as Sari lunged in the trailer. Ron pulled his shirt collar over his nose and mouth. He had no choice. He stepped out into the driving sand.

He bent his head, squinting at the ground, but the snaking patterns of sand hid the road from him. The wind's hot breath shrieked and moaned in his face, blocking all sound from the trailer. Hunched over, he edged step by step toward the back of the rig. He reached out to steady himself with the side of the trailer, but his hand met only a prickly wall of sand. His heart pounded. He turned to his left and rushed a few steps, swinging his arm in broad strokes. Nothing. He turned in a circle, looking through the slits in his eyes, but the earth and sky were invisible behind the sand. He knelt down, afraid to move farther. His knees sunk in a small berm, the road no longer beneath him.

The horse pulled back and tried to rear as wind and sand hammered the trailer. Antonio struggled to his feet in the darkness and stepped toward her, feeling for her neck. He moved his hands between her ears and withers, trying to calm her. The vibration of the truck's door slamming assured him help was coming.

Moments passed. He glanced at the trailer door. With little more than shadows to guide him, he felt his way to the back of the carrier and pressed against the door. It was locked. He stood, waiting for the man who had helped him, but he heard only the vicious clawing of the wind.

Certain knowledge seized him. He turned on his heel and moved back to the front of the trailer. He felt along the front wall and took a loading rope off its hook. Finding the horse's head, he ran his hand down her lead. He felt the tie and yanked the knot. It seemed secure. Still, he doubled it, then slipped around the mare to the feed door. Snorting with fear, she tried to rear, then lunged, her hoofs scraping down his leg, narrowly missing his foot.

Working his hand through the bent metal, he managed to open the door. He tied one end of the rope to the same ring that held the horse, tied his shirt over his nose and around the back of his head, then, with all the strength he could muster, climbed through the opening. He fell onto the pavement.

Still holding the rope, he edged up to the truck and felt for the door handle. As the door opened a crack, the light came on inside. Empty. He let the door shut.

"*Amigo,*" he called against the wind again and again, but the wind spit his words back in his face.

He continued moving forward, pulling the rope to its full length. Tiny knives of sand whirled around him, slashing his skin. About ten feet beyond the front fender, he felt the rope tighten. He dropped to his knees and crawled in a wide arc as he fought his way to the back of the trailer, searching the ground around him with one hand, clinging to the rope with the other.

When he'd searched as far as the length of rope would stretch, he stood and listened. The wind was abating, allowing light. He scanned the immediate area around him. A man struggling to rise faded in and out of sight only a few yards away.

"*Amigo.*" This time the wind carried his voice.

The man who'd saved him stumbled toward him, hand outstretched. Antonio grabbed his arm and guided him to the rope. Together they fought their way to the back of the trailer.

Ron felt the trailer rock as Sari struggled against the tie that held her. He unbolted the door and climbed into the trailer, the Mexican right behind him.

Light filtered in through the opaque, side windows. "Whoa, girl." Ron ran his hand over Sari's back as he moved toward her head. "This is precious cargo, *amigo*. If anything happened to her, I could lose my job and my reputation. It's a miracle she didn't pull loose."

He yanked on her tie, checking it, then saw the double knot. He looked at the Mexican. A moment passed. "*Gracias.*"

Ron put his hand on the man's shoulder and pointed to

55

the clean hay where he had been lying. "Rest, *amigo*," he said, then turned and stepped out of the trailer.

As he walked back to the truck, he took a last look down the road he'd just traveled. Far into the distance he could make out the flashing lights of a police car, resting at a tilt a few feet off the road. He stopped. Did the officer need help?

He jumped up on the running board for a better look. A flatbed truck had pulled up next to the cruiser.

"Looks like he's already called somebody."

He stepped back down on the road and ran his hand over the door panel, feeling the pitted surface. "Sheesh. I wonder if my insurance company will say this was an act of God and refuse to pay for repainting?" He put his hands on his hips. Sometimes God let things happen that didn't make sense at all.

He got in the cab and started the engine. As he pulled away, he glanced in his rearview mirror. Little eddies of sand danced across the road behind him, obscuring the police cruiser as it disappeared in the distance.

Ron's headlights lit the REST STOP AHEAD sign. He looked at his watch: 10:15. Putting on his turn signal, he eased off the freeway and parked the truck and trailer a little distance from two eighteen-wheelers already shut down for the night.

He opened the back of the trailer. "Hey, *amigo*."

"*Sí?*" The Mexican stood and gave Ron a broad smile.

"You're looking pretty bright-eyed and bushy-tailed since we stopped and ate." Ron stepped into the trailer. But before he could move up to Sari's stall, the Mexican took a few steps backward and eased in front of the mare to untie her lead. He looked at Ron for approval.

"*Bien, bien.*" Ron stepped out of the way.

The Mexican man made a soft clicking sound with his tongue as he guided the mare backward. She balked at the edge of the trailer, switching her wrapped tail back and forth. It hit the metal sides of the trailer like a bat. A white ring appeared around her eyes as the banging continued. Her shoulder muscles tightened, and she tried to rear. Ron stepped forward to grab her halter, but the Mexican took a small step back from her.

Ron stopped, his adrenaline pumping.

The Mexican started to hum, moving his hand lightly up and down the mare's neck. A full minute passed, then he stepped toward her, exerting a slight pressure on her chest while stroking her neck. His head was next to her cheek and ear. "Shhh, shhh." The mare's ears flicked back and forth.

Ron watched, waiting for any sign Sari would bolt. But the mare backed halfway off and stopped. So did the Mexican. He stepped a few inches away from her and whispered. Her ears flicked forward. Curious, she extended her nose toward him. He stepped toward her, again exerting a slight pressure on her chest. One step at a time, she backed the rest of the way out of the trailer.

Ron let out his breath and studied the young Mexican as he stooped and ran his hands over Sari's leg wraps. The man was relaxed as he spoke to the mare, reassuring her, soothing her fears. He worked with a quiet self-confidence that seemed at odds with his circumstances. Ron wondered how his son would feel in a foreign country, without any money, unable to speak the language, and riding with a stranger to some unknown place.

The Mexican looked up at him, and Ron gave him a

thumbs-up. The young man stood and walked the mare up and down the paved lot. Ron watched for a few minutes, then got back in the truck. He closed his eyes to rest for a minute.

When he opened his eyes, he looked at his watch. It was 2 a.m. He jumped out of the cab and ran to the back of the trailer. The Mexican was sitting on the edge of the open doorway, holding Sari's lead rope as she ate from a small pile of hay he'd put on the ground. Ron saw her soiled hay had been moved to one of the empty stalls.

"*Buenas noches, señor.*" He stood up.

Ron pointed to the road. "Let's go. *Vamos, amigo.*"

The Mexican loaded Sari and got in the trailer with her.

"No, you come up front with me." Ron motioned him out.

The man stood looking at him, not moving.

"Come on out. Up front with me."

Still, he stood. Finally, Ron took the young man firmly by the arm and guided him to the passenger's side of the truck, opened the door, and guided him in.

Ron got in and started the truck, then turned on his headlights. SHERIFF. The bold letters jumped out at him from the side panel of the door of the car just pulling off the highway. He glanced at the young man next to him. The Mexican's face was calm, but his eyes were focused on the car.

Surely they weren't looking for this man all the way up here. Had the officer who stopped him put out some kind of bulletin? Ron's mind raced. Maybe he shouldn't have tried to help. It really wasn't his problem. He was helping this man break the law. That was wrong. Still, he'd known so many of these poor Mexicans in his years hauling, about the desperate situations in their homeland that drove them across the border. But did that make it right? He wished he had the wisdom of Solomon.

Not get involved. That's probably what he should have done in the first place. But it was too late for that now. He looked at the Mexican again, and his own son's face came to mind. *God, forgive me if I've made a wrong judgment.* He drove slowly toward the exit, passing the sheriff as he turned onto the road.

For the rest of the trip, each time they pulled over, the Mexican jumped out of the truck and went to the back of the trailer to check Sari's wraps and clean out the soiled hay. He worked with a respect for the needs of both man and animal.

While they rode, the young man sat looking forward, his hands in his lap, his feet directly under him. He smiled when Ron spoke to him, but whatever he understood, he kept to himself.

It was midmorning when Ron turned into the long drive of Regalo Grande. As they approached the big hacienda, Ron saw the gates were open. He drove through them, pulled into the parking area next to the indoor arena, and honked the horn. Chick came out of the hay barn.

"Hey, Chick," Ron shouted, opening the truck door.

"Hey, buddy. Good to see you. Did everything go okay?"

"Pretty good. You know how high-strung this mare is. Glad I had someone with me to help keep her calm." They walked to the back of the trailer.

The Mexican was already there, untying Sari. "Shhh. . . . Shhh," he whispered, stroking her neck. She nickered and backed out.

"Hey, I'm impressed." Chick raised his eyebrows. "You sure you didn't give her a tranquilizer?"

"The vet at the breeder's said no way. I'm telling you, the kid really has a knack with horses."

"Really." Chick put his thumbs in the top of his jeans. "How long's he been workin' for you?"

"Oh, he's just helping me out. He's looking for steady work."

Chick's face lit up. "Really." He walked around the Mexican slowly, looking him up and down. "We might be able to help him out. Ms. Amante was just sayin' she'd like to have some more help around here. Let me call up to the house. If she's home, maybe you could talk to her about it."

"I'll get that, Poppy." Angelica ran to answer the phone.

It was Chick. "The hauler just brought Sari back, and he's got a Mexican with him that's lookin' for work. The hauler says the guy's real good with horses. Maybe you should come and talk to him."

"I'll be right there." Angelica walked out the back door and down the hill.

A gentle summer breeze was in the air, snatching fragrance from the flowers along the drive, wrapping her in a scented veil of jasmine. She took a deep breath. For a moment nothing existed but the natural beauty around her. *This is the day, this is the day that the Lord hath made.* She began to hum.

Her step was light as she approached the barn. "Good morning."

"Mornin'." Chick stepped to the side and introduced her to the heavyset man with the deep tan standing with him. "Ron, this is Miss Amante."

"Pleased to meet you, ma'am. Your dad's spoken of you many times."

She shook his extended hand. "How was the trip?"

"Well, fortunately, I had some help." Ron motioned toward the trailer and the person standing there.

She followed his gaze. The man straightened and brought his heels together. The trailer cast a shadow across his face. All she could see was his hands, as if the sun were highlighting them. One firmly gripped Sari's halter, the other gently held her lead.

Angelica turned to Ron. "Chick just told me this fellow's looking for work."

Chick took the lead from the Mexican and stepped back.

Before Ron could answer, a gust of wind blew through the barn. The door Chick had just walked through slammed shut, and Sari reared, pulling back on her lead. Chick snapped the rope to pull her down, but her nostrils flared, and panic filled her eyes. She reared again, her front hooves lashing out. Chick gritted his teeth. Angelica saw the rope burns on his fingers as he struggled with the mare and grabbed for the rope, trying to help.

Sari lunged to the right, trapping herself between the barn wall and Ron's truck. She stood wide-eyed, trembling. Chick swore under his breath.

Suddenly, the young man who'd come with Ron was facing the horse holding his hand out. "Shhh. . . . shhh. . . ."

Sari stood, muscles tensed, trembling. Angelica's heart pounded. If Sari bolted, she would tear up the underside of her belly on Ron's truck. The Mexican took a step toward her. "Shhh. . . ."

The mare's ears pointed forward. Her full attention was on the man who spoke quietly to her. He stood still for a

61

few moments, his hand extended. Without a sound, he took another step toward Sari and took hold of her halter. He whispered to her, clucked his tongue, and leaned into her chest. As he encouraged her, step by step, she backed out from between the truck and barn.

Angelica released her breath.

"Wow. What was that?" Angelica glanced at Ron.

"Just Sari being Sari," he said with a nervous laugh, clearly shaken.

Chick examined the burns on his hand, then looked back at the Mexican. "He knows how to handle a horse all right. We could use that kind of help around here."

Angelica nodded. "We sure could. And Sari seems to have taken a liking to him." She turned to the quiet young man holding Sari by the halter. He looked down at his feet. "What's his name?" she asked Chick.

"It doesn't matter what you call him. He's just a Mexican."

Angelica winced. "What's that supposed to mean?"

Chick's face reddened. "Uh, nothin'. It's just they usually pick up a nickname along the way."

"Would you ask him his name?"

"Sure. *Cómo se llama usted?*"

"Antonio Perez, *señor*." The man kept his head down.

Angelica pursed her lips. "Who does he work for now?"

"Nobody right now," Ron answered. "I brought him along to help me. I thought maybe somebody'd be looking for a good worker."

Angelica looked at the Mexican again. He was thin, but it was easy to see his chest and shoulders were well developed. He seemed a lot taller than the other Mexicans who worked on the ranch while she was growing up. She noted

62

the threadbare, dirty shirt, the torn, baggy pants, and the scuffed, broken sandals. The end of a rope hung out from under his shirt. His hair clung to his neck; he hadn't bathed in a long time. Still . . . he stood straight, steeled under her gaze. There was a presence about him, a quiet dignity. She sensed an inner strength.

Angelica bit her lip. *How thoughtless of me. Here I am gawking at him like I've never seen anybody who works for a living, talking about him as if he weren't even present.* She made up her mind. "Chick, why don't you and Antonio put Sari in her stall? Tell Antonio he has a job with us."

"Will do, Ms. Amante." Chick smiled broadly, pulled the barn door open, and made a sweeping motion with his hand. "*Ven conmigo.*"

"Did you have Pasha's water trough cleaned yet?" Angelica called after them.

Chick glanced back at her. "Not yet. I was just going to do that when they drove up with Sari."

"Well, that can be Antonio's first job. You two go ahead. I'll be there in a minute to show him where it is."

The two men disappeared into the barn.

Angelica turned to Ron. "Where's his stuff?"

"He's got about everything he owns with him right now."

She tried not to look surprised. "That makes it easy. What was he making at his last job?"

"I'm not sure. But most folks pay about five hundred a month, food, and a place to stay."

"That sounds fair to me. I'll have Chick tell him. Thanks so much for all your help."

Ron nodded a farewell as he got back in his truck.

She watched him drive away, turned, and headed into the barn to find Antonio—she wanted to make amends. Chick

63

had him hauling a bale of hay to Sari's stall. He carried it with ease, hoisted above one shoulder. He set it down with care, then picked up the few wispy, oated stems that had fallen from it and pushed them back in the bale.

"Chick, tell him we're going to pay him two hundred fifty dollars every two weeks. Tell him to come with me. He can get started right now by cleaning Pasha's trough."

Chick turned to the man and spoke in Spanish.

"*Sí.*" The young man nodded his head.

Antonio followed behind Angelica as they walked to the pasture. At the gate, he rushed in front of her to open it. She smiled and got a quick look at his face. Her eyes widened. He was handsome in the classic sense, with his square jaw, dark eyes, and deep tan, but there was something else, a strength that didn't threaten.

He waited for her to walk through, then closed the gate. She saw Pasha trotting playfully toward them, prancing and tossing his head. "Go on. Get." She waved her arms at the horse. He gave an indignant snort and took off at a gallop.

They walked across the pasture to the trough. "This is a slimy, filthy mess. It isn't fit for Pasha to drink from," she said out loud, then flushed, realizing he couldn't understand her.

She pointed to the trough. "You clean." She made a scrubbing motion with her hand. Suddenly, she realized she hadn't brought anything with her so he *could* clean it—no rags, Ajax, steel wool.

She was about to signal him to sit down so she could run back up to the house and get something when he began looking around in the field. He picked up a rock with a flat side and studied it. Then he returned to the trough, kneeled down, let the water out, and began to scrub. Amazingly, the filth fell away and the metal shone through. She watched, curious and fascinated. He'd solved the problem with a rock.

Then she noticed his smile. It lit his face as he worked, patiently keeping at the task, whistling softly. He did his work with a kind of quiescent joy. His quiet, simple way touched her.

She stood silent, watching him. The minutes passed. The beautiful spirit revealed before her, there in the field at the dirty water trough, sparked an inner longing. How could this delight for life have survived the poverty and nothingness, the years of hunger and want that drove so many from his homeland? She lowered her eyes. His humble act, done with such willing care, somehow seemed more noble than any clever application of the law she had made.

When he finished, the trough looked new. He stood and took a few steps back from her. "*Bien?*"

She hadn't spoken Spanish since she took it in high school. But even if she hadn't remembered that *bien* meant "good," everything about him said he valued doing a good job: the concern in his voice, the way he leaned forward to catch her answer, the way he gripped the rock, but most of all his face, which was open, honest, waiting. Yet there was a ruggedness about him that didn't bow to her position, only respected it. So unlike her co-workers in their professionally starched and pressed shirts, tucked into Armani pinstripes, bowing and scraping before the kingmakers at Czervenka and Zergonos. This man drew her in a way she didn't understand.

He flashed a smile at her, revealing white, even teeth.

"*Muy bien.*" She smiled back, then looked away.

The world sure would be a different place if everyone approached their jobs with as much care as he cleaned a water trough. But that wasn't the way the world was. Her stomach knotted.

She looked at him again. He was standing, patiently waiting. He'd set the rock on the lower edge of the trough, a tool in its proper place. "Antonio, I think you're just the guy we need to whip this place into shape."

A warm breeze blew through the pasture. For the first time since she'd arrived home, she felt like everything was going to work out.

She just needed to get a copy of his papers.

5

Angelica stood in front of the big picture window in the living room, looking down past the gates of Regalo Grande. Poppy should be arriving with her parents any minute. She played with the pearl dangling from the chain around her neck. This was going to be hard. Her mother had been told she could never have children. Her parents still called Angelica's birth, eighteen years after their marriage, their little miracle. It was important to her that she make them proud. *Dear God, please prepare their hearts for my news.* A red flicker of metal flashed beyond the oaks. She walked to the far corner of the window for a better look. A car turned into the drive.

She ran out the front door and waited beneath the archway. When her parents had called on the night she'd arrived home, her mother had refused to give her any details as to why she'd accompanied her father on his trip, and Angelica hadn't been able to pry anything out of Poppy. Was she going to reopen her interior design business? Many of her professional contacts had been in Los Angeles. But why the secrecy?

Perhaps her mother had made a new circle of friends in Los Angeles, where many of her father's partners lived. Angelica rolled her eyes. Did they have eligible sons? Her mother never missed an opportunity to let her know it was time she got married. She wanted grandchildren. Angelica gasped. Surely they weren't bringing any "new friends" home with them! And here she was standing out front like Bachelorette Number Two.

As Poppy pulled in front of the big arches, Angelica was relieved to see her parents sitting by themselves in the backseat. She could see her father's big frame and her mother's tiny one silhouetted in the back window. Before she got down the steps, Poppy was opening her mother's door.

"Oh, honey, I'm so glad you're home. You look beautiful," her mother called out over Poppy's shoulder.

Her father came from around the back of the car, but instead of greeting her, he stepped in front of Poppy. She could hear his deep, gentle voice. "Here, Gen, turn your legs toward me." He put his hands under her mother's thin arms and lifted her through the door.

Angelica's eyes widened. Her mother's face was wan, and she was much thinner than the last time Angelica was home. Her father supported her as she stood.

"Mom, what happened? Were you in an accident?"

"We'll talk, honey. But right now, give me a hug." She extended her free arm toward Angelica.

Her father smiled as mother and daughter embraced. Angelica stepped out of the way as Poppy handed her mother a cane.

"Dad, are you okay?" She put her arms around him.

He patted her back, never comfortable with such displays

of affection. Years in the operating room had burdened him with the knowledge that too often life and death were separated only by a split second or the cold, metal blade of the surgeon's scalpel. Better not to feel too much or too deeply.

"I'm fine, honey." She felt his hand linger on her shoulder as he stepped away. "Let's go in. Your mom and I are starved. Poppy, I'll get the suitcases. You go ahead and start lunch."

After the suitcases were unloaded, phone messages checked, and the mail rifled through, they gathered at the table on the big, tiled patio overlooking the estate and valley to wait for Poppy's lunch. The sky was cloudless, the air crystal clear. The view stretched as far as the eye could see.

"Mom, now tell me what happened."

"Do you remember when I got the flu?"

"No."

"You remember. I joined that walking club, trying to get a few pounds off. I'd finally worked my walk up to three miles a day, then I had to quit."

"You mean over a year ago? Last summer?"

"Yes. It seems like that's when this whole thing started. I just never got my energy back. Then a few months later, I was sick again. I went to the doctor, and they did a lot of tests, but nothing showed up. They told me it was a virus, to rest and drink a lot of water."

"You seemed fine at Christmas. Why didn't you say something then?" Angelica sat back in her chair and folded her arms, looking from her mother to her father.

Her father answered. "There was really nothing to tell. It just seems to come and go. The doctor thought it could be a virus or even something brought on by stress. Your mother hasn't been immune to the pressure I'm under." He reached over and took her mother's hand in his.

"That's why I went with your dad to Los Angeles. There's a specialist down there who Dr. Bell referred me to."

"So what'd he say?"

"They just don't know. I've been tested for MS, lupus, mycoplasma, and everything else. I'm getting scared. This last time it hit me, my legs went numb, and I couldn't get out of bed for over a week." Her voice faltered, and tears welled up in her eyes.

Angelica got up, hurried to her mother, and wrapped her arms around her mother's thin shoulders. "Don't worry. You're going to get better. Dad and I are going to find out what's wrong, and we're going to take care of it." She spoke with more conviction than she felt.

Angelica laid her face against her mother's hair. Its dry coarseness pricked her cheek. She closed her eyes tight and pressed her lips together. There would be time for tears later.

Poppy whistled as he stepped onto the patio. He carried a big tray of sandwiches, deli meat on thick slices of San Francisco sourdough, in one hand and fresh fruit arranged on large, crisp, lettuce leaves, likely picked from his garden that morning, in the other. He set them on the table. Poppy took the placemats and plates from under his arm and placed one in front of each person. "You come now, Miss Angel, and sit down. You need eat."

"Poppy, I left a message for the vet. Be sure and let me know if he calls. I want him to check Sari before I send the stud fee."

"I do that, Dr. Amante." Poppy disappeared into the kitchen.

Her father chose a sandwich and put it on his plate.

He seemed to have aged a lot since she'd seen him last Christmas. His hair was much grayer, the lines of his face deeper. Circles under his eyes showed through his dark tan.

"Well, we couldn't be more proud of you, young lady. In the midst of all this, you're our one bright spot."

A smile lifted her mother's hollow cheeks. "You couldn't have picked a better time to visit. I just wish we'd known a little sooner. We committed to our cruise dates before we knew you were coming, unfortunately we leave a week from Monday. I'm going to call our travel agent and see if there's any way that can be changed, but I kind of doubt it since it's been changed once. I was just too ill to go earlier this summer."

"Don't worry about it, Mom. We're going to have lots of time together." Angelica took a deep breath. Here was an opening.

Her mother rushed on. "I'm not going to worry about it now. Tell us about you. We know you've been swamped since that man died and they gave you all his cases. Didn't you say some of them might be precedent setting?"

"I told your mother you'd thrive on a challenge like that." Angelica noted the sparkle in her father's eyes. "Mark my words, they'll be offering you a junior partnership before it's over. Fill us in on all the details." He picked his sandwich up with both hands and took a bite.

Angelica floundered for an opening sentence. "Uh, there'll be plenty of time for that. I want to hear about what's new with you. What happened at the meeting with your partners?"

Her father swallowed and set his sandwich down. "It was a board meeting for New Life. We're concerned about the continued delays we're encountering from the Federal

71

Drug Administration. We should have received approval on Thrombexx by now."

"It does seem like it's been in the pipeline forever. You thought it was only months away from approval when I moved to New York."

He shrugged. "We're at the mercy of the government, honey. I have complete confidence in our research and trial data. Thrombexx was tested at over fifty centers here and some in Canada. The suppression of the cells in the blood vessel walls of the new hearts was dramatic. We've provided everything they've asked for and more."

"It'll be worth it, Dad. Your company's going to end up with a proprietary interest in the product, aren't they?"

Her father's face glowed with pride. "You're something else. Always thinking. Absolutely. That's why we formed the company and I invested in it. As soon as we get the FDA approval, we're going public. I've worked on this for over eight years, and I'm sure this drug is going to all but eliminate the problem of chronic rejection syndrome in transplant patients."

Angelica picked up a slice of apple. "There's no chance that the FDA won't—"

"Oh, honey, don't even say that. Your dad borrowed against most of our assets to make this investment."

Angelica frowned. "Mom, I'm an attorney. I get paid to think of the downside." How thoughtless. Her mother was under enough stress, and she hadn't even heard the news Angelica had to reveal. "I'm sure Dad knows what he's doing."

"If things work out as I plan, you and your mother and your children and their children will be financially secure." As always, her father's primary concern was his family.

Her mother tapped her father's arm, and he looked where

she was pointing. "Ben, there's a strange man down there. Look, walking on our drive. He's going into Pasha's pasture." She shaded her eyes with one hand. "I'm sure that's not Chick."

Her father started to rise when Angelica cut in. "That's Antonio. Chick just hired him to take care of Sari and the other horses. He's great with her."

"I'm glad he did. We needed somebody." Her father sat back in his chair. "I planned to talk to Chick about that new pasture I had fenced. It's full of rocks. I want them cleaned out before we let any of the show horses exercise in there. They'll nick their hooves."

Angelica's eyes sparkled. "Dad, why don't we go down after we finish eating? When you've finished with Chick, we can take a ride."

He smiled broadly. It was clear he had missed her. "Great idea. When we finish eating, I'll change my clothes and meet you down there. Now, tell us all about this new position they gave you."

She'd wanted to tell them, to explain everything . . . so they would understand.

"Angelica?"

Poppy hurried across the patio. "Dr. Amante, Dr. Williams on phone for you."

"Wait, Angel. I'll be gone just a minute." Her father excused himself.

Angelica looked at her mother. "Who is Dr. Williams?"

"He's the vet your dad hired to handle the breeding program. After you went to school, your dad kind of lost interest, but he always hoped you'd get involved again after you got settled in your career. So he's kept his finger in showing and breeding. He says it's been a good tax shelter for us." She reached over and rested her hand on Angelica's. "And

73

you know, I love seeing the horses in the pastures, racing around with their tails held high, tossing their heads. It always reminds me of when you used to jump up on Pasha's back, no saddle or bridle, as free as the wind, the two of you. You've been our joy." She started to say something more.

Angelica looked at her mother. "And?"

"Oh, we weren't going to tell you. We wanted to surprise you."

"What?"

Her father returned to the table.

"Ben, I know it was going to be a surprise, but I'm going to tell her now."

The excitement in her mother's voice brought a smile to her father's face. "Go ahead, honey."

"We've decided to plant the seventy-five acres over the ridge in grapes. It's been a dream of ours for years . . . to have our own label."

"How exciting." Angelica pushed her plate to the side and leaned forward in her chair.

"Well, that's not the surprise. I mean . . . it's part of it. But anyway, we've been having some work done on the land, and we thought what a great place to have a little party for you when you got home. To celebrate your promotion and share our news about the vineyard. I hired a party planner. There was no way I could do it myself. We're having a tent set up and a caterer, and we've invited lots of friends." Oblivious to Angelica's silence, her mother rushed on. "I didn't have contact information for hardly any of your friends, and I couldn't ask you since we wanted it to be a surprise." She caught her breath. "But there's still time. It's more than a week away."

Her father sat down. "Mom's even planning to take you

shopping in the city for something special to wear." He looked at his wife. "Should we tell her the rest of it?"

Her mother hesitated, then smiled. "No, let's keep that a secret."

Angelica fought back tears. Her mother glanced at her father, then back to Angelica. "What's wrong?"

Angelica took a deep breath. "Mom and Dad, I need to tell you something. The only reason I didn't tell you before now was I wanted to tell you face-to-face. I've made a decision about working in New York. I won't be going back."

All the words rushed out at once. Not at all like she'd planned. Her mother's fingers flew to her lips.

"*What?*" Her father's voice cut through the air like a surgeon's scalpel.

"I didn't make this decision without a lot of thought."

"You never discussed it with us."

"Dad, it had to be my decision."

"What happened?" Her father's voice took on a professional tone. He folded his arms across his chest.

"When Bill O'Connell died, the firm gave me his files."

"And a promotion," her mother added.

"Yes, but as I began to get into the cases, I realized that the client was cheating their employees."

"How could that be legal?" Her father's arms relaxed a bit.

"Well, the employees were illegal Mexicans working the crops, and what the company did was withhold their pay. You know, told them the head office was late, or the mail was lost or something like that, usually a couple of months. Then they'd call immigration and have them deported."

"It must have been legal, or your firm couldn't have represented them." His words were clipped.

"Dad, this isn't about what's legal, or what can be

75

framed as legal. It's about what's just. What they are doing is wrong."

Her father looked mystified. "Angelica, the world is full of injustice. You can't make it your business to pass moral judgment on every case your firm handles. You don't have all the facts. Maybe they weren't good workers. Maybe they created other problems. I don't see why that would be any of your business. Your responsibility is to your firm and to the client. I hope you'll reconsider this."

"Why don't you call them and tell them you'd like some time to think this over?"

"I can't, Mom. My things are on their way out here." Angelica brushed her hair away from her face and lifted her chin. "They fired me."

"They fired you!" Her father's arms dropped to his sides, and his mouth hung open.

Her mother's face was pale, filled with concern. "Why are you throwing everything away? We put you through school. We did everything in our power to help you. How could you do this to us?"

Angelica felt tears well up in her eyes. "It isn't about you. It's about me." Angelica spoke with a deliberate calm. "I've given this a lot of thought, and I've made a plan."

"Well, I can't wait to hear what it is, young lady." Her father had never talked to her with such a hard edge to his voice.

"I'm going to apply for a job as a public defender." She clenched her fists under the table.

"Public defender? That is ridiculous. You can't do that. You won't make enough to live on. Public defenders are attorneys who can't find better jobs, settled for less because they had to." He pushed his plate away, his sandwich unfinished.

"That's not true, Dad. There are plenty of competent attorneys who got into the law profession to help other people. And who needs more help than the indigent? Besides, it's an excellent way for me to get trial experience."

"If you want trial experience, why can't you apply at a firm in the city?" The force of his words didn't invite an answer.

"Why? Why can't I be what I want to be? Why do I have to justify everything to you and Mom? You're right. I won't make much money. I'll work long hours at a third of the pay. But I've thought about that." She braced herself. "I have the money in my trust account. I can use that to help me get by."

"Your trust account?" He jabbed his fist at the table. "That money was never meant to be used for something like this. That was to be used for your first home, to further your education, to make investments."

"I am making an investment. I'm investing in myself. And after I've got some experience under my belt, I want to open my own office and take pro bono cases."

"Where on earth did this thinking come from? You left here focused and on track."

Tension hung like a curtain between them.

"Dad, you always taught me to stand up and be counted, to follow my dreams, to never quit. You know ever since I found out the details about Poppy's life when he came to America . . . no, it was even before that, when I went with him to visit Helena's grave, that I was determined to make a difference in the lives of people like that. That's what I'm going to do now. I admit, I got sidetracked, but now I'm going after what I want. I'm not going to look the other way anymore."

"Angelica, that was just idealistic, childish fantasizing."

He waited for her to comment, his face firm, his eyes never leaving hers. Moments passed. He looked away, a grudging respect flashed across his face, and he shifted in his chair. "It seems like you've made a final decision."

"Yes, Dad. It's going to work out. It's the right thing to do. You'll see." Angelica reached out and laid her hand on her father's arm. "Give me a chance. Please, support me in this."

Her father folded his hands in front of him. "Angelica, you're our only child." He looked at her mother. "I think it's safe to say I'm speaking for both of us." His voice softened. "We can't support this, but we won't oppose you. You're home now. Maybe being here will bring you back to who you really are. What I am going to ask is that you give this more thought. Promise me you won't apply for any jobs right away—that you'll take more time to think this through."

Angelica put her hands in her lap. Her heart went out to her parents. Her mother sitting there, clutching the table to steady herself. Her father, choosing his love for her instead of his anger. She didn't need more time to think about it, yet she wanted to be fair to them.

She would honor her parents' request . . . for now. Her hands relaxed. "I promise."

They rose from the table in silence. As Angelica followed her parents into the house, she looked back down to Pasha's pasture, where her mother had seen Antonio. There didn't seem to be anyone there now. As she turned to go back into the house, her eye caught movement. She squinted, trying to make out what it was. She realized it was Antonio's back. He was bent over the water trough, scrubbing the ledge where he'd laid the rock. She watched for a moment. A little of the tension lifted as she thought about the time she'd spent with him at the trough—he, so untroubled by his circumstances, whistling softly.

A breeze kicked up, and she scanned the sky. Clouds gathered in the distance, casting a shadow over the pasture where Antonio worked, reaching up to the patio where she stood, and turning the summer air cool. Angelica closed her eyes and lifted her face toward heaven. *Lord, I want to trust You, but You make it hard.*

Chick stood next to Angelica's saddle. He rubbed polish on a silver concho, then wiped it off with a rag. The polish that got on the leather he wiped off with his finger. The Mexican watched him.

"That's how you do it," Chick told him in Spanish. "And you'd better do it good. This saddle belongs to the *patrona*. I'll leave this stuff here so you can do this later. Right now, we're goin' to go to the stables so you can do the feedin' for tonight."

They walked out of the barn. "Hey, look. It's the doc and Angelica." Chick pointed to the path that led from the house to the horse facilities.

"Dr. Amante." Chick wiped his hands on his pants, then shook his boss's hand. "How was your trip?"

"Lots of long days. I'm glad to be back. How'd everything go around here?"

Amante's idea of a long day was eighteen holes. "Well, the news, as I'm sure Angelica must've told you, is that Sari's back from Texas."

"So she said. I've already asked the vet to come out and check her." Dr. Amante turned to the Mexican. "And this is the young man you've hired? Angelica says he's very good with Sari. Tell him 'Welcome.'"

79

Chick translated.

Angelica reached out and touched the Mexican's arm. "I welcome you too, Antonio." She tilted her head, trying to look into his face.

He glanced at her, shifted his feet, and looked back at the ground.

What a wimp. If he's as dumb as he acts, this could work out better 'n I thought.

Angelica turned to her father. "In his country, the classes just don't mix. This is probably making him uncomfortable. Chick, tell him that in America we look at each other when we talk. We all have the same right to speak."

"She says to look at her when she talks to you," Chick told him in Spanish. The Mexican raised his head and looked at her.

"*Bien*, Antonio." Angelica patted his shoulder.

He responded with a silent, courteous smile.

That's right, beaner. You know your place.

Angelica put her forefinger on her lower lip. "You know, I think I'll brush up on my Spanish. My old high school textbook is still in the bookcase in my room."

Chick caught his breath. Last thing he needed was the boss's daughter sticking her nose in his business. Better nip this in the bud. "Oh, he doesn't speak that kind of Spanish. He speaks the Spanish of the *campesinos*. It isn't Spanish. It's Mexican."

"I bet he'll understand me." As usual, Angelica seemed sure of herself, no matter what anyone else said. Just like an uppity woman. "I want him to be able to help me with the horses, so we have to find some way to communicate. Have you shown him where he's staying in the bunkhouse?"

"He'd rather stay in the barn," Chick said. "He's not as Americanized as some of the other Mexicans we've had work for us. I know his type. Believe me, the barn is better than what he's come from."

Angelica frowned at that. "Chick, Dad had the bunkhouse built for the hired help, and Antonio might as well start getting Americanized if he's going to work for us. Don't you think so, Dad?"

Chick saw the approval in the doctor's eyes and forced himself to smile. "Sure, no problem. It was just that Ron said Antonio stayed in the barn at his last job, so I just thought it'd feel familiar to him." Chick patted the Mexican on the shoulder.

"What about getting him some clothes, Chick?"

"I was thinking the same thing, Dr. Amante. There's always some old clothes lying around the bunkhouse. And if I can't find anything that fits him, I'll take him with me to St. Vincent de Paul the next time I go to town for feed. Or maybe Poppy can see if his church has anything."

"Tell him you'll show him his living quarters, but he can choose where he wants to stay, and that you'll be getting him a few things to wear as soon as you can."

Chick turned to the Mexican. "This is the boss. He said you can sleep in the barn. If they like your work and decide you can stay, they'll get you some better clothes."

"*Bien, señor.*" The Mexican stared at his feet.

"Good." Dr. Amante smiled, clearly pleased. "It's settled then. Right now I want him to pick up the rocks out of the new pasture. He can use a pick to dig out the bigger ones, and I want them carted and piled behind the barn. We may want to use them for drainage somewhere else on the property. Any that will stack well we can use on the stone wall out front."

Making sure his tone was friendly, Chick translated. "Go to the barn and get the cart and pick. It's by where you got the hay. Hurry up, these are important people, and we don't have all day."

Chick turned back to Dr. Amante. *Yep, I think this is gonna work out real fine.* He tipped his head and smiled. "He'll be ready in a minute, sir."

He glanced back toward the young man who'd broken into a jog. *Yep, he's nothin' special. Just another Mexican.*

While Antonio was gone, Angelica, her father, and Chick walked through the pasture, checking the new fence. She observed the rocky ground around her. *There's no way anybody could pick up all these rocks.*

"Dad, look how many rocks there are. Do you really expect one person to do all this work?"

"Don't be silly, honey. Look over there. He's already started."

Angelica looked where her father was pointing. Antonio had taken the wheelbarrow to the front corner of the pasture. He stooped down and picked up a rock and put it in the wheelbarrow. He bent down again and dug with his hands around the next one and lifted it into the wheelbarrow. He worked with purpose and without hesitation. He didn't seem to see the hundreds of rocks before him. He saw only the job at hand. He didn't even look up as they passed.

Dusk faded into night, and about ten o'clock, Angelica went up to her room to get ready for bed. She slipped on her silk nightgown and turned off the light. She opened the bay window and sat down on the plush pillows. The full moon lit the Sonoma Mountains. Shadows played in the canyons and danced beneath the trees.

A clicking sound came to her, steady and incessant.

She looked out past Pasha's pasture, trying to pinpoint the

source of the annoying interruption to a beautiful evening. There, outlined in the moonlight, was Antonio, still digging up rocks and putting them in the wheelbarrow. She watched him move from rock to rock, bent over, not bothering to stand, until three or four were dislodged. Then he gathered them and put them in the wheelbarrow.

Angelica's eyes filled with tears. Something about the mechanical, repetitive ritual made her think of the Mexican laborers working for the clients of Czervenka and Zergonos. The breeze came from the valley floor, carrying the sound of rock hitting rock as the wheelbarrow filled. *He's a laborer, just as they were laborers. This is who they were. Ortega, Ramirez, Martinez, Herrera. They were real men with real families. They deserved better than what they got.*

Tears trickled down her cheeks. These thoughts always brought her back to Poppy and the callous act that had left him and his pregnant wife homeless. Immigrants with nothing but the pittance they earned from what work they could find. *There's nothing I can do about that, but I can help Antonio.* The clicking stopped.

She looked out her window and saw the Mexican pushing the wheelbarrow toward the back of the barn. It wobbled under the weight, and he struggled to keep it upright. He disappeared into the shadows, reappearing a moment later empty-handed. She watched him walk into the barn, and the tears flowed in earnest. Her privileged past pressed upon her. "Oh, dear God . . . bless *him*," she whispered.

Angelica got up and went to the bookcase built into one wall of her bedroom. She flipped the switch that lit it. Shelf by shelf, she looked at each book. There it was, her high school Spanish text. She pulled it out. The book next to it tumbled to the floor. She picked it up. It was her Bible—the one Poppy had given her when she started junior high school.

She'd forgotten all about it. She ran her finger over the gold scrollwork etched in the cover. The leather was soft and worn. She used to read from it every morning. She and Poppy would talk about the verses as he drove her to school. It pleased him so when she'd quote a scripture to make her point.

Angelica took the books to her bedside table and set them down. She opened the cover of the Bible. "To Miss Angel—John 3:16." She thumbed through the pages of John. *John 3:8, I love that one.*

She'd always loved the words in red. Poppy told her some words were in red to remind her that Jesus shed His blood for man. There it was, John 3:16. Poppy had underlined it.

She thumbed through a few more pages, then her eye was drawn to a verse: "If you ask anything in My name, I will do it."

She read it again. "If you ask anything in My name, I will do it."

She closed her eyes, the power of the promise present with her. She knew God's Word was truth. She had accepted Christ as her personal Savior when she was ten. But the events of the past few months had made her wonder: Did He really hear *her* prayers? Did He really have a plan for *her* life? And if He did, would He forgive her for working on the cases at Czervenka and Zergonos? Could she forgive herself?

She read the words again. "If you ask anything in My name, I will do it."

"Jesus, forgive me and bless Antonio."

She rose and returned to the window. She couldn't change the past, like what had happened to Poppy's wife and baby girl. She couldn't help those who'd been wronged by Czervenka and Zergonos, but there was something she could do, and with God's help she would. She walked to her bedside table and set her alarm.

6

THE SUN WAS just beginning to light the Sonoma Valley when Antonio stepped out of the barn to begin his first full day of work. He'd slept well in the stall next to Sari after raking it out and putting down some fresh rice hulls and several leaves of hay.

He headed for the stream across the drive and down the hillside. Passing below the big house, he looked to the upstairs window where he had seen the *patrona* sitting the night before. The window was still open, but she wasn't there.

The man she is married to is a lucky man.

He'd never forget the moment he first saw her. Memories of her appraising stare replayed in his mind. He shook his head, remembering. *Her husband must be a strong man. She is strong with men.* Images of the sunlight on her beautiful face, when he opened the pasture gate for her, returned and chased away that thought. *But he is a lucky man.* He tried to put it out of his mind. It wasn't right for him to think of her.

"*Gracias a Dios,*" he whispered. He had a job and would

soon have money to send home. The risks he had taken had been worth it. He would be able to help his family. The *mayordomo* had said he would get two hundred dollars every two weeks. What a generous man, the *patrono*. Antonio determined to do a good job for them so they would be glad they had given him work.

He ducked under the oaks and took off his shirt, pants, and sandals before stepping into the stream. He washed himself as best he could in the shallow, cold water, then quickly stepped back onto the riverbank and put on his pants. The words of the *mayordomo* came back to him: "If they like your work and decide you can stay, they'll get you some better clothes."

He picked up his shirt and looked at it, then knelt down and put it in the water. He wrung it out, put it between his hands, and scrubbed it. Then he rinsed it again and hung it on a little branch so the warm summer breeze could dry it. *When they see me working today, they will see I don't need any new clothes. They have done enough for me.*

While he waited for his shirt to stop dripping, he sat down on a big branch that had fallen across the riverbed. He reached down and picked up one of his sandals. Pressing on the back of the sandal, he worked his finger into a slit between the heel and the sole. He eased the paper from its hiding place. Smoothing it open, he ran his hand over the words written there: "Church of Our Lady, Elena Perez, Acatic del Astillero, Jalisco, Mexico." This was his only link to his home and family. This is where he would send the money he earned. On the journey to America this was the one thing that he did not want to lose, his paper, this very, very important paper.

The missionaries at the church just outside Guadalajara often helped the desperately poor Mexicans who came to them. They filled out papers to file for a birth or death. Sometimes they gave away clothes or blankets. They taught songs and verses from the Bible. These services had been provided for many years, and the church workers were known and trusted by the Mexicans. The church workers wrote the address for his mother when his father first left for America.

This was the church where his mother would go the day after the moon was full, hoping to find an envelope. She would walk for miles to catch a bus. Many times he had gone with her only to find there was nothing waiting for them—no envelope, no word. Then his mother would cross herself and tell him God would provide their food until the next time.

Antonio refolded the paper and slid it back into his sandal. The thoughts of his family filled him with resolve to work hard and do well so he could return to them someday. It was his dream to stay in America until he'd earned enough money to buy land of his own in Mexico, raise a family, and be able to help care for his parents. Others had done it, and he could too. God had given him favor on his journey. God was with him.

He crossed himself, overcome with gratitude at the opportunity that lay before him. He put on his sandals and checked his shirt, pleased to find it still damp—it would keep him cool through most of the morning. After putting it on, he smoothed the front and arms with his hands, pressing it as best he could.

As he ran his hand down his sleeve, he felt a small, soft object under the thin fabric. Keeping his finger on it, he pushed his sleeve up to see what it was. A small bug. He pinched it between his fingernails, carried it to a rock, and set it down. He bent close, studying it. He knew many creatures of the land were friendly and good, like the fish and deer and armadillos that gave food and those that flew above the earth and gave song. But some were dangerous and would steal, like the coyotes that killed the chickens and livestock of his people and left them hungry. He observed the small bug, its eight dark legs and pale body. He had seen this insect before. It could make people sick with its bite. The sister of his *padrino* had suffered long with the illness. He picked up a small stone and crushed it so it could not hurt anyone else who came to the water.

His stomach growled. Yesterday, the *mayordomo* had showed him a building by the barn and told him it was where he would eat. He'd gone there last night. It had a big room with beds, and there was another room with tables. There was an icebox full of cartons and bottles, like the iceboxes in the markets of Guadalajara, but there was a light inside this one. He'd looked at the food, but he didn't know what some of it was or if it was all right for him to eat it. He found a bottle of Coke, but he didn't have a coin to open it. Finally, he found some bread that had been left on one of the tables and an orange in a bin. He had eaten those things. Many nights in Mexico there was no food at all—or only enough for the little ones. He could wait a little longer. If no one mentioned anything about meals by midday, he'd ask.

He thought for a moment about the *mayordomo*. The man had not taken him into the building, only pointed at it. And there was something else. When the man spoke to the *patrona*, he smiled and laughed. But when they were alone, his voice was hard, without cause. Maybe he should not say anything to the man whose moods were as different as the two colors of his eyes. Yet he did not want to judge the *mayordomo* without giving him a chance to show himself. *Dios, You have never let me starve. I will trust You now.*

Antonio took one last look at his shirt, rolled up the cuffs to hide the frayed edges, then stepped out from under the oaks. As he made his way back to the barn to get the wheelbarrow and pick and head to the new pasture, his thoughts returned to the *mayordomo*. He'd heard him talking to someone else through the wall of the stall where Antonio slept. His voice was low, dark. He did not understand the words. Except for one—Texas.

Angelica awoke to the ringing of her alarm and the aroma of freshly brewed coffee that had made its way up the stairs to her bedroom. 6:00 a.m. She jumped out of bed and grabbed her robe.

As she passed her open window, her ear caught the clicking sound, rock upon rock. A quick glance outside confirmed that Antonio was already at work. She rushed down the stairs to the kitchen. Poppy was slicing something when she walked in.

"Morning, Poppy. I thought for sure I'd beat you down here this morning."

"Good morning, Miss Angel. You sleep good?" He poured coffee into a thick mug and handed it to her.

"I sure did. What a beautiful day we're going to have." She slipped onto one of the stools pulled up to the counter. "I've got to get busy this morning."

"Why you busy? You just got home."

"I've been thinking about something." She ran her finger around the rim of the mug. "When I told Mom and Dad that I wanted to become a public defender, they asked me not to rush into it, and I promised them I wouldn't. But late last night I saw Antonio, that new man we hired, working in the pasture. He must have been tired. The whole thing reminded me of those men my firm was deporting." She took a sip of coffee. "Then I got an idea. And the more I thought about it, the more sense it made." She set her cup down and folded her arms on the counter. "I'm going to teach Antonio to speak and read English."

Poppy tried to hide his smile. "That sound like not rushing into it."

"Well, it isn't. One, it will give me a chance to work with someone just like the people I'll be helping as a public defender. You know, see what it's really like. Two, Antonio will learn English. And three, I'll learn Spanish."

"You sound like you in front of a jury." Poppy put on his apron.

"Well, I'm not going to just sit around licking my wounds while I sort this out with Mom and Dad. Soon I'll be speaking Spanish like a native. Being bilingual will be a big plus on my résumé no matter where I work."

"You speak Spanish when you in high school. You know many words."

"That was a long time ago, and I really never used it that much, but it won't take long to refresh my memory. And I want to find a children's book, you know, the kind that has simple words, to use when I teach him to read. What do you think?"

Poppy reached across the counter and put his hand on hers. "It sound to me like you want to help those men your company send back to Mexico." He smiled at her, his face tender. "My Jesus know what's in your heart. I think it a good idea, and I will ask Him to use your idea for His purposes." He stepped back and put his hands on his hips. "What I fix you for eat now?"

90

Having Poppy's approval felt like a spiritual confirmation. She had a very good feeling about the whole thing. "Oh, Poppy. You know what I like."

Nearly every Saturday morning while she was growing up, she would wake up to the delicious smell of French toast made with Poppy's special recipe. He used thick slices of Italian bread soaked in whipped eggs. He grilled them until they had a paper-thin crust, then he dipped them in cinnamon and maple sugar. She tried to make them herself in New York, but somehow they never turned out the same as Poppy's.

"Lucky for you, Miss Angel. I happen to have my bread ready right here on the counter."

She smiled. How precious he was. He had already heated the griddle, and she saw a plate of cinnamon and sugar next to it.

"I can't wait. Just fix two, or I won't be able to fit into my jeans."

"You too skinny. I no like to see you so skinny. God no make people to be skinny. He make you perfect. You eat till you not hungry and you no worry about jeans. Your mom buy you new jeans if you need jeans."

Angelica laughed. "Oh, Poppy. Mother and I are going shopping next week. We've planned a day in the city. She isn't planning on buying me jeans, though. Silk slacks, maybe."

"I hear you all talking on patio yesterday. You still going shopping for new dress?"

Angelica's voice sobered. "We talked some more last night, and they're going ahead with the party. They feel like they have to. They're going to announce their plans for the vineyard. Mom told me to invite whoever I wanted, but I haven't kept in touch with anyone really. I was so much younger than everyone else in high school. We didn't have that much in common. I was into my academic life, and they were into their social life."

"What about Brad?" Poppy studied the French toast sizzling in the pan.

Angelica didn't answer.

Poppy looked at her. "You miss him, no?"

Poppy knew her so well. "I have. He was everything I thought a man should be: smart, ambitious, driven. It was hard when we broke up. I was in love with him. Sometimes I still think about him. If he could have moved to New York, we'd probably be married by now."

"I know your mama crazy about him. I think they still talk sometime."

"If they do, she never mentioned it to me. I think Mom was crazy about the idea of me marrying into that family and giving her grandchildren."

"You hard on your mother. She just want you to find nice man, a man that understand you. I pray for you too. I ask my Jesus to send you nice man. He know what man is perfect for you, and He will send him."

Angelica smiled at the little old man. She realized she had drifted away from the teachings of her childhood. Then it had seemed so easy to accept Poppy's simple faith.

As soon as she finished breakfast, Angelica went back upstairs, dressed, took her Spanish book, some paper, and a pen, and sat down on her window seat. She drew a T-chart. On the left side, she wrote: yes, no, day, what, who, house, Mr., Miss, Mrs., the days of the week, the months of the year, and the numbers one through ten. On the right side, she wrote: *sí, no, día, qué, quién, casa, señor, señorita, señora*, the days of the week, the months of the year, and the numbers one through ten in Spanish.

She took another piece of paper and made another T-chart. On the left, she wrote words she wanted to relearn and spent the rest of the morning thumbing through her Spanish text, reviewing verbs and looking up words to add to her T-chart.

About noon, she marked the "Conversational Phrases" chapter of her book, stuck her charts in it, and headed to the new pasture. She stopped in the kitchen and set her things down on the counter.

"You're still in here, Poppy? What are you doing?"

"I just finish clean the refrigerator."

"I'm going down to start Antonio's class. I thought noon would be a perfect time. He'd be breaking for lunch anyway. I need more paper though. A tablet or something."

"Your dad have big yellow pads in his office. On shelf behind desk." Poppy looked at the book on the counter.

"Great idea." Angelica hurried down the hall. When she returned, Poppy was gone. She reached for her book and papers, then stopped. Another book had been stacked on top. She picked it up. The Children's Living Bible.

She flipped it open and saw the little gold stars beside verses she'd learned as a child. She looked down the hall toward Poppy's room. "Well, I guess if it was good enough for me, it'll be good enough for Antonio."

She headed to the new pasture.

"*Buenos días*, Antonio," Angelica said as she approached him.

He stood up. "*Buenos días, señora*," he answered with a quick nod of his head. He smiled and wiped his hands on his pants, then extended his arms to take her books.

Angelica stared at him, surprised. *He called me Mrs.!* She shook her head and waved his hands away. "I'm no *señora*, Antonio. I'm *señorita*."

His smile broadened. "*Señorita?*" He shifted from one foot to the other.

"*Sí*, I'm *señorita* Angelica." She nodded her head in an exaggerated motion.

He looked down at the ground, and she noticed the reddening of his neck. *What* had she said that could have embarrassed him? She touched his arm and tilted her head so she could see his face. "Antonio?"

He glanced at her. "*Sí?*"

He seemed so uncomfortable looking her in the eye. She would have to work on that. She opened her Spanish book and read the phrase she wanted to him, pronouncing each word slowly and carefully in Spanish: "*No . . . hablo . . . español.*" Not that she needed to tell him she didn't speak Spanish. It must be obvious.

She looked at him.

A grin tugged at his lips. "*Sí.*"

"You . . . *usted* . . . *no hablo* . . . English," she improvised from her limited Spanish.

"*Sí.*"

"*Es necesario* you *englase*, me *español.*" Good heavens. She could only hope he understood.

He thought a moment and then nodded. "*Sí.*"

Good. She looked through her Spanish phrases. "*Cómo está usted?*" she asked clearly and carefully in Spanish. "How are you?" It was as good a conversation starter as anything.

"*Hambre.*"

She turned to the back of the book to the dictionary, running her finger down the list of words. "*Hambre, hambre* . . . Oh! Hungry?"

"*Sí.* Hungry."

Her thoughts returned to the night before. Rock against

94

rock. *He must be starved.* But his face showed no emotion, and once again she was struck by his quiet dignity.

She looked at her watch. It was almost one o'clock. "Well, come with me." She pulled on his shirtsleeve and motioned him to follow her.

He put the rocks he'd been stacking into the wheelbarrow and followed her to the bunkhouse.

Angelica had rarely gone into the bunkhouse. It was just a place where the hired help stayed. But she was not going to have someone who worked as hard as Antonio go hungry. They went inside. She set her book and papers down, then went into the kitchen area to look around. In the refrigerator, she found everything she needed to make a sandwich, and there were plates and glasses in the cupboards. She rummaged through the drawers and found a bottle opener and knife.

Antonio stayed a few steps behind her, watching everything she did. When she dropped a piece of bread, he picked it up and handed it back to her. When she dropped it in the sink, to rinse it down the drain, he picked it up and put it on the counter. She pushed it back in the sink, down the drain, and turned on the garbage disposal. She noticed him flinch as the motor started. She looked at him and smiled, then finished making the sandwich and put it on a plate.

It didn't look like much for a hungry man. She put a few more slices of meat and cheese on it. It still looked kind of dry.

Poppy's garden was just a few yards to the west of the bunkhouse; she could get a tomato there. She walked outside, Antonio right behind her. She walked through the rows of onions, radishes, and cucumbers to the tomato patch. Bending down, she examined several. She poked one.

Antonio eased in front of her, picked a big, red tomato, and held it out to her.

"*Gracias.*" She took it from him.

He picked another one and offered it to her.

He was at least six feet two and muscular, yet he looked like a little boy standing there with the tomato. She laughed and shook her head. "No. No more."

He started laughing. "No?"

As they stood there in the garden, she was aware of the crystal blue sky behind him and the gentle breeze blowing his hair. How odd that they were laughing together, she and one of her father's workers. Yet she felt so comfortable, as if she had known him a long time.

It's good to be home. It's so good to be home.

Antonio took the first tomato from her hand and motioned her ahead. They walked back to the bunkhouse kitchen.

She sliced the tomato, put it on the sandwich, then cut the sandwich in half and put it on a plate. She opened a Coke and poured it in a glass with some ice, then carried the plate and the glass to one of the tables and set it down. She stepped back, so he could sit down, but he pulled out the chair in front of the plate—for her.

"No, you sit," she said in English. He kept standing. She went and got her book and turned to the phrase chapter. "*Por favor . . . sientese,*" she read from the book.

He sat down and picked up the sandwich with both hands.

Angelica sat down next to him. "*Muy bien.*"

Still holding the sandwich, he raised his eyes to hers. Only a few inches separated them. "*Muy, muy bien, señorita.*"

She felt her neck reddening, and she quickly looked down at the Spanish phrases in the open book. She put her finger on the page and ran it down the blur of letters, but none of

96

the phrases made sense. None except the one that surfaced in her mind: "The eyes are the windows to the soul."

"Would you like to learn to read? I brought a book. I thought it might help." She felt like a babbling idiot. What was the matter with her? She took a deep breath. "Look." She opened her Children's Bible and turned it toward him.

He gently touched the page. "Bi-bul."

"*Sí, Biblia.*" Oh, for heaven's sake. Now she was speaking Spanish, and he was speaking English.

Through the open window just behind Antonio, a movement caught her attention. She focused, then saw Chick move away. He had been standing there listening to them. Why?

7

ANGELICA STOOD ON the patio and called down to the vegetable garden. "Poppy, are you about ready?" She watched him with his big basket, going from plant to plant, deciding which vegetables were ready to be picked—not too green, not too ripe, just right.

"We leave in maybe twenty minutes, Miss Angel. Church start at eleven o'clock."

"I'll go down and tell Antonio we're taking him to church."

Angelica ran across the grass and down the steps that led to the stables. Walking along the well-worn path, she thought about the many, happy years she had spent on the ranch. To her right, across the green, irrigated pastures, was a large cluster of oaks where her father had built her a playhouse when she was six. She hadn't wanted her playhouse too close to the big house. After all, she was six and didn't need a babysitter anymore. He had honored her request, and it wasn't until years later that she'd realized Poppy had an unobstructed view of her little house from his living quarters, just off the kitchen. The family had always joked about her independent streak. Her parents teased that her first word was "No" and her first complete sentence was "I do it *myself*." Well, now her independent streak had cost her her job, but for a good reason. She needed to put it behind her. Focus on getting her license to practice law in California.

As she continued down the hill, just in front of her lay the big, circular, outdoor arena. She'd spent many hours there after school and on weekends exercising Pasha and practicing for horse shows. She rode western and competed in pleasure classes. Pasha was well trained; it was she who had to spend time practicing. Her mother had arranged for her to take private riding lessons at the ranch. She learned to keep her hands still, not move her feet, and signal Pasha to change his gait by using the slightest pressure of her legs. She wanted to win, as much for herself as for her parents. Soon a trophy case was built above the bar in her father's study. Its blue ribbons and silver trays boasted of her success, and every visitor to Regalo Grande was afforded the pleasure of seeing them.

When she reached the stables, she found Antonio cleaning the area where the farrier had shoed horses on his last visit. Chick sat on a bale of hay, chewing a piece of straw, watching him.

"Isn't this Antonio's day off, Chick?"

Chick spit the chaff from his mouth. "Nah. He just got here. No need for a day off till he's put in at least a full week's work. Besides, he doesn't have anythin' else to do."

"Well, as a matter of fact he does." Angelica folded her arms across her chest and leaned against the stable wall. "Poppy and I are taking him to church in Glen Ellen. The church has a ministry for the Mexican laborers who work the grapes around here, so we're going to get him some clothes and shoes."

"Lucky guy."

She frowned at his sarcasm. "Did you have him move into the bunkhouse?" She looked at him as she waited for his response.

Chick picked at his fingernail. "I was gonna have him do that today. Maybe when you guys get back, he can pick out a bunk and put his stuff there."

Angelica noted how Chick avoided her eyes.

"*Antonio, aquí, por favor.*"

Antonio put down the box into which he had been throwing bits and pieces of horse hoofs and horseshoe nails. "*Sí.*"

"Hey, you're gettin' good with the Spanish, Miss Amante. Been studyin'?" Chick broke off an oated stem from the bale, stripped the grains from it, and stuck the end of it in his mouth.

Again, she noticed he avoided her eyes. "I've been brushing up on my Spanish. It's still pretty rough, but it won't take me long. Please tell him we're taking him to church, and after that we're going to get him some clothes. We'll pick him up here in the car in a few minutes."

Angelica listened as Chick translated what she had said. She couldn't put her finger on it, but there was something in Chick's manner, not just when he talked to Antonio, but in general, something not quite right. She listened to the words he was using and recognized many of them. He seemed to be doing just what she asked. Maybe she'd just been an attorney too long.

Antonio brushed off his pants, tucked his shirt into the waistband, and retied the rope belt. Then he asked Chick a question. When Chick answered, Antonio took off at a trot.

Chick inclined his head to Angelica. "He's going to wash his hands, then he'll be ready to go."

Angelica had just entered the house and changed into a skirt and some sandals when she heard Poppy give a short honk of the horn. She grabbed her Spanish book and ran down the stairs. She climbed into the seat next to Poppy and barely got the door shut before he stepped on the gas.

Poppy stopped on the drive next to the horse facilities and honked. Antonio ran across the open space and got in the back seat of the car.

Angelica opened her book and began looking through the "conversational" pages.

"Poppy, I've got to get a little Spanish phrase book. You know the ones I mean. You've seen them before."

"Yes, Miss Angel. Your dad have one in his study. He use it sometimes to talk to Rafael, the gardener."

"I'll ask him if I can have it."

Angelica continued looking down the page of her book. "Ah, here it is." She turned toward the backseat and told Antonio they were going to church.

He smiled and nodded.

"They might have some clothes for you. *Ropas por usted.*"

"*Sí, señorita.*"

"*Me llamo* Angelica."

"*Sí, señorita.*"

"No, my name is not *señorita.*" Convincing him to call her by her name was going to be harder than she thought. "*No señorita. Me llamo* Angelica."

He looked at her intently. "*No señorita? Señora?*" His face was a mix of confusion and concern.

"No, no. *No es señora*. I am *señorita* Angelica," she said, tapping her chest.

"*Señorita* Angelica." He tipped his head toward her, smiling. "*Me llamo Antonio Perez*."

Was he teasing her? Why did she feel like he had somehow gotten the upper hand? He was probably just being polite. She nodded her head toward him, then turned around and gazed out the window. What a beautiful smile.

"You know, Poppy, all my things from New York, including my car, should be here tomorrow or Tuesday."

"That be good, for sure."

"I've been thinking about it. Since I don't know exactly where I'm going to be working, I'm going to put all my furniture in storage. Then I'm going to go to Hastings and visit with some of my old professors to reestablish those contacts. Let them know what happened and ask if they'd be willing to give me a reference again. It's kind of embarrassing having to explain you were fired, but I think they'll understand. What do you think?"

Poppy tapped the brakes as they came up behind a pickup hauling a trailer. "I put that on my prayer list. I ask my Lord to show you what He has for you. You need put it on yours. He have a plan for your life, Miss Angel. His plan better than our plans." The old man patted her hand. "His ways mysterious sometimes, but He always let us know His will."

"Poppy, why did Mom and Dad change churches? I was surprised when I found out they weren't coming with us."

"Your mom say she like go to Santa Rosa better. She tell me more of their friends go there. I hear her say on phone that the service start later and the chairs more comfortable. I say she lucky woman their friends pick that church." Poppy slowed as the truck and trailer branched off onto one of the many drives along the road.

Angelica giggled. "Sometimes Mother is pretentious. I could see her picking a church for the wrong reasons."

Poppy turned and looked at her, his face full of interest. "Tell me, Miss Angel, what church you pick in New York?"

Angelica looked away and settled back into the seat, her cheeks flushed. There just hadn't been time.

With the road clear before them, the car wound its way toward Glen Ellen Faith Church. Angelica rolled the window down, turned her face into the warm, summer breeze, and closed her eyes. Poppy's words played back. "His ways mysterious sometimes, but He always let us know His will." *God, show me Your will. Show me Your plan.*

She felt the wind making a mess of her hair. She closed the window and took her mirror from her purse. Reflected just behind her shoulder was the handsome face of the Mexican man sitting in the backseat.

Poppy parked the car, and the three of them walked toward the sanctuary. "You in for a treat, Miss Angel. My pastor, he wonderful speaker. His sermons very powerful. He know his Bible, and he let the voice of the Lord speak through him. Sometimes I think maybe he raise the roof. My Jesus, He know about this place."

Once inside, Poppy found the preacher. "Pastor Steve, I want you meet my Miss Angelica Amante."

"I'm so pleased to meet you, Angelica. Poppy has spoken of you many times."

Angelica tried to hide her surprise. The pastor was a slight man, soft-spoken, quite ordinary.

"And he speaks highly of you as well." Angelica turned toward Antonio, who stood with his hands clasped across his waist, hiding his rope belt. "This is Antonio Perez. He works on our ranch."

The pastor extended his hand. "Pleased to meet you, Antonio."

Antonio hesitated, then extended his hand. "*Buenos días, señor.*"

The pastor answered in Spanish, his eyes as welcoming as his voice.

"Poppy says you have an outreach program here, clothes for those who need them. We thought maybe Antonio could get some things."

"Oh, the King's Closet—it's in the basement. Gretchen Sneidmiller's in charge of it. It's open after every service. Just go down to the basement and help yourself. Gretchen usually goes down there right after the service is over."

The church bells began to ring.

"I'd better get going." The pastor made his way to the platform.

Poppy nodded toward the front of the sanctuary. "I like sit up front, Miss Angel, so I can hear good." They slipped into the second pew.

The choir of about twenty members stood on a small, raised platform just behind the lectern. When the soloist stepped forward to sing, Angelica could see the name "Gretchen" printed on her nametag. A rather large woman with short, gray hair, she appeared to thoroughly enjoy her performance. She held the microphone in one hand and snapped the fingers of her other hand as she walked back and forth across the stage. Angelica turned to Antonio to see if he was enjoying the music. His face was somber. She glanced around the church, trying to see what could be bothering him. What did he see that she didn't?

Most of those attending seemed to be families. Everyone dressed casually, and there were crayons and coloring tracts in holders on the back of each pew. There were a few Mexican men sitting in the very last row. One was dressed nicely and had on a big Stetson hat, but the others looked like they'd walked directly from their work in the vineyards to the church. She looked at Antonio again. He seemed sad. Maybe he was thinking about home. She shrugged her shoulders.

After the opening music, the service started with announcements. Everyone laughed when the pastor said his wife had not yet returned from visiting her parents and that he had found the real meaning of Jesus's words "man cannot live on bread alone." There was another song. Some raised their hands in worship.

Angelica watched Antonio take the Bible from the holder in the pew directly in front of him and thumb through several pages. He looked at the little girl next to him, who was coloring a picture that rested on top of her Bible, then he crossed himself and bowed his head. What could be bothering him?

Frowning, Angelica took the program and Bible from the holder in front of her. It listed today's sermon as one in a series on the Beatitudes. The sermon was titled: "Blessed are the meek: for they shall inherit the earth."

She listened as the pastor spoke of the Sermon on the Mount and of how it dealt with the heart and mind. How the life of the believer, described by Jesus, was a life of humility, grace, and character that reflected Jesus Himself. Her eyes drifted to Antonio's bowed head and dark, calloused hands, folded in his lap.

The service ended with an altar call followed by a final hymn.

When the service was over, Angelica touched Antonio's arm and motioned him to follow her.

They found their way to the basement at the bottom of a short flight of stairs. The room was filled with rows of racks full of clothes. They were divided—men's clothes on the right side, women's on the left. Then they were divided again by size. Antonio followed her as she moved down the rows looking for his size. When she found it, she motioned for him to look through the shirts and pants. She left him and started to the back of the room where she saw rows of shoes and boots.

"Miss!"

Angelica looked toward the stairs.

"Miss!"

Gretchen Sneidmiller hurried toward her.

"Tell him not to touch everything. Some of our things are quite nice, and we really prefer that those people have someone help them."

"Exactly what do you mean?" Angelica's neck stiffened.

Gretchen raised her eyebrows and took a step back. "Well, you know. They just aren't used to nice things. Look how rough and calloused his hands are. He could snag those knit polo shirts. Some of them still have the tags. Of course, it wouldn't be on purpose, but we do have local people who are trying to find work. They come here to get clothes when they have a job interview. We like to save those nice things for them."

"Oh, really?" Angelica knew she was being curt, but she didn't care. "Well, this man already has a job and just needs a few things. The pastor said you're in charge of this ministry. Perhaps *you* could help him." This was exactly why people like Antonio needed an advocate.

Gretchen Sneidmiller turned on her heel in the crowded basement. Before she had taken more than a few steps, she stumbled over the leg of one of the clothes racks. Angelica watched as she fell headfirst toward the sharp, steel edge of the clothes rack marked "L." Angelica's anger turned to horror as the woman's full weight drove her forehead toward the scissor-sharp edge of metal. If it were not for the rough, calloused hand that slipped between her head and the rack just as she hit it, she would have received a disfiguring gash across her face. Instead, the blood that dripped on the floor was from a dark-skinned hand.

Angelica watched as Antonio gently lifted the injured woman to her feet. He wiped his hand on his pants, so as not to soil her clothes, and helped her to a nearby chair. She limped badly.

Angelica rushed over to her. "Are you all right?"

"I feel faint." She was trembling.

Antonio knelt beside the woman and looked at her foot. He eased her shoe off, and Angelica watched, surprised how his touch seemed to comfort and calm the shaken Gretchen. He began to rub her ankle, his fingers moving with a smooth confidence, as though he'd dealt with this kind of injury before. She watched him work with compassion and care, unconcerned about his own wound.

Suddenly, tears began to roll down Gretchen Sneidmiller's cheeks.

"Gretchen, what happened?" The pastor came running down the stairs. Poppy was right behind him. "What was that crash? It sounded like something fell."

"I tripped. I think I'm going to be all right. If you'll help me upstairs, my husband will take me home."

As the pastor and Poppy guided her up the stairs, Angelica took Antonio's hand in hers. "You okay? *Bien?*"

"*Sí, bien.*" He looked down at her, making no attempt to remove his hand.

She examined the cut, which had stopped bleeding. Then her eyes traveled to his face. The humble, gentle spirit reflected there made her feel pretentious, with her designer handbag tucked under her arm and two-hundred-dollar sunglasses casually pushed back in her hair. He'd shown more class than she or the other woman. Her cheeks flushed.

"I'm glad you're okay." She stepped away, breaking the moment. "Let's find you some clothes."

They spent the next twenty minutes looking through the racks and left with some shirts and pants, one pair of boots, a belt, and a straw hat, which Antonio put on as soon as he stepped outside the church.

"There's Poppy, waiting for us in the car."

Poppy pulled up, and they got in.

"I felt so bad when Mrs. Sneidmiller fell, Poppy. But I wish you could've heard her when we started looking at clothes. She didn't want Antonio to touch anything. Can you imagine? Thank heavens he couldn't understand a thing she said. If he had, I bet he wouldn't have been so nice to her when she fell."

Poppy's wise eyes sought hers. "We must pray for her, Miss Angel. She don't know no better. God have His way to correct us. He will correct her, His way."

She felt Poppy's gentle reprimand. "Oh great, in the meantime, how many other poor people will get only the leftovers from the King's Closet? The true King wouldn't run it that way."

"It look like Antonio got some nice things."

Angelica turned around and looked over the seat at Antonio sitting proudly with his clothes folded neatly on his lap. He'd even found a belt to replace the old rope he'd been wearing. She'd pointed out that the buckle was broken, but he seemed to want it anyway. It was the only one that fit him.

Poppy looked in the rearview mirror. "I see he have new hat. It like the one Rafael wear."

"Maybe it's a custom to wear a hat when you work. It's so hot down in Mexico, they probably need one to keep the sun off their heads."

When they got home, they let Antonio off at the stables. "Enjoy your day off. I'm going riding now, but later today I'll help you with your English," she called after him.

He turned and tipped his new straw hat to her as they drove off.

"Oh, Poppy. I'm always breaking into English with him. He couldn't have understood a word I said."

"You no worry, Miss Angel. I have feeling he understand you."

Poppy fixed Angelica lunch. After she ate, she went into her father's study and found the little phrase book. She left him a note saying that she'd taken it, then headed down to the stables.

She found Chick sitting on the same bale of hay watching Antonio cleaning up after the farrier.

"Chick, I think we need to go over some things with Antonio."

"Sure, Miss Amante." Chick jumped up. "Like what?"

Angelica noticed a little bead of sweat form on Chick's forehead. He eyed the book in her hand.

"I just want to go over a few details. Please call him over here, and let's go to the bunkhouse kitchen."

"Hey," he shouted to Antonio, waving him over.

Antonio came to join them, and Chick explained what Angelica wanted. They all went to sit around one of the tables in the bunkhouse dining area.

"Please tell him this is where he's to eat whenever he's hungry. Tell him he can have any food that's here, then ask him what he likes to eat so Poppy can get it when he shops for you guys."

Chick translated.

"*Yo quiero frijoles, arroz, tortillas* . . . *y* kookies." Antonio grinned.

Angelica laughed. "Cookies! Okay! I'll be sure to get you some." She looked at Chick. "Please tell him he can take vegetables from Poppy's garden if he would like."

Chick raised his eyebrows. "Since when will Poppy let someone in his garden?"

"Since I said so. Just tell him, please."

Chick translated.

"Also, I was thinking that every day on his lunch break I could meet with him here to help him with his English—and maybe he can teach me a bit of Spanish. Ask him if that would be okay."

"There's really no need for that, Miss Amante. I don't have no trouble talkin' to him."

"I wasn't doing it for you. I was doing it for him."

Chick shrugged, then told him.

Antonio's face lit up. "Yes, is good."

"See, he's learning already. Maybe you saw us in here yesterday at noon?"

"No, can't say I did."

"I thought I saw you outside the window."

"Mighta been just passin' by. Can't say I remember."

Angelica didn't take her eyes from Chick's face. "Maybe so. Well, if you'd take him into the bunkroom—let him

110

pick out a bed and give him a drawer for his stuff, I'd appreciate it."

"Will do, Miss Amante." Chick and Antonio headed to the bunkroom.

"Oh, Chick." Angelica ran after them. "I forgot. Tell him that Sunday will always be his day off, and he can do whatever he likes. If he wants to go to church, we'll take him."

"Or." Chick hesitated. "I was thinkin'. If he wanted to, I could take him over to Lo Bianco Vineyard. Mario's got a lotta Mexicans workin' there. He could visit with his own people."

Maybe she'd been too quick to judge Chick. "What a great idea."

Antonio found himself alone in the bunkhouse—his new clothes stacked on the bed with the sleeping bag the *mayordomo* had given him. He sat down on the mattress. He bounced up and down lightly, then lay back, stretching his legs out, wiggling his toes, which hung several inches past the end of the bed.

He picked up his clothes and took them to the drawer he'd been told was his. He neatly folded two of the three shirts and one pair of the pants and put them in it. The boots were set next to the dresser. He took one shirt, one pair of pants, and the belt with him.

He went into the kitchen and made a sandwich, just the way he had seen the *patrona* do it, then folded it in some paper on the counter and set it on top of his clothes. He picked it all up and walked to where he'd been cleaning up after the horseshoer. He looked through the box there and picked out four nails—one long one and three short

111

ones—and a long piece of baling wire. He rolled up the wire, then stuck it along with the nails in his pants pocket and walked to the stream under the oaks.

The sun filtered through the branches of the big trees. He sat down by the stream and unwrapped his sandwich. He chewed slowly, listening to sounds that were so familiar: birds above, a cricket somewhere on the other side of the stream, the water flowing by, the rustle of the leaves, the whisper of the wind.

When he finished his sandwich, he dug in his pocket for the horseshoe nails. He chose one of the short ones and then picked up his belt, studying the broken buckle. He pushed the nail through the leather, where the original hook had been. Next he took two small rocks and pressed them on one end of the nail, bending it into a hook and securing it into the leather. Now the buckle worked. He smiled remembering how the *patrona* had tried to talk him out of choosing it. Her accent was so heavy he could hardly understand her. At one point she'd said, "The buckle isn't good." As if the buckle had behaved badly. She often used the wrong word when trying to speak to him. He bit his lower lip and stifled a laugh, still respecting her, even though she wasn't present.

Antonio removed his old clothes, put on the new ones, worked the belt through the loops, and fastened it. He fished the remaining three nails and wire out of his old pants and put them in his shirt pocket; then he washed his old clothes in the stream and spread them on a rock to dry.

He sat on the big, fallen branch that lay partly in the stream, where he had sat the first time he'd been under the oaks. Had it been just a few days before? So much had happened, but he'd been treated well.

The *mayordomo* had said they were taking him to church. Could it be this was church in America? The ladies and children did not wear dresses, and their heads were uncovered. The men wore shorts. People laughed out loud, right in the church, when the priest spoke. Sadness stirred within him. The little girl next to him used her Bible like a table and colored on top of it.

Maybe this was not church. Maybe he had not understood.

He took the nails and wire from his pocket, laying the two short ones flat side to flat side on top of each other horizontally, making one piece. Then he placed the long nail behind them vertically. He held the wire on the back side and wrapped it in a crisscross pattern, securing the horizontal and vertical pieces together, making a cross.

He held the cross to his lips and prayed. *Lord, I come to You with nothing to give You, yet You have given me Your favor. You made a way before me and have brought me here, to this place, and provided much more than I need.* He sat silent, overcome with the truth of his prayer. *Give me strength and wisdom that brings honor to You and to my people.* He sat still before the Lord.

The shrill voice of the woman at the church as she spoke to the *patrona* echoed in his mind. Somehow he had offended the woman by his presence. Perhaps he shouldn't have been there.

He lowered his head and fingered the cross. *I do not know what I did that was wrong, but because You are good, You touched her with my hands. Your breath was upon her. Breathe upon her heart, if it pleases You, and make my peace with her.*

The leaves of the oaks swayed and danced above him, drawing him out of his prayer. He lifted his head, acknowledging the wind that whispered through the branches. *Lord, are You speaking to me?* The sun cast shadows on the tangled

113

mass of leaves that floated freely above him . . . like dark, flowing hair . . . like dark, flowing hair. He closed his eyes and found Angelica's striking beauty waiting there. *Lord, be with her. Keep her safe. I see her walking or riding or leaving the ranch—always alone. A woman should not be alone.*

Her silhouette the first night he picked up rocks, a solitary figure in the window, intruded on his thoughts. What was she looking for? *What is her heart's desire? Give her her heart's desire, if it pleases You.*

Antonio opened his eyes. As he ran his fingers over the cross, he noticed his cracked, calloused hands and stained fingers. These were not hands meant to hold her. These were hands meant to labor, day and night, and to feed his family in Mexico. His heart wrenched. He put the cross and his hands in his pockets. "*Dios*, I will bear it all if You will bless *her*."

His thoughts were interrupted by the sound of something coming under the trees farther upstream. He stood and looked.

It was Pasha. Angelica was sitting on his back with no saddle or bridle, just her hand in his mane. The horse went to the stream, and she let him drink. Antonio stepped into the shadow of the trees, unsure what to do.

The sunlight played across her dark hair and lit her beautiful face. He stepped forward to say something. *What can I say?*

He would call her name, as she had asked him to. But before he could call out, Pasha lifted his head, his ears pointed forward. He looked directly at Antonio.

"Finished, boy?" Angelica patted the horse's neck and leaned to the right, turning Pasha around, galloping away with her head against his mane and her dark hair flying.

"Angelica." His whispered word floated heavenward, alone. He raised his face, as if to follow its flight. "Give her the desires of her heart."

He turned to walk up the hill to the barn, then stopped to make one last request. He bowed his head. *Then have mercy on me, and heal the wound in mine.*

He squared his shoulders and strode up the hill, to the job that would secure his future in Mexico.

8

"ANGELICA, THIS TRAFFIC is terrible."

"Mom, it's no worse than it was yesterday when I met the movers in Mill Valley and put my stuff in storage. At least we're in my two seater and not in your tank." Angelica whipped her Mercedes in and out of the heavy traffic on the Golden Gate Bridge, working her way to the off-ramp to downtown San Francisco.

"That's true. It's so good to have you home, honey, even though I wish it were under different circumstances. We did so many things together when you were in law school. Remember how I used to pick you up and we'd have lunch downtown? I wish I felt better so we could do more."

"Don't worry about it, Mom. We're together today, and that's what's important." She gave her mother a sideways glance. "I think it's great that you feel well enough to go shopping in the city, especially after that trip down south. Any particular reason?"

Her mother's insistence that they embark on a search for a "perfect" dress for Angelica to wear to the upcoming party wouldn't have been that unusual before her mother's illness. But to invest what little energy she now had into finding Angelica a "perfect" dress hinted at something more. Asking her mother point-blank what she was up to wouldn't do any good. She'd learned that years ago. It would take some sleuthing. Changing the subject was a standard diversionary tactic her mother employed when secretly planning a blind date, the most likely explanation for her mother's behavior.

"Look, Angelica. Oceanside Cinemas."

Angelica hid a smile. Something was definitely up. She looked at her mother again, dainty hands folded in her lap. With two years' experience in New York, surely she was more skilled at advancing her agenda than the diminutive woman beside her. She'd bide her time and wait for another opening. "Remember that time you and I went there, to that big movie premier you'd heard about, and it turned out to be an X-rated movie?" She giggled. "It was just plain lucky that our bright and shiny faces didn't show up in any of the pictures that the paper printed in their coverage. Can you imagine? Dad opening the entertainment section, and there's his wife and daughter, front and center."

Her mother grimaced. "As soon as that stripper scene started and we figured out where the story was going, we were out of there." They looked at each other and burst out laughing.

"I'll let you off and park in the underground lot." Angelica moved to the right lane as she approached Union Square.

"The doorman can take the car at Saks. You won't have to worry with parking."

"I'm not worried about parking. I'm worried about you doing too much walking."

"The doctor said it was good for me." She picked up her cane.

Angelica turned her face, pretending to look out the window. She didn't want her mother to see the fear she felt. Her mother seemed to be deteriorating before Angelica's eyes. Forcing a smile, she turned back and said, "Let's go bend some plastic." She looked at her watch. "It's almost noon. Do you want to eat first or shop first?"

"Well, let's do a little shopping, then we can go to the St. Francis and have lunch. It's better later—not so crowded. Besides, it'll give me a chance to rest. I think they even have a high tea there if you want to do that. Then we can go on to Maiden Lane and see what Gucci and Hermes have for the fall line."

"Oh, fun, but I really don't need anything, Mom."

"Now, now. You know that's when you find the cutest outfits. Just when you think you don't need anything, you find out you do."

Angelica looked at her mother's drawn face and sweet smile. They'd had lots of fun together over the years. "Yes, Mom, sometimes you do." She reached over and tucked a wisp of hair behind her mother's ear.

As they looked through the racks, her mother's prediction proved true. Angelica found a beautiful summer dress of white chiffon. The front had a deep V-neck, which would have been too revealing had it not been for the delicate, scalloped ruffle appliquéd on its edges. The top tapered to her slender waist and flared out to a full skirt that fell over a silk underskirt. When she modeled it for herself in the store mirror, more than one head turned to admire her.

"You absolutely *must* have that, darling." Her mother's eyes glowed with pride. "It will be perfect for the party Saturday night."

Angelica looked at the saleslady. "How much is it?"

Her mother put her hand on Angelica's arm. "Don't worry about it, honey. I want you to have it. Your dad told me before we left to be sure you got something real pretty."

The willing accomplice exposed. "You sure, Mom?"

"I'm sure you'll be the prettiest girl at the party Saturday night." Her mother's eyes sparkled with mischief and mock innocence.

Time for the opening salvo. She'd take her best shot. "Do you think the handsome young attorney you've invited will think so?"

"Really, Angelica. Everyone will think so, dear. Let's go take a look in the men's department. I'd love to find something for your dad."

"A reward for the accomplice?" Angelica gave her mother a wicked smile. She was closing in. She'd have the details by the time they finished lunch.

"No, they're having a sale."

In the men's department, her mother asked for a particular salesman, Pierre.

"Mrs. Amante. How good to see you again. How may I help you today?"

As Pierre extended his manicured hand to her, monogrammed cuffs peeked out from under his Armani jacket. Angelica couldn't help but take a quick look at the cuffs of his tailored pants. Yep, they fell exactly midway between the top and toe of his shoes.

"The holidays are coming, and my husband and I will be attending several functions. I'd like to look at some formal wear."

"Of course. And that's why you're here." He glanced toward Angelica. "And who is your beautiful friend?"

"Oh, I'm sorry. This is my daughter, Angelica."

Pierre gave a slight bow. "I should have guessed. You look just alike. Now, Mrs. Amante, let me show you what's new for the season." As they turned to go, her mother gave her a wink.

Angelica followed behind, looking in the glass counters on either side of the aisle—wallets, sunglasses, shaving kits, belts. The image of Antonio's broken belt, and of the rope it had replaced, drifted into her mind. She stopped and looked in the display case.

A salesman appeared across the counter from her. "May I show you something, Miss?"

She hesitated. "No, just looking."

The belts were beautifully made of Italian leather, some with designer-logo buckles and some with simple, silver ones.

Antonio. That first day at the water trough . . . the tireless hours in the pasture . . . the sandwich he offered her when he was so hungry . . . the selfless help he offered Gretchen Sneidmiller . . . the used clothes, boots, and broken belt that he accepted with such gratitude . . .

Joy, peace, goodness, kindness, gentleness—she'd seen them all in him. She set down the box holding her new dress. He deserved better than his lot in life, much better.

She called to the man behind the counter. "I've changed my mind. I'd like to see that black leather belt on the end, the one with the silver buckle."

He handed it to her. She held it up, looking at it, feeling the rich leather. The image of Antonio's hands folded to hide the rope around his waist when he met the pastor flashed in her mind. "Gift wrap it, please."

"What kind of paper? Birthday, wedding?"

"The store wrap will be fine." She paid for it, took the bag, picked up her box, and went to find her mother.

120

She found her browsing in men's shoes. Her eyes lit up when she saw Angelica's package. "What'd you buy?"

"A belt for Antonio. He had to get a broken one at the church, and I think he deserves something nice. He's such a hard worker. Such a nice person." Why did she feel like she had to justify everything she did? Her mother thought nothing of spending a fortune on a dress Angelica didn't need and would probably wear once.

Her mother frowned. "You shouldn't concern yourself with the hired help, honey. Chick can take care of them."

Angelica gritted her teeth. Maybe she'd give him the belt *and* invite him to the party.

By the time they got to the sidewalk, Angelica wondered if her mother would need a cab just to get across the street to the St. Francis. "Here, Mom, let's sit on the bench for a few minutes and people watch. My feet hurt."

"That's okay by me."

Angelica helped her sit, then sat next to her. This might be a good time for a conversation about the guest list.

"Did you invite the Callens?" Their son had just graduated from medical school.

"Angelica, look over there."

Her mother nodded her head toward the homeless people sitting across the street in the palm treed and manicured plaza. "Do you think it's safe?"

"I'm sure we'll be fine. About the Callens?"

"Angelica, I'm not comfortable here. Look."

Angelica followed her mother's gaze. Just a few yards from where they were sitting, a man was reaching in a trash receptacle, looking at the contents. "He's just hungry." She reached for her purse.

"I certainly hope you're not going to give him money."

"I was thinking of buying him some food and giving it to

him." Angelica noticed the doorman from Saks approaching the man from behind. She could hear him speak, even though he kept his voice low.

"Get. Go on. The people shopping here don't want to look at you."

The man stooped farther into the trash, his shoulders even with the rim of the can, continuing to dig.

"Move on or I'll call the cops." The doorman looked around to see if there was a foot patrol nearby. "You're no better than the trash. Get out of here."

"See, Angelica, they shouldn't be in our shopping area. He's just asking for trouble. I'm sure this city has places for homeless people. Look how he just ignores authority. Defiant. That's what he is."

A police officer hurried down the block toward the two men. "What's the problem?"

"Can't get this guy to move, officer. I've asked him nicely, and he just ignores me."

The officer leaned toward the man. "Hey, move on or I'll have to arrest you."

There was no response. The officer waited a moment. "I said move it," he repeated, his voice rising. The man ignored him, digging deeper in the trash. The officer grabbed one of the man's arms and twisted it up his back, jerking him out of the bin. Angelica started to rise.

The man arched his neck back and moaned, his face contorted in pain. Stringy hair covered his eyes, his mouth a yellow slash in a grizzled face. In his free hand was a piece of a dirty, smashed sandwich. He began waving his free arm in spastic movements, bringing his hand repeatedly to the side of his head, as if trying to put the sandwich in his mouth, but hitting his ear. He struggled against the officer

122

like a trapped animal, spewing guttural growls, terror in his eyes.

The doorman knocked the sandwich out of the man's hand, but he continued the ritualistic flailing, poking at his ear, then his mouth, shaking his head violently. Through it all, shoppers, annoyed at finding their path blocked, skirted the scene, then continued on as if it were nothing out of the ordinary. It finally dawned on Angelica what was wrong.

She jumped up and shouted, "He can't talk." She rushed across the sidewalk. "Can't you see? He can't talk. He's deaf."

The officer relaxed his hold slightly and took a look at the man, then turned to Angelica. "Who are you?"

The doorman stepped back, recognition dawning in his eyes, a polite nod. "Miss?"

The homeless man's eyes were wide, his face panicked and his attention focused on Angelica. There was a stench about him that made her take a step back. "I'm an attorney." The officer's grasp loosened a bit more. "Are you arresting this man?"

"Why are you asking?"

"Because he's a human being who is starving, and the only thing I saw him do was try to get some food. Is that a crime?"

The doorman began to back away. "I should get back to my post."

Angelica turned to him. "You're the one who started this. I heard what you said to him." The doorman looked at the ground. "What if it was your brother? What would you have done then?" She turned to the policeman. "Don't you have a mission or a shelter around here? Isn't there someone you could call to get this man a meal? Is jail the first option?"

The homeless man struggled from the officer's hold and loped down the street. The officer gave her an icy stare, watched the man disappear, then, without answering, walked away.

"Sorry." The doorman hurried back to the gilt-edged entry to Saks Fifth Avenue.

Angelica returned to the bench. "Let's go, Mom." She took her mother's arm and helped her up.

It was two o'clock by the time they sat down in the ornate dining room of the St. Francis Hotel.

Lunch was presented on fine china and the water in crystal goblets, poured from a sterling silver pitcher. The wait staff stood close by as the two women had their lunch.

"Angelica, why are you so quiet?"

"That whole thing on the street. It was upsetting."

"Yes, it was. The panhandlers are aggressive, and the homeless people ruin it for the rest of us. I could smell that man from where I was sitting. There is absolutely no reason why those of us who work hard should have to be subjected to something like that."

Listening to her mother, Angelica realized that she had grown apart from her. Her mother lived in the privileged world of money and pampered naïveté. She knew nothing of the poverty and hopelessness that was the daily life of much of the world. *Ortega, Ramirez, Martinez, Herrera . . .*

Angelica's stomach knotted. She stopped her thoughts just as her mother was saying, "It certainly was upsetting. But let's not let it spoil our plans."

Plans. *"God have a plan for you, Miss Angel."* Poppy's words came to her.

"Mom, you're a Christian. You go to church most Sundays. You know what the Bible teaches. Can't you see that people like that need help? They need an advocate."

124

"How do you know they aren't right where they are because of their own actions? Most of them are drunks or druggies. They've made choices in their lives, and they're living with them."

"So then, throw them away. Is that what you're saying?"

"No, I'm saying keep them away from me. I've made choices in my life too. You know I worked in college and then helped your dad through medical school. We made sacrifices all our lives to get where we are today and to give you the life you have."

Her mother's words brought back memories of the loneliness she felt growing up in their absence. "Yes, you *certainly* did."

"Angelica Cianna, watch your tone. I just don't understand what's gotten into you. You've always been so level-headed. It never crossed our minds you'd walk away from your job in New York. It was everything you ever dreamed of."

"I never dreamed about taking advantage of people who have nothing and can't defend themselves."

"Really, Angelica. You're blowing this way out of proportion. Those people know they're taking a risk. You were just doing your job."

"And so were they. Only I got paid for doing mine."

"We understand that you were put in a difficult situation. But do you have to write off your entire future because of it?"

"It's not just that situation. You know I first took an interest in the poor way back in high school, when I found out how Poppy's wife and child died. It took me weeks to find that article in the archives of the San Francisco paper. That landlord wasn't even charged. He should have been found liable for what happened. Forcing a pregnant woman into the street for the lack of twenty dollars in rent money—it's a crime. No woman should have to have her baby in an alley, and when that baby died, someone should have been held accountable. If more people like me were interested in advocating for the poor, things like that wouldn't happen."

At the mention of Poppy's loss, her mother changed tactics. "Angelica, you can make a difference anywhere you are. Work doesn't have to be your only outlet. You can volunteer."

"Volunteering isn't the same kind of commitment. It'd be giving what's left over of my time, and most of the time that would be zero. Look at all the displaced people out there in the Square. Don't you believe you should love your neighbor as yourself?"

"First of all, they aren't our neighbors, and second, I do love them. I just don't love what they do."

Pat words that sanitized her mother's position. Pat words like, "Deportation is the natural consequence. . . ." The kind of words that doomed the less fortunate to their circumstances. Angelica bit her lip. There was no point in trying to convince her mother of her reasons to get involved. Suddenly, it was clear. God did have a plan for her. There was nothing more to think about. She *would* become a public defender, even if her parents continued to discourage her. A new dress and a party certainly weren't going to change her mind.

She looked at her mother sitting across from her. There was no need to tell her at this very moment. She would tell them both . . . later.

When they stepped into the house, the delicious aroma of baking biscuits greeted them.

They ate in the formal dining room. Built to take full advantage of the valley view, it was just off the main hall. A series of stucco arches framed its entry, and a step down led to the floor of handmade Mexican tile.

The centerpiece of the room was the table. Large enough to seat twenty comfortably, it was made from the wood of an oak cut on the ranch. High-backed, armless chairs covered in a rich, dark fabric with a Native American motif complemented the highly polished, rough-wood table. A huge wrought-iron chandelier that held twelve candles hung from a beam at the apex of the twenty-foot ceiling.

Angelica's mother saw the room in *Architectural Digest* and insisted that the picture be followed to a T—no electric lights allowed. She even found the beeswax candles shown in the picture and made sure a supply was kept on hand so they always had fresh ones for unexpected company.

"How did you girls make out today?" Angelica's father pulled out her mother's chair for her.

"It was an interesting day." She glanced at Angelica. "Angelica found a beautiful dress for the dinner Saturday night. Honey, you must wear your Dior, diamond-drop earrings with that dress. I found a new purse and matching shoes at Gucci's. I looked for something for you, dear, but I just didn't find anything I liked."

Her mother's comment about an "interesting" day was surely directed at the incident with the homeless man. Angelica needed to tell them about her decision—there was nothing more to think about. She would be applying for a position of public defender, and she would go wherever it took her. Angelica looked at her parents, about to start their evening meal. This wasn't the time.

"Mom, what are you serving on Saturday?"

"I ordered hors d'oeuvres and finger food. And Ben, I told the caterer that we'll need some servers, don't you think?"

"That's fine. And tell Poppy if they need more help, use one of the laborers."

At the mention of the laborers, Angelica looked at her father. "We took the new man, Antonio, to Poppy's church. There was a whole basement of clothes that were free for the taking. The next time you clean out your closet, Mom, we should take your stuff down there."

"I usually donate my cocktail and party dresses to the consignment shop run by the community theater group. It's important to support the arts."

"I don't think those are the kind of things the King's Closet is looking for. I meant your everyday stuff: pantsuits, skirts, sweaters, you know."

"That's fine, dear. Remind me this fall when I put away my summer clothes. I should have some things then."

Angelica looked at her father. He didn't seem to be listening. Even in the soft candlelight, she could see dark circles under his eyes.

"Hey, Dad, anything new on the drug approval for Thrombexx?"

"It should only be a matter of weeks now. As soon as we get FDA approval, we'll be launched."

"Then we can really move on developing that seventy-five acres for our vineyard, can't we?" Angelica's mother looked to her husband.

"We've already got quite a bit done. The road's cut in, and the soil work is done. Now I'm working on having it split off as a separate parcel so we can carry it as a separate business."

"Just think—we're going to have our very own label." Angelica's mother picked up her wine glass and raised her hand, toasting them all. "To Amante Vineyards and a wonderful party." Then she turned to Angelica. "And a special surprise."

When dinner was over, Angelica went up to her room. Without a doubt, she was going to have to endure "the surprise." She changed her clothes and looked out her window hoping to see Antonio. In the dim light, she saw him dragging a hose to the sheep pasture. She went over to the shopping bags she'd thrown on her bed and dug around for the box with the belt.

She took it out and considered what she should do. At the time she had bought the belt, it seemed perfectly reasonable—Antonio needed one; his was broken; he deserved it. He was a hard worker and had absolutely nothing. But now that she was faced with giving it to him . . . it suddenly seemed overbearing. She had no right to impose her standards on him. His clothing wasn't her responsibility. Maybe he didn't mind a broken belt or a rope. She couldn't give him a card with the box saying, "Welcome. We appreciate everything you do around here. Thought you might like this." He wouldn't be able to read it, for one thing. Yet she wanted him to have the belt. She didn't want his experience in America to be like that of so many of the Mexican laborers who worked in the fields. Still, what would he think?

Poppy finished cleaning up from dinner and went to his room. This was his favorite time of day. All his work was

129

done, and he could sit and read his Bible and have his evening devotionals. His old, comfortable chair faced the window, which had a beautiful, pastoral view of the surrounding tree-studded hills.

He sat and looked out at the natural beauty, preparing for his prayer time. The beautiful view never failed to fill him with peace and bring into focus God's greatness. Once he'd read a poem, "The Color of Light." The closing lines revealed that the colors man sees in nature are really,

> All from white light diffused
> through a prism of unceasing love.
> The evidence of God's presence.
> The color of God's glory.

The truth of the poem had moved him so much that he had cut it out and kept it in his Bible.

The sun had not fully set, and tonight he was particularly aware of the twilight colors outside his window and the words of the poem—the presence of God, everywhere for everyone. The God who hears and answers prayers.

As was his ritual, before he started his evening petitions, he picked up the faded, black-and-white picture from the table next to his chair and kissed the face of the young, pregnant woman. "I love you, Helena. You two rest under pinions of God's wing until He bring me to you." Images of that tragic day often intruded on his thoughts at prayer time, but he would not allow it. He chose to forgive all who had turned from him in his time of need and instead dwell on the stranger whose kindness had provided the money to give his Helena a burial. "My Jesus, You bless that man who find me in that alley. He such good man. He come from nowhere, and then he disappear."

He picked up his prayer list and went through it. Then he

began to praise the Lord for His faithfulness. "Thank You, Jesus, for this beautiful life You give me. You bless me with family and job. I ask You bless my savings and show me who need Your blessing from it." He asked God to watch over the president and all the leaders of the world. Next he asked God to send His Holy Spirit to soften Benito Amante's heart. "Whatever You need do, Lord . . ." He put the name of Geniveve Amante before the Lord repeatedly, as he pleaded with God. "Send the person You have to heal her."

Then he prayed for Angelica. "My Jesus, You love her and have a plan for her. I ask You, show her Your plan for her life. Show her what job You have for her, what husband You have for her, what Your will—"

There was a knock on the door.

"Poppy, I need to talk to you."

He turned to the door, pleased at the sound of his Angel's voice. "Come in, Miss Angel."

The door opened, and her lovely dark eyes peeked in at him. "Am I interrupting you?"

"No—" He held his hand out to her. "I do my prayers. You remember you ask me to pray for you. I do that."

"I'm glad you do, Poppy. Things are becoming clearer." She sat down on his bed. "I need to ask you about something. Remember I told you Antonio got a broken belt when he picked out clothes at the church?"

"Yes."

"Well, when Mom and I went shopping today, I saw a nice belt and got it for him. But now I'm not sure I should give it to him." She tilted the wrapped package back and forth in her hands.

He studied the emotions crossing her lovely features. "Why is that?"

"I don't know. Maybe he'd take it the wrong way. You

know, like I think I'm better than he is. I can't explain anything to him. My Spanish isn't that good. And really, I'm not sure what I would say or why I feel funny about it."

Such a kind and caring heart. "You good girl, with good heart. You give it to Antonio. I no think he take it wrong way. I think he understand."

"Do you think so, Poppy?"

The hopeful look on her face caused him to smile. "Yes, I think so, Miss Angel."

Angelica was quiet for a minute, pensive. "I hope so." With a sigh, she rose. "I think I'll just leave it for him down at the bunkhouse. I'm sure he'll know it's from me, because I'm the one who tried to talk him out of getting the broken belt at church. But this way it won't put him on the spot or embarrass him. If he feels awkward, he can just put it away."

She turned to leave, then glanced back at him. "I love you, Poppy. Thank you for praying for me, but be sure to pray for Mom too. I'm worried about her." She blew him a kiss and shut the door behind her.

The old man settled back in his chair. As he looked out the window at the beauty it framed, he smiled. He knew Angelica so well. He recognized her uncertainty for what it was: the stirring of something more than the simple desire to give a needed gift to the handsome, Mexican boy who had come so unexpectedly to the ranch.

"Thank You, my Jesus," he whispered to the God who hears and answers prayers.

Angelica went through the kitchen and out the door to the deck that overlooked the horse facilities. She could see

Antonio was still down in the sheep pasture by the water trough. She went to the bunkhouse.

There was no one in sight. She had never been in the room where the beds were set up. Stepping into it, she saw there were eight beds. The mattresses were set on narrow, plywood frames, and there were sleeping bags on top of some of the mattresses. Only two beds had the sleeping bags unrolled and stretched out. One would be Rafael's, and one would be Antonio's. She stepped closer. There, placed neatly beside the bed in the corner, were Antonio's worn and broken sandals. She took the box and put it on top of the sleeping bag, then left.

She smiled as she walked back to her room. Yes, she had done the right thing. Antonio was such a nice person. Had he ever had a gift that was wrapped? What did he do at Christmas and on his birthday? When was his birthday? She wanted to know more about him.

When she got back to her room, she took her Spanish book and began to look up phrases.

She practiced out loud. "How old are you? *Cuántos años tienes?*"

She took a sheet of paper, smiling as she wrote out questions in Spanish that she wanted to ask him. She stopped and chewed on the end of her pen, then spoke as she wrote in Spanish, "Do you have a . . ." She picked up the Spanish book and turned to the English to Spanish section. She ran her finger down the English list under G. There was the Spanish word she wanted. *Novia.* She finished the sentence. Do you have a . . . girlfriend?

By the time Antonio finished watering the sheep, it was getting dark. He wanted to try to use the shower in the bunkhouse that Chick had shown him. He preferred the stream, but he knew the moon would show its fullness only a few more times before it would be too cold to bathe there.

He went into the bunkhouse, then stopped midstride as he walked toward his bed. There was a package on it. He looked around the room. No one was in sight, and there was nothing on any of the other beds. His eyes returned to the package.

He found the switch he had seen Chick use to turn on a light. He took his thumb and forefinger and lifted the switch up. Light filled the room. He pushed the switch down, the light fled. Up and down, up and down . . . How did it know what he was doing? How was it so quick to answer him? He commanded the light to appear with a final flip of the switch and strode back to his bunk.

He sat down on the bed near the package, looking at it. Who would bring him a gift? He felt the gold stripe that ran vertically through the paper. Turning the box, he saw how the paper was folded in perfect points at each end and then taped. He put it back on the bed. *What's in it? Is it really for me? Maybe somebody meant it for Rafael.*

He decided to go take his shower and change his clothes. If the box was still on his bed when he finished, he would open it. Stopping at his drawer, he lifted out the neatly folded black jeans and red cotton shirt. They were the finest clothes he'd ever owned. Wary of the dirty clothes he was still wearing, he carried the new ones so they wouldn't touch him. He looked at the box one more time from the bathroom door.

The faucets waited silently above the tub. He turned the one with the blue letter, as Chick had shown him. The water flowed. He turned the one with the red letter—nothing happened. He stood staring. Soon a little trail of steam rose from the faucet. Smiling, he watched the water run. He pulled the lever up, and the water came spraying out of the shower pipe. He stepped out of his clothes and into the tub.

It wasn't quite as nice as standing under the waterfall that fed the river at home, but it was better than standing under a tree with a bucket of water and pouring it over his head, as he often did when the fields had to be plowed and there was no time to go to the river.

I'd better not use too much water. They must need it at the big house. He turned the faucets back to where they were, wiped the water off his body with his hands, and dressed. Before he finished buttoning his clean shirt, he stuck his head out the bathroom door to see if the box was still on his bed. It was.

He sat on the bed and picked the box up again. He studied how the paper was fastened. He took his fingernail and loosened the tape. After several minutes, he'd worked the paper off without tearing it. He folded the paper and laid it on the bed, then lifted the box lid. A belt, coiled in a tight circle and lying on a bed of transparent white paper, was inside. He took it out. The thin, silver buckle caught the light. He flashed the buckle back and forth, making the light dance.

He slipped the horseshoe nail out of the belt hole and took off the belt he was wearing. In a minute, the new belt was through the loops and fastened. He walked to the bathroom and stood on the edge of the tub to look in the mirror above the sink. It didn't matter that the sleeves of the red shirt bunched up at his wrist and the button was broken just above the belt looped through the faded jeans. These were fine clothes, worthy of a smooth, black leather belt and a shiny, silver buckle. He stepped off the tub and

135

went back to his bed, running his fingers around the silver buckle as he walked.

He pulled the belt from around his waist and sat down, looking at it. *Angelica.* She knew the belt he had was broken; she tried to get him to leave it at the church. She left the box. *Why is it wrapped like a special gift?* His face lit up, and a smile spread across his face. *Chick said if they liked my work, they would get me some better clothes.* This was America; this must be their way. They must like his work. Still, wouldn't that have come from the *patrono*, the man who paid him? Only Angelica knew about the belt. He felt the heat coming to his cheeks. The thought was impossible, foolishness.

He remembered stories he had heard from the Mexicans who returned to the fields of Guadalajara to visit their families after working in America. Some of the stories were unsettling, and he wondered if they were true . . . but some of the men told of Christmas gifts, like this one—usually money wrapped in a box. He looked in the box again and took out the thin, white paper and shook it. Seeing nothing else, he recoiled the belt and put it back in the box.

What good people they are, Angelica especially. The thought of her made his heart skip a beat. "Horse . . . clean . . . Sunday . . . come . . . go . . . good." He said the words out loud in English, with a heavy accent. He took a deep breath: "O . . . K." The pronunciation was perfect. He had learned the two words from listening to Chick. He was saving them to surprise Angelica. He pressed his fingers to his forehead and repeated all the words he knew in English again.

He reached in his front, jeans pocket and took out the primitive, metal cross he always kept with him. "*Gracias a Dios,*" he said looking at it. "God is with us." His mother's familiar words crossed his mind. "If you are still, you can feel His breath. It is His Holy Spirit. It is everywhere, at all times, to do His will." He raised the cross to his lips. *Glory to You, Dios, for the things You have done.*

He picked up the box and paper and went to his drawer. He put them under his clothes. Just as he shut the drawer, a breeze came through the room. Had someone opened the front door to the bunkhouse? He looked, but no one was there.

9

IT WAS SATURDAY, and Angelica wanted to be sure that she spent some time helping Antonio with his English. It was important to her that he learn to speak English so he could advocate for himself someday, but it was also important that she become fluent in Spanish to improve her chances of getting a job in the public defender's office. Besides, teaching Antonio would help her take her mind off the party her parents had planned for that evening. Something was up. She could feel it.

She'd only been able to visit with him a few times during the past week, but she'd already discovered he was a fast learner. If she repeated an English word for him a few times, he got it. He was a pleasure to teach—so willing to learn.

She went over the list of questions she'd written in Spanish the night before, hoping he would understand the textbook phrasing. Chick had been right. Antonio's Spanish and hers didn't match word for word. Whenever she noted a difference, she adjusted her Spanish to match Antonio's.

She picked up her books and stuck the list in one. As she

walked down to the stables, her thoughts wandered to the party planned for that evening. Whatever the surprise was, she would endure it. Poppy said God worked in mysterious ways. Maybe the Callens' son would turn out to be Mr. Right, or maybe someone at the party would lead her to a job opening.

As she approached the barn, she saw Chick working one of the horses on a lunge line in the arena. "Hey, Chick. Where's Antonio?"

"He's cleanin' the stalls. Should be finished anytime."

Angelica walked into the stables. The tang of fresh hay and sweet grain was in the air. Twelve stalls lined one side of the cement walkway. Each one opened out to an adjoining paddock. The next to the last door was open, so she walked down and looked in.

Antonio was working in Sari's stall with his back to Angelica. She noticed the boots he'd chosen at the church, but he wasn't wearing his new belt. She watched him rake the dirty rice hulls and then shovel them into the wheelbarrow, whistling all the while. He'd put the mare in her paddock, and the animal was leaning over the half door, watching him. With the wheelbarrow full, he grabbed the handles and headed out the stall door. He looked up just as she was about to jump out of the way. He came to an abrupt halt.

"*Perdone, señorita.*"

"*No problema, Antonio. Fini?*" She knew that wasn't exactly the right word, but it was close.

"*Una más.*"

"*Una más?* One more?"

"*Sí.*"

She set her books down and opened her little dictionary. *Let's see . . . go . . . go to your house . . .* "*Vamos a su casa cuando termines, estudiaremos Ingles hoy.* We study English

139

today." It might not be perfect, but she was pretty sure she got the point across. She glanced up at him.

"Okay." He pronounced the word perfectly.

She clapped her hands. "Hey, good."

"Yes, good." He tipped his hat to her, then pushed his wheelbarrow out the door, whistling loudly.

Frowning, Angelica watched him go. Once again she got the feeling that he had gained the upper hand. He didn't know more than five words in English, yet somehow he made her feel like he knew plenty.

In the bunkhouse kitchen, Angelica got a Coke and sat down at one of the tables. She wondered why he wasn't wearing his new belt. She looked inside the bedroom at his bed. There was no sign of the gift. She decided to wait and see if he said anything.

Before long, Antonio came into the dining room. He removed his hat and sat down at the table with Angelica. As he sat, she got a quick look at his belt. She could see it was the one from the church, but it had some kind of spike holding it shut. She wanted to ask him why he wasn't wearing the new belt, but she decided not to say anything.

They reviewed the words that she'd been practicing with him. He knew them all. *He can't be studying. He doesn't have any books.* The feeling that maybe he was a better student than her pricked at her. She bit her lower lip. *No way.* She pulled out the sheet of questions that she'd worked on. First, his age.

"*Cuántos años tienes?*"

"*No sé, posible diecinueve o viente.*" He shrugged his shoulders.

"You don't know! Er. Uh. *No sé?*" He smiled, obviously amused by her reaction.

He repeated. *"No, señorita. No sé. Posible diecinueve o viente."*

She realized he was saying he was nineteen or twenty, but he didn't know which. She couldn't imagine not knowing her age, and he certainly looked older than nineteen or twenty. *I wonder how many are in his family?*

"Cuántos son en su familia?"

"Doce."

Twelve! Angelica tried not to let her astonishment show. As their time together passed, she learned that besides his parents there were five younger brothers and four younger sisters. Antonio had helped raise them since he was twelve, when his father came to America to work. Until that time, the whole family had worked on ranches around Guadalajara, milking cows or working the fields for property owners.

She read in Spanish from her list. *"Qué edad tenías cuando empezastes a trabajar?"*

"Probablemente cinco." He held one hand about four feet above the floor, showing how tall he was back then.

He started working when he was five? Again, she couldn't imagine it.

They continued in her broken Spanish and his broken English. She would read her question, and he would answer. From what she could tell, he'd started helping his family earn money at the age of five by filling milk cans from the buckets his father and mother used to milk the cows. Later, he worked for a flower grower, planting and picking flowers, earning five pesos a day. Then somewhere around age twelve, when his father left for America, he took his father's place in the fields, planting corn and sugar cane. He slept in the fields where he worked, under one of the tractors if it was cold, and walked home on weekends with his wages in his pocket. He gave all of his money to his mother and then spent his days at home helping her plant crops, haul water, wash clothes, and whatever else was needed.

As Angelica pieced together his story, she got a glimpse of his world. She couldn't help but feel grateful for the life of wealth and privilege she enjoyed. He seemed to see nothing unusual about a five-year-old working from dawn till dusk under the hot, summer sun, a child working beside grown men and expected to work with their tireless discipline, or a twelve-year-old stepping into his father's position as head of the house. She could see his job at Regalo Grande was just the next step in a predestined life of selfless, thankless labor. But what surprised her most was the way Antonio spoke matter-of-factly. She didn't detect any resentment or regret in his voice or features as he spoke of the hardships that defined his childhood. Instead, there was a tone of gratefulness for his good luck in always finding work.

I wonder if he thinks of himself as lucky? She opened her dictionary and found the word she was looking for: *suerte*. Lucky.

"*Usted piensa que usted a tenido suerte en la vida?*"

"No. *No, señorita. No suerte.* Is more."

"Is more?"

He smiled, his lips together, and then broke into a broad grin, as if deciding to share a secret. "*Sí*, is *mucho* more."

He put his hand in his pocket and took it out, rolled into a fist, hiding something. Then he turned his palm up, showing her the primitive cross made of horseshoe nails.

"*Es Dios.*"

She was struck by his confidence. How was it he was so happy with such a hard life?

He looked at the cross for a moment, as if it held some mystery, and then put it back in his pocket.

142

His papers. She wanted to get a copy of his work papers. *"Papel?"*

He looked at her a moment. *"Papel?"*

Don't tell me he doesn't have any papers. She looked in her dictionary, papers, *papel.*

"Sí, su papel. Es muy importante." Even though this wasn't perfect Spanish, every Mexican knew about the important papers.

Antonio's face broke into a smile. *"Sí, tengo el papel importante. Es muy importante tenerlo."*

Well, he definitely understood how important it was. Still, she'd better be sure they were talking about the same papers. "Where did you get them? *De dónde obtienes?"*

"Guadalajara."

She wondered who had helped him. There wouldn't be any way he could have hired an attorney. *"Quién ayudó?"*

"Los misioneros."

"But you *tienes?"*

"Sí, señorita, en un lugar muy seguro."

He said they were in a very safe place. Still, she should make a copy. She looked in her dictionary. *"Yo necesario copia."*

"Good, *señorita. Te lo traigo."*

He would bring them to her. Good. She looked through her dictionary and chose some words, then asked him if he wanted to become a citizen of the United States.

"Porqué?" He tilted his head.

"Why?" She drew back. Didn't every illegal who came here from a third-world country want to become a citizen? *"Porqué?* America is *muy bien."*

A patient look settled on his face. *"Sí, pero Mexico es muy bien."*

Through broken Spanish, a little English, and sign lan-

143

guage, she came to realize that Antonio loved and missed his country. His desire was to work hard and earn money to help his family and build a future there, not to forsake his homeland.

She bet he was sending all his money to his mother. "*Va a enviar el dinero que gana a su madre?*"

"Yes, *señorita*. You *pagarme?*"

After struggling to find the word *pagarme* in her dictionary, she told him she thought her father paid the workers every other Sunday. Then she paged through her dictionary again, managing as best she could to tell Antonio that he would be paid next Sunday and she would help him get a money order.

He smiled and sat back in his chair, visibly relieved. Perhaps she could put in a note telling his mother he was all right. The missionaries who had helped him with his papers could probably read English. She pieced together some words and asked him if he'd like to mail a letter with his money.

The look on his face said more than words. "*Muy bien.*"

It didn't seem right that something as simple as writing a letter could mean so much to him. She looked forward to doing it. "*De nada.* You're welcome. But call me Angelica."

He leaned toward her. "*Muchas gracias, señorita.*"

Once again, she was struck by the depth of his eyes, his black hair, his straight, perfect teeth, so white against his dark skin, and his incredibly masculine presence. It was a struggle not to giggle under his gaze.

What's the matter with me? He just wants to be respectful to his boss. It's probably considered rude in his country to call your boss by a first name. That's what it is, plain and simple.

But that wasn't what it was, and she knew it, plain and simple. Antonio was ruggedly handsome and intelligent and had an inner strength and confidence she didn't understand, a charisma that drew her.

She looked down at her list again. Her question written in English, "Do you have a girlfriend?" jumped out at her.

"*Novia*. Girlfriend. *Novia*." She quietly tested her pronunciation, then raised her head, ready with her Spanish words.

He'd leaned forward, perhaps trying to catch her whispered words. His dark, discerning eyes, shadowed by black lashes, were inches from her. Her mind went blank, her heart raced, and her lips parted in surprise.

"Is he gonna work anymore today?"

Angelica jumped. Chick stood at the door. She looked at her watch—an hour and a half had passed. "Uh . . . sure, Chick. We're through for today." She stacked her papers and books on the table. She'd pick them up when she got back from riding. "Chick, please ask him if he wants to go to church tomorrow."

Chick translated.

"*Yo prefiero no ir*."

His answer surprised her. She wanted to ask him why he didn't want to go, but she'd asked enough questions for one day. "*Adios*, Antonio."

"Uh, Miss Amante, since he doesn't want to go to church tomorrow, maybe I'll take him over to Lo Bianco Vineyard."

She shrugged her shoulders. "Whatever he wants to do on his day off is fine with me."

She hurried out the door and across to Pasha's pasture. Her whistle brought him running. She hoped Antonio hadn't heard her say *novia*. What must he think? Why was she going to ask him a stupid question like that anyway? "Pash, get me out of here."

She decided to head up to the ridge. Riding past the sheep pasture, she noticed Antonio had moved the irrigation pipes and was latching the gate as he left. Chick was parked next to the sheep fence and was pulling a salt block off the back of his pickup.

About halfway up the mountain, she heard someone shouting. She turned Pasha around and could make out Chick jumping into his truck, racing toward the drive, trying to get around a stampede of sheep headed to the open ranch gate.

She kicked Pasha and started down the mountain. As she got closer, she saw that Chick had driven in front of the frightened animals, then leaped from the truck. He was waving his arms at them and shouting, trying to scare them back toward their pasture. "Ya! Ya!"

She saw Antonio circling around behind Chick, through the field. He walked with his head down, looking through the grass as he covered the ground. When he reached the drive, he picked up a stick. Chick didn't see Antonio until the Mexican stepped in front of him and walked toward the stampeding sheep.

Angelica stopped Pasha under the oaks. She could see everything, yet stay out of the way.

Antonio walked back and forth in front of the approaching sheep, waving the stick in front of him. "Shhh. . . . Shhh." Chick didn't make a sound or move.

He repeated the sound over and over. "Shhh. . . . Shhh." The frantic sheep slowed to a choppy, quick walk. He kept waving the stick.

As they neared him, he walked directly toward them, still making the quiet, calming, "Shhh. . . . Shhh" sound.

He looked the sheep over as he walked into the middle of the milling herd. He singled out a big one and tapped it on its rump. Within a few minutes, the sheep began to calm down, and the big sheep that Antonio tapped with his stick slowly turned back toward the pasture. The other sheep began to follow. He made no loud noises, just a calm and urging "Shhh. . . . Shhh." Soon the herd became a tight circle, heads gently bobbing behind the ram as he led them back to their pasture.

Angelica watched Antonio walk behind the circle of sheep, shepherding them up the drive. As the last sheep passed through the open gate, a breeze began to blow through the oaks in the pasture. The leaves rustled, "Shhh. . . . Shhh." The sound carried across the fields.

Angelica rode up to Chick. "What happened?"

"I guess the Mexican didn't shut the sheep's gate."

"I think he did. I was riding right past him when he latched it."

"Well, guess he didn't latch it good enough." Chick shouted up the drive to Antonio, motioning him to come. "Hey, Paco!"

Antonio jogged to join them.

Chick began to speak to Antonio in Spanish. His voice was not loud, and at first Angelica thought he was just discussing the incident with him. But a look of concern crept across Antonio's face, then a flash of anger.

Chick spoke so quickly, Angelica wasn't sure if she understood, but she thought she caught a few words: *no more job*, *stupid*, *last time*. She frowned. "What are you saying to him?"

"I'm just tellin' him to be more careful. He didn't shut the gate good."

Angelica looked at Antonio. His mouth was a thin line, and his eyes were focused on the sheep pasture.

Angelica tried to reassure him. "*No problema. Accidente.*"

He didn't move or look at her. He was focused on the sheep pasture. He fixed his darkened eyes on Chick. "*A las borregas les gusta la sal fresca.*" His voice was firm.

Chick spoke to him again.

"Well, Miss Amante, guess we'd better get back to work. You can see this guy needs to be supervised."

Antonio followed Chick up the drive.

Angelica gave Pasha his head and started back up the mountain. *What was that all about?* Just above the sheep pasture, she stopped and looked down on it. The sheep were clustered around the new salt blocks. *What was it Antonio had said? "La gusta la sal fresca." Something like that. "La sal fresca." The salt fresh. The new salt. They like the new salt. That's what he said.* Angelica watched the sheep licking the fresh salt blocks. *The salt was in Chick's truck before the sheep got out. Chick went in there to put the salt in after Antonio latched the gate . . . and Antonio knew it.*

She stroked Pasha's neck. "He didn't even raise his voice. He should've punched Chick on the spot for blaming him. You know, Pash, he held his own right there. His way."

She scanned the surrounding fields and spotted Chick's truck. She could see the two men, one swinging a pick, digging a hole, and one . . . supervising.

Angelica leaned back, signaling Pasha to stop, and watched for a moment. Her thoughts returned to the embarrassing scene at the table. Of course he had a girlfriend in Mexico. Why was she going to ask him that anyway?

Thoughts of Brad surfaced, bringing with them a twinge of loneliness. She had come back to California to start over in her professional life. Maybe it was time to start over in her personal life too. Maybe the party tonight was as good a place to start as any. She turned Pasha and started up the hill, then turned for a last look over her shoulder, at Antonio. Maybe.

The weather was perfect for the party under the open-air tent. A parade of well-wishers traveled up and down the new road that led to the vineyard property on the ridge. Angelica kept her eye on the arriving cars, trying to glimpse the occupants, as she chatted with Mrs. Marley, the ninety-five-year-old widow who owned the acreage next to the ranch.

The Gritzmockers, driving a restored 1930s convertible, parked on the mowed hillside, followed by the Scotts: he a former test pilot, she a former model. A few minutes later, the Wybrews, her parents' dearest and oldest friends. The Callens . . .

"What's the matter, dear?" Mrs. Marley's surprised voice interrupted her thoughts.

Angelica glanced in her mother's direction to see if she'd noticed the latest arrival. "Uh, nothing. Could you excuse me, please?" She quickly walked to one of the tables of food and gave a casual glance to the young man walking in with the Callens. It had to be their son, although he certainly didn't look like the geeky intern whose picture had been in the paper her mother sent her. She lifted the lid of a chafing dish and looked in his direction. Nope, geeky would not be the word.

She put the lid back on the dish, smoothed the skirt of the new dress, and walked over to meet the Callens.

"Good evening. It's good to see you again." Angelica gave Dr. and Mrs. Callen a quick hug.

"This is our son, Jason."

He extended his hand, and Angelica shook it. His firm grip fit perfectly with his broad shoulders, chiseled features, and wavy, black hair. He looked like an ad for a fitness center.

Dr. Callen turned to her. "How long will you be visiting? Your mother's kept us up-to-date on all your successes in New York."

"I don't believe we've missed one," Mrs. Callen added sweetly.

Angelica scrambled for a tactful way to break her news. She didn't want to embarrass her mother. "Actually, I've decided to make a career change."

"She hasn't decided exactly what that will be," her mother interrupted. "But we couldn't be happier that she's decided to make a change to the Bay Area. We've missed her."

Angelica heard her father's voice behind her. "So glad you could come. Is this Jason?"

"Yes, I was just telling Gen that Jason has been visiting us, and we're on the way to the airport. He's flying out to start his residency in Chicago."

"Isn't that wonderful, dear?" Angelica's mother seemed genuinely happy to hear of not only the young man's opportunity in Chicago, but his imminent departure.

"Tell me, what are you planning to specialize in?" Her father put his hand on Jason's shoulder, and the two of them walked toward the refreshment table. Angelica followed close behind.

For the next thirty minutes, the two men exchanged stories of their residencies. Angelica waited for an opening to join the conversation, but she didn't get one until Jason's parents interrupted to say good-bye. "We'd better hit the road. You never know what the traffic is going to be like going to the airport."

"It was nice meeting you." Angelica spoke her first and final words since they were introduced.

She noticed her mother continued to crane her neck every time a new guest arrived. But as dusk darkened, fewer and fewer cars came up the hill, and by the time night had settled in and chilled the air, the parking area began to empty.

Angelica's father watched the final set of taillights disappear down the hill, then let out a big sigh. "Wow. What a night. I'm bushed." He looked at Angelica's mother. "You must be exhausted."

"I'm doing fine. Setting a chair up for me here where everyone came in was a great idea."

"Angelica, the caterers are going to finish cleaning up. I'm going to bring the car right here next to the tent so Mom can just step in. When I pull up, would you help her?"

"Sure, Dad."

As they waited for her father, Angelica decided to ask her mother the question that had been on her mind since they'd first told her about the party. "Well, you said that there was a surprise. And, I have to admit, I'm surprised."

"Me too, honey." Her mother's voice was subdued.

"*Now* will you tell me what this was all about?"

Her mother thought for a moment. "Angelica, it's no secret that your father and I are disappointed with some of the choices you've made recently. We hope that as you spend time here and renew acquaintances, you'll get your focus back."

This wasn't the time to tell her mother of the decision she'd made at Union Square. "I am getting my focus, Mom."

Her mother's face brightened. "I hope so. Your dad and I know getting fired kind of threw you for a loop. We want to support you in every way we can to become the person we know you are. You've got a real gift for the legal field, and we hate to see you waste it."

Angelica chose to ignore what her mother was implying. "So what was the surprise?"

Her mother hesitated. "I invited Brad."

"You what?" Angelica took a step back. "I can't believe you did that."

"We've known Brad for years. When you two broke up, it didn't end our friendship. We've stayed in touch with him."

"Mother, that's fine, but you had no right to set me up like this. I was so in love with him. When we couldn't work things out, it took me months to get over it. And it's obvious he'd just as soon leave things the way they are. He didn't show."

"Angelica, it was his idea."

"*His* idea?"

"When he found out you were home to stay—"

"And exactly how did he find out?"

Her mother straightened in her chair. "I called him."

"I knew it. I knew something was up." Was this the way it was always going to be? Was she ever going to be able to run her own life?

"We ran into him a few months ago at Jack Wright's campaign fundraiser. Afterward we went to dinner. He poured his heart out to us. He said he'd been a jerk and wished he could have a second chance."

Angelica thought about the weeks after their split. The flowers he'd sent her, the phone messages he'd left her . . . the ones she never answered.

"He was supposed to come before things really got started.

152

So you could have time to talk. If you still felt that it was over, he was willing to accept that."

"I can't believe this." Angelica could see her father pulling up. "I can't believe that you would go behind my back." Memories and feelings overwhelmed her.

Angelica's father got out of the car. "What happened?" He looked from mother to daughter.

"I told Angelica that we invited Brad."

"Oh." Her father shook his head. "Leave me out of it, Gen. I told you we should have let her know right at the outset." He reached toward her to help her out of her chair.

"You could have told her any time you wanted. No one was stopping you." Her mother's voice began to quiver. She pushed Benito's hand away and struggled with her cane, trying to stand up.

Angelica was upset with both her parents. But there was no point in discussing it until everyone calmed down. "I really don't want to talk about this anymore tonight. Let's go."

"A very good idea," her father snapped.

No one spoke on the short drive home. As they headed up the drive to the entryway, Angelica squinted through the darkness. "Who's that?" A car was parked in front of the arches.

"I don't know." Her father pulled their car next to the parked vehicle. "Maybe somebody missed the turn up to the ridge."

"Mother, is that Brad's car?"

"Honestly, I don't know. After the fundraiser, we met him at the restaurant. I didn't notice what he was driving. Did you, Ben?"

"No, but this is certainly getting to be a mess."

Angelica waited for her mother to get out, then slammed the car door behind her.

Her mother stopped and faced her. "If it is Brad, be civil. He still cares for you. There's no need to take your anger out on him."

Angelica walked behind her parents as they went through the front door and toward the living room.

"How are you, young man?" her father's voice thundered.

Emotions flooded through her. Angelica leaned to the side, looking around her father's broad shoulders. Black hair slicked back, firm chin, hooded eyes flashing cobalt blue. She wanted to run, both away from him and into his arms. The whole thing seemed surreal, in light of the conversation she'd just had with her parents.

Brad strode toward her, reached for her hand, and clasped it between his. She hoped he couldn't feel her trembling.

"Angelica, it's so good to see you."

Low and intense, Brad's voice washed over her. The last time she'd heard it had been over the phone on a rainy spring night, telling her if she really loved him, she'd move back to San Francisco. It seemed like a lifetime ago.

"It's good to see you too." She felt the heat of his hands.

Behind Brad's back, her father gave her mother a piercing glare, then gestured toward the couches. "Let's all sit down. I'll go tell Poppy we need some refreshments."

"I have right here." Poppy stood in the doorway. "I visit with Mr. Brad while he wait for you. When I see you come home, I know he going to visit longer." Poppy carried the tray to the coffee table.

They seated themselves, Brad choosing a chair directly across from Angelica.

The mood lightened as the conversation ranged from horse breeding to Brad's position at his father's law firm. As they talked, Angelica studied Brad. They'd shared lots of great times together. She'd had a huge crush on the popular, charismatic upperclassman that first year she'd been in college. He wasn't quite six feet tall, but when she'd met him, he seemed to tower over her. A champion debater, he could trample his competition, no matter which side of the issue he was given, by disguising his temper as passion. He'd never even noticed her. Not until she faced him at the debate championships and then walked out with the trophy. Their friends never let him forget he lost the debate. He never let them forget he won the girl. A smile began to tug at her lips. Her eyes wandered over his blue blazer and khaki pants. She shifted in her seat. In a way, he seemed more preppy than manly.

"Angelica?" Her mother's voice broke into her thoughts. All eyes were on her.

"Uh . . . yes?"

"What do you think about Brad's news?"

"Sorry." She turned to him. "What were you saying?"

"I was just saying that my dad wants to open another office in Tiburon. Some of our biggest clients are in Marin County. I'm going to be handling the case that the Bay Area Preservation League has filed against our clients, the Fosters. They own Marin Heights Development."

"What's the case about?" Angelica leaned forward.

"The Bay Area Preservation League claims the project is not aesthetically pleasing. They've fought every project that's been proposed over the past fifteen years. And there are concerns about part of it being in a slide area. I think we're going to get media coverage, so it's a great chance for me to get my name out there."

155

"Sounds like you're well on your way, son."

"If I win the case and get the subdivision approved, I will be." He winked at her father.

Her father looked at his watch. "Well, Gen, it's getting late." He stood and helped her off the couch. "I think we'll go on to bed. You kids have some catching up to do."

Brad stood as her parents left the room. "Good night."

When they were gone, he sat back down. "I'm sorry your mom's not doing better. I hope this specialist she's seeing can help her."

She tilted her head. "You seem pretty up-to-date about what's going on around here."

"I've stayed in touch." He held her gaze.

"So I've heard." She waited for him to reply. The silence was awkward. "I thought you were supposed to be here early this evening."

"Is that what your mom told you?" A look of alarm spread across his face. "Don't tell me you've been waiting for me all evening."

"Not quite. I just found out about it a few minutes ago." His nervousness touched her.

"I was planning to come up early, but the more I thought about it . . . I just wasn't sure. . . . I didn't know how you'd feel about it."

"Brad, I don't know what to say. I don't know whether I'm glad or mad. This is a total surprise to me."

He rose and sat down next to her. "Angel, there hasn't been a day since that phone call that I haven't thought about you." He turned toward her. "When I heard you were coming home to visit, I made up my mind to see you, to talk to you."

He hesitated, his face serious. "I was wrong when I tried

156

to make you choose me over your career." He took her hand in his. "I want another chance." His eyes held hers.

This was the Brad she remembered. No wasted words, Angelica pulled her hand to her lap, breaking the moment. "A lot of time has passed. I just don't know."

"Why? What's to know? You still care."

The tone of his voice, the force of his personality—both were as much a part of his speech as his words. She knew admitting he'd made a mistake was a huge concession for him. But she also knew he was willing to make it because he was sure of himself. He was right. She still cared.

He took her face in his hands and kissed her. Their time apart vanished.

She turned her head. "It's too soon. A lot has happened."

"And we have lots of time to talk about it."

"So you know about that too?" Her words had an edge. When would her mother stop meddling?

"Your mom just said you'd come back to look for a new job."

"I have. I've decided to become a public defender."

"You what?" His eyes widened, and his voice rose.

"Oh, brother. Not you too? Nobody seems to think it's a good idea."

He reached for her hand. "No. No. I'm not saying that. It's just kind of a shock. I mean, last time we talked, you were so committed to your job."

"You mean, and *not* to you?"

"Let's not go there. Please. Can we just spend some time together?"

Yes, she wanted to spend time with him, but she didn't want to fall under his spell again. This time she wanted it to be on her terms.

He continued. "Next Saturday I'm going sailing. A friend

of mine is having a get-together. We're meeting at her house in Tiburon. We'll sail for most of the afternoon then go back to her place for a barbeque. Come with me."

"Wow. What a speech." She couldn't resist. "It almost sounded like you rehearsed it." She saw the color rush to his cheeks.

"Well?" He waited for her answer.

"*Her* house? You sure *she* won't mind?"

"It's not a couples thing. I've already called and told her."

"Told her? Pretty sure of yourself, aren't you?"

He ran his finger down the line of her chin. "I'm sure how I feel about you. Give this a chance."

She felt the lure of his charm. "How about I meet you there. You live in the city, and there's no point in you driving all the way up here and then back, and then here again to bring me home."

"I'd drive anywhere to be with you. I would have driven to New York, if you'd let me."

If things were going to be on her terms this time around, she might as well start now. "No, I'll meet you there." She scooted away from him and stood up.

He rose, and they began to walk toward the front door. "I'll call you next week and give you directions," Brad said as she opened the front door.

"I'm looking forward to it."

He stepped onto the pavers of the entry, turned, and leaned toward her. She moved back inside the house. "One step at a time."

The breeze from the valley whipped through the arches, creating a draft, slamming the door closed between them.

Angelica pulled the door open. At the sight of Brad's startled face, she laughed. "Sorry. It was the wind. Talk to you soon."

She gently shut the door and leaned her back against it, allowing herself a moment of truth. There was so much history, her first kiss . . . other girlfriends and broken dates. Still, he was the first and only man she'd ever loved, and that pull was strong. The heat rushed to her cheeks. She bit her lip. Enough. It had been a long day, and it was time for bed.

She passed by the kitchen on her way back to the stairs. Poppy was drying glasses, and Antonio was sweeping the floor. From the corner of her eye, she saw Antonio straighten up and tip his head in her direction.

Brad. It was as if his charismatic presence were following her down the hall, smothering her with thoughts of him, creating confusion. Why did she feel so unsettled? Why did she still care?

Poppy said he prayed that God would send her a husband, and she had prayed God would show her His plan. She felt a twinge of excitement. Maybe this was what it was all about. This was why God had allowed her to be fired in New York, so she would come back home to Brad.

10

"GOOD MORNING, MOM." Angelica joined her mother at the kitchen counter.

"You ladies want breakfast?" Poppy slipped a crisp, white apron over his head, tied it behind his back, and began rolling up his sleeves.

"No, I've got a million things to do today. We're leaving on our cruise tomorrow, and I'm not close to ready."

"How about you, Miss Angel?"

"Just an egg and a piece of dry toast, Poppy. I've been eating too much. Are you going to need any help, Mom?" The argument the night before seemed overblown this morning. Seeing her mother sitting there, her nightgown clinging to her thin body, Angelica couldn't help but wonder if her mother was overdoing it. Her parents had postponed this trip once because of her illness. Angelica's heart went out to her.

"No, honey, I'll be fine." She rose to return to her packing, then stopped and put her hand on Angelica's arm. "Is all forgiven?"

"Oh, Mom." She stood and embraced her mother. "I'm

sorry I got so angry. It's just that I had no idea you guys were still communicating." She stepped back. "Brad and I talked last night . . . and . . . I'm glad we did."

"Do you think you'll see him again?"

She didn't want to tell her mother about the date. What if it didn't work out? The last thing she wanted was constant phone calls every time the ship docked. Still, she didn't want to lie. "Yes, I think I'll see him again. But please don't ask me any more about it. Deal?"

Her mother could barely hide her excitement. "Deal." She rushed out of the kitchen and down the hall. Angelica hadn't seen her move so quickly since she'd returned home.

Angelica poured herself a cup of coffee while she waited for Poppy to finish making her breakfast. "Are you going to church this morning?"

"Of course. Why?"

"I was just wondering. I asked Antonio if he wanted to go. He said no, and I do want to help Mother with her packing after I finish breakfast. There's no point in her exhausting herself before they even start their trip."

"Maybe I talk to Antonio about going to church. He need fellowship. There some nice Mexican men there."

It was all Angelica could do to keep from giggling at the thought of Poppy trying to talk to Antonio. "As a matter of fact, I think Chick's going to take him over to Lo Bianco Vineyard this morning so he can visit with some of the Mexicans who work there."

"That not church, Miss Angel. They all need be in church on Sunday. Including you." Poppy frowned at the egg.

Bless his heart. He wanted to be sure the Lord's work was done. Well, if it wasn't, no one could blame Poppy. "He'll probably go next Sunday. It'll be a nice break for him on his day off to go to a place where he can be with his people."

Poppy's face broke into a smile as he put her egg on top of the toast.

"When Chick gets back this afternoon, I'm going to ask him to take me to Mill Valley so I can get into my storage bay. I need my study table and chair and a filing cabinet. The setup I had in my apartment will work perfectly in my bedroom. If I'm going to find a job, I've got to get organized."

Poppy raised his eyebrows. "I thought you tell your parents you going to think about it some more?"

"I've thought about almost nothing else since I've been home." The filthy man clutching the dirty sandwich in his hand rose from the shadows of her mind, briefly blocking out the beautiful kitchen of Regalo Grande. "When I saw those homeless people in Union Square, I made up my mind about getting a job as a public defender." Poppy put her hot breakfast in front of her.

"I bet those homeless people never think they make such a difference in your life." Poppy touched the tips of his fingers to his heart. "That my Jesus. He work *all* things together for good."

You precious man. Poppy had no idea what effect one homeless Greek immigrant had had on her life. The young man who didn't speak the language, had nowhere to turn, no one to help him. Who one cold, wet December night, huddled in an alley, surrounded by trash and the stench of rotting garbage, and watched as death took the two things he loved most in the world. He had never mentioned the incident, and she had never told him what she knew. Tears sprang to Angelica's eyes.

Poppy's face filled with concern. "Why you upset, Miss Angel? You afraid to tell your papa and mama you make up your mind?"

"No." She blinked away her tears. "I want to. There just hasn't been the right opening." She cut into her egg.

He patiently prodded her. "Maybe you need make the opening."

There was no fooling Poppy. She dreaded another confrontation. Besides, they were looking forward to their trip. No need to cast a pall on it by upsetting them. She promised herself she would tell them as soon as they returned.

She chewed slowly. Her thoughts returned to what Poppy had said. The idea that anything good could come out of that terrible incident with the homeless man was something she hadn't even considered. If only she could have his simple faith that everything worked together for good. She looked at Poppy, smiling as he carefully scraped the frying pan, the breeze from the open kitchen window teasing the hair on top of his head. There was something vaguely familiar about the way he was cleaning. It reminded her of something. She took another bite of her breakfast. What was it?

When she'd finished eating, she helped Poppy finish cleaning up, then went to get dressed. As she walked down the hall, she saw her father was in his study writing out checks.

"Hi, Dad. What time are you guys leaving tomorrow?"

"Your mom said we need to be at the airport at nine in the morning. We'll probably be gone when you get up."

"Where is your cruise stopping?"

"We fly to Miami to board. The ship stops in San Juan, St. Thomas, St. Martin, and Antigua."

She sat down in the chair by his desk. "Sounds wonderful."

"We'll have fun, but the timing couldn't be worse. This is the anniversary trip we had to cancel the last time she became sick. Then I had the time. Now, I need to be here and be

163

available in case something breaks with Thrombexx. I just didn't think it would take this long for the approval."

Her father looked tired. "Anything I can do while you're gone?"

"Just keep your eye on the mail and check the answering machine. I'm paying all the bills and leaving checks for the help. Give Chick the paychecks next Friday. He'll cash them and pay everybody." He pushed the checkbook to the side. "There's really just Poppy, Rafael, and the new man right now. And Poppy takes care of his own check. When we get the vineyard going, there'll be a lot more."

"Are you going to hire more Mexicans to plant the vineyard?"

"I'm sure we will."

"Is Chick going to be the boss? Won't you want a Mexican foreman?" Surely Antonio would have legal status by then.

Her father considered her question. "I've never had one. We've always managed. Anyway, that's a ways off yet." He hesitated. "Angelica, have you given this idea of being a public defender any more thought?"

"Uh. Yes."

"And?"

Her eyes searched his face. "Can't this wait until you get back?"

"That kind of a question makes me think you've made up your mind." He folded his arms across his chest and sat back in his chair. "Well?"

"I have, Dad. I've thought about it a lot. In a way, I've thought about it ever since I first found out what happened to Poppy when he was a young man. You know I thought about that incident when I wrote my valedictorian speech. But there was another part of me that didn't want to disap-

164

point you and Mom. I love you both, and I wanted you to be proud of me."

Her father ignored her reference to Poppy.

"And we have been. Very proud." His face softened. "You were an idealistic kid. That was fine then. Now you need to focus on the long term. You've got your entire life ahead of you, and your mother and I are behind you." He hesitated. "You could even have a political future. Don't throw it away. Make something out of your life."

Angelica sat stunned. She'd known he wasn't happy about her pursuing a career as a public defender, but she'd never realized he considered it throwing her life away.

Her father looked at her, as if she should continue. Slowly, his face filled with disappointment. "I hope you change your mind while we're gone."

Angelica could feel the tears in her eyes, but she held her father's gaze. "I won't, Dad. I want to do what you're asking, but I can't. I tried it your way, let me try it mine now."

Her father picked up his pen and pulled the checkbook in front of him, dismissing her.

Angelica left her father's office, her heart heavy. It seemed like her life was in a downward spiral. At least she'd leveled with him. This time apart would do them both good . . . she hoped.

In her room, a wave of loneliness passed over her. She picked up a picture from her dresser. Her parents smiled from behind the glass. Her father held her high school diploma. He told everyone he met at her graduation ceremony that she'd been accepted at Hastings law school. His dream was that she'd become an attorney. "What a bright mind. She's the youngest student they've ever admitted," he said over and over, waiting for each person's response. If they didn't say anything, he closed the conversations with "Isn't

165

that something?" and moved on, looking for someone else with whom to share his news.

"You're on your way, Angel," he'd told her. "Nothing can stop you now."

She realized that that was when it had started. The subtle pressure, the velvet glove, guiding and molding her future. The well-connected friend of her father's, whose unexpected phone call had led to the interview at Czervenka and Zergonos. That was when she'd lost herself, when she'd embraced the dream of her father and taken the path of least resistance. But she wouldn't let it happen a second time.

She wandered to the window seat, cranked open the bay window, and sat down in her favorite spot. She could see Pasha in his pasture. Maybe she'd wash him later. He hadn't had a bath since she'd been home. She saw Antonio walking up to the fence. He was dressed in clean clothes, ready to go with Chick. He jumped up on the fence. Pasha trotted over to him and butted him in the face with his nose, knocking him off balance. Antonio reached over the fence again and rubbed Pasha's neck and shoulder and scratched Pasha's ears.

Angelica smiled and leaned forward, putting her chin in her hand. He was always the same—kind and patient. She remembered him showing her his cross and how blind he seemed to the desperate hardship of his childhood. She didn't understand how he could be so happy and content when he had nothing, not even much of a future. He'd never really make it in life—have a car, house, family, money. He must want a better life, yet he seemed to simply accept what came his way. She sighed. What did he know that she didn't?

Antonio heard Chick honking the horn. He latched Pasha's gate and ran to get in the truck.

"What took you so long? I've got a lot of things to do today. I don't know why I'm takin' my day off to run you around."

Antonio understood Chick's Spanish easily. He looked at Chick and offered a smile. "Why are you taking me?" Even though the *patrona* had said Chick should take him to Lo Bianco, he had a definite feeling that there was something in it for the *mayordomo*. He'd heard Chick say the words *Lo Bianco* and *Texas* several times, his voice always low, as if whispering a secret to the telephone. Maybe they had cockfights there on Sunday. He'd heard from the men at home about the cockfights in Sacramento. Maybe they brought the birds from Texas.

"First I'm stoppin' at the gas station."

The truck bounced along the winding road, and before long Chick pulled it into a gas station. Chick jumped out, and Antonio watched him put a card in the gas machine and then pull it out, fast, as if he'd burned his hand. He rolled down his window to ask Chick if he was all right.

"Don't just sit there. You need to learn a few things if you're gonna be worth anything."

Antonio opened his door and got out.

"Look over there. See that hose? Bring it here."

Antonio pulled the thin hose to him.

"Take the cap off them stems."

Antonio did as he was told.

Chick grabbed the hose from him and bent down. *CHOOOSH.*

Antonio jumped back, then leaned forward. The hose blew air into the tires. He watched Chick move the stem, and the air came back out. Where did the hose get its power?

167

Frowning, he followed the line of hose to its source, a hole in the concrete.

He trailed Chick to the front of the truck and watched Chick open the hood. His *padrino* had a friend whose brother had a truck. He'd never been allowed to actually touch anything under the hood, but he'd watched. Chick pulled out the oil rod and looked at it. Antonio spoke loudly in English, "Oil."

Chick glanced at him. "Duh." He put the rod back into the engine.

Next the *mayordomo* wiggled the hoses that went to the big black box on the side of the engine. Antonio'd seen sparks come from it once in Mexico. There had to be fire in the box, or the engine wouldn't run.

"Get back in. We're gonna leave."

Antonio got in the truck and was shocked to see Chick get in, start the truck, and drive off. He looked in the side mirror to see if the police were behind them. He looked at Chick. He seemed awfully calm for someone who had taken gas without paying. He went over in his mind everything that had happened at the gas station. He hadn't seen any money change hands. Then it occurred to him, the card. The man who had brought him to the ranch had done that same thing to the gas machine when they stopped along the way. Antonio relaxed in his seat. This was America—the card must pay the machine . . . but how did the card get money? It seemed like buying something without paying. He wanted to learn more about this.

As Chick drove, Antonio recognized the scenery. It was the same road that the old man had driven on to go to church. But as soon as they crossed the bridge, Chick turned away from the church. Antonio leaned forward in his seat, taking notice of the landscape as they passed. Soon they were surrounded by many hectares of vines, staked in wide, straight rows, full of fruit. And among the fruit were many men of dark skin. He turned into the window. His people.

Chick drove up in front of a big building, put the truck in park, and got out. A man, short and thick, walked up to meet them.

"Hey, Mario."

The man spoke English to Chick.

"Get out, Paco."

Antonio got out. The man looked him up and down.

"I've got some business to do. You go down there by the oaks, where those trailers are. That's where the Mexicans live."

Antonio got out of the truck and looked where Chick was pointing. He could see a path, past the barn and down a hillside. He followed it to the oaks.

"Good morning." Antonio tipped his head to a man about the age of his father, sitting in an old chair that was shaded by the spreading branches of the big trees.

"Good morning," the man responded.

"May I sit?"

"Of course, please." The man gestured to a branch that hung low next to him.

Antonio straddled it and politely waited to see if the man wanted to talk. In a moment, another man joined them. He sat on the ground between the chair and the branch. As the minutes passed and observant eyes from trailer doors and windows caught sight of Antonio sitting on the branch, more men decided to take a seat under the big oaks. Soon there were about fifteen men of many ages.

"Cigarette?" the man between the chair and the branch asked Antonio.

"No, thank you." When his father was home, he smoked,

169

and it took money that they needed for food. And though his father promised he would not smoke, he always did. The cigarette was more powerful than his mother's tears. Antonio would not smoke.

"Coke?" a boy asked, holding out the Coke he was drinking.

Antonio thanked him and took a drink.

Someone asked, "Where you from?"

"Jalisco." Antonio took another drink of the Coke.

"Hey, Ramauldo. He's from Jalisco."

A man sitting on a trailer step walked over to Antonio, his hand extended. "Welcome. I'm from Jalisco. What's your name?" He leaned against the branch Antonio was sitting on.

Soon the conversation began to flow. Antonio found out three of the men were from the area around Guadalajara. Though they couldn't discover any mutual acquaintances, they knew the territory well and had relatives who worked on farms around Guadalajara.

One man's wife had just given birth. "When I pick the grapes and the sun is very hot, I think of my daughter. It is like a drink of cool water."

One man's brother had experienced bad luck. "Immigration picked him up in the tomato fields before his *patrono* had a chance to pay him." The man shook his head. "Very bad luck. He had waited for two months, and he was finally going to get paid the very next week when Immigration came."

Everyone nodded in agreement. This was very bad luck.

"You going to work here, Antonio?" Ramauldo asked.

"No, I came with the *mayordomo* from my ranch. He said he has business here."

"That his truck up there?"

Antonio could see Chick leaning against the front of the truck talking to a man. "Yes, the blue one."

Ramauldo chuckled. "The Coyote."

"The Coyote?" Antonio thought about the coyotes who had left him in the desert.

"We call him that because he finds our people work and . . . he has the eyes of a dog. He comes here to see Mario. Sometimes he brings in men; sometimes he takes men out."

Antonio set his Coke can down on the ground.

"Seems he always has jobs lined up somewhere. Texas, I heard. But not today, I guess."

"Why do you say 'not today'?" He was curious about this news of Chick and his business in Texas.

"The truck has no camper on the back. When he comes with the camper on, he is either bringing men in or picking men up. He is good for the men who need jobs."

Antonio heard the horn of the truck. He jumped off the branch. "I'd better get going. I hope I can come again soon."

He heard friendly farewells as he ran up the path to the truck, but his mind was on the news he'd heard. He thought about Mario, his black eyes intense and penetrating. He felt a chill. Why had Chick brought him here?

Angelica cross tied Pasha in the washing area. She soaped and rinsed him as he snorted and high stepped. While he dried, she conditioned his mane and tail and braided them so they would be silky and curly when they dried. As Angelica was growing up, her mother had called Pasha "Angelica's doll." She'd never played with dolls other than those that

171

rode her plastic horses. When she finished, she tied him out in the sun to finish drying.

The slam of a door caught her attention. She walked around the corner and ran into Chick and Antonio.

"Hey, guys." She looked at her watch. "You're back early."

"He had plenty of time to visit the Mexicans at Lo Bianco."

"It's fine with me, Chick. I was hoping you would take me down to Mill Valley so I could get some stuff out of storage."

Chick gave her a blank stare. "I wasn't plannin' on working this afternoon. I've been killin' myself these past few weeks, and I've got things I need to get done." He looked at Antonio. "Tell ya what." He stuck his thumbs in the top of his pants and leaned back on his heels. "I'll let you use my truck, and Antonio can help you. He's got nothin' else to do today. And he's young—hard work don't bother him a bit."

Angelica chewed her lip. It didn't seem fair. Antonio worked harder than Chick by far and got much less time off. But she needed somebody to help her. "Okay. Tell him to come with me. He's going to earn a little extra money this week." She'd pay him well for working on his day off. He needed it.

Chick straightened up. "Uh. Well maybe I *could* change my plans."

"Oh, I wouldn't dream of it. You're doing enough, letting me use the truck," Angelica said. "Go ahead and tell him."

Antonio listened as Chick translated, then nodded his head. "Is good. Thank you."

Angelica understood his heavily accented English easily.

"*Muy bien*, Antonio. Tell him I'll meet him at the truck in a few minutes. Pasha got me soaking wet. I'll put on some clean clothes and be right back."

Smiling broadly, Antonio spoke before Chick could. "O K."

She hesitated, surprised that he had understood her. "Good. Chick, throw some blankets and a rope in the back of the truck, please."

Angelica took off at a jog up to the house. How was he learning English so quickly? She wondered what other surprises he had up his sleeve.

By the time Antonio finished loading the truck, Angelica had a new respect for him. The movers had managed to get all her belongings into the small bay, but there hadn't been an inch to spare. It had required a lot of patience, shifting, and lifting to get to the table, chair, and cabinet she wanted. He wouldn't let her help him. She wasn't sure if it was because he considered her his boss or if it was because she was a woman.

Antonio moved things as if they were museum quality, being careful not to bump into anything and estimating accurately how much space was needed to extract them from the stacks of boxes and furniture. He even arranged them in the truck so they fit together in the bed snugly, with blankets protecting them from each other.

Angelica returned to the storage unit. She could see the wardrobe boxes that held her work clothes lined up along the back wall. With any luck she'd be interviewing over the next few weeks, and she'd need some of her clothes. She scanned the bay. There was no easy way to get to them.

It would require an hour or more of moving things. She looked at Antonio.

No. It was his day off. She'd asked enough of him. She glanced at her watch.

"Come on, Antonio. We're going shopping."

As they got into the truck, she teased him about the efficient job he'd done. "What are you, a professional mover?"

"Professional, *sí*," he repeated back to her.

He gave her a wide grin, his straight, white teeth a handsome contrast to his deep tan. . . . Had he winked at her? Maybe he hadn't . . . she wasn't sure. She looked straight ahead and turned the ignition key. Nothing happened. She turned the key again. The truck didn't start. She fumbled with the keys.

Antonio looked at her. "*Problema?*"

"*Sí.*" She reached for her purse. As she dug around for her AAA card, Antonio got out of the truck. He walked to the front and bent down examining the grill.

Angelica crammed everything back in her purse and got out to see what he was doing. To her surprise, he poked his finger in between the metal, then ran his finger over the grill.

"Oh." She went back to the driver's side and pulled the hood release.

Finding the latch, Antonio lifted the hood. He stood with his hands on his hips looking at the engine.

Angelica stepped next to him. "Hmm," she commented. She'd never looked under the hood of a truck in her life.

Antonio fingered the top of the dipstick, then moved his hand over the battery. He wiggled the cable. She saw the nut move around the battery post. Leaning over the hood, she took a closer look.

"The cable is loose." She tried to tighten it with her fingers. It didn't move. "Just a minute. *Momento.*" She got back in the truck and opened the glove compartment. There was a flashlight, a small screwdriver, and a pair of pliers. She took the pliers.

The sun beat hot as she tried to tighten the cable clasp. Antonio gently took the tool from her and tightened the bolt.

Angelica got back in the truck and turned the key. The engine started.

With a huge grin, Antonio slammed the hood down and got in the passenger's side. Angelica didn't try to hide her admiration. "You figured that out. *Cómo usted sabe?*"

"Chick. I see." He pointed to his eyes.

"Chick?" She raised her eyebrows. Would wonders never cease? Antonio must be a quick study.

Angelica got on the freeway and headed north.

"*Cómo usted sabe* English?" She knew she was speaking Spanglish, but he'd understand. "*Usted comprende* many words."

He gave her a patient smile. "I see, I hear." He tapped his eye and ear.

So, there was a simple explanation. He paid attention to what was going on around him. She should have been able to figure that out, it was the same way she would have learned were she in his situation.

As they drove along, Angelica switched the radio on. Country western music blared from the speakers. "Ouch." She turned the volume down and pressed the search button a few times, looking for rock music. The button stopped on a classical station, a news station, a Spanish station. She and Antonio looked at each other at exactly the same time. "Hey, that's great." She turned the volume back up and settled into her seat.

By the time she got to the Valley Mall, it was after three o'clock. "Antonio, I need *comprar ropa. Usted* want to go in *tienda?*"

"*Sí.*" He hesitated. "*Pero no dinero.*"

She knew that. How thoughtless. First she'd acted surprised that he'd learned English while living in an English speaking country, and now she invited him to shop without paying him. Well, that was because people in America always had money in their pockets. At least the people she knew . . . Her thought convicted her.

There was a lot she needed to learn about her future clients.

"Let me pay you *por* your *bien trabajo.*" She took a hundred-dollar bill out of her wallet. "Here."

He didn't move.

"I want you to have this for your good work. *Por su bien trabajo.*"

Despite her assurance, he didn't take the money.

Angelica shifted in her seat. *I guess it is a lot of money to him for a few hours' work. But he needs it. And I would have paid a mover every bit of that and more.*

His eyes met hers, as if he were reading her thoughts. His expression told her he wanted to earn his way, not receive charity. Once again she wondered if she'd disrespected him.

She took his hand and pressed the money into it. "Please, *señor?*"

He folded the bill and put it in his jeans.

The mall was full of people shopping the back-to-school and summer sales. Angelica and Antonio walked along looking in the windows.

"Antonio, a men's store." She tilted her head to see if he was interested in going in. He wasn't behind her.

176

She spun around. She looked in the store they'd just passed. Nothing. She retraced her steps, scanning the people around her. Directly across the wide aisle, she saw him standing at the counter of Fantastic Hair. She hurried across to the salon. Just as she stepped in the door, she heard the pretty girl behind the counter ask him, "What's the name?"

"Name Antonio."

Angelica backed up a few steps.

The girl wrote it down. "Take a seat over there." She pointed in the direction of a long bench.

Angelica walked behind him, and when he sat down, he saw her. He looked surprised. "Sit, *señorita*?"

Angelica picked up a hairstyling magazine. She thumbed through it. "Look, Antonio." She pointed at the hair of the male models. "*Bien?*" She'd help him find a style he liked.

He shrugged his shoulders. "*Yo no sé.*"

"You've got to tell them how you want your hair cut. Don't you do that in Mexico?" She spoke in English, as if he could understand.

He smiled, seemingly amused.

Well, fine. She shut the book and put it down.

Soon his name was called. He followed the stylist, a young woman with a short, tight skirt and bleached hair, to her station and sat in the chair. Angelica followed behind.

"How do you want it?" the stylist asked him.

"Just kind of follow what you see," Angelica answered for him.

"What about his sideburns?" The young woman looked at Angelica, as if Antonio weren't there.

"Make them even with his ear."

The stylist wet his hair with a water bottle and began running her comb through it.

Antonio lifted his hand, put it on top of the comb, and

gently took it from her. He leaned toward the mirror, parted his hair on the left, combed it over the top of his head, and then combed the left side straight down.

The stylist recognized the basic cut. "Whatever you say, Antonio." She took the comb back from him and touched his sideburns with it. He pointed to the bottom of his ear lobe. "Oh, the Elvis look?" She laughed and began cutting.

Angelica went back to the bench and sat down. She could see his face in the mirror. He showed no emotion but watched every clip of the scissors. As the long hair fell away, he suddenly looked older, almost polished. Everything about him was symmetrical. With the hair cut away from his face and shoulders, she could see his cheekbones and square chin. His neck looked thicker; his shoulders were broad. He was heavier than he'd been that first day—a kid standing with his head down. Now that she could look at him unobserved, *kid* was the last word she would have used to describe him.

The woman took a razor and made a straight line at the bottom of his ear and trimmed his sideburns. She put some gel in his hair and combed it as he'd shown her.

Angelica got up and met them at the counter.

"He cleans up pretty good," she said to Angelica.

"How much does he owe?"

The stylist looked at Antonio. "*Ocho dólares.*"

He handed her the hundred-dollar bill.

Angelica watched him take the change and put it in his pocket. No tip. Didn't they tip in Mexico?

"*Gracias,*" Antonio said, nodding his head.

The girl smiled and reached out, laying her red, manicured nails on his forearm. "Do come back."

Angelica turned on her heel and followed Antonio out.

"Angelica! Angelica!"

178

She looked around and saw two women approaching her.

"Angelica. It's me, Jill. Jill Anderson. I haven't seen you since we graduated from high school. How are you?"

Suddenly feeling conspicuous, with one of the ranch hands at her side, Angelica glanced quickly at Antonio.

"Jill! It's great to see you. You look wonderful."

"I read in the paper that you landed some big job in New York with an international law firm. What're you doing here?" She adjusted the leather shoulder strap of her Chanel purse.

"I'm planning on moving back. What've you been up to?"

"I work at a travel agency. This is my friend Mary. She works with me." She glanced at Antonio, then back at Angelica.

"Uh, this is one of our laborers." Thank heavens he'd had his hair cut.

Jill raised her perfectly shaped eyebrows.

"He's been helping me today." This felt awkward, and Jill wasn't helping by acting so "holier than thou."

Jill went on without acknowledging Antonio. "We're in a hurry, just going back to work from lunch, but let's get together soon."

"Yes, let's," Angelica answered.

"Call me at work next week, Time For Travel."

Angelica watched the girls walk away, then looked at Antonio. His dark eyes looked directly into hers. He knew. She'd been embarrassed to be seen with him. She hadn't even used his name when she'd introduced him.

She looked down, quick heat rushing to her cheeks. What did it say about her? Did she only care about him, and the less fortunate who had so affected her, from a high place, allowed by her position of privilege?

179

She looked at Antonio again, standing patiently at her side. Did she really consider him her equal, as he was in the eyes of God? God looked on the heart. If He were looking on their hearts right now, they were certainly not equals. Not even close. She felt ashamed.

Antonio gently touched her elbow. "Is OK, *señorita*."

Angelica blinked back tears as she looked up into his face, searching for some sign of anger, but she found only humble absolution there. She took a deep breath. She wanted to go home. Her stomach was in a knot. She started to turn toward the exit.

Suddenly, it occurred to her that Antonio might think she was leaving because he was with her. If only she spoke Spanish better, she could explain everything. It wasn't about him; it was about her. The thought echoed back to her and spoke to her heart. That was the problem. It was always about her. She'd had him work on his day off so *she* could get her furniture. She'd brought him to the mall so *she* could buy a dress for *her* interview, and now *she* would take him home because *she'd* acted like a jerk. It was time to start walking the walk. She could shop anytime, this afternoon it was going to be about him. She turned and faced him.

"Antonio. *Usted* want to look *en tiendas*?" She pointed at the stores.

A smile tugged at his lips. "*Posible*."

She slipped her arm in his. "Let's go, *señor*."

They walked through the mall, stopping at stores that displayed men's clothes. At their first stop, Angelica helped Antonio explain to the salesman that he was looking for some casual clothes. By the time they went into the second store, he'd caught on to the routine of looking, picking out things, and trying them on. When he came out of the dressing room, if he wanted the item, he'd wear it up to the counter and hand the cashier the old clothing he'd taken off. The cashier would clip the tags off what he was wearing and ring it up, and he'd walk out with his old clothes in a bag. By the time they got to Macy's, he was wearing a pair of chinos, a sports shirt, socks, and a pair of cowboy boots, and he carried a blue blazer slung over one shoulder. With his cowboy boots on, he towered over Angelica. She had the strange feeling she'd come in with one person and was leaving with someone else.

As they moved along, Angelica wondered if he noticed the difference between the clerk in the first store who ignored him and the clerk in the last store—the one who offered help the minute they walked in. There was no way to tell. Antonio was always courteous but cool. He answered, "*No, gracias,*" to their questions, then moved away, giving the impression of being someone above it all, who didn't want to be bothered. It delighted Angelica, and she stayed as uninvolved as she could.

When they left Macy's, Angelica noticed a woman shopper give her a disapproving look. Apparently, she didn't think the tall, handsome, well-dressed man wearing a navy blazer should bother with a young woman in worn jeans and scuffed boots.

"*Tienes hambre?*" Antonio asked her.

Angelica realized she was famished. "*Sí, señor.*"

He pointed to a restaurant across the promenade.

Angelica read the sign. "Mi Mama's Cocina. Yum." She patted her stomach.

As they waited to be seated, Angelica noticed a big poster taped on the wall. "Flamingo Hotel—Mariachis—Bands—Folklorico. Friday, September 5."

"Look, Antonio." She pointed to the poster that showed some mariachis gathered around a microphone. "*Es aqui, en Santa Rosa.*"

He stepped closer to the poster, studying it. The hostess appeared and asked if they were ready to be seated.

"Yes, we are. A window seat, please."

The hostess nodded. "Of course."

"Do you know anything about that event at the Flamingo next Friday?" Angelica asked as she seated them.

"Not really, but the manager does. I'll ask him to stop by your table." The hostess gave them their menus.

Angelica looked at hers. Antonio picked up his and looked at it.

"What? *Qué gusta?*" she asked him, pointing at the menu.

Knowing he couldn't read English, she pointed at the pictures, which were numbered. Then she pointed to the corresponding numbers on the menu: #1 was one enchilada, beans, and rice, #2 was a tamale, enchilada, beans and rice, #3 was a tostada; she went on down the list. When she was finished, he pointed to #2.

She pointed to the number two. "*Qué es?*"

"*Dos,*" he answered.

She pointed to the three.

"*Tres,*" he answered.

The biggest number printed on the menu was fourteen, which he recognized. She was surprised. She pointed to the prices, but he just shook his head.

The waitress came and took their order. While they waited for their food, the manager came to their table. His greeting was warm. "*Buenas tardes.*"

Angelica smiled at him. "Could you tell us about that event you have posted by the front door?"

"Oh, that's at the Flamingo Hotel. Every month they have music there for the big Mexican community that lives around here. It's advertised across Sonoma County, and people come from all over." He went on to tell them they could buy tickets at the door and the event began around eight in the evening. As he left, their food came on big plates with a stack of hot tortillas in a basket. As soon as Angelica started eating, Antonio picked up a tortilla and began scooping the food into his mouth with it, biting off part of the tortilla with each scoop.

Angelica froze. She hadn't even thought about his knowing how to use a knife and fork. If she told him to use his fork now, he'd be embarrassed. If she didn't, he'd be embarrassed when he figured it out. "*Es bien utilizar.*" She pointed casually to his fork.

He set his half-eaten tortilla on his plate, picked up his fork, and shoveled some beans onto it. She turned back to her food.

From the corner of her eye, she saw the telltale redness crawling up his neck. She bit the inside of her lip. An idea came to her. She'd have Poppy invite him to lunch at the house one day this week. That way he could figure it out in private.

And so the meal continued. He used his spoon to stir his Coke when he saw her stir her iced tea. He wiped his mouth with a napkin every time she did. She acted as if she didn't notice and practiced English with him. Soon the waitress appeared, and Angelica asked for the check. She left a tip on the table and went up to the cashier. When she put down her money, Antonio took out all the money left in his pocket and handed it to her.

She added the three dollars and forty-four cents to the money on the counter. "*Gracias*, Antonio."

Before they stepped out the door, Angelica dug in her purse and got a paper and pen. She copied down the address

183

of the Flamingo Hotel and the phone number. She glanced at Antonio. *What would it be like to dance with him?*

Antonio looked at her precisely at the moment the thought crossed her mind. She caught her breath and looked away.

Maybe it *would* be better if Chick took him and dropped him off.

11

THE HOUSE WAS quiet, empty. Her parents and Poppy had left for the airport. There were homemade muffins on top of the oven and fresh cut fruit in a small glass bowl on the counter, coffee ready in a sealed carafe. She unscrewed the lid, poured a cup, picked up the fruit, and walked back upstairs to her room.

She sat down in her window seat and put the bowl of fruit in her lap. Looking across the valley, she sipped her coffee and thought about the shopping trip with Antonio. Being with him was so easy. They could hardly speak each other's language, but it didn't seem to matter. She felt like she'd known him all her life. She grinned. They had a connection she didn't understand, but it felt right. Had he noticed?

She looked toward the barn and stables. No one was in sight. Once again loneliness swept over her. Why did she feel like this? She'd always been on her own. She'd never needed anyone, not really.

Setting her fruit and coffee aside, she rose, stepped to her bookcase, and picked out a book of poems she'd written. She ran her hand over the paper cover. She'd written many of them during the years Poppy cared for her—when she was alone while her parents traveled and worked. Some of the poems reflected the sense of abandonment she often felt, the loneliness. Her parents had a good life, had made a good life for her, but she realized now that life hadn't given her what Poppy gave her. Suddenly that seemed most important.

Something stirred in her. She wanted more than her parents had—to give something more to her own children. Not just the trappings of "success." But exactly what it was she wanted and how she'd go about getting it, she didn't know. She sighed and put the book back. It wasn't that they hadn't been good parents. They'd given her everything money could buy, from the ranch to graduate school. And they loved her deeply. In their way. But something was missing in her life.

Well, there was no point in dwelling on it now. She had things she needed to do.

The most important thing first. She called and made an appointment for that afternoon with her college professor and mentor, Dr. Maddox, at Hastings. This would be a critical meeting. Not only did she plan to tell him about her plans to become a public defender and ask his professional opinion, but she wanted to get a letter of recommendation.

By the time Poppy got home at noon, she had lunch set with Jill for Tuesday, she'd been on the Internet and looked at the websites of surrounding counties, and Brad had called and given her directions to his friend Lindsay's house in Tiburon. He also piqued her curiosity by saying he wanted to talk to her about her job search when he saw her.

As she ran down the stairs, she heard Poppy in the kitchen. "See you later," she shouted to him on her way out. "Oh, please get the mail for me. I'm supposed to go through it for Dad. Love you."

As she opened the front door, she heard Poppy's voice from down the hall. "Jesus, You take care of my Angel today while she on those roads. She got no top on her car."

On her way to the city, she thought about her college years. Dr. Maddox had taken an interest in her from her first day as the youngest student to ever attend the school. How many times had he encouraged her when she felt like quitting? He'd even been there for her during her ups and downs with Brad. She dreaded this meeting. He'd had such high hopes for her, and she'd let him down. Maybe she wouldn't even ask for another reference.

She pulled into the familiar parking area that served his office, parked the car, and slowly walked to meet him.

As soon as she stepped into his office, he rose and opened his arms, turning his palms up. "Angelica, I'm so glad you could come." She shook his hand.

His white hair pointed wildly in every direction, his "magnifiers" were balanced on the end of his nose, and the flesh-colored plastic hearing aid still gripped his right ear. The brilliant and fiery-eyed professor of philosophy hadn't changed a bit.

"Sit. Sit." He pointed at the chair in front of his desk. "Tell me about the great things that have happened to you since graduation. Has that firm in New York given you the opportunities you hoped for? When you applied there, I wrote them a letter that left no doubt about your capabilities." He didn't hide the pride in his voice.

When the professor had settled behind his desk, Angelica took a deep breath and began to recount the events that brought her to his office. His face was intent and his eyes penetrating as she poured out her story. She included her parents' disappointment and her personal quandary.

"So you see, things have changed." She gave him a tentative smile.

"No, Angelica, I would say things have not changed at all."

His face was a mask. "How on earth could you say that? I had everything going for me there, and now I don't even have a job."

He tapped his forefinger on the desk as if tapping on a blackboard. "Follow my analysis. Apply that bright mind of yours, young lady. *Then*, you sat in front of me and read your valedictorian speech, saying you must never forget the intent of the law. *Now*, you sit in front of me and tell me that you could not do a job that asked you to do just that. The only difference is, then you spoke from the naïveté of youth, and today you speak from experience. The latter being much more impressive, I might add. This is exactly what Edmund Burke was referring to when he said that the only thing necessary for the triumph of evil is for good men to do nothing."

A weight lifted from her shoulders. "You mean you don't consider me a failure?"

"A failure? Nothing could be further from the truth." He slammed his hand on the desk. "You're a force to be reckoned with, Angelica. I'm glad to see that you're finding your passion. Some people never do."

"You mean you could see me just being a public defender?"

"No, not at all. Never *just* being a public defender, but being a fine attorney who chooses to work in the public defender's office, making a real difference in people's lives, leveling the playing field for people who can barely stand on their own two feet." He winked at her. "I must say I've never forgotten a certain young scholar or the story she once told me of her esteemed friend Poppy. It's good to see her back."

A smile began to spread across Angelica's face. She'd forgotten she'd shared that with him. His reference to it somehow validated everything she'd been planning. "Any advice?"

The professor sobered. "Do your homework. Immerse yourself. Spend time with the kind of people you'll be defending. The more you understand where they're coming from, the better job you can do for them because they'll be real people, not just names on a file."

Ortega, Ramirez, Martinez, Herrera. The wisdom of the professor's words stirred her memory. Angelica stood. "Thank you so much. And Dr. Maddox, would you mind giving me a reference if I need one?"

"You won't. Anyone who talks to you for five minutes will see you're not only qualified, you're committed."

By the time she got home, Poppy had gone to his room. The house was dark except for the light in the kitchen where he had left a thick stew simmering on the stove and a bowl and ladle on the counter. It looked and smelled delicious.

So much had happened. She wanted to talk about it. She got a spoon from the drawer and walked down the hall to Poppy's bedroom.

Poppy had just begun his regular evening appointment with the Lord, on his knees beside his chair, when he heard Angelica in the kitchen. "Thank You, Jesus, for bringing my Angel home safe. I worry about her, Lord. You know she getting grown-up and she have no husband." He thought about the time he'd spent with Brad the night of the party. "I think You bring Mr. Brad here for her. I visit with him, and I see he love her, for sure. But he no love You. I ask him where he go to church, and he couldn't remember the name." The uncertainty he'd felt about Brad the night before returned to him. "Paul say in Your Word that a man should love his wife as Christ love the church. I want that for my Angel."

At the thought that Brad might not be saved, great concern welled up in Poppy. "Oh Lord, send Your Holy Spirit to Mr. Brad. Draw him to You."

Angelica's voice at his bedroom door interrupted him. "Poppy, may I come in?"

"Give me wisdom, Lord, so I know how to pray for my Angel and her Brad." He got up from his knees and sat in his chair. "Yes, Miss Angel, come in."

She walked in and sat on the end of the bed, balancing her bowl on her knees. "This smells delicious. Thanks so much for keeping it warm. I'm starved." She took a bite of the stew. "Poppy, I want to talk to you about something," she said, her mouth full.

He folded his hands in his lap. If his girl wanted to talk to him, he wanted to listen. "You tell Poppy about it."

She swallowed. "Today I went in to see one of my old professors. I told him about what happened in New York and how I've decided to become a public defender. He totally supported my decision."

"I think that good."

"But what about Mom and Dad? They're so upset about everything."

"You need honor your papa and mama, but they need respect you too."

"I told him I plan to be working with the less fortunate in

the future, and I've made up my mind to help the Mexicans in particular."

Poppy felt the presence of the Spirit. The image of Antonio in the church basement crossed his mind. God had already been at work, preparing the way. Antonio's presence at the ranch became clearer.

"You have good opportunity for that right here at home."

"You mean Antonio?"

"Antonio, and there many Mexican people at the church too."

"Professor Maddox said I should immerse myself in this. Really get to know the people I'm going to advocate for. I thought about it while I was driving home. It makes a lot of sense. For one thing, it makes me feel like I'm moving forward with my career even though I haven't really resolved this with Mom and Dad." Angelica took another bite of stew.

"Sound like a plan to me." Poppy gave a nod of approval.

"Here's something else I've been thinking about. When I took Antonio shopping yesterday, we went to lunch. He used his tortilla like a shovel. When I asked him to use his fork, he tried, but it was kind of awkward. Could you eat with him a few times so he can practice?"

"Yes, Miss Angel. I need fatten him up. I can ask him help me in kitchen, then he can eat with me." He smiled with confidence, pleased to be included in her plans.

"That's perfect. Why not make some Mexican food? That's fattening." She scraped the side of her bowl.

"I not know too many Mexican dishes. I know Greek and American food best."

"There's lots of cookbooks in the kitchen. I can help you." Angelica's face lit up. "I'll even help you cook."

191

A chance to spend time with my girl. His wise eyes observed her. *And a chance for her to spend* time *with Antonio.* "Yes, you help me."

⁎

Angelica hoped Poppy hadn't noticed the quick heat she felt in her cheeks at the thought of cooking for Antonio. Somehow the idea was very appealing.

He'd ordered a tamale and enchilada combination plate at Mi Mama's Cocina. She wanted to cook something better than that, something special. "Why don't we fix *carne asada*, beans, Mexican rice, and salad. The steak will give him a chance to use a knife."

"I go shopping on Wednesdays. When should we have dinner? Maybe Thursday?"

She jabbed her spoon in the air, going down the imaginary list. "No, I have to go to the city on Thursday, and Friday there's a big dance for the Mexican community at the Flamingo Hotel. I saw a poster about it when we were at the mall." She lowered her hand. "I thought I'd ask Chick to take Antonio to it on Friday, if Antonio wants to go. But, after talking to Professor Maddox, I'm thinking maybe I should go with him." Dancing with him would really give her a feel of the culture. She slowly closed her eyes.

"Miss Angel?" Poppy's voice broke into her thoughts. Her eyes flew open, and he was studying her. "If he no want to go, you could go anyway, for your career."

He knew her so well. She needed to be careful. She wasn't at all comfortable with her thoughts, and she certainly wasn't ready to share them. "I could. But I'd just be an observer. If he goes it'd be a *lot* more worthwhile." She looked at him innocently, licking her spoon.

"I'm sure that true," Poppy answered.

Heat crept up her neck, yet his eyes never left her face. She needed to close the subject. "I'll ask him about it the next time I see him."

"I say that a sure thing." He looked quite pleased with himself.

She rose and kissed him on the cheek. "This Wednesday we'll have our dinner. Thanks for listening. Good night."

Angelica closed the door behind her and leaned against it for a moment, relieved to be alone with her thoughts. It was true, she should learn about the Mexican culture, but she couldn't deny that learning about Antonio made it a whole lot more enjoyable. . . . His strong arms . . . his dark eyes . . .

She took a deep breath, why was she thinking such things? He had his job on the ranch, and she had her career. He thought of her as his boss and nothing more. Maybe she and Brad should take Antonio. She tapped her finger on her chin.

Maybe not.

Poppy picked up his Bible and ran his hand over the cover, thinking about Angelica's interest in the hardworking young man. "Oh, my Jesus," he whispered. "I did wonder why You bring this man to ranch. Your ways are mysterious, but Your plans, perfect." A spiritual knowledge pressed upon him. God was working in the lives of these two young people.

The old man knelt down by his chair and put his Bible in front of his knees. He opened it and took out a piece of paper, tear-stained and wrinkled, smoothing it out carefully on top of the Bible cover. Then he leaned forward until his forehead rested on it. Now he knew exactly how God wanted him to pray. "Draw my Angel and Antonio to You so they grow to know each other in Your arms. And use me, Lord, to bring Mr. Brad to the saving grace of Jesus Christ."

The week passed quickly. Angelica set a work area up in her room. She put the table and filing cabinet at an angle next to her window seat so she could enjoy the view of the valley while she worked. She made numerous professional contacts, set up her computer, started files on job possibilities, and began the process to activate her license. The dinner she and Poppy planned got completely out of hand when Poppy decided to serve it in the formal dining room with a full, formal place setting. Poppy seemed oblivious to the difficulty this created. She spent the whole time trying to figure out Spanish words for soupspoon, butter knife, and other such things, which caused the dinner to go on for hours. It finally ended with them all laughing as they ate homemade Greek jelly cookies with their hands and licked their fingers.

Friday evening Angelica called the bunkhouse to let Antonio know what time they'd be leaving for the Folklorico that she'd told him about.

She looked through her closet but couldn't decide what to wear. What did one wear to a traditional Mexican dance? She didn't want to overdress. She wanted to fit in. Most of the people would be from the ranches, wearing their work clothes, she guessed.

She picked out a pair of cotton slacks and a simple blouse. She looked through her jewelry box and settled on a pair of small, gold, hoop earrings and a necklace with a single pearl. She kept her eye on the bay window, and when she saw Antonio walking up to the house, she ran down to meet him.

It was after eight when they arrived, and Angelica couldn't find a place to park. Finally, she pulled up to the hotel and asked the doorman to take the car. He opened her door. When she got out, Antonio was already waiting for her.

She asked at the front desk where the Folklorico dance was located.

"Bay six. Down that hall." The woman behind the counter pointed behind them.

They could hear the mariachis before they got to the bay. As they walked along the big hallway, they passed groups of people, clustered together, talking and laughing. Angelica was completely surprised by what she saw. Families—parents, children, grandparents—everyone was dressed like they were going to a wedding.

The ladies wore satiny dresses, many had lace shawls, and some had woven flowers in their hair. The children were dressed up as well. All the little girls wore party dresses. Most wore shiny black shoes with lacy, white socks, and every one of them had little earrings sparkling in their pierced ears. The little boys were wearing white shirts and dark pants, and some even had on ties. She looked down at her cotton slacks and white blouse. She was completely underdressed.

As they waited in line to buy their tickets, Angelica observed the people around her more closely. The dresses were cheaply made, and the little girls' shoes were plastic, not patent leather. Some of the women wore hose but didn't shave their legs, and none of them wore much makeup. Most of the boys' clothes fit like hand-me-downs. Some of the men wore bow ties. One man was wearing a T-shirt with a tuxedo printed on it.

But everyone stood and walked and sat as if they were wearing the finest fashions of the season. She suddenly realized they were a proud people. They knew they were poor—their country was poor. They'd come to America to partake of her wealth, but they had no desire to forsake the motherland they loved. They were here to celebrate their culture.

Angelica paid for tickets, and they went in to find a place to sit. She was the only woman in pants. She felt the curious eyes of the people as she and Antonio walked around, looking for a table. She was the only fair-skinned person in the room. *What if they think I don't own anything better?* She suddenly felt self-conscious.

There were no empty tables. Finally, they stopped near the stage. Antonio pulled out a chair for her at a table that was nearly full. She hesitated.

"*Siéntense. Siéntense, por favor,*" said the man across from her as he waved his hand, motioning her to sit. She looked at Antonio, who smiled and nodded his head. She sat down. Seated next to the man opposite her was a woman holding a baby, two more children next to her, about three and six, Angelica guessed. The children sat quietly. In fact, most of the children in the room were either sitting at tables or standing next to their parents.

Antonio was waving his forefinger at the baby across from him, a little girl; even she had on a dress. The father saw him and took the baby from her mother, handing her to Antonio. Angelica's eyes widened. Antonio took the baby with ease and bounced her on his lap. The two men laughed and spoke, but she couldn't understand what they said. An older man passing by stopped, and he took the baby. The three men began talking together. The baby's mother seemed to find the men's behavior quite ordinary.

Angelica felt out of place but not unwelcome. Many conversations went on around her, but she had no idea what was being said.

Well, she had come to learn about the Mexican people, might as well start now.

"*Me llamo es Angelica,*" she said, introducing herself to the woman across from her. "*Cómo se llama usted?*" She asked the woman her name, in perfect textbook Spanish.

The woman answered politely. "*Me llamo Isabella Rodriquez de Garcia.*" She was soft-spoken.

Angelica winced. Was she saying her name was Isabella Rodriquez of Garcia? As in belonging to Mr. Garcia. Is that how these women thought of themselves? Thank heaven they'd come to America. They'd have a chance to find out they could be their own person. They didn't have to be dependent on a man. Isabella didn't look as old as Angelica, and already she was strapped with three children. What did she have to look forward to? Angelica smiled at her. *Poor thing*.

Just then the little boy sitting next to the woman stood up. "*Mama.*" He opened his arms, reaching for her neck.

She pushed her chair back a bit and lifted him to her lap. He took his chubby hand and put it on her cheek, drawing her face to his. "*Te amo, Mamá.*" He gave her a big, toothy grin and laid his head on her shoulder. His eyes closed, and his big grin became a contented smile of perfect peace as he fell asleep in her arms.

Angelica's eyes drifted to the mother's face. The joy she saw there brought tears to her eyes and an empty ache to her heart. This was what she had to look forward to, and she wasn't even as old as Angelica.

The mariachis sang, and the music echoed through the room, reminding Antonio of his home.

Several people were dancing, some on the dance floor,

others in the aisles. Antonio talked to the two men at his table. They were from his state of Jalisco and had worked in the United States for many years.

"*Pardone.*" Angelica tapped Antonio on the arm and got up. The three men stopped talking as she asked them, "*Coka?*"

Antonio smiled at her kindness. "*Posible.*"

She left them, and he watched her make her way to the refreshment table at the front of the room. He could tell she didn't feel at ease. Perhaps it was because she couldn't understand what people were saying, or because she was dressed so differently. He grinned. He knew the feeling well. He would try to make her feel included.

Señor Garcia leaned toward Antonio. "Who's the pretty *americana*?"

"I work at her family's ranch, Regalo Grande."

"Why'd she come here?"

"She told me about it and offered to bring me."

The older man raised his eyebrows. "You're a lucky guy."

"Yes, it's true. I was lucky to find work right away with such good people."

Señor Gonzalez put his hand on Antonio's shoulder. "What he means is most *patronas* don't spend time with poor Mexicans."

The older man nodded. "That's right, my friend, but then a handsome man is never completely poor."

The two men laughed, and despite his discomfort, Antonio knew they meant no harm.

Angelica returned with two Cokes and handed one to Antonio. When she sat down and turned her attention to the stage, the older man winked at Antonio.

The mariachis lifted their voices, ending their song, then bowed, signaling a break. They carried their guitars and walked down the stage stairs just a few feet from her table. There was something vaguely familiar about the second man in line. Angelica looked at him. Where could she have seen him before?

He looked at her, and recognition flickered across his face. His eyes moved to Antonio, and his face broke out in a broad grin. He walked toward their table, putting his guitar under his arm and stretching out his hand.

"Welcome, *amigos*," he said with a heavy accent. "How good of you to come."

Antonio and Angelica shook his hand.

"You come from the church, no?"

That was it. The church. He'd been sitting in the back. He'd had on a Stetson hat. "You go to Glen Ellen Faith Church."

"*Sí*, I go to that church. Name's Manuel. I put a poster there last week. You see it, no?"

"I didn't go to church last week. I saw a poster at Mi Mama's Cocina at the mall."

"Oh, yes, very good place to eat. The manager's here tonight."

The mariachi pulled a chair up to their table, then turned to Antonio and spoke to him in Spanish.

Manuel spoke easily in both English and Spanish. Angelica learned he worked on a horse ranch near the church. He had been there for ten years. His family lived in Puerto Vallarta.

As Manuel and Antonio talked, she found out that Antonio's father worked somewhere in the fields around Sacra-

199

mento, but he didn't know where exactly. He told Manuel that his mother kept envelopes with return address labels on them. The missionaries at the church, where his mother received the money, had explained to her about the return address. But the address changed with the seasons, so they were never really sure where he was. She always worried that someday her husband might never come home, and that was the only link she had to him.

As Manuel translated, Angelica was deeply moved by what she heard. Antonio spoke of his mother with such compassion and respect.

She put her hand on Antonio's arm. "Manuel, please tell him his mother sounds like a very special and brave woman. I hope I can meet her someday."

Manuel translated.

Antonio looked at Angelica, his eyes filled with emotion. "*Muy especial.*"

Manuel slipped from his seat and laid his guitar on the table. "Excuse me, *un momento.*" He moved on to another table and began speaking with the family there.

Angelica felt privileged that Antonio had shared his mother's story with her. She sought out his eyes. "Thank you."

Antonio reached past her and picked up the guitar. He pushed his chair back a little farther from the table and strummed the strings.

"*Sabe?*"

"*Un poco.*" He strummed a few chords.

The two men across from them stopped talking and looked at him, but he didn't notice. His head was down, and he seemed completely absorbed with the guitar and his own thoughts. He continued to strum softly. The music was hauntingly beautiful. It gave her goose bumps.

Hearing the music, Manuel returned to the table. "So you play?"

"*Un poco*," he answered.

"Manuel, would you ask him where he learned to play?"

Manuel did so, then told Angelica. "He say that many of the men who come home to visit from America bring guitars and radios and records and tapes. They listen to the music and then try to play it on their guitars."

Did he have a guitar at home? "*Usted*, guitar in *su casa?*"

"*Yo no, pero mi padrino sí tiene.*"

"*Padrino?*" Angelica looked at Manuel.

"That's his godfather. *He* has a guitar."

Lights flashed above them. "Oh, that's for me." Manuel took his guitar from Antonio. "Time for me to play. I hope I see you in church again." He left them for the stage.

Angelica turned to Antonio, looking at him with a mixture of surprise and admiration. She'd always loved music and had taken piano lessons on the baby grand in the living room as a child, but she hadn't thought about playing in years. She was too busy getting good grades, then building her career. She wondered if he had talent. Maybe he could get an inexpensive guitar and continue to learn to play.

When Antonio scooted his chair back up to the table, she realized she'd been staring at him. She looked toward the stage, pretending to watch the mariachis.

People began to fill the dance floor—husbands with wives, fathers with daughters, even older children with their younger brothers and sisters. Some of the little children stood on the dance floor just clapping their hands. Angelica was struck by the sense of family. The very old were treated with respect;

the very young looked after with delight. She glanced at Antonio. Did women ever ask men to dance?

As Angelica looked on, she wondered what kind of dance they were doing. It resembled a polka, though some of it seemed like a cha-cha. There was a definite rhythm, but it was foreign to her. Antonio sat back in his chair, tapping his foot. She watched him watching the dancers. Should she ask him?

The couple across the table from them were standing and motioning Angelica and Antonio to join them on the dance floor. The woman handed the baby to her oldest child.

Angelica looked at Antonio. He smiled and shrugged his shoulders. She stood, and they followed the Garcias to the dance floor.

On the floor, Antonio turned to her and took her hand. She felt a warmth flow through her. He began a pattern of steps, and they moved in a circle around the floor. She was surprised at his light touch. The top of her head came just under his chin, and she could smell the fresh, clean scent of soap.

He didn't hold her close, so she was able to watch his feet as they moved. Within a few minutes, she'd caught on to the simple pattern and was able to follow him without looking down. Hoping he would notice . . . maybe pull her a little closer, she casually looked around at the other dancers. But Antonio continued with gentlemanly decorum.

Don't be shy, we're dancing. Angelica adjusted the hand she had on his shoulder, moving it to his back, pressing ever so slightly. Just then, the song ended.

She looked up at Antonio. Quite openly he studied her—without a trace of shyness on his handsome face. He tipped his head and looked in her eyes. *"Gracias, señorita."*

Her heart fluttered. Time stopped as she lost herself in his gaze. She couldn't breathe, couldn't think. There was nothing but Antonio's dark, beautiful eyes, drawing her from the crowded room into a private moment alone with him.

She looked away. "Let's *sentarse*," she sputtered, feeling foolish, as they followed the Garcias off the dance floor.

They stayed until eleven o'clock, when the music stopped, but they didn't dance again. Driving home, Angelica tried to find out more about Antonio's interest in music, but the language barrier stopped her from learning much. *Sí*, he would like to have a guitar. No, no one else in his family played. *Sí*, he would like to see Manuel at church again.

She dropped him off at the bunkhouse.

"*Muchas gracias, señorita.*"

"*Buenos nochas*, Antonio." She grinned. "My name is Angelica," she teased.

"*Sí*," he replied and shut the door.

As she drove up to the house, she reflected on the evening. It had been well worth going. Just as Dr. Maddox had predicted, it had given her a perspective she never would have gotten working in a public defender's office. She thought about how underdressed she'd been. There *was* a lot she didn't know about the Mexican people.

She felt a little tug in her heart. She wanted to know more.

In the bunkhouse, Antonio changed into some clean work clothes. He'd hammered a few horseshoe nails into the wall next to his bed, and there he hung the shirt and jacket with the store bag covering them. He took the cross out of the front pocket of his chinos, folded his pants, coiled his belt before putting it back in the box, and then put everything in his dresser drawer. He slipped his feet into his sandals, picked up his cross, and walked outside.

He was restless. He jogged across the drive and down the hill to the stream. Once there, he walked along the stream, up toward the ridge. Finally, he sat down on a big boulder and turned his face to the starry night. The moon flickered through the leaves of the oaks. He pressed the cross to his lips.

"*Dios,*" he whispered. Thoughts crowded into his mind—riding in the car to the dance, Angelica dressed so beautifully, Manuel, the guitar . . . touching Angelica, holding her. He took the cross from his lips. When Manuel had left with the guitar, she'd stared at him as if she wanted him to play more. It was almost as if she knew.

Since he was very young, he'd been able to hear music and pick it out on the guitar. It was known among the people who lived in the fields of Guadalajara. The gift, *un regalo*, they called it. Whenever families gathered for holidays or celebrations, they wanted Antonio to play. They would hand him a guitar, and he would sit quietly a moment, until he heard the music. Then he would begin, his fingers moving effortlessly across the strings, releasing the music in his mind. Many times, when he went to Guadalajara with his mother, the vendors would let him borrow a guitar, and he'd stand on the street and play, hoping passersby would throw him a peso.

Sometimes, when they found no check had come to the missionaries, his mother would walk with him to the vendors and sit with him, and he would play for her. He would stand and play, looking only at her. He did not want to see the strangers who dropped a coin in her lap or pressed one into her hand with a look of pity. They did not know about the gift. There was no need for pity. He would play until she said it was time to go. Then they would stop and buy food and walk home. He pressed the cross to his lips. *Dios, You have been good to me.*

The oaks swayed in the summer breeze that blew up from the valley, bringing him back to the present. Angelica. He remembered the scent of her perfume as they danced. Thoughts of her pushed everything else from his mind. His heart ached. What could he do? He could not deny what he felt. He wanted to be with her, to be near her, to touch her hair, to touch her face. But he had nothing. She could never care for him. He was poor, and she was rich. Maybe he should leave and go back to Mexico . . . but his family needed money, and above all he must work hard at the job God had given him.

He stood up. She deserved the finest and the best. He had nothing to offer her. Nothing. He could never ask her to love him. She must never know how he felt. He could never have her—he could only love her.

Raising his hand, the cross wrapped in his fist, he turned his face to God. "If it can be, let me give her this one thing. Your gift, *un regalo*. I can play Your music for her. It will speak of my love to her. I beg You, make a way for me. Let me play Your music for her. Let me give her this gift—*un regalo grande*." He dropped his hand, surrendering to the outcome.

As he walked back along the stream, the breeze through the oaks picked up. He was filled with a peace that passed his understanding, filled with the indwelling Spirit of the God who hears and answers prayers.

"*Dios*, I will watch for Your answer."

12

ANGELICA LAID HER clothes out on her bed. It was going to be a beautiful day for sailing. She tried to put the dance the night before out of her mind, but her thoughts kept returning to Antonio—how handsome he was, the way it felt to be in his arms, the image of him holding the guitar. She got chills again.

She shook her head, trying to clear it. She had to stop thinking of him this way. He was a laborer, with his own goals and dreams, and achieving them would take him far away from her. They were two very different people, from two very different worlds. And her parents. If they couldn't understand why she wanted to advocate for the poor, she could just imagine what they'd think if she told them she had feelings for one of the laborers, a Mexican. She shook her head again. *God, help me forget about Antonio.* A beautiful chord of music echoed in her mind. She sighed. She needed to get ready for her date with Brad. He deserved the chance he had asked for.

It was hard to know what to wear in San Francisco, especially on the water. A beautiful, sunny afternoon could turn cold in a matter of minutes if the fog rolled in.

Layers were best, so she chose a sleeveless turtleneck to wear under a V-neck sweater. She set out the new red, white, and blue windbreaker she'd bought in Walnut Creek so she wouldn't forget it.

The weeks at home had convinced her that coming back to California had been the right move. Even though her parents had not supported her decision to become a public defender, they had not closed the door completely.

And Brad. So easy to be around, so much a part of who she was. She looked forward to seeing him again and meeting his friends. They'd agreed to meet at Lindsay's in Tiburon at eleven o'clock, then all drive over to the marina.

Her thoughts turned to his cryptic comment about wanting to talk to her about her job search. His father's firm was well connected, perhaps he'd made some phone calls. Maybe Brad had gotten a lead on a position that was opening in San Francisco County. Or maybe even something at the federal level.

She finished dressing and went downstairs. She stopped in her father's study and browsed through the mail Poppy had stacked on the desk. One of the return addresses caught her eye; it was from New Life, Inc. She opened it. The letter confirmed her father's purchase of $500,000 worth of stock options. She could see from the account statement it wasn't his first purchase. When he'd told her he'd invested in the new organ-rejection drug, Thrombexx, she hadn't realized he'd invested so heavily.

She understood how it worked. He invested in the company by buying options to purchase their stock, based on its future, higher value. That value would come when the drug hit the market. But if the drug wasn't approved, for any reason at all, the options were worthless. The company would have no way of repaying her father the money he'd invested, and, in turn, her father would have no way of repaying the loans he'd taken to raise the money in the first place.

Concern crawled along Angelica's nerves. Surely, he knew what he was doing. He'd worked in the field of organ transplants for forty years. He'd felt confident about the approval. She put the statement back in the envelope. "Oh, dear God, don't let anything bad happen," she murmured. "I'd better get this on Poppy's prayer list."

She continued going through the mail. The last piece was a letter from the County of Sonoma saying her father didn't need to go through a formal filing to split off the seventy-five acres from the rest of the ranch. He could do a "short plat" by having the land surveyed and the map recorded. He'd be happy to hear that. He'd wanted to keep it as a separate business, plus it would be much more valuable as a separate piece. She glanced at her watch. It was time to go.

"Poppy. Poppy," Angelica called from the door.

"Yes, Miss Angel?"

"I'm leaving now to go meet Brad. I'm not sure when I'll be home."

"You drive careful."

"I will. Love you. Bye."

Angelica took the top off the car and headed to Tiburon. She found Brad's directions easy to follow and was soon driving down Tiburon Boulevard. Right on Seaview, left on Bay Court—5236, but there was no place on the street to park. She circled the little court and saw that someone was having a garage sale. One of the bargain hunters pulled out, and she pulled into the space.

She grabbed her windbreaker and purse, walked up to the door, and rang the bell. Brad answered.

"Come in. Come in." He gave a sweep of his hand. "You look great."

"Thanks."

He took her purse and jacket. "Follow me. The rest of the group is out on the patio."

They walked through the kitchen and breakfast nook to the backyard. He laid her purse and jacket with a pile of other things.

"Hey, everyone. This is Angelica."

There were three young women and one other man. "This is Lindsay, Renee, Mariclair, and Scott," Brad said, pointing to each one.

"Here, sit down." Lindsay pulled an empty chair around, making a semicircle. "Would you like some coffee or rolls?"

"No, thanks. I'd better save my appetite for this afternoon." Angelica took the offered chair.

Everyone was friendly, and soon she found herself part of the conversation her arrival had apparently interrupted.

"Don't tell me there's not a glass ceiling in corporate America." Lindsay crossed her arms. "The *Wall Street Journal* just had a story on that."

"I didn't have to read it in the *Wall Street Journal*," Renee said, sitting back in her chair with her cup of coffee. "I'm the executive secretary to the CEO at one of the biggest firms in the financial district. I know what people are making. Women are paid less to do exactly what a man does. It's an open secret."

Scott threw his feet off the lounger and sat up. "Hey, ladies, wait one minute. Are you telling me you are ready to put your lives on hold to pursue a career? That's what it takes if you want to move to the top of a major corporation. That means no time for husbands or kids. It means work."

"Oh, please." Mariclair glared at Scott. "Are you saying women are afraid to work? Besides, I'm not planning on having any children. We're not even talking about getting to the top. We just want equal pay for equal work at midlevel, especially in areas like human resources and staff jobs. What do you think, Angelica?"

Ortega, Ramirez, and all the hundreds of others had never been paid at all. "I agree. There are a lot of inequities in employment law, particularly with minorities." She said it with more passion than she intended.

"That's right." Mariclair nodded toward Angelica. "Women are a minority group, and there's no reason why we should put up with sex-based discrimination. The lawsuits that have been filed and won are proof of it. In fact, a friend of mine just joined the Equal Rights Law Center. Women's rights are their top priority."

Brad held up his hand. "Hey, wait a minute, everybody. It's Saturday, and the workweek doesn't start 'til Monday. This all sounds too much like work to me. Let's go sailing."

Angelica caught the wink Brad gave Scott.

"Who are we meeting down at the marina?" Scott asked, getting up.

"Riley, Bonnie, Kathleen, and Bryan are meeting us there." Lindsay pushed her chair back. "We're going on Riley's and Bryan's sloops."

"Who's driving?"

Brad put a hand on Angelica's shoulder. "Why don't the three of you go in Scott's car? I'll take Angelica and meet you there."

Everybody grabbed what they could carry from the pile of coats, coolers, and backpacks Angelica had seen when she first walked in and headed out the door.

"Hey, Lindsay. Why are there so many cars on the street?

I could hardly find a place to park when I got here," Renee asked.

"There's a garage sale at that blue house." Lindsay pointed to the back of the court. "The boy who lives there is a Boy Scout, and he's doing some kind of a fundraiser for one of his badges. He stopped by my house and asked if I could donate anything."

"I love garage sales." Mariclair peeked over Lindsay's shoulder. "Maybe, if it's still going on when we get back, we could go look. I found a great old side table at a garage sale once for seven dollars. There might be something there with my name on it."

Lindsay shrugged. "Sure, if it's still on when we get back. Probably won't be much left by then, though."

"If you're meant to have it, it will be there," Renee chimed in.

"Hey, wouldn't it be great if life worked that way." Brad laughed. "Let's go."

Scott shut the trunk, and the three girls piled into his Mustang. Brad and Angelica followed in Brad's white BMW.

Brad reached across the console and took her hand. "Have you thought any more about what I said?"

She had thought about it a lot. "I'm here, aren't I?" She gave him a mischievous smile.

When they got to the marina, they found the rest of the group already at the dock, stowing their gear. Scott and the three girls decided to go with Riley and Bonnie on Riley's sloop. Angelica and Brad joined Bryan and Kathleen on Bryan's boat, *Free Spirit*.

Bryan called to Riley across the slip. "Let's meet back here at three o'clock."

"See you then, if not sooner," Riley called back.

211

The day was warm and the breeze gentle as they moved out of the harbor to the open waters of San Francisco Bay.

Bryan guided the sloop out of the marina with the auxiliary motor. "Hey, Brad, give me a hand with the sails."

"Sure thing."

In a few minutes, the big red, white, and blue mainsail was set, embracing the sea breezes and sending the sloop skimming over the water.

Angelica put on her windbreaker and sat down on the side deck. She raised her face toward the sun and closed her eyes. *Heaven.*

Brad came and sat down beside her. "Having fun?"

She turned and smiled at him. "I could get used to this."

"Doesn't this remind you of college? Remember Colin's sloop? How many summer nights did we all go out in it?"

Angelica reached for his hand. "I haven't thought about that in ages." She leaned back. Brad slipped his arm around her and lowered his cheek next to hers. He pulled her closer.

"I lov—" A gust of wind caught the sail, tilting the boat port side and throwing him off the side deck.

Angelica grabbed the gunwale. "You okay?" Her look of concern dissolved into laughter.

Brad scrambled to get his balance. "Yeah, fine."

"Hey, buddy," Bryan shouted. "Now you know why I call her the *Free Spirit*. She has a mind of her own."

"Anyone want a drink?" Kathleen asked.

"Coke." "Perrier." "Got anything diet?" Everyone made their requests at once.

Kathleen opened the cooler and gave Bryan a Coke. She took the rest of the drinks and joined Brad and Angelica on the side deck. "Isn't that Riley and the others over there?"

212

"It sure is." Bryan waved. "Anybody feel like racing?"

"Yee haw!" Kathleen raised her Perrier. "Let's do it."

"I'm going to set the *Spirit* free." Bryan pushed the tiller starboard, the wind caught the sails, and they were off.

Seeing the sloop suddenly heading his way, Riley gave Bryan a thumbs-up and swung his boom around, and the two boats headed across the bay amid screams of delight and good-natured dares.

One race wasn't enough, and soon the two sloops were battling to win the best two out of three, then three out of five. By midafternoon, the talk turned to the upcoming barbeque at Lindsay's.

"I guess it's about time we started back to the marina. Everybody's starved." Bryan pointed in the direction of the Golden Gate Bridge. "Besides, it looks like we've got some fog rolling in." He signaled to Riley that they were turning back. Riley turned his sloop to follow.

The boats sailed toward the Tiburon Peninsula. Angelica and Brad sat on the bow. As they cruised past the forest-covered hills of Angel Island, Brad took her hand.

Angelica saw Fort McDowell. "Look, there's the North Garrison, where the Immigration Station used to be. I did a report on that in high school."

"What about it?" Brad asked.

"Well, back at the turn of the century, it was called China Cove. It was where the Chinese were processed to enter the United States—a detention center, because of the Chinese Exclusion Act of 1882, which was passed to prohibit the immigration of certain nationalities and social classes."

He pulled her close to him. "You know, on the Statue of Liberty it says, 'Give me your tired, your poor, your huddled masses yearning to breathe free, the wretched refuse of your teeming shore. Send these, the homeless, tempest-tost to me, I lift my lamp beside the golden door!' Remember?"

He suddenly seemed so dear, so sweet. She had practiced her graduation speech a hundred times with him. The reference to that time of their life dimmed the recent past. They had history together. Really, as she thought about it, they had broken up because he wanted her to be near him. Why had that seemed so unreasonable then? Funny how things had worked out. The very thing that had broken them up had resolved itself.

"Yes, Brad, I do." She settled back into the warmth of his chest and his words. "You said that you wanted to talk to me about my job search. I'm hoping you can help me."

"Oh. Yes." She heard the excitement in his voice. "I've been thinking about it since I was at your house. I know how upset your parents are about your decision to become a public defender, and I think I've come up with the perfect solution." This was going to be interesting. "Remember, I told you my dad was opening up a new office in Marin?"

"Yes."

"Well, I had a talk with him about you."

Angelica sat up and looked at Brad, his hair tousled by the sea air, his blue eyes sparkling. "Me?"

She could see he was quite pleased with himself. "Yes, you. He wants to add at least two more attorneys to the staff. And." He stopped a moment and looked in her eyes. "He would like the firm to do some pro bono work."

Angelica saw right through Brad's effort to make this seem like a natural fit. She was sure he'd presented the idea to his father, of having the office perform some legal work, free of charge to those who needed it, only to help her. "That *is* something to think about."

He pulled her back to him. "Angel, we're just starting that office. You'd be in on the ground floor. You could

214

handpick the pro bono work the firm accepts. It could be your little project."

"It takes a lot of work to get a new office up and running. When you work for free, you get all the work you want, but it doesn't pay the bills," she countered.

Brad stroked her hair. "Let me worry about that. It's a perfect setup for you."

And for him. He'd be fully involved in her life. But there was no denying that it was an offer to consider. Especially since her preliminary searches hadn't turned up any job openings.

"Thanks, Brad." She patted his hand. "Let me think about it."

She closed her eyes and let her mind wander. This was something to keep on the back burner. If nothing opened up in the county or federal offices for her, then this might be something she should seriously consider. Not her first choice, but a good second choice. She wanted to be a full-time advocate, not just do some work on the side. Working for Brad's firm would mean giving prime time to the work that the paying clients required and giving only the time left over to the cases that mattered to her. It was a compromise.

"Hey, you two. I need some help docking." Bryan's voice broke into her thoughts.

Brad jumped up, and Angelica followed. They secured the boat and helped the others tie down theirs. Everybody loaded the car trunks.

"See you guys at Lindsay's." Brad took Angelica's hand, and they walked to his car. He opened the door for her, and she got in. Then he jogged around to the other side of the car and started it.

"I had a great time today. I'm glad you asked me to come." Their eyes met.

215

"I'm glad too." He leaned toward her and kissed her.

"Guess we'd better be on our way," Brad said without moving.

He kissed her again.

"I guess we'd better." Her eyes held his.

Brad turned back to the steering wheel, cracked the window, and put the car in gear.

They pulled up behind Scott's Mustang as Brad turned onto the boulevard. "Wasn't it funny when Riley made that steep port tack to beat us around the buoy and Bonnie fell in?"

"I laughed so hard, I cried." Angelica started giggling.

Brad looked at her and burst out laughing.

By the time they got to Lindsay's house, the group was on the patio, and Lindsay had the coals started in the grill.

"Looks like that garage sale's still going," Mariclair said to no one in particular. "Anyone want to come with me to check it out?"

"Come on. Let's all go." Lindsay jumped up. "By the time we get back, the coals will be ready, and we can start cooking."

Scott stretched out on a lounge chair. "I think I'll pass."

"Good." Lindsay clapped her hands. "Then we won't have to hurry. The steaks are marinating on the kitchen counter. When the coals are ready, put them on the grill for me, will you?"

"No problem. Take your time."

Everyone walked down to the end of the court. The guys headed for some skis that were leaning up against the front of the garage. The girls scattered among the card tables set up in the driveway. Angelica glanced at the few things displayed: an alarm clock, a pen set, some assorted knives, a barbeque fork. *Pretty picked over.*

She wandered into the garage. On one side there was a nearly empty clothes rack, and on the other side another card table. A boy in a Boy Scout uniform sat behind the table.

"Hi." Angelica walked up to the table. "Are you the one having this garage sale?"

"Uh huh."

"Looks like it was pretty successful."

"I've made $228.64, so far."

Angelica smiled at his excitement.

"How much do you want for this canteen?" a man called from behind the clothes rack.

The boy got up from the table to see what the man was holding. His foot knocked over something that was leaning against the table leg. "Crumb, who put that there?" He picked it up and laid it on the top of the table.

Angelica's eyes widened as she picked it up. A guitar. It felt light in her hands. It had a blond front and darker sides and back. The lacquer on the front was full of hairline cracks. The neck seemed short and the body deeper than other guitars she'd seen.

Brad walked up to the table. "Hey, what'd you find?"

"Do you know anything about guitars?"

"Not really." He took it from her and strummed it a few times. "Sounds fine to me. Do you play?"

"No, but one of the ranch hands does. He might like it."

"Aren't you a nice lady."

The Boy Scout returned to the table with some money in his hand.

"Is this yours?" Angelica asked the boy.

"No, my friend's mom gave it to me for the sale. She said it'd been in her garage for at least a couple years. A foreign exchange student left it a long time ago."

217

Angelica looked it over. "It's kind of beat up. How much do you want?"

"Fifteen bucks? I've even got it tuned up."

"Five."

The boy's face fell.

Brad's mouth dropped. "Whoa, you're tough."

The young man picked up the guitar and strummed it a few times. "It plays real nice, lady." He dropped his hand to his side.

The stroke of the boy's hand . . . the strains of music . . . the mariachis . . . Antonio's hands. Her memory stirred. The hands that had held the guitar the night before, the hands that had held her on the dance floor. How many times had *he* been bargained down, cheated out of a fair price? Was this how the flower grower had agreed to pay the fatherless young man five pesos a day for his hours of backbreaking work under the hot summer sun? Was she so steeped in the high-stakes competition of corporate America that she couldn't give a Boy Scout a fair price for a used guitar? Did everything have to be negotiated?

She dug in her purse and got her wallet. "What are you going to do with the money you're making?"

"Our troop is going to make a donation to the March of Dimes."

She handed him two tens and two fives. "Here's fifteen dollars for the guitar and fifteen for your cause." She took the guitar and gave the boy a wink. "You're a good salesman. Reminding me how nice a guitar sounds was exactly what I needed."

Brad started laughing. "Boy, you really had me going." Then he turned to the young man. "The March of Dimes, you say?" He dug in his pocket. "Here's another ten dollars."

Angelica looked at him. "Why are you doing that?"

"My mother lost her first child, a girl, to a birth defect, and our family's been involved with their annual fund-raising event in San Francisco for years. This year my dad's on the entertainment committee for the evening ball that's held the first weekend of December."

In all the years she'd known him, he'd never mentioned it. The look on his face told her not to question him. At least not now.

"Well, be sure to let him know what a big contributor I am," Angelica teased. "Maybe I'll get a free ticket to the ball."

"I have a feeling he was already planning that." Brad winked and took her hand. "Ready to go?"

"Yeah, I'm starved."

"We're going back to the house. You guys ready?" Brad asked as they passed Lindsay and Renee.

"Come on, everybody," Lindsay called out. "Let's go eat."

When they got back to the house, Angelica smelled the steaks Scott had put on the grill. Everyone pitched in, and soon all the food was set out on the patio table, buffet style. Angelica realized everyone had brought something.

"Gee, Lindsay. I wish Brad had told me to bring something."

"Don't worry about it. You're his guest, and he brought dessert."

"He probably had Aunt Safeway bake it." Angelica laughed. "Anyway, I can help you clean up."

They filled their plates and sat wherever they could. Talk turned to the afternoon antics.

"Hey, Bonnie, what's with you trying to beat the sloop to the buoy?" asked Bryan.

"Very funny. You think I fell in? Are you forgetting who

the captain was? I was the only one in 'pushing' distance when Riley saw you were beating us . . . with four on your sloop and six on ours."

"Hey, it was an accident. Really." The young real estate broker answered with the conviction of a guilty man.

Everyone burst out laughing.

"Angelica, Brad said that you moved here from New York. Where in New York did you live?"

"In Manhattan. I worked for Czervenka and Zergonos."

Bryan gave a low whistle. "Wow, talk about being connected. Don't they represent a lot of interests in Washington?"

"That they do. Although I worked in the International Office handling immigration issues."

Bryan shook his head. "Bet you were busy. Immigration's a big problem. Everybody wants in. It's just not possible. The Mexicans have just about taken over Southern California. There're illegals sneaking in every day."

"Yeah, have you guys been following that news story about the guy who came over illegally trying to get drugs?" Riley asked.

"There are plenty of drugs in Mexico. Why'd he come here?"

Everyone laughed.

"Not illegal drugs. Medicine. It was a big story here in California earlier this year, but it's kind of died down now."

"What happened?" Angelica asked.

"The family lives in one of those shanty towns just across the border." Brad broke in. "The wife had cancer, and she needed a medicine that was only available here. Her husband tried to get visas for months so they could bring her here."

"Apparently they tried to raise money for the medicine

220

too. So if they got to the hospital they'd be able to pay. But they didn't have anywhere near enough. Their little town had come together, but those people could hardly feed themselves," Riley added.

"Anyway, after months of trying to get a visa and enough money, they were running out of time. She only had days to live. So he crosses illegally to try and buy the medicine and gets caught. He's in jail over here now, and his wife is dying in Mexico, or dead."

Renee put her plate down. "How sad. They shouldn't have put him in jail."

"They had to. He broke the law," Scott said, with his mouth full.

Lindsay shook her head. "Sometimes you *have to* break the law."

Antonio's voice, speaking about his mother, played back to Angelica. What if she were sick? Would he go to prison to save her? There was no doubt that he would. The thought was upsetting.

"Boy, if that doesn't sound like situational ethics," Bonnie countered. "When is it all right to break the law? When something's real important. What if everybody thought that? It'd be chaos."

Lindsay chewed her lower lip. "That's true."

Riley jumped in. "Besides, those people need to follow the rules. Yes, it's too bad that the family's in such a tough situation, but there are procedures they can follow. They should've started trying to get visas sooner, not waited till the last minute. It wouldn't have mattered anyway because he didn't have enough money for the medicine."

"That's not true." Renee spoke up. "The reporter said that the cancer center takes a certain number of charity cases

221

every year. So, he might have gotten the medicine. But he couldn't do anything if he couldn't get over here."

"If they take that free medicine, then an American who could have gotten it isn't going to get it."

"So what are you saying? An American life is worth more?" Lindsay shot back.

"Of course I'm not saying that. I'm just saying there have to be rules and order so you don't get in messy situations like this."

Brad turned to Angelica. "You haven't said a word. What do you think?"

She looked around the room at the people whose friendship was only hours old, then spoke from her heart. "I wonder—if it was your mother or your wife . . . or you. What would you think then?"

For a moment, no one spoke.

"Hey, Counselor, that's a hypothetical." Bryan broke the awkward silence, striking a pose that mocked seriousness.

"But if she's right, what then?" Lindsay shot back.

"Angelica, surely you're not saying it's all right to break the law?"

"I'm saying, as human beings we have a responsibility to each other, and borders or race or economic status shouldn't change that. Of course it's not all right to break the law. Sometimes the laws that are made by man need to be changed. Only God's laws are infallible. Sometimes you have to fight for what's right. Laws should stand up under questions like, 'What is morally right?'"

"Hear. Hear." Lindsay raised her Coke can.

"And may your wildest dreams come true." Riley raised his Evian toward Lindsay. "How about giving me some justice, then. Admit it. I won that race fair and square."

"Speaking of wild dreams. Have any of you guys seen

222

that new release playing at the Corte Madera Cinemas? The one that was filmed in San Francisco."

"You mean *The Scanner*?" Scott asked.

"Yeah, it's made more at the box office than any other movie this year."

"I heard that's because of the special effects they used in the dream sequences," Mariclair added.

"So did I," said Renee.

"Have you seen it?" Brad asked Angelica.

"No, but I'd like to."

"Why don't we go next weekend?"

"We'll meet you guys there," Renee said. "Want to, Mariclair?"

"Sure."

"Well?" Brad looked at Angelica.

She hesitated. "Sure."

The gathering broke up about eight o'clock. Brad helped Angelica and Lindsay clean up.

"Thanks so much for everything." Angelica gave Lindsay a hug.

"Me too." Brad planted a friendly kiss on her cheek.

Angelica put the guitar under her arm and picked up her purse.

Brad walked her to her car. Before he reached to open the car door, he took her free hand. "Hey, you've been kind of quiet. Everything okay?"

"Yeah . . . I don't know. It bothered me, that story about that poor man trying to get medicine for his wife. Who's going to defend that man? That's exactly the kind of work I ought to be doing. Don't you think so?"

Brad turned her toward him. "I *think* you're awesome."

She tilted her face to his, and he pushed a wisp of hair away from her eyes. "I'm looking forward to seeing you again. How about dinner after the movie?" he said softly. "My friend Chris is the maître d' at Marin Joe's. I'll ask him to reserve a table for us."

"Sounds wonderful."

He bent down to kiss her, but the guitar neck, sticking out from under her arm, jabbed him in the ribs.

"Ouch."

Angelica backed away. "Oh! Sorry. You okay?"

Brad started laughing. He was still holding her hand, so he patted it. "I'll call you soon." He opened the car door, and she set the guitar on the passenger's seat and got in. As she pulled away, she waved.

She frowned at her passenger. "Stupid guitar."

She thought about Brad and their date all the way home. When she tumbled into bed later that night, she pulled the covers up under her chin and closed her eyes. She felt the gentle rocking of the sloop and Brad's cheek next to hers. In the free and benevolent place between waking and sleeping, unfettered by worldly cares, the warmth of his embrace encircled her.

He loved her. She could feel it. Other differences could be worked out. Love was the only basis for marriage. That's why she'd agreed to marry him . . . she loved him.

13

Angelica walked into her father's office and picked up the paychecks. She thumbed through them: Chick, Rafael, Poppy, Antonio. She put them in her pocket. Before she settled down in her room to develop a phone list of professional and personal contacts, she wanted to get the checks to Chick. She had to start thinking outside the box, search for jobs in the surrounding counties. Going through ordinary channels to try and find a job had yielded nothing. As she turned to leave, the phone rang.

"Hello."

"It's Mom."

She smiled at the distant voice. It was good to hear from her. "How are you?"

"We're in port at Aruba. How was it?"

"How was what?"

"Your date, of course."

Angelica pulled the receiver away from her ear and looked at it. She shook her head and put the phone back to her ear. "It was fine, Mom. I had a good time. How are you feeling?"

"Are you going to see him again?"

"Mom, I had a great time, and I'll tell you all about it when you get home. How's Dad?"

"We're having a wonderful time. Here's your father. He wants to talk to you."

Her dad asked how she was, then asked what was really on his mind. "Have you been going through the mail? Anything about an approval on Thrombexx?"

"No, but you received an account statement from New Life, and you got some good news from the county. You don't have to do a formal split for the vineyard. They're going to let you do a short plat."

His excitement sang through the phone lines. "That's great news. Would you call the surveyor tomorrow and tell him? His number is there in the file."

"Sure, Dad. You guys having fun?"

"We are. Your mom's been resting a lot." Angelica thought her father's voice sounded tentative. "We'll be home next Friday. We'll talk more then." She hung up, then sat for a moment.

Why had her father been so reluctant to talk about her mother? She's "resting a lot," he'd said. Not, "she's been shopping" or "she's playing bridge" or "she's getting brown as a berry."

Points of fear pricked at Angelica, and a longing for her mother welled within her. She was being silly. Her mother's voice sounded strong. She was fine.

She went to find the surveyor's file on her father's desk and put it by the phone. That done, she picked up the checks and walked to the bunkhouse.

Chick sat in the dining area reading the Sunday *Chronicle*.

"Here are the checks my dad left." She handed them to him.

He went through them, taking his out and putting it in his shirt pocket.

"When do you give the workers their money?"

"I go into town tomorrow and cash these, then I pay them."

"Antonio wants a money order to send to his mother. Can you get that?"

Chick hesitated. "How much does he want?"

"I don't know. Is he here?"

"No, he went outside a while ago. I'll see if I can find 'im."

Angelica heard Chick calling Antonio. She looked out the window of the bunkhouse hoping to see Antonio. Soon she saw him running across the drive, up the hill from the oaks.

He came into the bunkhouse out of breath. "*Sí?*"

Chick followed him in.

"Chick, tell him today is payday. Ask him how much of his check he wants in his money order."

Chick translated.

"*Doscientos.*"

"Two hundred," Angelica repeated. He must have wanted to keep fifty dollars for himself. She was glad. "*Bien*, Antonio."

"Tell him you're going to get his money order for him tomorrow."

Chick translated. Antonio spoke back to him.

"He's askin' about a letter to his mother."

She'd forgotten all about her promise. It certainly wouldn't

227

be convenient now. Her day was mapped out. She hoped the work she did today would help her plan a specific strategy for tomorrow. She looked at her watch. If she hurried, it probably wouldn't take more than a few minutes to write the letter.

"Come." Angelica motioned for Antonio to follow her.

They walked up to the house and into her father's office. Antonio took off his hat. Angelica pulled a chair up to the edge of the desk so he could sit down. She moved behind the desk, took the yellow legal pad that her father kept by the phone, tore off a few sheets of paper, and picked up a pen. She looked at him. He looked at her.

"*Uno momento.*" She jumped up and ran to her room, then returned with her Spanish book and dictionary.

"Okay." She studied her book. "Let's start with, 'Mama, how are you? I am fine.'" She repeated the greeting to Antonio in Spanish, and he smiled and nodded. She copied the Spanish phrases from her book, making sure she got the spelling right.

"*Aquí está mi dinero,*" she said, looking at him for approval. *Here is my money.* It was always a good idea to let the receiver know you'd sent money in the letter . . . just in case.

Antonio nodded, and she wrote it down. After thinking a moment, Angelica took her dictionary and found the word she wanted. "*No preocuparse?*" Antonio smiled and nodded again. Clearly he liked the idea of letting his mother know she didn't need to worry.

"Hmm. Let's see. Here's one," she said, looking through her phrases. "I miss you?" she asked in Spanish.

"Good," he said in English.

She glanced over her phrases again. "I love you?" she asked in Spanish.

He drew back in his chair.

"I love you, Mother?" she asked again, lapsing into English.

"Love?" he repeated back to her in English with a heavy accent.

"Love. *Amor*." She pronounced it slowly. "La . . . v."

"La . . . v. Yes," he answered in English, then whispered it a few times, pronouncing it carefully, as if it were an important addition to his stock of English words.

She wrote it down as the closing sentence.

She wanted to write a few things for the missionaries and managed, with the help of her dictionary, to ask him if that was okay. He agreed, so she wrote in English, "I am Antonio Perez's employer. He is working at our ranch in northern California. I believe that the people receiving this letter speak and write English. If you do, please tell his mother that he is doing very well, and if it is possible, could you reply to this letter? Also, could you ask where his father is working? I would appreciate any help you can give." She wrote her address at the bottom and turned the paper so Antonio could see it.

He drew himself up and took a deep breath as he looked at it, then took her pen and made an X carefully at the bottom.

She took an envelope and put the letter into it. She needed the mailing address. "*Quién? Qué números?*" She tapped the face of the envelope. "I need. For *busón*."

"*En mi casa.*"

She asked him to bring it to her tomorrow with his money order. He nodded. That reminded her. "And your papers too. *Su papel importante.*"

"Okay." He held out his hand for the envelope.

His hand. The guitar. She'd almost forgotten the guitar.

229

For a moment, she hesitated. Her morning was going to be gone, and she hadn't even started the list. She looked at her watch.

"I have something for you, *un regalo, por usted*." Angelica hoped he wouldn't mind. "A gift, for you."

He studied her a moment. "*Regalo?*"

"Yes, a gift. *Es en mi car-o*. Come." She stood.

He followed her to the entryway and out to the front of the house, where she'd parked the car the night before. She opened the passenger door and took out the guitar.

"Here." She held it out for him to take.

He stood silently, his mouth slightly open. "*Un regalo . . . Dios,*" he finally whispered.

"*Dios?*" she said with surprise. What did God have to do with it?

"*Por usted,*" she told him. "For you."

He held it as if it were made of glass. He looked at it, inch by inch, slowly turning it over in his hands.

He lifted his eyes to hers. Time stopped. She was aware of the sweeping valley stretched out below him and the cloudless, bright blue sky open behind him. An overwhelming sense of peace filled her as she stood beneath his gaze.

He pulled the guitar to his chest and closed his eyes, and his fingers gently passed over the strings, releasing a chord, breathy and sweet, as tender as a first kiss. Then another chord—slowly, gently, the music floated around her.

The touch of his fingers quickened, building, bringing the music to life—rich and full. As he played, the music became a living thing. It held her transfixed, increasing in intensity to a deep, penetrating, bass sound, rushing through the air. Her heart began to pound—feelings flashed through her—something she had never felt before, something she wanted to feel forever. Antonio's practiced fingers flew, creating musical prisms of blinding beauty. Bursts of tonal color refracted through the notes, dancing around her, leaping to a crescendo, culminating in the rapid repetition of a singular treble note. She couldn't breathe.

Then by degrees, through beautifully balanced phrasing, his touch lightened to almost a lullaby.

Spellbound, she couldn't move. Caught in a vignette of time, she witnessed something she did not understand, something beautiful and powerful and pure.

His eyes were still closed as the last note lingered. The look on his face brought tears to her eyes—his love of the music revealed there. As she looked at him, his eyes opened, connecting with hers. For a split second, the truth of the moment was unveiled before her. The love she saw reflected in his eyes was the love not of the music but of her upturned face.

She didn't move. "Antonio, that was beautiful, thank you." *Don't stop.*

"*Gracias.*"

She pulled her eyes from his and stepped away from him. "Well, well." She forced a lightness to her voice. "What a beautiful day. Go now. *Adiós.* It's your day off."

He tipped his head to her. Was he acknowledging her thoughts or her actions? She wasn't sure. Then he turned and walked down the drive with the guitar under his arm.

She watched him until he disappeared under the oaks. "Wow." She fanned her face with her hand and started through the entryway.

"Poppy," she called out before reaching the front door. She began to run. "Poppy. Poppy." She looked in the kitchen, but he wasn't there. She ran down the hall and burst into his room. "Poppy, did you hear that music? That was Antonio."

231

Poppy started to get out of his chair. "I was talking with my Jesus, Miss Angel. I no hear anything. What happen?"

"I just had the most amazing experience. You know I went on that date with Brad yesterday."

"Yes." Poppy sat back down.

"Well, there was a garage sale on the street where I parked, and I found an old guitar. I don't even think I told you that when we went to that dance at the Flamingo, Antonio picked up the guitar of one of the mariachis and played it a little. Anyway, I thought it would be nice if he had a guitar. So yesterday I saw one at the garage sale and got it. I gave it to him this morning, and you should have heard him play. It was music I've never heard before. I can't even describe it. Beautiful. No, beautiful isn't good enough. Out of this world. That's closer."

"Like the angels?" Poppy suggested.

"Not really like angels. More like God Himself. Isn't that something? That somebody working in our stables would have a musical talent like that. I'd love for him to play for an audience. I wonder where he learned to play. I've got to find out more." She looked at her watch. The list would have to wait.

Angelica started out the door, then paused. "You know, Poppy, it was kind of odd. Right at the end, when he finished, he looked at me in the most intimate way." She felt the heat rush to her face. "I mean . . . Well, it's hard to explain."

Poppy nodded his head slowly. "Yes, Miss Angel, some things hard to explain. Some things can't be explained. And for some things no explanation necessary."

She looked at the old man. Seeing him sitting there, the deeply etched lines on his face, his hands wrinkled and spotted, folded on his Bible, he seemed so frail, so vulnerable. Her heart filled with love for him. Suddenly, the thought of

232

losing him swept through her, and she ran to him, putting her arms around his neck.

"Poppy, I love you so much. You'll never leave me, will you?"

"I leave when my Jesus call me. But my Jesus, He never leave you. I ask Him take care of you, Miss Angel, show you His plan for your life." He took her face in his hands, his wise eyes full of tenderness. "I tell you a truth, my Angel, God love you through me. Love is stronger than death. That's the power of the cross."

She blinked back tears and kissed his cheek. What a precious man. What would she do without him? *No one could ever love me like he does.*

She went back to her father's office and for the next hour wrote out sentences in Spanish. "Where did you learn to play the guitar?" "Would you like to play and be paid?" "You could perform in a big stadium." "You could be famous and rich."

When she finished, she looked out her window but didn't see Antonio anywhere. She folded the paper and put it in her pocket and went to look for him.

She jogged down to the stables and looked in the barn and bunkhouse. She didn't see anyone but Rafael, the gardener, taking a nap.

Finally, she found Chick in the kitchen, making himself dinner.

"Where's Antonio?"

"I don't know. The last time I saw him, he was walking across the drive, down toward the oaks."

"Thanks." Angelica headed toward the oaks.

When she got there, she didn't see anyone and decided to walk along the stream. Before she had gone far, she saw

Antonio sitting on a rock, his back to her, his head down. He seemed to be looking at something.

"Antonio," she called out.

He jumped up and turned around. Whatever he had in his hand, he stuck in his pocket.

"*Sí, señorita?*"

"*Siéntese, por favor.*"

He sat on the rock. She sat on the fallen oak branch just across from him, took the paper out of her pocket, and unfolded it. She asked him in Spanish where he'd learned to play the guitar.

"*No lo sé.*"

She stared at him. Had she understood? "*No lo se?*" How could he not know?

"*No lo sé,*" he said, smiling.

"What kind of an answer is that?" Her voice rose.

His expression became one of concern. She realized he had no idea what she had just said. She tried using Spanish, asking him if he'd like to play and be paid.

He frowned, as though unsure what she meant. "*Qué?*"

She sighed and read the explanation she'd written down so carefully, telling him he could perform in a big stadium. And he could too. His music wasn't like any other. It was simply amazing. She told him what she thought and that he could be rich and famous.

He looked at her, uncertainty and disbelief evident in his features. He fingered the cross in his hands.

"*Qué?*"

She bit her lip. If only she spoke Spanish better! She read the explanation again. "*Usted famoso, mucho dinero.* Famous. Much money."

He sat on the rock, silent.

What on earth could he be thinking about? Of course, the

answer was yes. She noticed his black hair, neatly combed, though a small piece had fallen across his forehead, his handsome face in deep thought, his square shoulders and broad chest, all of it somehow at odds with his station in life.

Suddenly, he stood and walked over to her. He knelt beside her. "*No, señorita.*" His tone was so quiet, his manner so gentle, she couldn't take offense.

She stood up. "*Porqué?* Why?"

"*No es posible.*"

"*Es posible.* It *is* possible. This is America. It's possible." She folded her arms across her chest. "It happens all the time. Nobodies become somebodies." She realized she had again lapsed into English. "*Es posible.*"

He looked at her, almost as if she were a child with whom he had to be patient. She suddenly felt foolish standing there with her arms folded and her chin stuck out belligerently. "Never mind. *No es importante.*" She folded the paper and put it back in her pocket. "This is stupid. *Buenos noches,* Antonio." She turned on her heel and left. To think she'd given up her valuable time to try and help him. She should have stuck to her original plan of getting together her list of contacts. God helps those who help themselves.

As Antonio watched Angelica walk away, a deep sadness filled him.

"*Stupid.*" He knew this American word. He had heard it many times in the streets and in the shops of Guadalajara, from the children of the rich American *touristas. Stupido,* they would say and point at his bare feet or torn clothes.

Dios, I love her, but it is Your gift. I cannot sell what is not mine. It is not possible. Fame and money too are Yours to give, not mine to take.

He sat on the rock, alone with his despair. *Stupido*. The word seemed to hang in the air around him.

He pulled a piece of cloth from his pocket, opened it, and took out the eight silver conchos he'd unscrewed from Angelica's saddle. Laying the pieces of silver on the rock, he found the unpolished one: small, delicate, exquisite. Holding it near his lips, he breathed on it, obscuring its beauty, then rubbed it gently with the polishing cloth. He ran his calloused fingers over the delicate pattern of wispy curls. *I have been a fool. I am here to work, help my family, and return to them. My future is in Mexico.*

Over and over he rubbed the cloth on the silver face. He held the concho up to look at it. It sparkled and shone, more beautiful than ever. He set it to the side, then repolished and shined the others as long as there was enough light to see. With the sun's last light, he gathered all the pieces into the cloth and put them in his pocket, then set off at a jog, uphill, along the stream.

As the twilight deepened, he began to tire. Finally, he sat down by the stream where the water pooled around a cluster of boulders. His heart ached. She could never love him; it was not meant to be. He leaned against a rock, closed his eyes, and surrendered to the certainty of his thoughts. He needed to accept the truth. It was not God's will. Still, he would be everything to her that honor would allow.

The night breeze swept over him, and the presence that had sustained him through years of poverty and hunger and nothingness and want covered him, renewing his spirit. As he slept beside the still waters, the Spirit hovered over him, becoming light, hiding *God's* truth in his heart.

14

"Yes," Angelica shouted, jumping up from her computer. "Oh, Lord, You are awesome." She ran down the stairs.

"Poppy. Poppy."

Poppy came running out of the kitchen, wiping his hands on his apron. "What happen, Miss Angel?" His face was a mixture of excitement and dread.

"Our prayers have been answered. I just clicked on the Sierra County website, and they've posted a recruitment for a public defender." She grabbed Poppy's hands, and they danced in a circle.

"Praise You, Jesus." Angelica could see tears in Poppy's eyes as he let go of her hands and lifted his above his head. "Thank You, Jesus. Your name worthy to be praised." He closed his eyes a moment.

"Come up and look at it. I left it on my screen." Angelica pulled him up the stairs.

Moments later, Poppy stood in front of the screen with his

hands on his hips. "That say trainee class. You no trainee, Miss Angel."

"I know, Poppy. It's for an entry-level position in the Deputy Public Defender series. But I don't care. It's a foot in the door." She clasped her hands under her chin.

Poppy bent down and squinted at the screen, then stood up and looked at Angelica. "You read that salary?"

"It's not as much as I was making in New York, but it's decent."

"It decent for me. But I no shop at Saks." She saw a twinkle in his eye.

"I know. I've already thought about this. I have my trust account. God's blessed our family financially, and Mom and Dad have been generous with me. Knowing I have that in the bank was a big part of my decision to do this. I didn't know how long it would take me to find a job, and I didn't know what it'd pay. And even more important, you know I hope to open my own office. This job is just temporary, a good way for me to get the experience I need. My only concern is convincing them I'm not overqualified."

"That take some convincing." He looked back at the screen.

"Don't you think I'm doing the right thing?" A fiery dart of doubt pricked at her.

"You follow your dream, Miss Angel. You say you asked the Lord to show you His plan. Now, watch and have the faith."

Angelica put her arms around Poppy. "Finally. Finally. Something is going right. I feel like God is with me." Maybe this was the day things were going to turn around. She had something concrete to talk to her parents about. Brad's offer was no longer the only offer.

Yes, the worst was over. "I'm going to go call the surveyor

238

for Dad and get that out of the way. Then I'm going to start the application process with Sierra County."

Angelica went to her father's study, opened the file that lay by the phone, then dialed the phone number her father had written on the inside cover. While she waited for the connection, her mind drifted to the moment Antonio had played the guitar for her. She closed her eyes, hoping to hear the music again. There had to be a way to get him "discovered."

"Good morning. Brighton Engineering."

"This is Angelica Amante. Is Dick Brighton in?"

"One moment please."

"Dick Brighton here."

Angelica introduced herself, then explained about her father. "He asked me to call and tell you that the county has written him. He doesn't have to file a formal subdivision map to split off the seventy-five acres he's thinking about developing."

"That will really speed things up. Did he say if he still wanted to do a perc test? He thought he might want to build an office on that property. If it's going to have a bathroom, it has to have a septic system, which means perc tests."

"He didn't say, but he'll be back this Friday. I'll tell him to call you and let you know."

"That'll be fine. He can perc anytime. We've got quite a few projects pending, but we'll try to have the map drawn this week. When the map is complete he'll be able to pick it up and take it to the title company and get it recorded. Incidentally, while I was up there surveying, several people stopped and asked about the property. Is there any chance he wants to sell it?"

"None." Angelica made her tone firm. "He's going to develop a vineyard."

239

"He's got a mighty valuable piece of property there, now that he's having it split off."

"I'm sure he's not interested in selling. He and my mother have dreamed of having a vineyard for some time."

"Two of the people gave me their names and numbers. I put them in his file. Let him know if he changes his mind. They'll be there."

"I'll let him know." Angelica was cordial but less than encouraging. Why get his hopes up when she knew her father would never be interested? "Thanks for all your work."

She hung up the phone and sat back in her father's big, leather chair. There was no way her father would ever sell a piece of Regalo Grande.

Angelica spent the morning working on her application for Sierra County. She decided against submitting through the website. Her application would have a much more professional appearance if she submitted a hard copy in person. Besides, if she went down there, she could look around.

What she really needed was someone with connections to the county who could help her get an informal, informational interview. She thought about her list of personal contacts. Making phone calls would be the next item on her agenda.

As noon approached, she set her things aside, leaned back in her chair, and threw her feet up on the table. She'd accomplished a lot. Her mind wandered to Antonio. He was supposed to bring her his money order, the letter, and the address in Mexico so it could be mailed to his mother. And his papers. She looked at her watch. Surely he hadn't forgotten.

She thought about their conversation under the oaks. The whole thing was just stupid—trying to explain something like that to him without really speaking the language. How could she make him understand? She didn't want Chick to translate. It was none of his business. She didn't seem to be able to do it herself. She wasn't even sure how he'd be discovered, if he wanted to, and he'd already told her he didn't. She folded her arms across her chest and took a deep breath. She'd think of something. Getting him a chance to perform was a great idea, and he deserved it. She let her mind wander, working through the possibilities.

"Brad. That's it. Brad." She threw her feet on the floor and slapped her hands on the desk. "He said his father was on the entertainment committee for the annual charity fundraiser for the March of Dimes."

She pulled a yellow pad in front of her and began tapping it with the tip of a pen. If she could get Antonio to play for Brad's father, he might agree to let Antonio audition for the entertainment committee. But what would Antonio think if she asked him to play for Brad? He might not want to. She felt like it was a catch-22. She couldn't ask Antonio to play for Brad. If he said no, she'd have to drop it. She couldn't ask Brad to listen to Antonio because she couldn't be sure Antonio would play, and then he'd know what she was up to.

Her legal mind went into high gear as she considered every angle. There had to be a way to make Antonio see why he should seize this opportunity. She began to doodle on the top of the page, drawing a stick figure horse and rider. He could have everything he ever wanted. But first, she had to get him to play for Brad. She didn't have a single doubt that if Brad heard him, the rest would be easy. She put her pen down and rested her chin in her hands. She'd think of something.

She looked at the blank pad. "That's it." There on the yellow pad, right in front of her, masquerading as a stick figure, was the answer, as if subconsciously she was working it out all along. That was how she would get Brad and Antonio together. If it worked, Antonio was as good as on stage, and her dinner date with Brad would be the perfect time to put her plan in motion.

"Miss Angel, Antonio in kitchen. He have money order for you." She looked up to find Poppy standing at the door.

Angelica went to the kitchen. "*Buenos días*, Antonio."

"Good morning, *señorita*." His English was definitely getting better. He handed her his money order, the envelope with the letter, and the paper with the address in Mexico.

"He learning English." Poppy slapped the counter he was standing next to. "Praise be to Jesus."

"He's a fast learner. He just needs more practice." Angelica folded the papers he'd given her. "I'll put this in the mailbox today. *Hoy*."

"*Dónde su* other *papel?*" She hoped he hadn't forgotten to bring his papers.

"*Qué otro papel?*" He looked bewildered.

"*Su importante papel.* The one you have in a safe place. *En seguro* place."

Antonio pointed at the wrinkled, dirty paper with his mother's address. "*Este es mi papel.*"

"*Qué!* No, don't tell me that." Her eyes widened.

"*Sí, es mi papel importante.*"

"But I asked you if you had your papers. *Documentos.*"

"*Qué documentos?*" He showed her his empty hands. "*No comprendo.*"

"*Su documentos.*"

"*Mis papeles? Yo no tengo esa clase de papeles.*"

He was saying *papeles*, papers. He didn't have that class of papers. "*Nada?* Nothing? Zero?"

The truth began to sink in. Somehow he had misunderstood her when she'd asked him about his . . . *papel*, paper. Paper, papers, what was the difference? Obviously to him, there was one.

"Ohhh boy." She tried not to look alarmed as concern welled within her. This would have to be addressed, and soon. With all her experience dealing with immigration cases, she'd never been involved with helping an immigrant get an Alien Registration Card. It would mean working with the Department of Homeland Security, and for Mexicans already in the country and not married to a citizen, it was extremely difficult.

But more than that . . . how would this reflect on her? He was working on her ranch. Well, actually, technically, he didn't work for her. Her father was the one who employed him. That sounded like the voice of Constantine Czervenka. She was dangerously close to crossing an ethical line, and she knew it. And if she told her father, what kind of a position did that put him in? The law wouldn't accept ignorance as an excuse.

Her focus returned to Antonio. He stood calmly watching her, but she could see concern in his face. What about him? She'd only been thinking of herself and her family. Her actions could expose him to deportation and bring untold hardship to his family . . . but he had broken the law.

She looked at the man she had come to know. Standing straight, offering no defense, no excuse. She knew if she told him she was taking him to be deported, he would accept her decision and go with her.

Her heart filled with compassion. He had come to America out of desperation. He was here illegally, like so many thousands of other poor Mexicans. But he wasn't thousands of others; he was Antonio.

243

She'd come home to help people like him. There had to be a way. He'd have to get some type of temporary papers. She would contact the Bureau of Citizenship and Immigration Services and find out where to start. Maybe he could become a citizen . . . or, she realized, her thoughts in turmoil, he would have to go back to Mexico.

The week flew by. Angelica went to the Sierra County offices and turned in her application. Knowing she wouldn't hear anything until the recruitment period closed, she went to work trying to find out how to help Antonio. She decided not to say anything about Antonio to her father until she had some facts and knew what their options were. After all, she was the one who had told Chick to hire him when her parents were gone. Perhaps there was some temporary status he could be given. They were certainly willing to sponsor him.

A call to the U.S. Citizenship and Immigration Services sent her into a voice mail maze that ended when she slammed the phone down. A call to the Department of Homeland Security wasn't any better. Finally, she called Brad.

"So, I'm not having any luck finding out how to help him." Angelica waited as Brad processed everything she'd told him.

"Why don't you just call Immigration and forget about it? You're completely innocent in this."

"Because there may be some way of helping him, some way for him to become legal. To be sponsored. Something. I want to find that out first."

"It occurs to me that this is a perfect example of why you should come to work for our firm. That offer I made you still stands. Angel, this is exactly the kind of case you could handle pro bono. And you'd have great resources in our San Francisco office to draw on."

She thought about what he was saying. Unfortunately, it was true. "Brad, I've made a commitment to myself. Just Monday a position opened up in the Public Defender's Office of Sierra County." She took a deep breath. "I've applied for it. It doesn't mean I'll get the job. I don't know how many have applied or who they are. But it's the job I really want." She waited for Brad to answer.

"What does it pay?"

"It's not about the pay, Brad. I've got my trust account to fall back on. It's about doing what *I* want for once in my life. It's about being true to myself."

Friday arrived, bringing Angelica's parents home from their trip. As she ran to the entry, her head was spinning with all the things that had happened since they'd left. She stopped behind the entry door, gathered herself together, and put a smile on her face. *Lord, I need You now.*

But her welcoming smile froze on her lips as she watched her father and Poppy help her mother into a wheelchair.

"Here, Mom. Let me have that." Angelica took her mother's purse as they guided her to the front door.

Her father glanced at Angelica. "I think she'd like to lie down. Let's get her up to our bedroom so she can rest. Poppy, would you go ahead and unload the car?"

"I guess I wasn't as ready for this trip as I thought. I should've been fine." Her voice began to quaver. "I was getting better. I was. I don't know why this is happening. Why can't I get well?"

"You are going to get well, Mom. Dad, have you called the doctor?"

245

"I called when we docked in Florida. Thank goodness Ralph's a personal friend. He's dropping everything to see her. He's already ordered some additional tests."

Angelica and her father settled her mother into bed.

"Just let me close my eyes for a few minutes, then . . ." She slipped into an exhausted sleep.

Angelica followed her father downstairs to his office. "Has it ever been this bad before?"

"Not really. It seems like every time this virus strikes, it's worse than the time before. She had to use the wheelchair on the trip home. She said her legs felt numb."

"There has to be an answer." Angelica folded her arms across her chest. "What did the doctor say when you called him?"

"He's as frustrated as we are. He's consulted with all kinds of specialists. Blood tests don't really pinpoint anything, and her symptoms don't seem to be consistent."

Angelica sat silently for a few moments, the seriousness of her mother's illness filling her with dread. "Don't worry, Dad. We'll find out what's wrong. I'm glad I'm going to be here now. I can be of more help." She kept her voice light, hiding her fear.

Her father smiled at her. "I'm glad you're here too, honey." He picked up the opened mail she'd stacked on his desk. "Anything happen while we were gone?"

This wasn't the time to burden him with the news about Antonio or upset him by telling him she'd applied for the Sierra County job. It would have to be brought up later. She knew what was foremost on his mind. "Nothing came in from New Life. Do you think you'll be getting the approval on Thrombexx soon?"

The smile faded from her father's features. "I wish I knew. The Federal Drug Administration just won't get off the dime. It's coming up to two years now. Every month, I hear, 'It will just be a few more weeks.' I'm heavily invested in that enterprise. There's absolutely no reason why that drug shouldn't be approved. The data we submitted is thorough and completely supported by scientific fact."

Angelica heard the doubt in his voice. "Dad, level with me. What's going on?"

He hesitated, looking down at his hands. He raised his eyes to the window and looked across the stables and fields to the valley below. Perhaps a minute passed.

"Dad?" Angelica put her hand on his arm.

"We thought these delays were just standard procedure. The FDA is notorious for this kind of thing. But about a month ago, the research department heard through the grapevine that more testing was going to be required."

"Well, that's not so bad. Just do the testing they want. You'll still get your approval."

He seemed to age before her. "That would be fine, except the plan I made for this whole venture was based on a two-year approval process. Which, at the time, we figured was at least six months more than would be needed. We had plenty of turnaround room. I made my financial decisions based on the best advice I could get."

"If the FDA does take another six months, exactly what is your exposure?"

"I'm not sure. As you know, I'm the primary investor in New Life. I've financed this venture with my own money."

Angelica remembered the stock option statement she'd seen while her parents were on their trip. The same uneasy feeling she'd experienced returned. She tried to keep her face from showing her feelings. "How long before you have to cash in those options to pay off your loans?"

247

Her father looked at her, and the surprise in his eyes told her he'd suddenly realized she knew more than he had told her, more than he'd probably intended to tell her.

"It's not so much I need to cash them in. I just need to know the value is there. All of the loans I've put on my assets can be extended, if I can show the value of the company. But I originally asked for only two years, thinking that'd be more than enough time. The notes against the ranch and the Amante Trust are coming up for renegotiation."

"Then that's what we need to do. What kind of documentation can you get to make your case so you can get an extension?"

"I just don't know. I need to talk with the banks and get an update on my stock accounts and a profit and loss statement on the trust. Everything I own is tied up in this. I've thought about nothing else since we left on that trip."

Seeing the grave concern on her father's face, Angelica straightened in her chair and folded her arms. "There has to be a way to get those extensions. If we can't get the banks what they need, we'll fight for more time. Maybe there's some legal maneuvering we can do. Brad's a litigation attorney. He may have some ideas."

"Yes, Counselor." Her father's smile was weak, at best. "But I really don't want this to go any further than the two of us, right now. Your mother knows very little of how serious this could be. I don't want to burden her with this."

"Don't give it a second thought. You've got client-attorney privilege with me." She hoped her teasing would help him relax.

"Thanks, honey. I'd better get busy. I need to get on this first thing Monday morning." He stood.

"Dad, is there anything I can do to help? Do you want me to work with the surveyor on the lot split you're doing

248

for the seventy-five acres? That would be one less thing for you to worry about."

He started to say something—then stopped. With a look of resignation, he sat back down. "Honey, the seventy-five acres is liened as part of the security for the New Life loans."

Angelica had some knowledge of real estate law from her college classes. "Doesn't that mean the lien holder would have to release it for you to split it off?"

"Yes."

"It's just unimproved acreage, and when you consider the whole value of the ranch, the seventy-five acres by itself as pasture land shouldn't be worth that much. It's the grape potential that gives it value."

"That's true."

Angelica thought for a moment. "What time is it?"

"A quarter to five. Why?"

"Give me the phone. I'm going to call Brighton and see if the map is ready. If we can get it recorded before the bank has any red flags about the loans, I bet they'll process the release of the seventy-five acres without asking any questions. Don't talk to your banks until I find out if we can get the map recorded Monday."

"Why didn't I think of that?" The tone of his voice lightened. "Maybe we can get this worked out after all."

"Don't worry, Daddy. You didn't spend all that money on my education for nothing." She dialed the number and caught Dick Brighton just as he was leaving.

"Who in the office is drawing my dad's map?" Angelica asked.

"One of our staff, John Miller."

"Is it ready to be picked up?" Angelica glanced at her father.

"I haven't received it yet, and I'm the one who gives the approval to release it."

"We need that map as soon as possible. Monday, if not sooner."

"It's five o'clock Friday night." The engineer's words were decidedly clipped.

Angelica softened her tone. "I know that. Is there any chance of getting him to work this weekend? This is very important. We'll pay him well for his overtime."

"First let me see if he's still here."

Please. Please let this work out. Angelica held her breath until Dick Brighton returned to the phone.

"Miss Amante? John can work on it this weekend. He should be able to have it ready Monday morning, but I can't promise."

Relief filled her. "Great. That's all I'm asking. I'll call you Monday and see if I can pick it up."

"Talk to you then, Miss Amante."

She hung up and gave her father a thumbs-up. "Now don't worry, Dad. I'll take care of this." She stood. "I'm going to have Poppy fix us a light dinner and serve it on the patio. It's a beautiful evening, and I bet Mom will feel like eating a little something when she wakes up."

"That's a good idea. We've had nothing but airplane food today."

Angelica left her father's study, stopped by the kitchen to ask Poppy to start dinner, then went up to her room.

She sat on the window seat, mulling over the conversation she'd just had with her father. If she could get the split through, her father could develop the vineyard no matter what else happened. That property would be free and clear. But it would take money to start the vineyard. All the soils tests had been done, so they knew the grape potential was there. But would her father be able to borrow money to hire the workers and plant the vines? He had said all his assets were tied up with New Life.

A plan began to form in her mind. A plan that would take money to implement. A plan that would save her family from bankruptcy . . . but would end her dream of being a public defender.

Her mother awoke at seven, and the three of them spent the warm, summer evening together on the big patio overlooking the valley.

"How was your date with Brad?" her mother asked.

"I had a wonderful time." She thought about his offer. How things had changed since that Saturday afternoon on the sloop. This most recent news about Thrombexx put a new light on everything. She was going to have to make some tough choices if she was going to help her father. "Brad talked to me about going to work at their new office in Marin. He said they were going to do some pro bono work and I could handpick the cases."

"That's wonderful, honey. Isn't it, Ben?"

"I should say. It's the best news I've heard in a long time. When do you start?"

"I don't know. I'm still thinking about it. While you were gone, a position opened up at the public defender's office."

Her parents sat staring at her.

"I applied for it, but I haven't been offered the job. I haven't even been called in for an interview, and I'm still considering Brad's offer. In fact, we're going out tomorrow night, and I'm sure we'll talk about it."

She saw her father's shoulders relax. "Sounds like a perfect match. You can do your crusading, and he can do his lawyering." Her father grinned.

"If it worked out that way. But the truth is, paying clients end up taking all your time." She really didn't want to talk about it now. "Something else happened that was totally cool."

"What's that?" her mother asked, leaning forward.

"I found out that Antonio can play the guitar. I mean he has real talent."

"Oh." Her mother sat back in her chair. "That's nice."

Poppy came out and began clearing the table.

"Here, Poppy. Sit with us." Angelica patted the chair next to her. "I was just telling them how beautifully Antonio plays the guitar." She turned back to her parents. "In fact, I've been trying to think of a way to get him to play for Brad. His dad's on the entertainment committee of the March of Dimes. Their charity event is in December, and I know if Brad heard Antonio, he'd get his dad to consider letting him play there. Just one song would be great. But Antonio's kind of a private person. I don't think he would audition."

She realized her father was studying her.

"Angelica, why are you taking such an interest in that young man?"

A look of alarm crossed her mother's face at the question. "You've got your hands full, starting a new job. Important things. Why on earth would you get involved in something like that?"

Angelica rushed to answer. "When you hear him play, you'll know why. Wouldn't it be nice if something really great happened for him?"

"Getting to work in our country is pretty great for them, dear." Her mother smoothed her napkin on her lap. "And we always treat our Mexicans well. Don't we, Ben?"

"Angelica, let it be." It was a demand, not a request. "That boy needs to spend his time working for money to support his family."

She looked at Poppy for support. "You no worry, Miss Angel. If that in God's plan, it will happen. God allow things to happen to accomplish His purposes."

Her mother's face relaxed. "Yes, dear. That's the right idea, leave it up to God. Don't get involved. He's not in your class."

"Mother, we're not living in a caste system." She caught herself. There was no point in getting on a soapbox. Her parents knew where she was coming from. Unfortunately, in light of her father's potentially disastrous financial situation, finding a way for Antonio to be "discovered" might be the first and last pro bono work she'd ever have a chance to do. *Lord, I'm trusting You. Keep me in Your hands.*

Somewhere, in the shadow of memory, a hand passed over the strings of a guitar.

15

Angelica and Brad were the last two people in the dining room of Marin Joe's. The candlelight was dimming, and the restaurant was quiet. She'd been on the date for hours, and there hadn't been one good opening to put her plan into motion so Antonio could play for Brad.

"I can't eat another bite." She pushed her dessert plate to the side.

Brad had grown quiet. In the flickering light, she could see his blue eyes tenderly searching her face, her neck, her shoulders. But it stirred only inward questions, not emotions. She wasn't the same person she'd been when they were engaged. And whether or not he was remained to be seen. She enjoyed being with him, but somehow a future with Brad seemed like settling for less than she wanted in life. In every way.

"So finish telling me about this problem with the Marin Heights subdivision."

For a moment, Brad's face went blank. "Oh. Uh. After we got the suit settled with the Bay Area Preservation League, the county required more soils testing. It has quite a slope, and there is concern about possible sliding because of the development."

"What do you think's going to happen?"

He leaned back and fitted his fingers together. "I don't know. I told the Foster family that Brighton Engineering is one of the best around. They know how to put the most optimistic spin on the soils data."

"Brighton Engineering! They're the ones that did the soils work on my dad's seventy-five acre parcel. We're splitting it off, and they're handling that."

He smiled at her surprise. "Just about everybody north of the Golden Gate uses them, if they want it done right. They've had years of experience dealing with lot splits and subdivision approvals. I'm waiting for their package so I can present it to the county. I'm hoping we can designate the forty lots at the bottom of the hill for low-income buyers. It wasn't in the Fosters' plan originally, but as things progressed, they saw an opportunity to do it."

Angelica couldn't help but notice how easily she'd been able to turn the conversation to business. "That part of Marin is incredibly pricey. I'm surprised the developer would want low-income homes near his subdivision. That's great—I'm just surprised. Developers aren't usually that charitable."

Brad grinned, a dimple forming in his right cheek. "Always looking out for the underdog, aren't you? I told Ed Foster I thought there was a chance I could get it through if I packaged it right. It wasn't easy, believe me, but getting that development approved for Ed is going to be a coup. I'm his third attorney, and I want to be his last. I've taken complete control of it. If he retains me to handle all his business ventures, my career will be made."

Angelica studied Brad's face. As he spoke about the case,

he became animated. He thrived on the challenge. It was part of the reason they'd broken up; work came first. She'd forgotten how intense he could be.

Brad reached across the table and took her hand. "My offer still stands. Come and join our firm. I can help you make your dreams come true." He ran his thumb down her ring finger. Heat brushed her cheeks, and she withdrew her hand.

The solution to everything was literally in front of her, and yet she hesitated. She could have a job that pleased her parents. She wouldn't have to worry about income or using her trust as a subsidy or coming up with the capital to start her own office. She wouldn't have to struggle anymore. She wouldn't have to do anything . . . but give up her dream.

She looked at Brad, who leaned slightly forward, waiting for her answer. "Some things have happened with Dad's drug approval that could affect my immediate plans. I'm waiting for that to play out. If he doesn't get his approval soon, then I may take you up on your offer."

"Is it that serious? Do you want to talk about it?" He seemed more delighted at the prospect of her changing her mind than concerned about the reasons for it.

"Not tonight." She could see in his eyes that he cared for her. But it was more conscious and thoughtful than passionate. For a moment, warm, dark brown eyes were before her, and the high vibrato of a single guitar string echoed in her ear, filling her with excitement.

"Hey, look. Someone must have opened a door and caused a draft. The candle blew out." Brad's voice brought her back to the present. "How about some coffee?"

"Sounds good."

Brad signaled the waiter and ordered for both of them.

Angelica straightened in her seat. It was time to lighten the conversation and look for an opening.

After the waiter served their coffee, Brad leaned forward. "When can I see you again?"

Her eyes widened. There it was, just the opening she needed. "How about going horseback riding? I love to ride on the beach." She hoped her words didn't sound rehearsed.

"You know, all the time we dated and talked about doing that, I don't think we ever did."

She had him. "Well, then it's about time, buddy."

Brad grinned. "Would I rent a horse?"

Angelica shook her head. "Of course not. We've got horses on the ranch you can ride. We've always kept saddle horses for company to use when they visit. Why don't we go next weekend? We can trailer out." *Say yes.*

"I'd love to, but I'm really under pressure right now preparing the Marin Heights package. What about in two weeks?"

Two weeks! She took a sip of coffee. She should have known, work came first. "Sure. Come to the ranch, and we'll trailer to the coast. There's a good place to ride near Bodega Bay. Come around eight o'clock."

Brad grinned at her. "Eight o'clock Saturday morning, two weeks from now. I'll be there."

And a few weeks after that, Antonio will be on stage.

On Monday morning, Angelica called Brighton Engineering and made arrangements to pick up the map for the seventy-five acres. She spoke to the title company and had them send a release to the bank holding the lien against the property. It would take a few days for all the paperwork to be completed, but when the releases were returned to the title company, they would record the map. She went looking for her father to let him know things were going well.

She found him in his study with Chick and Antonio.

"Am I interrupting something?"

"Oh, hi, honey. I was asking Chick to tell Antonio to check in with Poppy throughout the day for the next few weeks to see if your mother needs help being moved. Now that she's using a wheelchair, if I'm not here, there's no way Poppy could get it up or down the stairs or out to the deck. If she doesn't get better, we may have to have a glide installed."

A bolt of fear darted through Angelica. "Do you really think that's necessary?"

"Moving around exhausts her. She's going to see the doctor later today. We'll know more after that, but for now, it'll make her life easier."

Her father dismissed the two men.

"See you later, Antonio," Angelica called after them.

He tipped his hat toward her.

"What's that all about?" her father asked. "I thought he didn't speak English."

"I've been working with him so when he gets that audition, he'll be able to carry on some kind of conversation in English."

Her father's jaw tightened. "Angelica, sit down."

She sat in the chair next to his desk.

"Why are you taking such an interest in that young man? Your mother and I don't want to be in your face, but we feel you're far more interested in him than you should be."

"Dad, what's wrong with helping him? It takes very little of my time, and it can make a huge difference in his life."

He started to say something, then stopped. "Your mother isn't well. Don't add to her concerns."

258

"What are you talking about? What possible difference does it make to her if I help Antonio?"

His voice softened. "Honey, there's nothing to discuss. Just trust me, it upsets your mother. Please limit the amount of time you spend with that young man."

Her father sat back in his chair and let out a heavy sigh. "I've been on the phone all morning. The banks want to work with me, but they can't give me more than a few extra weeks on my payoff without some kind of definite information on the drug approval. I've talked to them all, except the one holding the lien on the ranch. Did you hear anything on the map?"

She couldn't help noticing his drawn expression, and her heart went out to him. "That's why I came looking for you. I just got off the phone with the title company, and the map is ready to be recorded. They've sent the release to Community Bank. They should have it back by Friday, if it goes through the bank's escrow department without raising any flags."

A little of the tension left his face. "That will be one worry off my mind."

She hesitated, then decided this was as good a time as any to bring up the plan she'd devised that might help her father with this financial crisis. "Dad, I want to ask you about something."

Her father's face seemed guarded. "What is it?"

"Well, I've been thinking. . . . You know I have my trust." There was over $150,000 in it.

"Yes, you said that you were planning to use it to supplement your wages and then open your own office."

"I've been thinking about it a lot, Dad. I won't be in a position to open my own office for quite some time. In the meantime, I can invest it and get a return on it."

His face relaxed into a smile. "What'd you have in mind—stock, income property?"

"A vineyard."

"A vineyard!" He chuckled. "Honey, you don't know anything about the wine business."

Angelica knew her father well and could tell by the way he studied her, he thought there was more to her idea than she was telling. And there was. "I know as much as you do. I'm talking about the Amante Vineyard."

"You don't need to invest your money in that. We're going to develop that through the Amante Trust. You'll be a part owner anyway."

"I know, but this way I can put my trust money to work." It was so good to see him free of his worries for a moment. She would never want him to know that her plan was driven by the fear that Thrombexx might not be approved and this would be the only asset free of that lien, if it was in her name. A possible source of income to help her family if everything else was lost. "Well?"

"Let me think about it. And talk it over with your mother."

"I'm going to write up a business plan. When you see it, I think you'll agree it's a smart move. As the business grows, I'll get a greater return on my money than I ever would if it sat in the bank."

Her father's expression filled with affection and admiration. "What I wouldn't give to be young again and have the world by the tail on a downhill swing. Bring me your business plan when it's ready."

The next two weeks flew by. Angelica knew that the recruitment period for the public defender position would close the following week, at which time they reviewed all the applications and sent letters out to the applicants whom they wanted to interview.

She wanted to keep that option open, even though her decision to use her trust money to help her father meant everything hinged on the FDA approving Thrombexx. If it was approved, she and her father would never have to worry about money again. If it wasn't, her trust money would be gambled on a vineyard, and she would have to take the job with Brad's firm to have any type of financial security.

She spent much of every day researching the wine business and refining her business plan, but she always broke at lunchtime to help Antonio with his English.

Brad called every night, usually between nine and ten, depending on when he finished at the office. Angelica found herself listening for the phone. When it rang, she grabbed it and took it to her window seat. They often talked more than an hour, about everything from grape stock to recent Supreme Court decisions. One night they got into a debate about the existence of God. Brad was the prosecution; she was the defense.

Several times she thought about bringing up her idea to have Antonio audition for Brad's father, but since she wasn't sure if Antonio would do it, she decided to wait and stick with her original plan. Saturday wasn't that far away.

On Friday, the title company called and informed her that the map was recorded for the Amante Vineyard and could she, at her earliest convenience, take a copy of the recorded map to Brighton Engineering. That would bring her one step closer to having to commit her trust money.

She dropped the phone into its cradle and chewed her lower lip. *Please, Lord, we desperately need that approval for Thrombexx.*

Saturday morning dawned bright blue. Angelica looked out her bedroom window at the beautiful fall day. She couldn't believe it was almost October. It was going to be chilly at the beach if the wind blew, as it usually did in the afternoon.

She dressed in a well-worn pair of jeans, pullover sweater, and sweatshirt. Then she brushed her hair, put on a little lipstick, and picked up her favorite boots.

When she reached the kitchen, Poppy had coffee and rolls set out for her on the counter.

"Good morning, Miss Angel."

Angelica responded by kissing his cheek. "Isn't it a beautiful day to go riding at the beach?" She pulled on her boots, then took a roll from the plate.

"In the Word it says, 'This is the day the LORD has made,'" Poppy answered, quoting the Psalms. "Every one of His days beautiful."

"I'd like to think this is the day the Lord has made, because today is the day Antonio is going to play his guitar for Brad."

"Oh my, this the day your big plan unfold."

She looked at Poppy with a sideways glance. She wasn't sure if he was making fun of her.

"Yep, it's going to be a day of surprises."

"I put on my prayer list that God use your plan for His purpose. So you no worry. God be with you."

Angelica gulped down the last of her coffee. *Such a dear man.* "Thanks, Poppy. And would you mind packing us a lunch to take? Love you."

When Angelica got to the stables, Antonio was cleaning the stalls, and Chick was working a horse in the arena.

Angelica called to Chick from the stables. He rode over to her. "Yeah?"

"I am going to take Antonio with me today. I'm going riding with a friend, and I want Antonio to help me with the horses. We're trailering to the beach over by Bodega Bay. I'm taking Pasha and Serif for my friend."

"You're the boss." Chick's voice was cool.

"Would you explain to Antonio that I need his help? Have him hose off the trailer, the one with the gooseneck. He can ride there. Tell him to be sure it's clean and to put hay in it. You know all the stuff that needs to be done. And when he's finished, ask him to go up to the kitchen and get our lunch from Poppy."

"You're the boss," he said again. He tied the horse he'd been working out and went to the stables.

Angelica got Pasha from the pasture and Serif from his stall, then tied them on the stable's wide, cement walkway. She groomed them for the ride—cleaning their hooves, brushing them, combing their manes and tails. She saddled and bridled both, pausing when she went to lift her saddle. The conchos sparkled. Angelica fingered them. They hadn't shone that much since they were new. And for once there wasn't polish all over the leather around the conchos. *Antonio.*

She led the horses to the trailer, which Chick and Antonio had just finished hitching to the pickup. A glance at her watch told her it was almost eight. Brad should be there any minute.

"Antonio, *muy bonito* my *conchos.* Thank you." She turned to Chick. "Didn't Antonio do a beautiful job?"

As she tied the horses, she heard the sound of a car approaching. It was Brad's BMW. Waving for his attention, she pointed to where she wanted him to park, then walked

263

to greet him. When he got out of the car, she stopped, mid-stride. He looked like an ad for Western wear. He had on new, stiff Levis, a shirt right off a Western apparel rack, a bolo tie, brand-new boots that didn't have a crease in them, and, topping it all off, a large Stetson hat with a sterling silver band.

"What do you think?" He beamed at her.

"You certainly dressed for the occasion." She turned her head just slightly to hide her smile.

"Well, you know, I thought that we might be doing this every once in a while so why not go ahead and buy what I needed. Everything but the hat. I couldn't find one that fit me. Guess my head's just too big. This belongs to one of my buddies. I had to swear on my life I'd take care of it before he'd let me borrow it." He gave it a little tap on the top, as if to make sure it was well secured.

Angelica put her arm through his, and they walked to the horse trailer. "Here you go, Cowboy. Meet Serif."

Brad patted Serif's nose with short, jerky jabs. "Nice boy."

Angelica hid a smile. "Do you want to ride him in the arena before we leave?"

"Okay. That's probably a good idea. I haven't ridden in years."

Angelica led both horses to the arena. She saw Antonio putting the lunch basket in the trailer.

"Hey, Antonio. Come here."

He set the basket down and jogged over to her. "*Sí, señorita?*"

"This is Brad."

Brad extended his hand. "Good to meet you."

Antonio shook it. "I am fine." He looked directly at Brad, smiling.

Angelica felt her cheeks grow warm. How many times had they practiced "How are you?" and the obligatory "I am fine"? Why hadn't she taught him other English responses to an introduction?

She put her hand on Brad's arm. "Isn't he doing well with his English? He couldn't speak a word a month ago. Thank you, Antonio." She handed Brad Serif's reins. "Ready, Cowboy?"

Brad got in the saddle, after a little push on his backside from Angelica. She put her foot in the stirrup and swung her leg over Pasha, and the two of them walked their horses around the arena.

"This is easy." Brad gave her a smile, clearly relaxing.

"Well then, let's trot." Angelica made a little clicking sound, and both horses broke into a trot.

Brad grabbed the saddle horn with one hand and his hat with the other. The reins dropped to the ground, and Serif stopped.

"What's wrong?" Angelica teased.

"Very funny," Brad answered. "Let's go to the beach."

Antonio was waiting for them by the trailer. His manner aloof, he loaded the horses in and opened the door to climb into the gooseneck.

Angelica said, "Antonio. Get *su* guitar. *Posible* you play."

"*No es necesario.*" His voice was firm, his face set.

"*Sí, es necesario,*" Angelica insisted. For a moment, she thought he was going to argue with her. *Please, Antonio, don't mess my plan up. This is important.*

His eyes didn't leave her face.

Then, almost as if he'd read her thoughts, his jaw relaxed. "*Bien, señorita.*" He walked to the bunkhouse and returned with his guitar. When he climbed into the trailer, Angelica started down the drive to the main road.

Chick waited until the trailer disappeared, then went to the tack room and placed a call.

"It's Chick. The guys from Hell's Canyon gonna be here like planned?"

"Same place, same day, same time," Mario answered.

"I'll be there with that Mexican I had up at your place." Chick cradled the phone between his ear and his shoulder and dug in his pocket for chew.

"That last spic you sent down there got killed. Rustling those wild horses off federal land is dangerous work."

"Well, there's plenty more Mexicans where these come from. And the more they need down there, the more money we make. With any luck, this one'll get himself killed too."

As they drove, most of the conversation was about Brad's big case and her plans for a vineyard, but Angelica's mind was on Antonio and his guitar. She had noticed how quiet he'd been since Brad's arrival. His manner was cool and professional. He wasn't acting at all like himself.

When they reached their destination, Angelica parked, and Antonio unloaded the horses. He avoided her eyes, but she did see him looking at Brad from time to time, and the expression on his face was one of . . . concern . . . jealousy? No. She shook her head. Impossible.

"Where to?" Brad looked around.

"We're going to trail ride first, double back down that bluff over there to the beach, then come back here. There's a footpath across the way that leads directly to the coastline. After we're through riding, we can load the horses and walk down to the shore with our lunch and eat."

Antonio stood, holding the horses. Angelica mounted easily, and Pasha sidestepped around behind Antonio, resting his nose on the Mexican man's shoulder. Both watched Brad take Serif's reins and struggle to mount by himself. Finally, Antonio gave him a leg up.

"*Usted esperar.* Wait here," Angelica told Antonio.

He nodded. There was no emotion on his face. Angelica paused. He was usually so animated, always smiling. "You okay?"

"*Bien, señorita.*"

As they neared the trail, Angelica took one last look back. Antonio stood where she'd left him, watching them ride away.

When Angelica and the man disappeared in the distance, Antonio walked back to the trailer. He found the hayfork and raked the soiled hay briskly to one corner of the trailer. So this was Brad, Angelica's boyfriend, according to the *mayordomo.* He was an important man, who worked in the courts.

The picture of Angelica's reddening cheeks when she introduced him to Brad intruded on his thoughts. *I made a fool of myself with my words, but she didn't want me to know.* He dropped his eyes, and his shoulders slumped.

This is the kind of man she will love. He can tell her what he feels without effort. He can give her anything she wishes for. His heart ached. *But will he love her more than life itself?* He sat on the edge of the trailer.

He spoke his thoughts as a desperate prayer. "*Dios,* for

You all things are possible. You make the sun show or hide its face. If it pleases You, take me to another place, to another job, where I will never again have to stand near her, unable to touch her. Why did You bring me here? So I might offend You? Why?"

The breeze blew up from the ocean, catching his words and carrying them heavenward. Bits of hay and dust kicked up around him, triggering memories—the desert, the sandstorm, the journey from his home to the very spot where he now sat—a path charted by a divine hand, for a purpose. A truth stirred in his heart. A revelation. Certain knowledge surged within him, and he knew the truth. He loved her, and it was right that he loved her. They had met not by chance but by appointment.

He turned to where he'd seen them disappear. He would pursue her. He spoke, as if answering the stirring in his heart. "I will find a way to show my love for her. And she too will know that it is right."

He stood and walked to the footpath that led to the beach. Picnic tables and benches filled a small area just to the side of the trail. He sat on one of the benches and leaned against the table. He chewed on his lower lip, thinking about all that had happened. His first thoughts were of his papers. She had wanted the papers that were impossible for him to get. Mexico was a land of laws, but the laws were not the same for everyone. The papers she wanted were meant for people who could read and who could pay for them. Not for people like him. But she had said that she would help him. Perhaps she knew which of the *federales* to pay. In his country, everyone knew which men to pay. But he had no money, and this was his obligation.

He fingered the belt buckle at his waist. He took off the belt and looked at it. The sun glinted off the smooth, handcrafted silver. *Angelica*. The buckle was made by man, for anyone who could buy it. Angelica was made by God, for him. He would sell the buckle and give her the money for the *federales*. Then he would be on equal footing with this man who pursued her. The next time the *mayordomo* went to Lo Bianco, he would ask to go. Maybe one of the men there would want to buy his belt.

His face broke into a smile. Surely he could win her from a man who couldn't even mount his own horse.

<hr/>

They rode side by side along the trail. A light breeze kept Brad preoccupied with his hat. When they got to the bluff, they dropped into single file. Angelica let Brad go first—Pasha didn't like a horse right on his tail. Brad held the saddle horn as Serif picked his way down the narrow path.

Angelica grinned. "Having fun, Marlboro Man?"

Before he could answer, Pasha stretched his neck out and nipped Serif's hindquarter. Serif responded with a kick, and Brad went flying. He landed on the ground with a grunt.

"Pasha!" Angelica jerked his reins. "Brad, I'm so sorry. Pasha's never done anything like that before. I don't know what got into him." Pasha pranced in place, nodding his head up and down.

Brad stood up, dusting himself off and eyeing her suspiciously. "Why don't you go first the rest of the way?"

Did he think she'd let Pasha do that? Or *made* him do it? "Pasha doesn't like a horse to walk right behind him. Come on. You go first. I'll keep Pasha far enough behind that he can't do that again."

Brad managed to get back up in the saddle. "Apparently Pasha knew more than I did about the danger of having a horse on your fanny." He sounded good-natured again, and Angelica smiled. The rest of their ride was uneventful, and in the early afternoon, they returned to the trailer. Antonio was sitting on the tailgate when they rode up. He and Angelica loaded the horses in the trailer.

"Where's Poppy's lunch?"

At Angelica's question, Antonio climbed into the gooseneck and brought out a big basket.

"Brad, would you carry our lunch?"

"Sure." He took it from Antonio.

"Where's your guitar, Antonio?"

He climbed back in the gooseneck. Angelica noticed the dampness in the air. She looked at the sky and saw it was clouding up. "Bring a blanket," she called after him.

He reappeared with the things she'd asked for.

"Come with us," she told him. The three of them walked down to the beach.

There were clusters of large boulders scattered along the shoreline. Angelica picked a spot, sheltered from the cool, ocean breeze by a big, smooth rock, where the ocean waves came close. It was far enough from the water that they wouldn't need to worry about getting wet.

She spread out the blanket and opened the basket.

"Wow," Brad said. "Who made all this food?"

"I have my sources."

There were assorted fruits and cheeses, sandwiches, pickles, olives, and cookies. At the bottom of the basket, wrapped in heavy tinfoil, were two burritos. They were still warm. Seeing what they were, Angelica smiled.

"For you," she said, handing them to Antonio.

He took them from her. "*Gracias, señorita.*"

"He sure doesn't talk much," Brad commented.

270

"He's kind of shy. After we eat, I'm hoping to get him to play his guitar for you. He's very talented."

"Oh, really? I don't know much about guitar music."

"I'm sure you'll know exceptional talent if you hear it."

A gust of wind came across the boulder, and Brad put his hand on top of his hat.

"Maybe I should take my hat off if it's going to get windy. I'll lose my best friend if anything happens to it."

"Nah, leave it on. I like it," Angelica said.

They ate their lunch as the sun peeked now and then through the thickening clouds.

"I wish we could build a fire. It's getting cold." Angelica began to repack the basket and glanced at Brad. "Do you have any matches?"

"No."

"There are some in the trailer. Chick always keeps them in case he has to camp in a rest stop when he's traveling with a horse."

"Why don't I run up and get them?"

She smiled at Brad's suggestion. "Oh, would you? It'd be fun to make a fire."

When Brad disappeared past the top of the bluff, she turned to Antonio. "Would you play for me?"

He picked up his guitar, and with a few strokes of his hand, she was transported to the first moments she'd heard him play. The exquisite purity and haunting simplicity of the notes touched her heart. It was more beautiful than she remembered. She put her hand on his. "Wait." She looked for Brad up the bluff but didn't see him. *Hurry up, Brad.*

Antonio's eyes followed hers. His face showed no emotion, but his hand dropped to his side.

"Help me gather some wood, Antonio."

271

By the time Brad got back, they had a squat circle of wood stacked near the boulder. Brad tried to light the wood, but the flame flickered out each time he lit a match.

"I think this wood's just too damp, Angelica."

"Do you still have matches left?"

"A couple."

"Maybe Antonio can light it. He never ceases to amaze me with his ingenuity."

Angelica looked at him and held out the matches. He took them and put them in his pocket, then turned and walked around the boulders.

Brad frowned. "Where's he going?"

"He's looking for something."

"What could there be on the beach that would start a fire? The wood's just too damp."

"Hold on, City Boy, I bet he gets the fire started."

In a few minutes, Antonio returned with some dried seaweed. He made a small hole in the center of the wood and put the seaweed in it. Next he broke some of the wood and made a little teepee over the seaweed. He knelt down, cupped his hand, and struck a match. A little flame started. He blew on it gently, encouraging it. As if on cue, the sea breeze picked up and fanned the small flame. Orange glowed, and the wood smoked.

"Told you." Angelica tried not to sound too smug as she sat down by the fire, her back to the ocean.

"Dumb luck."

"*Sentarse*, Antonio. Play your guitar for us." She pulled Brad down beside her.

Antonio picked up his guitar, sitting cross-legged, facing them. He strummed a few chords. Closing his eyes, he began to play. The music was soft and easy to listen to, but it wasn't the same.

"Where's the magic?" Angelica said under her breath. "Let's stand up. I think it's hard for him to play sitting like that."

They all stood. Antonio again strummed the guitar. His hands moved gently across the strings. The melody was sweet enough, but the genius was gone.

"He plays really well, Angelica. That's very nice." Brad nodded toward Antonio.

Angelica shook her head. "No, you don't understand. That's not him playing. I mean he plays differently than that." She put her hands on her hips.

"Maybe it just sounds different out here on the beach." Brad tapped his hat down.

"No, something's not right. Really, he plays differently than that."

"Again, please," she said to Antonio.

Just as his fingers brushed across the strings, the breeze gusted, blowing Brad's borrowed hat down the beach.

"*No!*" Brad took off after it.

Angelica wasn't sure what happened first—Brad running, the wind blowing, or the magic in the music—but suddenly she was alone, facing Antonio across the fire. A gusting breeze swirled around them. She felt as if she were in the center of a whirlwind. Nothing existed except her, Antonio, the music, and the fire. Diamond points of tone cascaded around her as his fingers caressed the strings. She looked at him and found his eyes upon her, reflecting a joy and a love she didn't understand. They were both present in a moment that they couldn't control. Alive and intense, his fingers flew.

She suddenly understood. There, nuanced between the rhythms, between the dynamics, between the finger and the string, was the essence of his music. It did not come from him. It did not come from the guitar. It came from his heart.

Intimate and bonding, the vibrato traveled between them. As clearly as if he had spoken, he declared his love for her, and without her consent, her heart surrendered to the life-changing power of a love that asked nothing in return. A knowing, a certainty filled her. This music was meant for her alone. It was a gift. His eyes still held hers as she accepted it. A silent acknowledgment of all that had passed between them escaped as a single tear down her cheek.

Slowly the wind subsided, and Angelica heard her name being called somewhere in the distance. She looked down the beach.

"I got it." Brad was waving his hat in the air. As he approached, she saw his pants were wet up to the knees.

"Wow, wasn't that something the way that wind came up? I thought I was never going to catch this hat. Finally, it blew into the ocean. Thank God the tide brought it to me. I was up to my knees in the water, and it was still floating away from me. I'm freezing. Let me stand by that fire." He moved in front of her so the warmth of the blaze could dry his pants.

Antonio stood across from him, holding his guitar.

"Go ahead." He nodded to Antonio. "I'm listening."

But Angelica knew it was no use. She met Antonio's steady gaze but spoke to Brad. "No, it's okay. It's too late now. It doesn't matter."

Brad nodded. "Yeah, it is getting late . . . and cold. Let's go."

They threw sand on the fire to put it out and headed back up the bluff.

Antonio followed behind Angelica and Brad as they walked up the trail to the trailer. They reached the bluff before he did and disappeared over the rim.

He stopped and turned toward the ocean. He had never seen the sea or its shore. The vast expanse of water stretched to the distant horizon. He could hear the waves crashing on the rocks. He put his hand in his pocket and pulled out his cross and held it in his fist as a sense of awe and wonder filled him. As it had earlier in the day, the sun broke through the gray clouds, sending rays of light across the water's surface. Antonio knelt where he stood and thanked the God who hears and answers prayers.

16

O<small>N THE DRIVE</small> home, Angelica couldn't keep her mind on what Brad was saying. He chatted about a deposition he would be taking the coming week, some engine trouble he'd had with his car, how great the lunch was, and how it was just plain luck that the Mexican got the fire lit. Angelica managed to keep the conversation going, but her mind was on Antonio, his music, and the incredible, life-changing moment they had shared on the beach. Most of all, her mind was on the unspoken promise of love he'd made as he looked at her. Her heart skipped a beat at the thought.

Finally, they turned up the drive to Regalo Grande. Angelica parked by the stables. Brad walked to the back of the trailer to help her unload the horses.

"That's okay, Brad. I'm going to have Antonio and Chick put up the horses. I just remembered something I've got to do."

Brad looked at her, his mouth open, his eyes wide. "What?"

"Oh, just something I forgot to do. Hope you had as much fun as I did." She turned and hurried up the drive to the house, leaving Brad standing with his mouth open, looking after her.

"Angelica. *Angelica!*"

She didn't turn around. She started to run.

She ran past Poppy, who was watering the plants in the entryway, through the front door, and up the stairs to her room. Crossing the room to her window, she saw Antonio unloading the horses and Brad getting into his car. The sound of squealing tires followed Brad down the drive.

Angelica shut her bedroom door, leaned her back against it, and took a deep breath. *What's the matter with me?* She walked back to the bay window and sat down. She took some of the pillows scattered there and propped them up behind her back, then leaned against them. As soon as she closed her eyes, the rush of the wind, the music, and Antonio's warm, loving eyes filled her mind. She shook her head and stood up.

What is this about? She sat down at her study table, put her elbows on it, and put her chin in her palms. Her mind was blank. What had happened on that beach? She sat back in her chair and folded her arms across her chest. No thoughts came.

She went back to her window seat and looked out at the valley. Evening was near, and she could see a few sparkles of light from the homes that were sprinkled across the valley. She cranked her window open. It was getting cool. She smelled the clean, clear air. The crickets were beginning to chirp, and a horse whinnied in the distance.

This was her life. There was no way she could ever make a life with Antonio. Her friends and family and colleagues would never accept him. It was impossible. Whatever happened on that beach, happened there, and must be left there. *Maybe nothing happened. Maybe it was my imagination. It was just windy, that's all. The wind made the music echo. It was all those bould—*

A knock sounded on her door. "Miss Angel, you okay?"

"Yes, Poppy. I'm fine. Come on in."

He stepped just inside the door frame. "What happen? I see you run in house. Your plan no work out?"

Tears began to fall. "Oh, Poppy, I don't know what happened." She took a deep breath, trying to calm herself. Crying wouldn't help anything. She looked out the window. "This is stupid. What am I crying about? No, I guess my plan didn't work out. It came to less than nothing. I don't know what happened. I asked Antonio to play the guitar for Brad, and the music just wasn't the same as when I first heard it. But then later, Antonio and I were alone, just for a few minutes, and suddenly the music was magical and he seemed magical and . . . well, this whole thing is stupid. Something happened on that beach. It's . . . it's as if Antonio was in love with me, and I was in love with him. But that's impossible."

She spun to look at the old man. Surely she'd shocked him. But there wasn't a trace of surprise on his face.

"My Bible tell me, all things are possible to him that believes."

"What do you mean, *him*? Do you mean Antonio? Do you mean me?"

"Yes." The old man's wise eyes met hers.

She turned back to the window. She gazed at the barn and stables and the pastures of Regalo Grande and the valley below—everything that had defined her life until this moment, but she didn't see them. She was standing in a

278

whirlwind, and there was nothing but the music, the fire, and the dark eyes that held her.

Poppy's words echoed in her thoughts. *"All things are possible to him that believes."*

The horseshoe nails . . . the cross. What was it Antonio had said when she gave him the guitar? She thought for a moment. *Un regalo, Dios,* that's what he'd said. He knew. He knew about the music. He recognized God had made a way for him. And then he'd played. He'd played for her. Slowly, the truth became clear. Antonio knew, and he believed.

"Poppy, my head and my heart are pulling me in two different directions. There is no way I could allow myself to love Antonio. We're from two different worlds. It could never work. It would tear up my family, he would never fit in . . . anywhere. That's the real truth, isn't it."

She turned back to him, wanting his answer, but he was gone.

It was after eight that evening when Angelica heard the phone ring. She was fixing a snack in the kitchen. It had to be Brad. She picked it up before the second ring, her words tumbling out before he could speak. "I owe you an apology."

There was no response.

"Hello?"

"Is Benito Amante there?"

Angelica's heart skipped a beat. A call this late for her father—could it be news on Thrombexx?

"May I say who's calling?"

"Russell Moore from New Life."

"One moment, please." Angelica put her hand over the

mouthpiece. "Dad," she yelled down the hall. "Where are you? Pick up the phone. It's New Life."

She heard him answer from his study and put the phone to her ear.

"This is Ben."

"Hi, Ben. It's Russ."

"You heard."

Angelica started. Her father's words were a statement, not a question. She held her breath.

"The approval was denied. More testing required." Moore's words hung in the air. "Ben?"

"I'll fly down there tomorrow. Call the board together so we can evaluate our position."

Angelica couldn't move. She couldn't take a breath. Dread filled her. *Nothing will ever be the same again.* The thought kept repeating in her mind. She hung up the phone and ran down the hall to her father's study.

His back was to her, but she could see he was rubbing his forehead with his hand.

"We've got to find a way."

Was that a tremor in his voice? In her entire life, she'd never heard her father's voice shake. This was the father her world rested on. Suddenly, the big office, oversized desk, and deep, plush, swivel chair dwarfed him. She lowered herself into a wingback opposite him and waited for him to get off the phone. Finally, he hung up and looked at her.

"We'll fight—" she choked the words out. "We'll bargain for more time. We'll get the testing done. I *know* we can work through this."

"I hope you're right." Was that fear in his eyes? "I'll know more after I get down there."

Her father picked up the phone and dialed Southwest Airlines.

Angelica drew a deep breath. "Show me where you keep the financial records of your loans."

He pulled out one of his desk drawers and showed her the files, each labeled with a title and a dollar amount.

She stood up and leaned across the desk. She tried not to look shocked as she realized there must be ten or fifteen of them. The first label was printed, "Cert. of Dep. $100,000," another, "Real Estate Investment Trust $700,000," another, "Regalo Grande $3,250,000."

Her father's voice drifted through the dread filling her.

"When is check-in?" He hung up. "I leave at six tomorrow morning." He didn't look at her.

"Are all these loans due at the same time?" She settled back into her chair.

"No, I got them over about a twelve month period. But they are all made by a handful of lenders and structured so that if one becomes delinquent, then all the loans with that bank become due. Regalo Grande is financed with Community Bank. They only do residential loans and wouldn't finance any of my commercial holdings."

Suddenly, she was the parent, and he was the child. She wanted to protect him. She would protect him. "Don't worry, Dad. It will work out. Between us, we'll come up with a good plan. Call me after your meetings tomorrow, and we'll sort things out."

He still didn't look at her. She walked around the desk and hugged him. He stood up and took her hands in his. "Angelica, this venture would have insured you and your children a good life for as long as you lived. I bet everything I had on it, and I still hope that dream comes true. But no matter what happens, no matter what I have to sell or give up, I promise we'll never lose Regalo Grande. I promise."

Angelica laid her head on his chest. Rather than calming her, the conviction in his voice made her feel there was something hidden in his words. "Don't worry, Dad. No matter what happens, I love you."

Her father stroked her hair for a moment. "Good night, my angel," he whispered, then left the room.

Angelica sat in his chair and swiveled around to the file drawer. She took out a handful of the folders and began going through them. The phone rang. It was Brad.

"Did you get done what you forgot to do?"

She wanted to pour her heart out to him, tell him about Thrombexx, the ranch, her mother's mysterious illness. He would have answers, and if he didn't, he'd have ideas about where to get the answers. Finding solutions was what he did for a living. But it wasn't the kind of thing you talked about over the phone.

"I'm sorry I acted like such a ninny. I don't know what got into me. There was something about the beach, the weather—I don't know. Anyway, I'm sorry."

"You had me worried there for a minute."

She heard the bewilderment in his voice and rubbed at her aching eyes. "Yeah. It's been a long day."

"You still sound upset."

"I'm just tired, and there's a lot going on right now."

"Is it something you want to talk about?"

She hesitated. "I do, but not right now."

"Why don't you get some rest, and we'll talk tomorrow."

She could hear concern in his voice. "That sounds like good advice."

"I'll call you soon."

"Good night, Brad." She hung up the phone and sat quietly for a moment, then turned her attention back to the files.

She lifted out the rest of the folders. The labels told the story: "Personal Line of Credit $200,000," "Stock Account, $300,000," and on and on. When she had looked at them all, she found there were nine files that summarized her father's secured loans and four files that documented his lines of credit.

She looked back in the drawer to see if that was all. There, lying flat on the bottom of the drawer, was a green folder. She picked it up—no label. She opened it. It contained mortgage insurance policies. In the event of his death, the property liens would be paid off. She quickly looked at the date. August 4, just last month.

Why now? What did it mean? Was it a wise precaution, or something else? Should she ask him? Her mind spun. She needed to get ahold of herself. Surely it was just a precaution to protect her mother and herself if anything should happen to him. Her hands were shaking as she put the folder back on the bottom of the drawer.

She spent the next few hours going through the files, reading the due-on-sale clauses, the accelerations clauses, and the release clauses. She wrote extensive notes and marked the sections she thought could be challenged. Finally, sometime after midnight, she put down her pen and went to her room, bone weary, emotionally drained.

Her bedroom was cool. She'd left the window open. Without bothering to turn on the light, she walked over to her window seat and reached for the crank. A strain of music reached her ears. She hesitated and then sat down, unsure she'd really heard anything. Then it came again, in the distance, as if calling to her. She cranked the window to open it farther.

There wasn't a single sound of anything else, not a cricket or horse or owl or even the valley breeze that so often swept into her room. It was as if all of nature bowed to the beautiful, haunting strains of music that came from somewhere outside her window. The music drew her. She wanted to see him. She needed to see him. Tonight the burdens of her heart were too heavy to bear alone.

Angelica slipped down the stairs and out the front door. She stood beneath the arch of the stucco entryway. She listened, trying to pinpoint where the music was coming from. She walked toward it. Finally, when she reached the drive, she realized it was coming from under the oaks by the stream.

The moon lit her path as she quietly picked her way down the grassy bank. She walked under the oaks. The music was clear now. She looked up the stream and saw him sitting on a branch that had fallen by the water, playing the guitar.

"Antonio."

He stopped playing and turned to her, but he said nothing.

She walked the short distance to the branch and sat beside him.

"Play for me," she whispered.

He began again. She closed her eyes and listened. Exhausted, she laid her head on his shoulder. Soon the night and the music and the beat of his heart became a dream. She slept in perfect peace, under the eyes of the Father the whole world rested on.

He didn't move. He hardly breathed, afraid he would disturb her. As the hours passed, he held her, where she had fallen in a half-sleep across his chest, as if she were a child.

"I love you," he whispered. "God brought me to Regalo Grande . . . and you to my arms."

He looked at her through the shadows that moved across her face as the night breeze cradled the leaves of the ancient oaks. He looked at her and memorized just how her eyelashes curved, how she drew a breath, how her hair fell across her forehead, how perfect her features were, how perfect she was. And he knew—if this were all he was ever allowed, it would sustain him.

17

ANGELICA CLOSED HER eyes, and for the hundredth time, relived the moment she had awoken in Antonio's arms, under the oaks. Opening her eyes and finding he had not moved for the hours she'd slept. She'd felt so protected, so cared for, so . . . loved.

And it seemed so wrong. She shouldn't have gone there. She had no right to seek him out for comfort and burden him with her family's problems. Yet here she was, standing at her mother's window again, thinking of him, hoping to catch sight of him, yearning to return to that circle of peace that surrounded him. Her cheeks grew warm remembering. Still, she must not allow that to happen again.

Angelica's father called her every night and gave her an update on the day's events at New Life. The news wasn't good. More testing was required, which could take months. They were trying to enlist other scientists to accelerate the additional testing. More money had to be raised.

She knew he didn't have months to meet his contractual obligations with his creditors, and he had no more avenues with which to raise money. The research and inquiries she and Brad had made, through attorneys specializing in contract law, convinced her that legal maneuvering was their only option. But even that would only buy time and would do nothing to move Thrombexx on to approval. There was no way to soften what her father needed to know, and she told him exactly what he was facing. Yet, they both agreed, her mother was to be informed with only the barest facts.

Angelica sat on the edge of her mother's bed. "You look like you feel better today."

"I do. I think this siege is about over. I'm going to try to walk with only my cane a little later." Her mother set her book on the side table.

"Don't rush it, Mom. There's no hurry." Angelica gently stroked her mother's forehead, brushing away thin strands of lifeless hair. "Poppy and Antonio and I don't mind helping you."

"But I mind." Her mother drew back from Angelica and pushed herself up against the pillows.

"Well, you shouldn't." Angelica gave a quiet laugh. "I'm glad I can be here, and I know Poppy and Antonio feel the same way."

"I'm not talking about you and Poppy." Her mother's voice began to fill with emotion.

Angelica searched her mother's face. "What do you mean?"

"It's that Mexican. I don't like him up here." Dry lips, closed in a thin line, marked the end of her statement.

"Why, Mom? He only does what he's asked."

"I see how he stares at you, Angelica. And I don't like it." Her eyes were fixed on Angelica's face.

Angelica tried to keep her emotions in check, but color filled her cheeks. "I've never seen him *stare* at me."

Her mother's voice rose. "Call it what you like. He looks at you like he was asked up here to watch over *you*, instead of moving me from one room to the other."

"He's a very caring person. If you'd take a little time to get to know him, you'd like him." Angelica tried to keep the frustration out of her voice. Her stomach churned.

"Don't defend him. You're already too involved. I see you going down to visit him each day at noon when I'm out on the patio for lunch, and your father's noticed it too."

"Mom, I'm helping him learn English, and he's helping me learn Spanish. Every time I've been with him, he's been a perfect gentleman." Angelica began to think back over the days her mother had been home. She could think of nothing that would cause this outburst . . . unless she hadn't been hiding her feelings as well as she thought. Her face grew hot.

"It's not about being a gentleman. It's about knowing your place. It's about not intruding where you don't belong. It's about not dragging people down. This is exactly what happened to Cianna."

Angelica stood. "What on earth are you talking about?"

"I'm talking about Cianna. You know she was as close as a sister to me."

Cianna! Angelica had not heard her mother mention her name in years. They had been friends long before Angelica was born. She'd once seen the woman's photo in a shoebox full of old pictures, but she knew little about her. "I know that, Mom. You gave me her name as my middle name. But I never met her."

"And she never met you, and she never became a doctor, and she never had a life. She drifted away after she married that Mexican she met on spring break. They were in love, she said. Then she married him, and that was the end of her dreams."

"How do you know that? Maybe she's been very happy."

"I know because I've seen how she lives." She began to weep. "She invited me to visit after they moved down there. Her life was hard. His family never really accepted her. They had nothing, and she was expected to stay home and take care of the children. She deserved better."

Her mother's condemnation of staying home and taking care of children brought up memories for Angelica of her own childhood and her feelings that her parents' absence was evidence that she had somehow failed them as a daughter. She ignored the familiar feelings of sadness.

"Did she say she was unhappy?"

"No, she didn't confide in me. She tried to act like everything was fine. Like he was still the man of her dreams, but she didn't fool me."

"I'm sorry if that's what happened to her. But what's that got to do with me?" Angelica got her mother some Kleenex.

"Nothing, yet." Her mother's eyes were accusing. "And I hope it never does. I've dreamed of your wedding day since I bought your first dress. Don't spend time with him, Angelica. He's not worth it."

The degrading tone of her mother's words sparked anger in Angelica. "He's a human being. He's good and kind. He's a beautiful person whom God has gifted with a musical talent. Can't you open your heart and let him in? Can't you get past the fact that he's Mexican? We're all one blood, Mother." Angelica stopped herself. It was all she could do not to tell her mother that her father's investment in Thrombexx was doing more to destroy her dreams than anything Antonio could have ever done.

The look on her mother's face said she had spoken with more passion and revealed far more than she intended. Jarred by that thought, she turned and left the room.

✳

Angelica's father returned to Regalo Grande on Wednesday night. He and Angelica mentioned nothing definite about Thrombexx or New Life during or after dinner. As soon as her mother went to bed, Angelica went to her father's study.

"Any new developments, Dad?"

"Nothing. What about on this end?"

"I've gone through all your files." Angelica walked around the desk and opened the top drawer, where she had put the pages of notes she'd made. They spent the next hour going over them.

Finally, Angelica sat back in her chair. "It looks like we have two weeks. The first loan that comes up for extension is Regalo Grande, with Community Bank, on October 15. They make only residential loans, so that won't trigger pay-offs on any of your other loans."

"I have nothing to show the bank that would justify an extension. If the drug were still pending, it would be one thing. I might've been able to stall. But with the drug approval denied, I have no way of convincing the bank there will be income for the foreseeable future." His voice was as hopeless as his situation.

"What about your partners?"

"All the partners who put up money are in the same position I am. Those who didn't aren't about to put their assets at risk."

Angelica sat looking at her father. He had aged over the few days he was gone. Her heart went out to him.

"I bring you some coffee and my special cookies."

Angelica turned at Poppy's voice to see him carrying a tray into the room.

"Thank you, Poppy." Her father's smile was weary but appreciative.

Poppy set the tray down on top of a low bookcase behind Benito's chair. "You no need me. I go to bed now."

"No, we're fine. Good night."

"Good night, Poppy. I love you," Angelica added.

Poppy turned to go.

"Uh, Poppy."

He turned back to her father. "Yes, Mr. Amante?"

"Would you pray for me, Poppy? I really need a miracle right now."

"I always pray for you. I pray for all my family. My Bible say: 'Whatever things you ask in prayer, believing, you will receive.' And I believe what my Jesus say. He say He even answer our prayers before we ask."

"I'm not a praying man, but maybe you could put a word in for me tonight."

"I go do it right now." He left the room as quietly as he had entered.

"Does Poppy seem a little tired to you, Angelica? I haven't seen him since I've been gone, and tonight he just didn't seem to have his usual spark."

"I think he just gets worried about us. Wouldn't it be great if life were as simple as Poppy says? Just believe what you read in the Bible. I mean—I believe the Bible is true, but it's just not that easy." Doubt pricked at her. Every time she trusted God, nothing worked out. Just this once she wished it could be different.

Poppy went to his room, shut his door, and turned on the floor lamp next to his favorite chair. Out of habit he looked out the window, but it was too dark to see much, other than the silhouettes of the trees clustered in the fields. He sat down and picked up his Bible from the side table. He opened the cover and took out his prayer list. After thinking for a moment, he added a few words to the bottom of it.

His eyes drifted to the black-and-white picture next to his Bible. Helena. Not a day had passed since the day she died that he didn't think of his wife and baby daughter. But lately she'd been on his mind more than usual, little vignettes of their time together flashing in and out of his mind as he worked. He set the picture down and listened. He thought he heard the wind. Why was it windy now? He glanced at the window again. It was closed. He listened. Was it a train? Impossible.

He tucked his prayer list back into his Bible. The distinctive sound grew louder. He sat on the edge of his chair. Yes, it was a wind. He was sure. Yet nothing moved in his room. He turned off his light so he could get a better look out the window. The silhouettes of the trees didn't move. He sat perfectly still, his Bible still in his lap.

He cocked his head, listening. As clear as a voice, the words came to him: "Well done, good and faithful servant." In the twinkling of an eye, he was consumed with a love so powerful that it became light. The light revealed the source of the sound that was now a deafening roar, a legion of angels surrounding him, the rush of their extended wings opening to form an infinite arc that reached to the heavens. There was no night or day. All the things of the earth vanished. And there, in the expanse between space and time, in spirit not flesh, emerging from beneath a gossamer shelter, was a woman and a child. He knew them. Heralded by the sound of a thousand trumpets, proclaiming victory over death, his soul took flight.

As quickly as it came, it was gone. No evidence remained of what had transpired—only a frail, empty vessel and the lingering echo of the last words he uttered: "Remember my prayers, O Lord."

"Gee, Dad. I don't think there's any more we can do tonight."

"You're right, honey. I'm going back to New Life on Monday. If I can't make any progress with the approval or financing there, we might as well go to the bank and lay our cards on the table."

"Something will work out." But there was no conviction in her words.

They walked together down the hall. Her father went to his room, but she stopped in the kitchen. She walked to the sink and got a glass of water.

What a beautiful, clear night. She took a few sips of water, then took a sweater off of the hook by the door and walked out on the patio. *Nothing will ever be the same again.* As the familiar thought surfaced, she let out a sigh.

She stood, letting her eyes sweep the valley. She wanted to remember just how it looked, just how the air felt in October, and to recall the scent of the flowers still in bloom. Memories of her childhood danced in the back of her mind—the day her father brought Pasha home, riding on the ridge, Poppy in the garden. This was the beauty and innocence of Regalo Grande that she had been privileged to know. She'd never been more aware of it than she was at this moment.

She sighed. The moment was fleeting, and she knew it. Tomorrow would come, and once again she would be faced with hard choices about her personal and professional life.

She looked at the starry sky. "Oh! A shooting star." She blew a kiss toward heaven, as she and Poppy had always done when she was a child. She smiled, remembering those long ago nights when her parents were traveling and it was just she and Poppy, sitting on the grass, long past her bedtime. When she saw the burst of light, she would point. "Look, Poppy!"

And he would answer, "That a soul, winging its way to heaven, Miss Angel."

It was just after five thirty in the morning when Antonio went into the bunkhouse kitchen.

Chick had called him from his work. It was good the *mayordomo* spoke Spanish as well as he did. Antonio appreciated not having to struggle to understand the orders he was given all day long.

"Hey, Paco," Chick said, "go up to the big house and get our groceries. I never did get them yesterday. If Poppy's not in the kitchen, he's around somewhere. Just get the groceries."

"Okay."

Antonio jogged up the hill to the kitchen and knocked lightly on the door. No one answered. He looked through the window, but there was no one in sight. He hesitated, then knocked again—no answer. He opened the door slowly and looked around. There weren't any groceries in sight.

He knew the old man slept in the room right across from the kitchen. He'd taken Antonio there once after they cleaned the kitchen, when he first came to Regalo Grande, and talked to him. He hadn't understood much of what the little man said—only that it was something about Jesus and the cross. When he'd shown him the cross in his pocket, the old man had said, "Yes. Yes."

Antonio stepped into the kitchen and shut the door behind him. "*Señor?*" There was no answer.

He walked across the floor and looked toward Poppy's bedroom. The door was closed. He walked quietly to it and knocked softly. Still no answer. He knocked again, and the door opened a few inches. "*Señor?*"

Pushing the door open just a little farther, he saw the old man sitting in his chair. Antonio immediately perceived there was no life in the room. There was only a likeness of the man he had known. He walked slowly to the chair and knelt beside it.

He did not fear death. He respected it. He understood its finality and its freedom. He knew it was sometimes directed, and sometimes allowed, by God. Death among the young was not uncommon in his homeland, and he'd been touched by it when sickness came to the families living in the fields of Guadalajara. The death of the young always brought despair for what might have been. But he'd also seen death visit the old. Often it was not only accepted but embraced. He took the cross from his pocket and bowed his head, acknowledging the Creator and His power to speak life and death into being.

Antonio rose and left the room, easing the door shut behind him. He hurried back to the bunkhouse and told Chick what he'd found.

Chick stared at him. "Are you sure?"

He nodded.

"I'd better call up to the house." Chick picked up the phone.

Antonio walked to the barn and sat where he could see Angelica's window. It was overcast, and he knew if she turned on her light, he'd see it. He longed to be with her. She loved the old man so, and she would receive his death with sorrow and grief. If only Antonio could comfort her, hold her and tell her death was not an ending but a beginning. He sat, waiting, and before long the light in her room went on. . . .

The keening scream that cut through the morning air took his breath away. He bowed his head and did the only thing he could to comfort the woman he loved. He prayed.

God, dry her tears with the breath of Your Spirit.

Benito sat on his daughter's bed, holding his only child, stroking her hair as she sobbed.

"No, Daddy. Don't let this be true." Her voice rose, hysterical. "Where *is* he?"

"Honey, the ambulance is on its way."

She struggled from his arms and threw back the covers. "Let me see him. I want to see him. This isn't true. It *can't* be true." She tried to get up.

He tightened his grip on her. "Angelica, I'm so sorry. I loved him too."

How many times had he watched this scene played out in a hospital waiting room? First the denial, then the anger, then the deep, consuming grief . . . and always the tears, that uniquely human response to pain. He handled it by distancing himself, and he needed to do that now, for her sake. "There's nothing that can be done, sweetheart." His voice was firm.

"Something can be done. Something has to be done."
He heard the frantic hope in her trembling voice. "Pray,
Daddy. That's what Poppy always says. He says his Jesus
hears and answers prayers. Pray that he's just asleep, that
he's not dead." Sobs racked her body, and she collapsed
against his chest.

Her plea left him desperate, searching for words to speak
to the God he did not know. His little girl needed him, she
wanted him to make it better, but he couldn't. How many
hearts had he made whole on the operating table? But here,
in his own home, when it mattered most, his talent, skill,
knowledge—it was all worthless. He could do nothing for
his suffering daughter.

His heart broke. *Jesus, who are You? Can You hear me?
If You're God, touch her heart and heal her of this grief. If
You're really God, do it today.*

He put his arms around her, and they cried.

Together, Angelica and her father rose from the bed and
made their way downstairs. She stood at Poppy's door, leaning heavily on her father for support. She saw her beloved
Poppy, sitting in his chair, his Bible in his lap.

"Oh, Poppy . . ." Her choked whisper seemed to echo
around the empty room. "Don't leave me. I need you."
She stumbled from her father's side to the chair, where she
collapsed, weeping at his feet.

The ambulance finally came. She stood beneath the entry
arches and watched it drive away. She took a deep breath,
trying to pull herself together. *I won't shed another tear.*
She squared her shoulders. She would handle it her way.
She wouldn't cry. Poppy wasn't really gone. *He's still here
at Regalo Grande.* She wrapped her arms around herself,

embracing the idea that she would always have her memories of him.

She wandered through the house most of the day. Passing her father's office, she saw he'd brought in the mail. Walking over to look at it, her eye fell on the tray sitting on the low bookcase behind her father's chair, where Poppy had put it the night before. The sight of the Greek cookies, lovingly placed in a circle on a pretty china plate, wrenched her heart. She turned away. She must take that to the kitchen for Poppy . . . later.

She sat at the desk, idly thumbing through the mail. There was the usual junk mail, bank statements, and a plain, white envelope with the return address "Church of Our Lady, Jalisco, Mexico." She lifted the letter from the pile and sat back, looking at it. It was addressed to Antonio Perez, C/O Angelica Amante. She thought about opening it. No. It was addressed to Antonio. She'd look for him later. She opened the top drawer of the desk and stuck it with her notes.

Her eyes widened when she saw the last letter in the stack. It was from Sierra County. She tore open the envelope. An appointment for an interview the following Monday. "Popp—" She caught herself. Poppy was gone.

An opportunity for the job she really wanted was suddenly in her reach. But she had vowed to help her family with her trust money and all but accepted Brad's offer. Still, that was before Poppy died. Somewhere deep within her heart, as she stood looking at the letter, her desire to help the poor was transfigured, becoming a desire to honor Poppy. If she had to live on the income of the job and nothing more, then so be it. *God, You have failed me.*

The thought repeated itself. Her life was devastated. God had failed Poppy too. Someone who loved the Lord with all his heart and soul and mind. First He took his wife and child from him forever and then left him to die alone in his room. A just God would never do that. Enough. She stood and straightened her shoulders. *I'm going to take control now.*

All day, Antonio could think of nothing but Angelica as he worked. He hoped she might come and see him at lunchtime, as she often did, perhaps to tell him what had happened. But lunch came and went, and Chick sent him to move the sheep to a new pasture. And so the day wore on. His thoughts were always upon her, and his eyes never rested as he looked for some trace of her—passing by a window, walking to the mailbox, sitting on the patio. At last the sun set, and his work was finished. He returned to the barn where he could sit and watch her window. The hours passed, but no light appeared.

Beneath the darkening sky, he walked down to the oaks and sat by the stream.

As night settled in, Angelica walked down to see Pasha. He must have heard her coming, because he was waiting at the gate. When she opened it, he followed her to the barn, where she fed him some grain and scratched his ears.

"Pash, I'm not going to cry anymore. It doesn't help. Anyway, Poppy's not really gone, is he?" She pushed the truth beyond the edges of her mind, behind a wall of tears.

Pasha pressed his velvety nose against her cheek.

She grabbed his mane, and after a quick, weak pull, he willingly kneeled. She slid onto his back, laid her head on his neck, closed her eyes, and gave him his head. His steps were slow and easy and rocked her gently. She paid no attention to where he was going. She didn't care. The familiar, steady gait lulled her into a safe place, where there was only Pasha's soft, silky mane and the bobbing motion of his neck. She didn't have to be fully present. She didn't have to think.

Leaves brushed across her face. She opened her eyes and saw they were at the stream. Pasha lowered his head, but instead of drinking, he knelt. Someone was beside her. Strong arms reached for her, whisked her from Pasha's back. She felt Antonio's strength as he pulled her to his chest. Through her tears, she saw his face, serious with concern. He pulled her head to his shoulder, and there, beneath the oaks by the stream, the cry from a father's broken heart was answered. The wall of tears crumbled, and truth was released to sow the first seeds of healing and prepare her heart for the new love that would grow there.

Poppy's funeral was held Saturday at Glen Ellen Faith Church. It was a crisp October day. Pastor Steve waited for the Amantes at the sanctuary door.

They arrived together, in the Lincoln, and Chick arrived in the pickup with two Mexican men. Pastor Steve greeted them at the door. "I'm so sorry for your loss." He led them to the front pew. There were about thirty other people who had known Poppy over the years seated throughout the church.

The pastor's wife played the organ from a hymnal. The large, freestanding cross that always stood behind the choir had been moved in front of the stage. The casket was displayed in front of it, just a few feet from the first pews. It was closed at Angelica's request. She said she wanted to remember Poppy peacefully sleeping in his chair.

The last strains of "The Old Rugged Cross" faded, and the pastor's wife took a seat near the organ.

"Welcome to you all," Pastor Steve began the service. "We're here today to celebrate the life of Plutarcho Mendopoulos. The man we all knew and loved as Poppy." He spoke of what a blessing Poppy had been to the church and recounted several stories of the old man's tireless service to the poor and sick and suffering. He asked if anyone would like to speak.

At first, no one came forward. Then, from the back of the church, an older man with a cane walked to the lectern. "I just want to say I will miss Poppy. My wife was ill for years before she passed. In the last months of her life, I had to care for her. Coming here on Sunday was the only time I allowed myself away from her. Every Sunday, Poppy brought me some prepared meals in a big basket. It really lightened my load at that difficult time. I will miss him."

The man turned and made his way back to his seat, passing a well-dressed, young woman in the aisle as she made her way to the front. "Five years ago, I was living on the street. No one cared about me. People didn't even look at me when they passed me sitting drugged out on the sidewalk. One day, on a bench outside Community Bank, I met Poppy Mendopoulos and his Lord and Savior Jesus Christ. Praise God, it changed my life forever. From that day, until this, I celebrate it as my birthday. It's the day I was truly born again."

Another person was waiting to speak before she finished. One by one, church members who had come to celebrate the life of the simple little man revealed his legacy. Pastor Steve looked toward the family. "Is there anyone else?"

Angelica tried to stand but sank back into the pew. She buried her face in her handkerchief. Benito Amante rose and walked to the lectern. "We were privileged to know Poppy for many years. He touched us all, and this world is a better place because Poppy Mendopoulos lived here." He sat down.

The pastor waited a minute or two, looking over the gathering. "Is there anyone else?"

He drew a breath to begin the closing prayer, then hesitated. He stared down the aisle of the church, not sure he was seeing what he thought he was seeing. All eyes followed his. Someone was walking to the casket. It was a Mexican man, carrying a guitar.

The man knelt in front of the casket and bowed his head, his back to the room. Then he stood and lifted his guitar, positioning his hands. When his fingers touched the strings, music filled the little sanctuary. Angelica lifted her head; her fingers flew to her lips. The music was a joyous sound, triumphant and powerful. The very air seemed to rejoice in the receiving of it.

Those who were there that day would speak of it for years to come. Some said they heard the most beautiful, angelic voices from above. Others said there was a glow that encircled the Mexican man and his guitar. Still others said that they had never felt such peace and that surely they had glimpsed a moment in heaven itself. All who came that day to remember the humble Greek man, known as Poppy, never forgot him or the Mexican who, for a few glorious moments, lifted the veil of death and revealed the essence of eternity.

18

ANGELICA WALKED DOWN the stairs to wait for the cab that would take her mother to the airport shuttle. The fog had rolled in the night before and hung across the valley like a damp shroud.

As she passed the kitchen, she thought about Poppy. The tears were still quick to come. She hated that. She needed to take control, to get on with life and focus on the financial problems that her father was facing—problems that wouldn't wait for her grief to fade. She needed to pull herself together; the interview was this afternoon. And she needed to work on plans for the vineyard, which now seemed more important than ever.

"Angelica, the fog is so thick I can't even see the end of the drive. I hope the cab can find its way."

"Oh, Mom, they've been up here enough times. It'll be fine." Angelica sat on the couch, next to her mother.

"I'm just thankful Ralph was able to get me in to the specialist in Orange County. Your father and I talked before he left this morning, and we decided I should join him in LA, then, when he's finished his work, he can drive me down to the appointment. To tell you the truth, I'm looking forward to getting away."

"I think it'll do you good, Mom. You've been cooped up here for weeks, and so much has happened."

"I know, still, I feel badly leaving you here. But this doctor is my only hope." Tears welled up in her eyes. "What if he can't find out what it is? I would give anything, everything, to know what is wrong. If this doctor figures it out, I'll be forever in his debt." She took a handkerchief from her purse. "You know Poppy said he prayed for me every day. He said God would send me a healing. I believed that until the day he died. But now, even that hope is gone."

Angelica looked at her mother with compassion. "We're going to find out. Try not to worry. Let's talk about something else." Angelica took a shaky breath.

The sound of the cab arriving interrupted her. "Here he is, Mom."

They went outside. The cabbie loaded the trunk, then Angelica gave her mother a kiss and watched the cab disappear down the drive.

She went to her father's office and gathered the files. With no one home, she'd rather work in her room with the view of the valley. She opened the drawer and took out her notes. Right on top of them was the letter to Antonio she'd put there on the day of Poppy's death. She picked it up and looked at it. With everything that had happened, it seemed like a lifetime ago.

Angelica picked up the phone and called the bunkhouse. Chick answered.

"Would you send Antonio up here? He has a letter. Tell him I'm in my father's study."

"Sure," Chick replied.

A few minutes later, Angelica heard the kitchen door open.

"I'm back here, Antonio."

"Good morning, *señorita*. How are you today?"

For the first time since the funeral, Angelica smiled. "Very good English, Antonio. I'm fine."

He took off his hat and sat down beside the desk.

"You have a letter." She turned the envelope so he could see it and then opened it.

There were a few English sentences followed by a half page of Spanish. Angelica read the English portion to herself: "I received your letter and relayed the information to the Perez family. You asked where his father is working. He's not working across the border. He is here. They have had some bad luck and very much appreciated the money their son sent. We are helping them with food until Mr. Perez can find work." It was signed "Carol Craig."

Angelica tried not to look alarmed. "The missionary wrote me in English. She says your father is home."

He sat straight up in his chair. "Father no work?"

Angelica read the Spanish to him, hoping he could understand through her American accent. His face grew concerned, and when she finished, he told her in Spanish that his family needed all his money. He asked her if she could send it right away and handed her a money order for two hundred dollars.

She wanted to ask him what exactly was wrong, but it was awkward since he made no explanation. She'd understood bits and pieces as she read, but there were many words that were unfamiliar. She took the money order and realized it was payday. "Did Chick give you the other fifty dollars in cash?"

He frowned, and she asked the question again in Spanish.

He shook his head and pointed at the money order. "*Este es mi dinero.*"

"You're paid two hundred fifty dollars every two weeks. This is only two hundred dollars."

Antonio frowned and tried to explain in English this time. "No, you make mistake. I get two hundred dollars, two weeks."

Angelica almost asked him to repeat himself, then reached for the phone. "We need to talk to Chick." She phoned the bunkhouse again.

Chick answered on the first ring. "Regalo Grande."

"Chick, could you come up to my dad's office?"

"Sure, boss." She heard the hesitation in his voice. "I'm just puttin' the camper on my truck. Thought I might go visit Mario over at Lo Bianco."

Angelica composed herself while they waited. Her mind wandered. There had been so many things. The disrepair of the ranch, that incident with the salt, the harsh words she sometimes recognized when she heard him speak Spanish to Antonio.

Chick walked into the room. "What'd ya need, Miss Amante?"

"Why is it that Antonio only gets two hundred dollars every two weeks when I told you he was to be paid two hundred fifty dollars each pay period, and my father's been giving you that much to pay him?"

Chick didn't answer.

"Well?" Angelica leaned forward, her arms folded on the desk.

The color drained from Chick's face. "Uh—"

"Yes?" Angelica's voice was deadly calm.

Chick shot an angry glare at Antonio. "He's just a Mexican. He's not worth more than two hundred dollars. He's

306

glad to get it, and why shouldn't I get something for running to town for his money order?"

Angelica was stunned by his blatant racism, his thievery. "And what about Rafael's money? Do you have a twenty percent charge for him too?" She knew her voice was rising, but she didn't care.

Chick's lips curled. "Look, lady, you're way too interested in these Mexicans—particularly *this* one. Don't think I haven't noticed how you watch him. And don't think he doesn't know a sugar mama when he sees one."

Angelica gritted her teeth against the rage boiling within her. She took a deep breath and put her hands in her lap. She wasn't going to let Chick get the upper hand by blowing up at him. Antonio, watching the confrontation escalate, stood and faced Chick, dwarfing him.

Chick took a step back, and Angelica allowed herself a small smile at that. "I'm not going to bother to count up how much money you've stolen. I'm just going to figure it's enough to cover what you're owed." She stood now. "Get your stuff and get off this property and don't ever come back here. If I ever hear from you again, you'll find yourself in court, charged with theft. And if I ever hear of you working on any of the ranches or vineyards around here, your employer will get a letter from me advising them to reconsider your employment."

Her firm tone left no doubt she would do as she said. Chick's face went red, then drained of color. Anger burned in his eyes.

"You're messin' with the wrong person, little lady. Don't worry. You won't be seein' me around here. But I promise you won't forget me." With that he stormed out of the room.

Antonio watched Chick leave. When Angelica eased back

into her father's chair, he sat back down as well. He leaned forward, putting his hand on her arm. "You okay?"

She took a deep, steadying breath. "I'm okay." She put her hand on top of his. "Antonio, why is your father home?"

"No worry. I send money."

She left it at that. "Why don't you go down below the gates and help Rafael. He's working on that stone wall. It might be better to wait until Chick's gone to finish the stables."

He looked amused by her request. "No worry for me, *señorita*." Then his face turned serious. His lips were parted, as if he wanted to say something.

Angelica waited. He was so near. His eyes searched her face, and he made no attempt to hide it. She felt a powerful pull. Then he rose and left without a word.

She watched him go. *What's the matter with me? I'm acting like a schoolgirl.*

But the perfect peace she'd found in his arms washed through her, and her stomach fluttered. She had to stop thinking about him. There was no way they could have a future together. The memory of Poppy's voice intruded on her thoughts. *"He have a plan for your life, Miss Angel. His plan better than our plan."*

She pushed his words to the back of her mind and tapped the edge of the letter in her hand on her lips, then folded it and put it in her pocket. She picked up the files and went upstairs to her desk.

She pulled the Spanish dictionary from the stack of books on the corner of the table and smoothed out the letter. Beginning with the first sentence, she wrote the English words above the Spanish words she recognized, then one by one, looked up the rest. "To our son of much esteem." *How true.* She continued, smiling. "We are so thankful to God for the money you sent." *How sweet. Such simple people.* "There is no food." Angelica's smile froze. "We are desperate. Your father was deported in a raid at his ranch." She caught her breath. *How terrible for him.* "The *patrono* had not paid him for months when Immigration came. . . ."

Angelica didn't finish the sentence. She stared at the paper. Slowly, the full impact of the words hit her. It couldn't be. It couldn't be what it seemed. *Ortega, Ramirez, Martinez, Herrera.*

How many files in William O'Connell's office had she seen with "Perez" written on them? Five? Six? *God, don't let this be true.* How could she ever tell Antonio? Why hadn't she left sooner? What if she had personally submitted his father's file? *How could he ever forgive me? He is good and kind and . . . and . . .*

"I love him."

The words seemed to spring from her lips of their own volition.

The day she'd given him the guitar, the wind and the fire on the beach, and the moments under the oaks came to her—still shots, hidden in her memory, brought forward now, tearing her to pieces.

"I love him," she whispered the words again. *But I don't deserve him.* She could never face him with this part of her life, tell him how she'd worked for a company whose mission it was to bring suffering to his people. She'd actually worked on the files. She walked to the window seat and stood looking out. What could she do? She couldn't tell him. *He'll hate me, and I don't blame him. If only Poppy were here.*

She stared out the window a long time, lost in thought. Where had it all gone wrong? It had started with the seduction of a job offer from Czervenka and Zergonos. And it had

309

continued with her choosing to follow her father's dreams instead of her own. It had been in the compromising.

Gradually, things became clear. The first thing she needed to do was tell Brad that she was not going to be working for his firm. She placed the call. He answered on the first ring.

"Hi, Brad. Can you talk?"

"A few minutes. What's up, sweetie?" She could hear the concern in his voice.

"I got a letter to interview for a public defender position in Sierra County, and I've decided to go for it. The interview is this afternoon."

There was silence on the line. Finally, Brad spoke. "You know I'm disappointed, but I understand. Try it. Maybe you'll find it really isn't your style. My offer still stands."

"I appreciate that. I'll let you go now. I've got some important things I need to do."

"I'll call you tonight." He hung up.

She quickly dressed for her interview, picked up her purse and her car keys, and went downstairs to her father's office. She got Antonio's money order. She addressed an envelope to Mexico and put the money order in it, then rummaged through her father's desk and found the key she was looking for. She looked at her watch. There was time before the interview. She ran out to her car and took off down the drive.

At Community Bank, she went in and asked for her safety-deposit box. After opening it, she took out the checkbook for her trust account, wrote a check for a thousand dollars, took it to a teller, and asked for two five-hundred-dollar money orders. Then she put the money orders in the envelope with Antonio's and sealed it. She looked at her watch, there was still time to make it to the post office

310

before the interview. She sent the envelope airmail, return receipt requested.

Driving to the Sierra County Human Resources office, her heart was heavy. She knew what she had to do. She must distance herself from Antonio. He could never know her part in what had happened to his family. She would do what she could to help him get his papers. Then he needed to get on with his life, somewhere else. She could continue to send money anonymously, as long as they needed it. He'd never know what she'd done. By the time she turned into the parking lot for her interview, her plan was set, and her heart was broken.

"Ms. Amante." The gray haired public defender pointed to a chair across from his desk. "My name's Dave McMahon. Would you please be seated." His voice was cool.

Angelica couldn't help but notice the dated cut of his suit and the mechanical, unpolished awkwardness of his introduction, so unlike her colleagues in New York. "Nice to meet you." She took her seat.

"Likewise." He opened her file. "You're certainly well qualified. We don't often see résumés like yours. What are you expecting from this position?"

There was a defensive edge to his voice. Her eye took in the credenza behind his desk—a picture of an overweight woman standing with two young children, a trophy with a bowling ball on top of it inscribed "Second Place," a coffee cup announcing "The Best Grandpa in the World." Clearly, the man across from her was intimidated by her application. Her credentials and sophistication were going to keep her from getting the job. She had to do something.

"I was fired from my last position. I'm hoping to start over." She heard him catch his breath.

"Excuse me." He closed her file. "Could you explain?"

Angelica talked for the next half hour, explaining what had happened in New York that had brought her to California. She answered all his questions honestly, and by the end of the conversation, she had confided in him about the recent death of her beloved Poppy and how she hoped someday to open an office that was dedicated to advocating for the poor.

"You've got a pretty ambitious agenda. I'm impressed. I'm just concerned that you may find that working here isn't challenging enough."

"The challenge for me is making a difference in people's lives."

He looked at her intently a moment, then spoke. "I don't think this position *is* challenging enough, but I do know that other positions within this department will be opening up in the near future." His face broke into a smile. "Might as well start at the bottom and work your way up."

Angelica refrained from the urge to run around the desk and hug him. "Are you offering me the position?"

"I can't do that yet. I have to complete all the scheduled interviews. I'll call you by Friday."

"Thank you. Thank you so much, Mr. McMahon."

For the next few days, Angelica immersed herself in the plans for the vineyard and the financial crisis that hung over her family, but she always stayed in earshot of the phone. She spoke to her father in Los Angeles every day, and slowly they both came to the realization that with October 15 just a week away, there wasn't going to be an extension of the loans that encumbered all of the Amante assets. She told him briefly about firing Chick and mentioned her interview with Sierra County. He didn't ask for details about either, because, although unspoken, it was understood that they were in the midst of far more serious matters.

Angelica avoided Antonio as much as possible. After telling him she'd find a replacement for Chick soon, she rarely spoke to him. She remembered Manuel, whom she'd seen at the church and met at the dance. A call to the church provided the phone number of the ranch where he worked as the *mayordomo*, supervising the workers, and she asked him to help her find a replacement for Chick, someone who could oversee the ranch and take care of the horses. She explained she no longer needed Antonio, who had been with her at the dance. If Manuel could help find him a job, she'd greatly appreciate it and would provide an excellent reference.

As quickly as the days seemed to pass, the nights seemed to stand still. She couldn't sleep. She spent hours thinking about the pending loan-call on Regalo Grande and her mother's illness. Inevitably sleep came, but her dreams were of an empty room and the faint smell of peppermint.

Each morning, she cursed the darkness she could not escape.

She turned her study table away from the window so that it faced her bookcase, and this afternoon, as she had every afternoon since her parents had gone to Los Angeles, she reread the release clause page of the lien documents.

She stared at the neatly typed words that hadn't changed since the first time she read them, then shuffled through the other papers in the file: a notary page, a legal description—that needed to be modified, now that the seventy-five acres had been split off—and an appraisal.

An appraisal.

Her mind began to race. She thumbed through to the last page. Appraised value: $3,250,000. Loan amount:

$850,000! The loan was for $850,000. Of course! Why hadn't she thought of this before? The bank hadn't lent her father one hundred percent of the value of the ranch, especially with the amount of other debt he was carrying. They'd only lent a portion. Was there a way to reduce the $850,000 enough to make the payments and keep that loan current? Her trust account. The $150,000 in it wasn't enough, but it was a start.

She sat back and folded her arms, mentally combing through everything she knew about her father's affairs. Nothing came to mind. Nothing that would significantly cut the $700,000 debt that would remain if she applied all her trust money to the loan on Regalo Grande.

She wouldn't be able to develop the vineyard property if she used her trust money to pay down the loan. *The vineyard property . . . the vineyard property . . . the surveyor . . .*

Dick Brighton's words came back to her. "While I was up there surveying, several people stopped and asked about the property. Two of the people gave me their names and numbers."

She ran downstairs to her father's office and found the surveyor's file. She dialed the number. In moments, she was talking with Dick Brighton, asking him about the people who had wanted to buy the property.

"Hold, Miss Amante. Let me get the file."

For the first time in days, she felt hopeful. If a sale of the vineyard property could be worked out and her trust money added, they'd be able to pay down the lien on the ranch substantially. It wouldn't save her father from financial ruin, but it might allow him and her mother to keep their home. At least it gave them a chance.

Dick Brighton returned to the line. "I have those names and numbers for you."

After writing down the information, Angelica hung up the phone. How much further should she go without talking to her father? There wasn't any question that this was by far their best chance to save the ranch. Still, it most likely meant there'd never be an Amante Vineyard. It would be his call.

She dialed the first number. "Is Mr. Gaynos there?"

"Just a moment."

"This is Nick."

"This is Angelica Amante. You gave your name to our surveyor and told him you were interested in our property on Sonoma Mountain."

"Property on Sonoma Mountain?"

"Yes, near Glen Ellen. You stopped by when the surveyor was flagging it."

"Oh, yes. Yes, I did."

"Are you still interested in the property?"

"Very much."

They spoke for about twenty minutes. She found out he already owned a successful vineyard in Napa, Lagryma de la Uva, but wanted to expand. His son Scott was in charge of the family business and would be in touch with her.

She dialed the second number.

"Is Glenn Wimer there?"

"He and Mrs. Wimer are in Europe for a month." That wasn't going to help her now. Angelica gave her contact information and hung up.

She leaned back in the big chair. She'd be able to get a quick appraisal of the seventy-five acres if she used the same people who had appraised the ranch for the bank. They had already done the research.

She continued to lay out a plan as she picked up the phone and dialed the number her father had given her for

New Life. When they told her he wasn't available, she asked them to leave him a message to call his daughter. She hung up and tried the Hilton, but there was no answer in her parents' room.

She stood, restless. There were so many things still up in the air. She needed a break.

She walked down to Pasha's pasture, relieved when she didn't see Antonio anywhere. She opened the gate. Pasha was drinking from the water trough. She walked over to him and began combing his mane with her fingers. He stood patiently, enjoying the attention from his mistress. She turned to lead him out of the pasture and found herself standing face-to-face with Antonio.

She drew her breath in. "You frightened me." She kept her tone indifferent, looking past him.

Concern shown in those dark eyes. "*Qué pasa?*"

"Nothing's wrong." She tried to walk past him.

He caught her arm, then reached out to turn her face to his. "*Qué pasa?*"

At the low, tender words, emotions raced through her. Fear. Anger. Confusion. She took a step back and tried to walk around him, but once again he intercepted her, his gaze trapping her, questioning her.

She didn't want to tell him what was wrong. *Everything* was wrong. She was no good for him. She'd helped bring misery to his family. But worst of all, she loved him, a man who didn't belong in her world and never could. It all rolled over her at once.

He still blocked her path. Fine, if he wanted to know, she'd tell him. "*Es el carta, de su familia.*"

At her mention of the letter from his family, he frowned. She felt trapped by her limited vocabulary, but she pushed on, telling him everything. How she knew what had hap-

316

pened to his father. That the company he worked for had deported him. Hadn't paid him. And that she'd helped companies do that when she worked in New York.

He stared at her, and she looked away, afraid of what she'd see in his eyes.

"*Necesito dejar.* You must leave here. Find another job." She wasn't sure she was saying it right, but she made sure her voice was cold. She was determined not to break down.

She couldn't let him know she was dying inside.

Angelica glimpsed his face as she pulled away from him. He looked as if she'd struck him. With a choked cry, she pushed past him. This time, he didn't stop her. She walked with quick strides toward the house. She couldn't let him see the tears pouring down her face. She managed to keep it together until she stepped through the kitchen door. Then she broke into a run, stumbled up the stairs, and threw herself onto her bed, sobbing.

As the room darkened, she began to pull herself together. She needed someone to talk to, someone who would understand how all of this had happened, someone who would not judge her. She needed Brad.

Antonio stepped out of the bunkhouse into the night, his guitar under his arm. He looked up at the *patrona*'s room. It was dark. He walked across the field to Pasha's pasture, climbed the fence, and sat on the top rail. He laid the guitar across his knees and took the cross out of his pocket. Pasha trotted over, stopping in front of him, nudging his hand.

"No sugar, boy." Pasha snorted and tossed his head.

He had not understood everything Angelica had said. He did understand that she'd worked for someone who had deported Mexican workers. And he understood that she felt great shame for that. He had heard it in her voice. The suffering she had caused his people had found its way back to her. Such was the way of life.

He'd seen her kindness to him, her love for the old man who had lived in the house, her dislike of the *mayordomo*. He knew that whatever she'd done, she regretted it. But why did she say he must leave and find another job? She delivered the words with anger, but he knew they were born of fear. What was she afraid of? He put the cross back in his pocket.

Pasha snorted again and walked to the water trough. As Antonio watched him drink, he remembered the day he came to Regalo Grande. He jumped off the fence, moving into the pasture. He walked to the trough and bent down. There, on the lower edge of the trough, where he had set it on that day that seemed so long ago, was the flat rock. "*Muy bien*," she'd said to him then.

There is more than she has said. There is something else she is hiding from me.

He recalled how she had stormed away from him, almost running to the house. *God, You know I wanted to follow her and hold her and comfort her, but she is proud and did not want me to see her tears.*

He looked toward the house, then went out the pasture gate and walked aimlessly. His feet took him to the stream. *Each day I have trusted You, and You have never failed me. I love her. I know You have made her for me. But only You can gather us together.* He sat on one of the boulders, beside the still waters, and pulled his guitar to his chest.

He closed his eyes and listened, but no music came. He looked toward heaven. "If I tell her how I feel, will You make a way for her heart to hear me?"

Again he closed his eyes. Instead of music, the faith that

had sustained him his entire life surged within him, and he was once again standing before her as she handed him the guitar. . . . He could see her exquisite face, and as he looked into her eyes, the hills behind her faded and became an ocean. He was standing on the beach in a whirlwind, watching a single tear roll down her cheek and drop into the fire between them. The fire became a stream of water flowing under the oaks, and he heard her whisper, "Play for me," as she sat down and leaned against him.

Then the image of Angelica dissolved into his chest and became music. So beautiful was the sound that he could not move his fingers. And there, beneath the oaks, as the anointed music played for him, he received his answer.

"Tomorrow I will tell her I love her."

19

ANGELICA STARED AT her glass of orange juice. Talking to Brad last night hadn't helped. He couldn't understand why she was so upset by what had happened to Antonio's father. His insistence that she was "just doing her job" in New York only left her feeling that she and Brad were not on the same page . . . about anything.

She finished her orange juice and rinsed out her glass. That was breakfast now that Poppy was gone. She sat at the kitchen counter, picked up the phone, and punched in the number for her parents' hotel. The front desk put her through to their room.

Her father answered. "Angelica, we were just talking about you. We tried to return your call yesterday, but you didn't answer."

"I was in and out." Thoughts of the day before overwhelmed her. If only she could pour her heart out to them about what had happened. How she was hurting; how she'd hurt Antonio. But they'd never understand. She was in this alone. "Is there anything new on Thrombexx?"

"Not really." She heard the concern in his voice.

"Well, I have some news that might help take the pressure off. There's someone interested in buying the seventy-five acres you had surveyed."

"And?"

"Well, it might be a way to pay down the debt on the ranch. I wasn't sure you'd want to do it, but I think it makes sense."

The line was silent.

"It might. When I get home, we can talk more about it. But if the lien can't be paid in full, we'd just be delaying the inevitable."

"I know, but I have some other ideas that might help." She tried to sound optimistic. "For starters, I'm going to take the recorded map to Brighton Engineering this morning."

"Might as well get that out of the way. But what we really need is a miracle."

She gulped hard. Sitting in the kitchen, Poppy's apron hanging on a hook and the smell of fruit coming from the basket by the sink, she felt as if Poppy might walk through the door any minute. "Poppy believed in miracles. Remember what he said that last night, Dad? Whatever you ask in prayer, believing, you'll receive."

"Yes, I do, honey. He meant well."

"I miss him so much. But I'm glad he didn't have to see what has happened." Angelica's voice broke.

"We'll be home tomorrow, and we'll all go out to dinner."

"Love you." She hung up.

The clatter of the phone in its cradle seemed unnaturally loud in the silent, empty kitchen. A sense of isolating loneliness chilled her. Her heart ached. If only Poppy were here.

She stood and slowly walked to the apron hanging on the

hook by the refrigerator. She pressed her face into the crisp, white cotton, breathing in the faint smell of peppermint. Deep within her a shuddering began. As it rose, it shook her entire body. Clinging to the apron, she slid to the floor and surrendered to the deep, racking sobs that called out for Poppy.

Angelica washed her face with cool water and dressed. She walked to her bedroom window and looked down the drive. Antonio's back was to her as he crouched down, working on the stone wall. A faint *click*, *click* vibrated through the window, bringing to mind a summer evening not long ago and the sound of rocks thrown in a wheelbarrow. . . .

She turned away, wanting to forget the past, forget him.

She looked at her watch. 9:00. The title company should be open. She grabbed her coat and purse and set off to town. As she sped down the entry, she kept her eyes focused on the driveway until she was safely past the section of wall where she'd seen Antonio working.

First, she stopped at the title company and picked up the recorded map. Next, she drove it to Brighton so they'd have it as the development process continued.

Angelica approached the counter of the busy office. "Is Dick Brighton here?"

"Just a moment please." The secretary picked up one of the ringing lines. "The surveyors have already left."

She turned back to Angelica. "Yes, Miss. Who'd you want to see?"

"I'm Angelica Amante. I want to give Dick Brighton a map that's been recorded."

The phone rang. "Excuse me, sorry." The secretary picked

up another line. "Brighton Engineering." She smiled at Angelica as she listened. "The Foster file has been submitted to the county." She cradled the phone between her shoulder and her cheek as she reached for Angelica's map. "Hold please, I'll get the file." She turned to Angelica. "Did you want to leave this? I'll see that Dick gets it."

"I was hoping to talk to him for a few minutes."

"Let me take care of this call, and I'll tell him you're here." She looked at the clock. "He's got a meeting in about five minutes, but maybe he can see you before it starts."

Angelica stood, waiting. *The Foster file.* There was something familiar about that. *The Foster file. Brad. That was Brad's client!* Angelica grinned.

The secretary returned with the file in hand and picked up the phone. "Yes, sir. The file was amended two months ago when our tests showed that the forty lots at the bottom are in a slide area." She tapped her pencil, listening. "I don't know if the county was told about it. The Fosters' attorney is handling it." She waited for the caller to finish speaking. "If the county wasn't given the addendum and told of the slide area, then they would have approved the forty lots as buildable." She held the phone away from her ear. "That's above my pay scale. You'll have to talk to their attorney about that."

Angelica's grin faded. Brad had told her just a few weeks ago that the bottom lots were for low-income buyers. The slide area. So, it was good enough for the poor.

The secretary turned to Angelica. "Sorry, I'm the girl Friday, the receptionist and everything else around here." She glanced at the bank of phone lines. "I see Dick's on the phone now. As soon as he's off, I'll tell him you're here."

"I was just talking to someone the other day about the Foster development in Marin." Angelica blurted the words

323

out. "I thought they were going to have low-income housing on those bottom lots."

"Don't ask me. We've done our work and given the soils results to their attorney. What the attorney chooses to give the county to get the approval is up to him. That's why people hire slick attorneys. You know what I mean?" She winked at Angelica. "But if you want to talk to him about it, he'll be here any minute. He's Dick's next appointment."

Angelica heard the office door open behind her.

"Here he is now."

Angelica whirled around as Brad stepped into the office.

"Angelica. Hey, what a pleasant surprise." He strode toward her.

She handed the secretary the map. "Just give this to Dick please, and tell him I'll call him later."

Angelica brushed past Brad and out the door. So this was what Brad had meant when he said it hadn't been easy to get the file through. He'd said it would be a coup since he was the third attorney. Maybe the other two attorneys didn't have the silver tongue of a champion debater who could take either side of a given topic and win. But really, how hard was it to steal from the unsophisticated poor? It didn't take a degree from Hastings.

Angelica walked, then ran, to her car. Her blood boiled as her heart sank. She'd seen it before at Czervenka and Zergonos. A young attorney was given a tough case and the unspoken message—sink or swim. If he pulled it off, he'd be on his way up; otherwise, he'd be just one of the masses.

"Angelica. Angelica."

Brad grabbed her arm as she reached for the car door handle. "Angelica. What's wrong?"

She turned, facing him. Vignettes of their time together ran through her mind—college days, their engagement, their reunion, his comforting words. She had history with him. She started to speak, hesitated, then suddenly her mind was focused and clear.

"What's wrong is you and your blind ambition. I happened to overhear the secretary in there telling someone about the forty lots in that subdivision you've been so dedicated to getting approved so they could be sold. Forty lots that are in a slide area. But, hey, the attorney misplaced an addendum, and who's the wiser. Right, Brad? The developer gets the kudos and the money for providing low-income housing, he unloads worthless lots, and, God willing it doesn't rain, those poor, naive buyers have a place to live. Everybody wins."

Anger flashed across Brad's face. "What are you talking about? I'm just doing my job. You know that."

"Yeah, advocate for the client, regardless, right? Do what it takes to get to the top, even if you have to step on the backs of hardworking people to get there. Been there, done that, and it turns my stomach."

"You're overreacting. The chances of that area sliding are minuscule. The report says so. The property's barely outside the acceptable stability ranges. It'll be fine."

"It will never be fine. It isn't just about charts and approvals; it's about cheating people, deceiving the public. It's about financial profits and moral bankruptcy."

Angelica pulled open the car door, got in, and shoved the gear lever into reverse. As she drove home, she thought about Brad. He had everything going for him: bright, ambitious, driven. He knew how the game was played, and he was playing it. Angelica slowly shook her head. She parked in front of the hacienda.

As she walked down the hall from the front door, her footsteps echoed through the empty house. She put her purse and coat in the hall closet and went into the kitchen. She drank a glass of water, then sat at the counter, drumming her fingers on the cold tile. Brad hadn't changed. He was still the same guy she'd broken up with. But she'd changed. There would be no more compromises. She was going to follow her heart and go after the man she loved. Tell Antonio she loved him.

The thought of actually standing in front of him and telling him she loved him made her knees feel weak. She needed time to think. Taking a deep breath, she headed toward the stables. As she neared Pasha's pasture, she whistled.

"Hey, boy." She opened the gate, and he followed her to the stables. Slowly, methodically, she brushed him and cleaned his feet. Then she jumped up on his back, and he carried her up the hillside.

Her thoughts returned to the events of the past few weeks, the devastating news of the FDA's denial of Thrombexx, Poppy's death, the letter from Mexico, Brad, the ache in her heart.

It was a gray, overcast day. She leaned her head against Pasha's warm neck, enjoying the gentle, rocking motion as he climbed the hill. Maybe there was no God. Maybe it was just fate and luck. If you were working at the wrong place at the wrong time, you got deported. If you were born poor, you were doomed to stay that way, and you'd never experience any of the great things in life or make a difference in this world. Poppy always prayed God would show her His plan. "Well, Pash, this must be God's plan. Poppy's dead, my family's going under, and Antonio's family is starving. Poppy always talked about the power of the cross—God's love—a love stronger than death. If this is what God's love brings, I don't want it."

Pasha snorted, put his ears back, and turned his head to nip at her foot.

"What's the matter with you?" She sat up and slapped his neck. "I'm running my own show now. I'm going to get that public defender position and . . . I'm going after the man I love."

* * *

It was midafternoon by the time she got back to the house. She went to the kitchen and looked in the refrigerator, but she realized she felt empty, not hungry. She walked back to the hall. Poppy's door was open. She hadn't gone into the room since the day he died.

She stood at the door—everything was just as he'd left it. She stepped in and walked over to the bed where she had sat and talked to him just the week before. *Oh, Poppy, if I could only talk to you now. You'd know just what I should say to Antonio.* She drew an unsteady breath, trying to get ahold of herself.

She wandered to the table beside his bed. On it was a picture of the two of them. She picked it up. The middle-aged man in the photo stood on the front lawn, holding the reins of a pony, while the little girl sat proudly in the saddle. Even now, so many years later, she could remember that moment. This was her first horse. Poppy had saddled him up while her father and mother kept her busy at the breakfast table. She closed her eyes. How big the pony had seemed. Poppy lifted her up on him, and she held on to the saddle horn with both hands. Her father laughed, and her mother clapped her hands in delight. "Isn't she darling, Ben?"

Suddenly, there, just at the edge of the memory, was the smell of peppermint. Angelica opened her eyes and set the picture back down, careful to place it exactly where it had been.

Her eyes drifted to a picture frame hanging on the wall. She stepped in front of it. "The Color of Light," she read silently. Poppy's favorite poem. How he'd treasured its words. She read them slowly.

> The deep, exquisite, nameless blue of
> The infinite sky, crowning the earth.
> The teal tint of the vast, tranquil ocean
> Stretching farther than man can see,
> Deeper than man can fathom.
> The pine green of the Pacific Northwest
> That delights the eyes and feeds the souls
> Of those who travel there.
> The incandescent orange of fall leaves
> Covering the east coast as the sun
> Slowly arcs to the south.
> The dusty, obscure shade of taupe
> Veiling the Grand Canyon at dusk,
> Awing the mind of man.
> The gilded yellow of the morning sun
> Rising with mystical certainty.
> All from white light diffused
> Through a prism of unceasing love.
> The evidence of God's presence.
> The color of God's glory.

She wiped away the tears that were sliding down her cheeks. She could hear Poppy's voice as clearly as if he stood beside her: "Look, Miss Angel, how blue the sky today," and, "See over there. See those flowers? Them, growing by the pasture. God Himself, He put them there. Look how bright their color, Miss Angel. God, Himself, He there, you know."

If only it were true.

She walked over to Poppy's chair. The headrest was frayed, and the footstool cushion held the impression of the heels that had rested there so many times over the years. On the table next to it was his Bible. She walked over and picked it up, running her hand over the worn cover.

There would be no more firsts to capture in pictures, no more comforting, late-night talks, no more wisdom to make things right. She pressed the book to her chest. She didn't try to stop the tears that fell on her hands and arms as she held it.

She sat in Poppy's chair and opened the cover of the Bible. Tucked just inside were several pieces of paper and a booklet. She took the paper on top and carefully unfolded it. It was Poppy's prayer list. So many times she'd heard him speak of it. She'd always thought it was a mental list, but here it was. At the top, printed in the uncertain stroke of an immigrant, he had written, "Lord, keep my Eyes on You and use me." Underneath that was a simple statement, "Keep Your hand on President." She smiled at the random use of capitals.

She read on. "Teach Mr. Benito to pray, so he will know you," then, "Send Mrs. A. someone to name her sickness." That was the one thing, above all others, that Angelica had hoped would be answered.

Under that he'd written, "Use my Angel's plans for Your purpose." She stopped and closed her eyes. Her plans. Her failed plans. *No one can use my plans.*

He'd drawn a line through his last sentence, but she read it easily. "Send my Angel husband that Love Her with Your Love." And next to it he'd written, "Praise You Jesus for Mr Antonio."

Angelica got goose bumps on her arms. She began to laugh and cry at the same time. Poppy knew. He'd known before she did. It felt like she was receiving Poppy's blessing. She closed her eyes for a moment, clinging to the sense of being with him again. How she'd taken him for granted when he was alive. She'd give anything to put her arms around his neck just one more time.

She wiped the tears from her eyes. Poppy's prayers died with him. Now they were nothing more than words on a paper. She refolded the list and put it back in the Bible.

She took out the next piece of paper and opened it. Written in Poppy's hand was a statement: "I have no living relatives. I leave everything my God did give me to my angel, Angelica Amante."

She gasped. She read it again. Waves of emotion washed over her as she realized the depth of his love for her. She closed the Bible's cover and looked at it. This was probably his most prized possession. She ran her hand over it. She reached beneath the cover for the booklet.

The phone rang. She set everything down and ran to the kitchen to answer it. It was the Human Resource Department of Sierra County.

"I start the first?"

"Yes. Just come in to our office anytime next week. There are a few details to take care of before you start."

"Oh?"

"Just a formality—an affidavit stating that you are a citizen, have no criminal record, and don't have anybody working for you who's here illegally. It's a requirement we put in place because there are so many people who hire Mexicans to do child care and housework and never check on their status."

"I see." Her stomach churned. "Uh, fine. I'll be there." She hung up the phone.

She felt as though someone had punched her in the stomach. Just a formality . . . a formality that put her in an impossible situation. *People hire Mexicans and never check on their status*. She'd checked. At least she'd tried to. But she hadn't fired Antonio when she found out he didn't have papers. She just couldn't bring herself to do it.

None of that mattered now. He worked for her. She walked upstairs to her bedroom and sat on her window seat, staring across the valley.

A thought passed through her mind. He didn't work for her. Not really. He worked for her father. Her father was the one who paid him. Of course. That was the answer. She could sign an affidavit that stated she personally didn't employ any illegals.

"We must not only defend the letter of the law, we must never forget the intent of the law. . . ." The words of her valedictorian speech played back to her. "Twisting the truth was an ethical sophistication she knew she would never be able to defer to." That's what she'd thought when Constantine Czervenka fired her. That was the kind of thing dishonest, high-priced lawyers in New York did.

"God, why are You doing this to me?" She leaned into the window.

She watched Antonio working on the stone wall, patiently repairing the weak spots. She would tell him how she felt about him. They would talk about what had happened. They would work through it together.

There was a truck backing up the drive toward Antonio. She knitted her brows together. It was Chick's truck, with the camper top over the bed. The hairs on Angelica's neck stood up as she watched Chick get out.

Chick walked to the back of the camper and opened it, then motioned Antonio toward him. They seemed to be talking. Antonio looked toward her window.

"God, *no!*" Chick was pushing Antonio into the back of the camper. *Please, no. Just this one thing, God.*

She ran down the stairs and out the door. She could see the truck speeding down the drive.

"Stop. *Stop!*" She ran until she reached the street, far below. Her lungs were on fire as she stood looking at the empty street.

What curse was she under? She raised her face to the darkening sky. "What kind of God are You? He trusted You! He believed in You. But You punish his family and now You do this to him? I *hate* You."

Fighting for breath, she ran back to the house, tearing through the front door, down the hall to her father's office. She would call the police. She grabbed the phone and pressed 9–1 . . . She couldn't call the police. They would ask questions. They would find out Antonio didn't have papers. They would turn him over to Immigration.

She slammed the phone down. She had to do *something*— find him, help him. She grabbed her purse and keys, then ran out to her car and sped down the drive.

Antonio sat, bent over in the back of Chick's truck. Chick had told him he was meeting some men who would take him to a job in Texas. He'd said if Antonio didn't leave Regalo Grande, he would call Immigration and have him deported, and that would bring trouble to Angelica and her family.

Antonio put his cross back in his pocket, then tapped on the little window that separated the back from the front of the truck. Chick had let him walk around the truck earlier in the night. He'd been able to see they were parked in a hilly area, and he had heard a stream.

"Whada ya want?"

"I need to stand up."

Chick got out and opened the tailgate. Antonio jumped out into the darkness.

"You stay here. I'm going to duck into those trees over there. Don't get no ideas. If I tell Immigration the Amantes hired you, they'll go to jail for it." Chick's lip curled. "You go anywhere, that's the first thing I'm gonna do. I'd like to see how Miss Priss would make out in jail." Chick left Antonio standing by the truck.

Antonio watched Chick walk into the trees. He'd been thinking about what Chick had told him. At the ranch, he'd thought that by going with the man he would save Angelica and her family from trouble, but Chick kept talking about how he could call Immigration any time. That meant he could call Immigration after Antonio was in Texas, still causing Angelica problems.

Antonio scanned the area around him, trying to get his bearings. He did not want to bring trouble to anyone. It was wrong for Angelica's family to suffer because of him. They had not known he didn't have papers. He needed to face Immigration himself. Tell the *officiales* that it was his fault and that punishment should be his alone.

He had been thinking about it for the hours he'd been in the truck. And he knew what he was going to do. A cloud passed over the face of the moon, casting a dark shadow over the truck.

He looked toward the place where Chick had gone. There was no sound. He bent down by the back tire, on the far side of the truck. It was so dark he had to feel for the metal stem. Then he did what he'd seen Chick do in the gas station. He heard the air going out of the tire. He watched for Chick as the tire went flat. He moved to the front tire and did the same thing.

"Hey, Paco. Where are you?"

Antonio stepped from the shadows.

Chick snickered. "Didn't think you'd be stupid enough to run off."

Stupid. How many times had he heard that in his life? How many times had he heard it from Chick? "Stupid Mexican" he called him, and sometimes Chick followed it with spit. Anger filled him. He knotted his fist and pulled it back.

Antonio's punch knocked Chick backward. As Chick struggled to get up, Antonio turned on his heel and strode away. As the distance from the truck widened, Chick's curses followed him. A vow to kill him. Then—a gunshot. He dropped to the ground and scrambled behind an outcropping.

Antonio crouched in the darkness, watching, listening. Minutes passed. He didn't hear anything. He started to run, keeping his head down. Headlights. Another truck.

He had to get away. Now there were more men. If they caught him, they would kill him. He fingered the cross in his pocket. With the darkness protecting him, he made his way through the trees, running until he was certain no one followed him.

A wind had begun to blow, clearing the sky, allowing the moon to show its light. He slowed his pace, then stopped. The night sky and the mountains that framed it were a God-given map. Many nights on the ranch he had studied them. He found his markers and started in the direction of the ranch. He would return to Angelica. He would have her call Immigration, and he would tell them the truth. He would remove any chance that she or her family might suffer for his actions. If it meant he would be deported, then . . . he would see his family soon.

Antonio came to a clearing and a bridge. He knew this place. He had crossed the bridge before. It led to Lo Bianco—and in the other direction, to Angelica. He looked toward Lo Bianco. In the distance, he could see headlights, coming directly at him. He glanced heavenward, at the moon and the stars, then ducked under the bridge. *Dios, light a path for my feet. I must return to Angelica.*

———

The rising sun lit the trees outside the window. Angelica looked at her watch, again. It was after seven.

She'd driven around most of the night. First she'd gone to Lo Bianco, but no one had seen Chick. Then she'd driven to the bus station, then down back roads and around the mountain roads. But there hadn't been a trace of Chick, or the truck. As the night wore on, her hope of finding Antonio faded. Finally, she'd returned home and stationed herself in her window seat, watching the drive, drifting in and out of an uneasy sleep.

Now, with the new day, came the crushing certainty—Antonio was gone. Everything that had happened in the last weeks rolled over her. Her grief was beyond tears. She was dead inside—without hope—without God.

Bereft and broken, she stood and faced the window. From a place of spiritual poverty and hunger and nothingness and want, she whispered, "Help me."

Suddenly, the autumn valley that stretched before her became a living thing. It seemed that every leaf on every tree stood out with brilliant distinction. Every wildflower, every blade of grass, though miles away, seemed imbued with color so intense it transcended the physical world, revealing spiritual truth. God was with her. He knew her, and He loved her. He was revealing Himself to her in this present age, as He had once revealed Himself to the world in Jesus Christ. The truth became Spirit, and she was filled.

She kneeled down, shaken but unafraid. She closed her eyes and surrendered her new life to the God who hears and answers prayers.

Minutes passed before she felt strong enough to rise. Using the windowsill as a support, she stood and looked across the drive to the valley, now only a carpet of muted colors.

Her eyes drifted to the gates. A man was walking on the side of the drive. "Antonio!"

She turned and ran down the stairs and out the door, shouting with joy. "Antonio!"

She fell in the entry, cutting her leg and tearing her pants. She didn't care. She got up, running and stumbling down the drive.

As he approached the gates of Regalo Grande, Antonio ended his silent prayers for Angelica. *And forgive me for the trouble I have caused and the wrong I have done.* He put his cross in his pocket. He took a deep breath and raised his head.

Angelica was running toward him. He took her in his arms. *Dios, please don't take her from me.*

He whispered into her hair, "I love you, Angelica." He could feel her trembling.

He tried to step back to look at her beautiful face, but she would not let him go. She pressed into him, then reached for his hand, pulling it to her lips. She kissed his fingers.

The sound of tires on gravel broke their embrace. A car engine shut off directly behind them. They turned. Immigration.

The *officiale* stepped from the car. The man asked him something in English. When he didn't answer, the man spoke to him in Spanish. "I asked you if this is your wife."

336

"No." He could feel Angelica's hand gripping his. She spoke to the man.

The *officiale* looked at Antonio. "What's your name?"

"Antonio Perez." The man's hand was resting on his gun.

"Can I see your papers?"

"I have no papers, sir." He saw handcuffs on the man's belt.

Angelica began to talk.

"She says that you've been working for her and that she's tried to find out how to get you papers."

"It's true. But I told her I had papers when I first came here. It's not her fault."

Angelica spoke to the *officiale* again.

He repeated his answer in Spanish. "There's no way for you to get papers when you've come here illegally, unless you have a relative who is here legally. Do you?"

Antonio shook his head.

The man spoke to Angelica, then spoke to Antonio. "When I drove up here, it seemed to me that you were more than just somebody who happened to work here." He waited for an answer, then continued. "But you say she's not your wife."

"No, she's not my wife, yet." He looked at her. How he longed to say it was true, that this was his wife.

"In the eyes of the law, your wife is considered a relative. If she was your wife, you would have legal status—temporarily. You'd still have to go back to Mexico and reenter, but you wouldn't be deported." The man folded his arms across his chest, observing them.

Antonio studied his face, the slight wrinkling around the eyes, the relaxed mouth, something in his voice that signaled things could be made right. The man was offering him a way out.

He couldn't take it. It wouldn't be right. This was not how it should be. He had not talked to her father, and more than that, he had never talked to Angelica about his feelings . . . about her feelings.

Beyond the *officiale*, drawing his eye, stretched the valley, peacefully resting between the mountains, as God had ordained it. Reminding Antonio, God's purposes and plans are assured. Time seemed to slow, as a certainty began to fill him, all that had happened had been by divine plan. This was a love ordained, a sacred trust. He would ask her to marry him—but not now, not like this. He would wait until he was sure this was what *she* wanted. He turned and faced her.

"Marry me, Antonio." Angelica's voice was breathless. "Say yes. Say *sí*." She jumped into his arms, her kiss telling him how sure she was.

The slamming of the car door brought them back to the present.

The *officiale* rolled down the window. "Young man, I'm going to be back up here next week. I hope I find that you're here legally." He rolled up his window and backed down the drive.

Angelica turned to Antonio and clapped her hands together. "We'll get married Monday. Married *lunas*."

With one hand, he easily captured both of hers, then put his forefinger gently on her lips. "No, *señorita*. *Primero*, I talk to *su papá*."

"Why?" She pulled back and put her hands on her hips.

He smiled. Such a strong woman, his Angelica. "*Respeto a* your *papá*."

She stared at him for a few moments, then kissed him again.

They walked hand in hand up the drive. The wind danced through the grasses around them. The cloudless, blue sky was above them, and the sun's light wove like tongues of fire through the brilliant, fall leaves of the trees, reflecting incandescent color all around them. He pulled her close to him.

Angelica and Antonio had cleaned up and were waiting at the living room window when the Lincoln turned into the drive.

Angelica squeezed Antonio's hand. "I wish I'd had time to prepare them, but I guess now is as good a time as any to introduce the man I want to spend the rest of my life with."

As they approached the house, Angelica saw her parents had caught sight of them. The shocked look on her parents' faces did nothing to ease the situation. She opened the door for them.

"What's this about?" Her father's words were terse. Her mother leaned heavily on her father, her face flushed and feverish.

Angelica tried to remain calm. "Let's sit down."

They followed her parents into the living room.

Her father guided her mother to the couch. Antonio stepped forward to help, but Benito stepped in front of him, cutting him off.

"Never mind."

Antonio moved back and stood. He studied her mother, his face showed no emotion.

"I'm sorry you're not feeling well again, Mom." Angelica stepped next to Antonio.

"I'd gladly suffer with this virus if it would bring my daughter back."

"Mom, don't talk like that. Let me explain."

The front door creaked.

"Angelica, go shut the door," her father snapped.

Before she could get to it, the door blew wide open, and the sound of water flowing through the fountain reached their ears.

Antonio tilted his head. The wind, the fountain, flowing water splashing on rocks, the stream under the oaks, one thought led to another. *The tick*. He'd seen it under the oaks that first day at the stream. And he'd seen the illness it caused in Mexico. He turned his focus to the *señora*. He thought about the pattern of the illness, the weeks he had moved her in the wheelchair, and the days he'd seen her walking. His eyes searched the exposed skin of her arms, neck, and legs. He didn't see the circular rash that was always a certain sign of the sickness. Still, he knew the illness lingered long after the rash was gone.

"*Una garrapata.*"

Angelica was walking back into the living room. "What'd you say, Antonio?"

"Mother sick. *Una garrapata.*"

"I don't know that word. Uh, *no sabe la palabra.*"

"I see. Mexico."

"Really, Angelica. This shows how ridiculous this whole thing is. You two can't even communicate, yet you're standing here with him as if he belonged in the house."

"Wait, Dad." Angelica ran from the room and up the stairs to her bedroom. She grabbed the Spanish dictionary off her desk, then raced back to the living room.

340

"G-A. G-A-R. Here it is, *garr-a-pat-a*. Tick. He's saying tick. He's saying she's sick from a tick."

"Angelica, she's seen the best doctors in the country. She's been tested for everything, including Lyme disease. We've been questioned about that a couple of times throughout this ordeal. Not to mention the fact we've never seen any ticks around here, nor has there ever been a case in our area."

Angelica turned to Antonio. "*No es posible.* No *garrapatas* here."

Antonio walked to the window and pointed to the oaks. "I see."

Her father slowly rose from the couch. "What's he saying?"

"He's saying that he saw a tick down by the oaks."

"Ask him if he could be mistaken." Her father's voice softened.

"*Positivo?*" Angelica held her breath.

"*Sí, positivo.* I kill." He pressed his forefinger and thumb together.

Angelica looked at her father.

Her mother burst into tears. "I couldn't bear to get my hopes up, then find out it was for nothing."

"Mother, it's possible Antonio's right. People get sick in Mexico, and they have to treat themselves. They don't have access to doctors and hospitals and medicine like we do. It's very possible people in his village have had this sickness."

"He's nobody. How could he know anything about diseases or ticks? How could he know something the best doctors in the country couldn't find out?"

"I'm calling Ralph." Her father turned and walked to his office. Angelica followed him.

Her father's hands were shaking as he made the call. "Is Dr. Miller there?" He tapped his foot. "Tell him it's Ben

341

Amante and I may have some important information about my wife's illness." He hung up the phone.

"Do you think it's possible, Dad?"

"No."

"Ben." They could hear her mother calling. "What's going on?"

Angelica and her father returned to the living room.

"I've left a message for him to call, dear. I'm sure he will as soon as he can. Now, Antonio, I think it would be best if you left us alone." Her father gestured to the door, then folded his arms across his chest.

Silence settled over the room.

Antonio stepped toward her father and stood in front of him, meeting his cold stare with quiet confidence. "*Permíteme, señor.*" Surprise and anger flashed across her father's face. Antonio's voice didn't waver. "I love her."

Angelica's mother struggled to her feet. "Make him leave, Ben. Don't let him say things like that. He's trying to ruin Angelica's life."

"Mother, that's ridiculous. He loves me . . . and I love him."

Her mother froze, her mouth open. She sank into the couch, slowly shaking her head. Angelica looked to her father, his mouth a thin line as he stared at Antonio.

Finally her mother spoke, her voice a whisper. "Why would you throw your life away? Everything we've worked for. He has nothing to offer you. You'll never have anything. You'll never be anybody."

"You're right, Mother. I'll never have anything but unconditional love, support, and loyalty. I'll never have to be anybody but who I am."

"Angelica, what's the matter with you? First you quit your job over some perceived injustice, and now you get involved with someone completely below your class. And listen to how you're talking to your mother. You've never been disrespectful. Is this what we can expect now that you've decided *he* should be part of our family? Look at the turmoil he's causing."

Antonio turned to Angelica and put his forefinger gently on her lips. "Shhh." Then he turned to her father. "*Señor. No es necesario*, this talk. You understand."

"I don't know what you're talking about. I don't understand any of this."

"You understand, *señor. Dios* give." He touched his fingers to his heart. "*Dios* put here. *Es un regalo. Es un regalo grande.*"

Angelica's eyes filled with tears at the beautiful simplicity of his words—words that meant so much to her. They embodied not only her father's love for her but the entire family dynamic.

For a moment, her father said nothing. Then, with grudging respect, he spoke. "What could you know about me or my ranch?"

Angelica took Antonio's hand and stepped beside him. "He knows lots of things, Dad. You'll see. Give him a chance."

The phone rang. A mix of fear and hope filled her father's face. "That could be Ralph returning my call." Her father rushed to his office.

343

20

ANGELICA TURNED OVER and looked at the clock beside her bed. 4:20 a.m., only ten minutes since the last time she'd looked. She got up and walked to her window seat and sat down.

Too much had been said. After the doctor had called and told them a false negative was possible, especially if a tick had been found on the ranch, her father had driven her mother to the clinic so she could give a blood sample. When they'd returned, their discussion had started all over again. This time, without Antonio.

It had only been a few hours since she and her parents had decided to call it a night. She had underestimated their opposition to her decision to marry Antonio. Explaining his legal status and all the rest of it only added fuel to the fire. "We'll just have to agree to disagree." That's how her father had dismissed her. It seemed like nothing she said could make them see Antonio as the hardworking, caring, godly man she loved and was going to marry.

"Lord, You and I are in this together. I know Antonio

is the man You have for me to marry, but my parents say they'll never accept him. My family will never be healed unless this is of You."

A breeze blew through the open window. The cool night air chilled her. She stood and leaned out to close the window. *Creak. Bang.* She looked out toward the barn, listening. Her eyes scanned the shadowy buildings. *Creak. Bang.* Pasha's gate. She must not have shut it all the way when she'd put him up after riding the night before.

She grabbed her jeans and a sweater, put them on, and took off for the pasture. Pasha wouldn't go anywhere, but he knew where the alfalfa was kept. A smile tugged at her lips. He'd done that before, gotten into the hay barn and made a mess. When he'd seen her coming, he'd taken off, tearing around the ranch with his tail up, snorting, daring her to catch him. She couldn't. Finally, he'd convinced her to make up with him, and she'd lured him back to his pasture with a carrot, a peace offering he grudgingly accepted.

She called into the night. "Pasha. Hey, Pash." She stopped, listening. She approached his pasture. The gate was wide open. "Pasha . . . Pasha."

Angelica jogged to the barn and switched on the flood-lights. Nothing. She turned to head for the stables, then stopped. The grain barrel, where the rich, "hot" grain for the horses was kept, was knocked over, grain scattered everywhere. "No. No. No." She took off at a run for the stables.

As she neared the paddocks, she saw her horse pawing the ground, turning his head and biting at his flank. "Pasha. Pasha."

As she neared him, he dropped down and began to roll, turning over on his back, then to his side, his hooves com-

345

ing dangerously close to the paddock rails as he rolled back and forth.

Angelica rushed to her horse. His flailing legs knocked her down. Scrambling out of the way, she turned her ankle and fell, hitting the side of her face on a rock. She tasted blood on her lips.

Colic. In all her years on the ranch, she'd only seen a horse act this way once before, and it had been fatal. Seconds counted now. She had to call a vet. She had to get Pasha help.

She struggled to stand. Suddenly, she was being lifted. "Antonio."

"I hear you. I see." He pointed to Pasha. "*Médico*, now. *Es importante*. Now."

Angelica began to tremble. The urgency in his voice and the concern on his face frightened her. "Don't let him die," she pleaded.

Antonio took her by the shoulders. "Go. Now." The feel of his firm, steady grip pressing through her sweater strengthened her. She ran to the tack room.

The phone book. Where was the phone book? She grabbed the phone and dialed information.

"The number for Dr. Jim Williams. This is an emergency." She wrote the number on the wall by the phone, shaking so badly that she could hardly hold the pencil.

"Dr. Williams' answering service."

"This is an emergency. You must reach him."

"Calm down. Give me your name and number. The doctor is out of town. Dr. Burns is on call. I'll try to reach him immediately."

Angelica's heart sank. The ranch would be hard to find if the doctor didn't know where it was along the road that wound up the mountain. "This is Angelica Amante. 555-

346

9468. I think my horse has colic. I'm at Regalo Grande on Sonoma Mountain."

"The doctor will call you as soon as he gets this message."

"Please hurry." She hung up the phone.

"What's going on?" The voice came from behind her. "I couldn't sleep, and I went to the kitchen for some water. I saw the lights on down by the barn."

"Dad." He stood looking at her, in his plaid pajamas and blue bathrobe. She ran into his arms. "Pasha's sick, and Jim's out of town. Some other vet is supposed to call me back." She clung to her father. "Can you do something? Don't let him die."

"Where is Pasha now?"

"He's by the paddocks. But we can't leave the phone. The vet's supposed to call."

Her father picked up the phone and called the house. "Gen, honey, Angelica says Pasha's sick and she's called the vet. I'm going to forward this phone to you. When the vet calls, give him directions." He hung up, then keyed in the forwarding code. He followed Angelica out to the paddocks.

Angelica stopped as they neared the paddocks. Antonio had a sheet tied to the paddock post and had managed to get it under the sick horse that now lay on his side. Standing, facing Pasha, the free end of the sheet looped behind his neck and gripped in his hand, he'd formed a makeshift sling. He whispered quietly to Pasha, then clucked.

Antonio took a deep breath and leaned backward, pulling the sheet taut, lifting the horse. Pasha turned, trying to get his legs under him. Again and again Antonio tried to help the horse stand. Finally, he stopped and bowed his head, as though speaking to an invisible partner. Angelica's father started forward.

347

Bending his neck back, raising his face to the night sky, Antonio leaned against the sheet with everything he had. And with a final Herculean effort, Pasha struggled up.

Angelica's father rushed to his side. "Let me help you."

"*Sí, señor*. Help." He motioned her father to Pasha's other side.

Her father stood looking at him across Pasha's back. "What do I do now?" he asked, palms up.

Antonio bent down and reached under the horse's belly, wiggling his fingers. "*Señor*. Down."

Her father bent over and could see that Antonio wanted him to grab his hands. They interlocked their arms, and he followed Antonio's lead as he thrust upward.

"I hope he knows what he's doing, Angelica."

"Have some faith in him, Dad. I just thank God somebody's here who knows what to do."

They repeated the thrusting motion every few seconds for several minutes.

"While you guys do that, I'm going to go get a halter and lead."

When Angelica returned, Antonio dropped his hands, took the halter, and put it on Pasha. He stepped beside the horse's stomach and put his ear to the horse's side.

He stood. "*Nada*."

"What's he doing, Angelica?"

"I'm not sure. But he's saying he doesn't hear anything when he listens to Pasha's side."

"What does that mean?"

"I'm not sure—" She was interrupted by the sound of tires on gravel.

"Maybe that's the vet."

The vehicle stopped, its headlights illuminating the scene.

They all looked toward the lights. "Dr. Burns?" Angelica called out.

"No, it's Mom. The vet is on his way. What's happened?"

"Pasha got out and ate the grain in the barn. He's so sick." She broke down. "Mom, I couldn't bear it if he died."

Antonio stepped to her and pulled her into his arms. "Shhh, *mi amor.*" He pressed her into his chest, holding her as she sobbed, and whispered to her, "No worry. He live."

He said it with such conviction that Angelica stepped away from him and looked into his face. But his eyes were on her parents; his face was filled with compassion. It struck her that he knew how helpless and frightened her parents were at this moment, when she needed them most. It was as if he worked to save the horse not just for her, but for them too.

Her father's face was a mix of fear and hope. "Whatever you can do, we'd appreciate it."

Antonio looked at her mother. Her mother's eyes were filled with tears. She averted her gaze and looked at the ground.

Antonio reached out and put a hand on her shoulder. "No cry, *señora.*" Her mother lifted her head and looked up into the compassionate face of the young man who comforted her.

Antonio reached into his pocket, then pressed the horseshoe cross into Angelica's hand. "*Dios. Es importante.*" Then he went to Pasha and gently urged the horse to walk.

"I'll get him some water," Angelica called to Antonio.

"No water."

Up and down the roadway, Antonio walked the horse, patiently urging him on, then letting him rest. The Amantes

349

sat on a bale of hay outside the barn, watching them. As dawn broke, the vet arrived.

Antonio brought the horse to him. Angelica and her parents waited for the vet's opinion.

"Well?" her father addressed the vet when he finished his examination.

"I'd say it *was* a case of colic. I don't think there's any doubt it could have killed him. Time is of the essence in a case like this. It's rare we find owners with enough knowledge to do what's necessary in the early stages to save the horse's life. They usually try to keep their horses lying down and give them water. That can be fatal." He looked around at the facilities. "Looks like you've got quite a setup here. I guess you've dealt with this from time to time."

"Not really. We don't have a ranch manager right now, and my wife and daughter and I really aren't involved with the day-to-day care of the horses. It was this young man here who took over." He gestured toward Antonio, who stood with his arm around Angelica's shoulders.

"Well, I'd say you've got someone who's more than capable of taking care of your horses." The vet reached out and shook Antonio's hand. "Maybe you've got a ranch manager and just didn't know it. He's somebody I wouldn't mind having work for me." He winked at her father. "Just continue to walk the horse, and keep him out of the grain. Bye now." He turned and went to his truck.

Angelica's mother took her father's hand. "You know, Ben, he might make a good manager if he got some tutoring and learned the language."

Angelica's father looked at Angelica, her head resting against Antonio's shoulder, the cross still clutched in her hand. "Yes, he might. And I don't think he'll have any trouble finding a tutor."

Angelica turned and faced Antonio. "I thought there was no *earthly* way this could work out." Still holding the cross, she pressed her hand into his. "I was right." She stood on her tiptoes and kissed him.

Angelica's mother pulled her jacket tight. "That breeze from the valley is chilly. Come on, Ben, let's get up to the house and make us all some coffee. I'm exhausted."

Angelica poured her father and Antonio another cup of coffee. "Dad, you and I need to sit down with your files and figure out what we're going to do this week about the loans."

"At this point, I think it's pretty clear. There's nothing to be done but to start trying to sell some of our assets." Her mother rested her hand on his arm.

Angelica couldn't help but notice the physical toll the crisis had taken on her father. He'd lost weight and aged dramatically. "I called those leads on the vineyard property from Brighton. I've left messages."

"I'm glad. But how many months will it take to put a deal together? I doubt we'll be able to save anything." The flat tone of his voice told her he'd resigned himself to the worst-case scenario.

"Dad, I'm not going to accept that. I'm going to pray with all my heart and work with all my might. If Poppy were here, he'd say, 'It all going to work out.'"

Her father and mother looked at her with surprise. Finally, her father asked, "Since when did you start quoting Poppy?"

Angelica thought a moment, then looked at Antonio. "Since I found out about Poppy's God. I found out He knows who I am, and He loves me."

"And?" her mother added, as if there were more.

"And He wants me to trust Him."

Her father raised his eyebrows. "I guess that's a good plan as long as you're working with all your might." He gave her a tentative smile. "Your mom and I have some work to do ourselves." He rose, then helped her mother get up. "We haven't unpacked a thing."

"Go on. Antonio and I will clean this up."

When her parents had left the kitchen, Angelica turned to Antonio and took his hand. "Can you believe it? We're going to get married tomorrow. *Matrimonio mañana.*"

He gave her an irresistible grin, which she promptly kissed. "And you know what else?"

"*Que, señorita?*"

"Oh, I won't be a *señorita* then." She stuck her tongue out at him. Surely he was not going to insist on calling her *señorita* after they were married. "I'll be a *señora*. And I'll drive right over to Sierra County Human Resource Department and sign a 'formality' that says nobody's working for me who's here illegally."

She could tell he hadn't understood a thing she said, but it was clear that he thoroughly enjoyed watching her say it.

Suddenly, his face grew serious. He dug in his pocket and pulled out his cross. He took her hand in his and pressed it into her palm. "Marry me."

She sat for a moment. The full impact of what he was doing revealed itself. He was asking her to marry him on his terms. She closed her hand around the cross. He was letting her know God would be the foundation of their marriage and their relationship would have spiritual order. It touched her deeply, this was the way it should be. "I will."

Tomorrow he would be her husband. She couldn't believe how lucky she was.

"Poppy's Bible." Angelica jumped up. "I don't want to forget to take it tomorrow. He must have told me a hundred times over the years that he wanted me to use it when I got married." She giggled. "I don't think he was thinking I'd be getting married at the courthouse though. But it wouldn't matter to him one bit." She grabbed Antonio's hand. "Come with me. It's in his room."

As they walked in, there seemed to be a brightness to the room that Angelica hadn't noticed before. It was hard to believe how much had happened since the last time she'd been here. She pointed to the table beside Poppy's chair. "There it is." She opened the cover and took the papers out. "We'll leave these things here." She looked around the room. "Is there a door or a window open? I feel cool air." The window was shut. She rubbed her arms.

She turned back to the papers, glancing through them. "His prayer list. His will. A passbook." She set the other papers down and opened it. "Antonio, Poppy must have had savings. He never said anything about it." She opened it.

There were pages of various amounts: one hundred dollars, five hundred, three hundred. . . . In December and on Poppy's birthday, they saw entries that equaled the bonuses he'd received. 1955 . . . 1960 . . . 1965 . . . 1970 . . .1975 . . . all through the years the entries continued. In the 1990s, there were several big deposits with the letters S-t-k beside them. Stock!

The last entry, made the week before his death, was for four hundred dollars. Angelica looked at the "Total" column and her eyes widened. $937,628.34.

She turned to Antonio, stunned. "Look. Poppy . . . money . . . bank."

He looked where she was pointing. "*Mucho dinero.*"

She dropped the book and threw her arms around Antonio. "It *is* all going to work out. We'll be able to help my parents, and yours too." She stepped back. "I'll be able to work as a public defender and then open my own office someday."

The look on his face told her he didn't understand much of what she was saying. But the look in his eyes told her that he too was realizing every dream *he'd* ever had. He pulled her to him. They kissed.

Surrounded by his protective arms, secure and warm, the things of the world did not exist. There was nothing but the moment, the beat of Antonio's heart, and the gentle breeze that filled the room—the winds of Sonoma, carried on the wings of a legion of angels, arching over them, joining heaven and earth.

Epilogue

Four Months Later
Guadalajara, Mexico

She laid wood on the fire, banking it for the night. She sat down near the heat of the flames and pulled the letter from her pocket. She held it tenderly, then gently opened it, smoothing the worn paper on her skirt.

Soon her oldest son would be coming home. God had given the boy favor when he'd left his family the summer before, leading him to a job at a big ranch in California. Each month he'd sent money, and sometimes there was a line or two with it, saying he was well.

Now this letter had come. He'd been given an important position at the ranch, *mayordomo*. And he was married. She ran her fingers over the letters where the missionary had shown her the woman's name. A-n-g-e-l-i-c-a. What was she like? Was she the daughter of one of the other workers? The

355

letter said he might be able to bring her to visit as soon as the *señorita*'s mother recovered from a tick bite.

She ran her finger over the blue marks and jots of the last word on the page.

A-n-t-o-n-i-o. The letter said he had made them. She took a deep breath, sitting straighter, lifting her chin.

She pressed his name to her lips and kissed it. How she had missed him. Tears came to her eyes as she remembered those moments over the many months, when fear pricked at her, planting dark possibilities in her mind. She had prayed every night by the fire that no harm would come to her child.

Now, he was married. Her son was coming home, bringing his bride to meet her. The night breeze fanned the flames, sending a cloak of warm air around her. She struggled to her knees on the rocky dirt, then bowed her head and thanked the God who hears and answers prayers.

AUTHOR'S NOTE

I HOPE YOU HAVE enjoyed the story you just read. It was inspired by a true story, my story. I married Antonio Perez Arana thirty years ago.

We now have two grown sons and live in Coeur d'Alene, Idaho, where I work as a real estate broker. My parents moved here shortly after we did. And I must let you know, despite what you've read, they adore Antonio.

The question I am most often asked is: does Antonio really play the guitar? I have to answer, not the way it's portrayed in the book. The guitar music is a symbol of Antonio's love for Angelica. And in that way, I hear the music whenever I am with him. While writing this book, I had hoped to find someone who played classical guitar who could work with me on a CD that would set some of the scenes to music.

Others wonder about the supernatural events: is there really a whispering wind and a Spirit who hovers over those who believe, becoming light, revealing truth? I can only tell you that God has a plan for every life. He revealed His plan for me when I met Antonio cleaning the stalls at my parents' ranch in the Sonoma Mountains. And each step of the way, through the joys and sorrows of life, God's Spirit has affirmed to me He is the God of love and power and purpose. A God who hears and answers prayers.

You can learn more about our journey together, and the Regalo Grande series, by visiting my website at www .nikkiarana.com, or you can write to me at P.O. Box 3781, Coeur d'Alene, ID 83816.

ACKNOWLEDGMENTS

Jesus said, "Therefore pray the Lord of the harvest to send out laborers into His harvest."

And so I began to pray when I first realized God was calling me to write this book. Praise God for His faithfulness. The laborers He sent were many.

The first to step forward were prayer warriors. Praying without ceasing that God would bring forth the book of His heart. Thank you for your unfailing commitment, Tex Gaynos, Glenn and Donna Wimer, Marvin and Pat Miller, and Renae Moore.

Equally committed, supportive, prayerful, and discerning is my agent, Natasha Kern, who continually called me to a higher standard. There isn't a doubt in my mind that God's hand was in our meeting. I love her like a sister and hold her just as close.

I extend a heartfelt thanks to Jennifer Leep, who is responsible for this book being published. Also, Eva Shaw, who was the first to encourage me to submit my work for publication, and Carol Craig, my editor, who worked tirelessly late into the night, so many nights, to help me craft my story.

I want to express my sincere and deep appreciation to Brandilyn Collins, Kathleen Miller, and Bonnie Allan, who were there for me from the beginning. Giving freely of themselves and asking nothing in return.

A special thanks to my parents, Col. and Mrs. Nicolaus Gaynos, my brother, Scott, family, and friends, who waited breathlessly for each page to be written. And most especially to my husband, who inspired this story.

Above all else, I am profoundly grateful as I look unto Jesus, the author and finisher of my faith; who for the joy that was set before Him endured the cross, despising the shame, and is set down at the right hand of the throne of God.

Coming This Spring

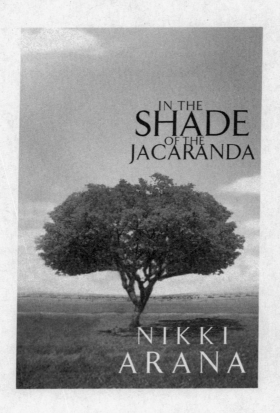

IN THE
SHADE
OF THE
JACARANDA

NIKKI
ARANA

1

Aₙɢᴇʟɪᴄᴀ Aᴍᴀɴᴛᴇ Pᴇʀᴇᴢ looked at her watch again. Thirty seconds had passed. The next two and a half minutes could change her life forever.

She walked to the living room, staring at the plastic stick from the pregnancy test kit, her heart racing. One minute had passed. No line. No red line to stamp across their lives, canceling everything they'd worked toward.

She laid the plastic stick on the coffee table and walked to the large window that faced the street of the little subdivision. The roses her husband had planted to climb the archway framing the small entry to their home in Valle de Lagrimas were in full bloom. She could see the pruning shears half hidden at the base of the arch. Since the day the bush had first bloomed, Antonio had never failed to rise before she awoke, cut a rose, and put it on the little table next to her side of the bed. It was often the first thing she saw when she opened her eyes. He loved her with a purity and devotion the first year of marriage had only deepened. She thanked God every day for the man He had brought into her life. Angelica walked back to the couch.

The sound of the phone ringing jarred her. *Mother*. She hadn't returned either of the calls that her mother had left at her work the day before. She put her hands over her ears. If only she'd turned the answering machine on before she'd started the test.

She counted the rings. If she didn't answer, and the machine didn't pick up, her mother would show up on her doorstep in twenty minutes. . . . She ran to the kitchen.

Mixed emotions surged through her. "Hi, Mom."

Her parents didn't understand why she'd chosen to marry Antonio instead of the bright, young attorney who'd pursued her. Even now, after almost a year and a half, they still didn't accept him. Thankfully, they kept their thoughts to themselves when he was present, but she'd heard the rude comments of others who moved in their circle—how the Mexican was lucky to marry the only daughter of the wealthy heart surgeon Benito Amante. Angelica knew the truth. She was the lucky one. What Antonio gave her, money couldn't buy. A rock solid partner. A man of honesty and honor. A man who understood her . . . a man who loved her. He didn't deserve their ignorant judgments, but the arrival of a baby would surely lead some to whisper how Antonio had trapped her and managed to tie himself to her family forever.

"Angelica, I was getting worried. Didn't you get my messages?"

"Just a second, Buddy's barking to get in." Angelica stepped to the glass slider and pulled it open. The tricolored sheltie looked at her, waiting for permission. "Hurry up." She nearly caught his tail in the door as she slammed it shut. Taking a deep breath, she returned to the phone.

"Sorry. I should've returned your call. But I haven't had a free moment since we got back from Mexico." Angelica turned, leaning her back against the counter, her eyes taking in the big kitchen. The down payment on the house had been a wedding gift. At least that's the way her parents had presented it. It was really their way of reminding her she was still a white, upperclass Amante, even though she'd married a Mexican. Reminding her appearances mattered. Reminding her that somehow their love for her was tied to her meeting *their* expectations for her life. She was their only child—born years after they'd been told her mother couldn't have children. It was almost as if, after waiting all those years, they wanted what was due them.

Antonio had recognized the gift for what it was and refused to accept it. He was determined they would make their own way. Angelica agreed with her husband. His wisdom and integrity were the very things that had drawn her to him, but she also loved her parents and knew it had hurt them when she'd married. Finally, to keep peace, Antonio had agreed to accept the money, not as a gift, but as a loan. The difficult compromise between her proud husband and her demanding parents had left both parties dissatisfied. It had also left her to figure out how to make the payments until Antonio's business created income. She clenched her jaw.

And now this. A possible pregnancy. She hadn't breathed a word of her fears to her mother. It would only upset her. Instead of seeing it as the early arrival of the most precious gift a married couple could receive, her mother would see this as interfering with her daughter's promising career. She would see it as an unplanned and unnecessary financial obligation the young couple was in no position to take on. Her mother would see the red lines as pointing the way to a downward spiral.

Angelica rubbed her forehead. "I've got twenty cases stacked up on my desk, and I'm trying to finish fixing up the guest room for Maclovia. She arrives tomorrow. I was going to try to get to the office for at least an hour today and review some depositions."

"If you'd accepted one of those offers you got from the big San Francisco firms, instead of taking that job at the public defender's office, you'd have an assistant." Her mother let a few seconds pass before continuing. "And there's no reason for you to be bothered with that guest room. If you would've let me send Maria down there to help you, you could've taken a nap this afternoon and been rested for our dinner tonight." Angelica waited through another carefully placed pause. "Why isn't your husband helping you? He doesn't have anything else to do, and it's *his* grandmother."

Angelica could hear the disapproval in her mother's voice. Her stomach knotted. Why couldn't her parents be happy for her and accept Antonio as the man she'd chosen to spend the rest of her life with? "He went to the community center to his English class." Her grip tightened on the phone. "He's studying hard to learn enough English to find work." She looked at her watch. Three minutes and fifteen seconds. "Mom, I've got to run. Anything you want me to bring tonight?"

"No, honey. Just yourself."

"Love you, Mom. We'll see you in a little while."

Angelica put the phone in the cradle, then turned and walked to the living room. As she reached for the plastic stick, her hand was shaking. She felt like she was observing her own life from some distant place.

Two lines.

One in the control window, one in the result window.

"A baby. I'm going to have a baby." She sank down onto the couch, staring at the stick. Two red lines, as clear as two red flags.

She picked up the little white paper that came in the early pregnancy test. "Over ninety-nine percent accurate."

She sat in lonely silence. It wasn't that they didn't want children; it was just that the timing couldn't be worse. She was pursuing her career as a public defender for Sierra County. Her boss had assured her, one more year of work as impressive as her last one, and she would be promoted; she would begin litigating felonies. Experience she needed. She straightened her back and ran her hand over her stomach. Eventually, she hoped to open her own firm and specialize in advocacy for the poor. Something she was passionate about after being fired from her job in New York when she had refused to exploit a legal loophole that allowed big produce companies to deport Mexican laborers like Antonio without fair compensation for their labor. Although she had lost her job, she'd never regretted the career-ending decision. But it had left her financially strapped, and she and Antonio had agreed—children would come when they were financially stable. That was how it was supposed to be.

She swallowed the lump in her throat. She was committed to a demanding job, to being a wife who supported her husband, a partner in Antonio's fledgling business, and now, the mother of an unborn child.

What was she going to do now?